BLACK PROFESSOR,
WHITE UNIVERSITY

BLACK PROFESSOR,
WHITE UNIVERSITY

BY DR. SAKUI W. G. MALAKPA

MILL CITY PRESS

Mill City Press, Inc.
2301 Lucien Way #415
Maitland, FL 32751
407.339.4217
www.millcitypress.net

University of Toledo
2801 W. Bancroft Street M.S. 954
Toledo, OH 43606
Tel. 419-530-2047 or H: 419-531-1866
Emails: smalakpa@hotmail.com; Sakui.malakpa@utoledo.edu

Printed in the United States of America

Library of Congress Control Number: 2020906053
ISBN-13: 978-1-6312-9161-6

ACKNOWLEDGMENT

No doubt, writing is a tedious undertaking. I therefore thank God for giving me strength and endurance to complete this work. Likewise, I'm most grateful to my wife Sue and the children for their patience during the preparation of this manuscript. Similarly, I am grateful to Professor Michael West, Professor of African and African American Studies at Penn State University, for reading the manuscript and providing incisive feedback. Ultimately however, I take full responsibility for this work.

SWGM

PREFACE

The literature and practical experiences are replete with instances of inequality, discrimination, and marginalization in the workplace. While these experiences are not limited to a particular employment milieu, this work focuses on higher education with emphasis on discrimination, marginalization, exclusion, non-promotion, and other problems of African-Americans, Hispanics, and other 'people of color' in higher education, especially those in predominantly white universities and colleges. Although the work is laden with realities gleaned from the literature and practical experiences of various individuals, and although, from the literature, authentic names, statues, court cases, and titles of books and journals are included, this is a work of fiction. Thus, the characters are fictional and any match of names, locales, and incidents is coincidental. Similarly, the work does not refer to any particular institution of higher education. Rather, it is hoped that the characters and the fictional institution, Southwest Achval University reflect an across the board picture of issues and problems of sub-groups of the population in predominantly white universities.
SWGM

DEDICATION

To My Lovely Children

TABLE OF CONTENTS

Chapter I:

THE INTERVIEWS

D
arrell Thomas endured many rocky experiences as a professor and it seemed he had come to the end of his rope. On his last day, he sat backwards one last time in his familiar chair, glanced at the now empty shelves and his old desk, stood up, looked around and walked out the door. He did not look back nor did he think he could ever return.

Upon leaving town, Darrell's first stop was definitely bound to be Ghetahzia[1] (pronounced with a hard G), his beloved hometown. In this small hot southern town, he was highly regarded. Both black and white older folks in the town simply called him Darrell while his peers referred to him as DD. Therefore, before he and his wife went anywhere, he wanted to familiarize himself once more with Ghetahzia, reminiscence a little, and reconnect with aging family members and childhood buddies.

Indeed, there was a plethora of reasons why Darrell wanted to spend some time in Ghetahzia before venturing anywhere else. He wanted to put most of his university experiences out of his memory and there was no better place for that than Ghetahzia. Besides, he was born here some sixty-eight years ago in a family of five children, three boys and two girls. He was

---

[1] A Loma word meaning "We have endured some or a lot."

1

the last of the five and his only living brother Tyrone (seventy) and sister Elayne (seventy-two) still lived in Ghetahzia. Many family members were buried in Ghetahzia. These included his mother, Clara, his father Dwayne, beloved siblings, and his beloved maternal grandfather, Darrell.

Waiting in Ghetahzia before the next step in life was customary to Darrell. When he completed high school, he waited there before going to college. After graduating from college, he waited in his beloved town for word from graduate schools. Similarly, in seeking his first major job, Darrell returned to Ghetahzia to await word on possible employment opportunities.

By the time Darrell returned to Ghetahzia to await word on his first major employment, he had completed a doctorate and was married to Vanessa, his college sweetheart; they had six children: Darrell (whom they called D3, the third Darrell after his father and great grandfather, was almost six), Kwame (five), Dwayne (four), Joseph (three), Clara Louise or CL (two), and Nabea (three months). With such a large family, he could not wait to start a full-time job. Because his parent lived in a small three bedroom house—the house in which he and his siblings were raised—his boys went to Auntie Elayne's while he, the girls and Vanessa stopped with Mom and Dad. As always, his mother was most patient and a source of hope and encouragement. "Well Baby," she sermonized, "the good Lord who put you through all those studies will make sure you get a good job for you and your family. You must wait for His time for His time is the best time. The good book says, 'my times are in thy hands'."[2]

Although when growing up in Ghetahzia, Bible reading, church attendance, and upholding high moral and ethical standards were required strictly, Darrell nonetheless softly swept aside his mother's comments. "I know Mom," he replied in a low husky voice as if to say, "you do not know how anxious I am to start working."

---

[2] Psalms 31:15 KJV.

His mother's support, lectures, and even Biblical references notwithstanding, the truth was, for Darrell, waiting for responses to his applications was torturous and the anxiety, mercilessly murderous. Yet, he handled the stress well. He visited a number of his high schoolmates in the area. He took the children out to games and regularly exercised, sometimes on the basketball court. Yes, he still could shoot a bucket or two. He also volunteered at the senior citizen home where he worked during his college days. Likewise, he volunteered in his brother's auto-mechanic shop to ameliorate his auto repair skills.

Vanessa too avoided boredom by keeping busy. The children were a handful while her mother-in-law, Clara, was another. For Vanessa and Darrell, this waiting time was a great opportunity to bond with the old folks. As Dwayne, his dad, was retired, he and Darrell took short trips—visiting nearby historic sites, fishing, or simply hiking in the woods.

Mid-way through the summer, letters began to come in. Most of them were what Darrell called "rejection letters." He learned not to take rejection personally; rather, as an economist, he attributed employment difficulties to the national economy. Before long, one letter invited him to an interview. The university was only seventy-five miles away so he chose to drive to interview for an administrative position although he dearly wanted to teach.

Before going for the interview, he emailed the job description to his undergraduate mentor, Professor Kwame and followed up with a long telephone conversation. "The job looks interesting but it does not seem like one cut off for you although that must not discourage you," the caring professor emeritus said. He advised Darrell to prepare a persuasive power-point presentation on his philosophy of higher education administration and leadership. In addition, he warned Darrell to be mindful of the fact that often, the hiring bar was set so high that only certain people could get the job. He said this was deliberately done with no consideration for people from diverse backgrounds, not implying that such persons were to be hired

irrespective of their qualifications or the lack thereof. He clarified this point by saying, "there are times when the hiring
requirements are set for the sole purpose of excluding certain
individuals or groups although often, this stratagem is masked
in different ways."

Despite prof. Kwame's sensitivity to barriers to the hiring
of African-Americans and others from under-represented
groups in predominantly white institutions, he encouraged
Darrell. "If you are not going up against an internal candidate,
you may have a chance. Good luck and be sure to be confident
and convincing."

The campus was beautiful and the faculty and administrators were incredibly friendly. The interview sessions were
lively and thanks to Vanessa, he did not only look elegant in
his suit but the power-point presentation was persuasive. In
one-on-one sessions with a number of administrators, and in
small group sessions over lunch or dinner, the young economist
effectively portrayed himself and eloquently explicated how
his educational background was appropriate for the position.

Going for a job interview is akin to standing in the light
while others watch you from the dark. Naturally, they can see
you but you cannot see them, know nothing about them, and
know not precisely how they are looking at you. Your best bet
then is to present yourself as strongly and effectively as you
can; you must market yourself well and Darrell did just that.

After hours of gruesome questioning and presentations,
Darrell finally sat to talk with the dean of the college, the man
who would be his boss if hired. He once more sold himself as
best as he could. "Like your CV or curriculum vita, you have
been very impressive Dr. Thomas," the man said. "Fact that
you published two refereed journal articles in prestigious professional journals and served as co-principal investigator on
two major federal grants prior to completing your doctorate
impressed us. But, do you have any questions of us?"

"Yes Sir," Darrell came back quickly. Initially, he refrained
from asking immediately about salary. Rather, he inquired about

the likely longevity in the position if hired and what were the benefits and advantages he could expect in the position. After a series of questions, he gravitated toward the salary range for the position. Finally, he asked, "Would you mind telling me the number of people you have interviewed and intend to interview and if there are any internal candidates?"

"Sure," the courteous gentleman replied. "We have interviewed three persons, one of them an internal candidate; you are the last to be interviewed. I must hasten to add," he tried to clarify diplomatically, "you being interviewed last does not mean you are last in consideration; it was strictly a matter of scheduling."

The dean looked at Darrell for any reactions or impressions. If Darrell had any doubts, concerns, or even misgivings, he did not show it. Instead, he tried his luck in a different direction. "If hired, what are the chances that my wife will get a job in the History Department as a lecturer?" He briefly touched on Vanessa's qualifications and teaching experience in literature as well as African and African-American history. Again, he got diplomatic answers.

Vanessa and Mom were preparing dinner when Darrell pulled up. The children ran out to meet Daddy and so did Vanessa. "How was it Honey?"

"You know Vanessa as I pulled in and saw you and Mom through the window, it dawned on me. My goodness, you and Mom are about the same height."

"Oh knock it off, Mr. Giant; so what? Without replying, Darrell started one of his interminable laughs which continued into the house. When he entered, the aroma of baked fish and steamed vegetables almost knocked him off his feet. Still laughing, he said he was so hungry, he could eat a restaurant.

"Must have been a good trip Vanessa; I hear your husband laughing his head off," Mom Clara said without looking up as she moved from one end of the kitchen to another.

Vanessa followed her husband into the house presumably looking for an answer to her question. "He has not said a thing about his trip Ma," she informed her mother-in-law. "He's laughing at our heights." Mom brushed aside the laughter as if to say she had heard that a thousand times before.

Although Darrell said the trip was O.K., at dinner, he reiterated what he had told his family before; that is, job search was a job in itself. In this particular case, he went on, he did not want to sound pessimistic but doubted if he would get the job. "First, there is an internal candidate and that's always a challenge for external ones although quite frankly, in some instances, that can be an advantage. Second, no matter how much my future boss tried to explain, being interviewed last is not a good sign. Third, I had the impression that they simply wanted to bring in a candidate from an under-represented group to show they considered candidates from diverse backgrounds thereby making diversity to work in their interests, not mine. Of course, my curriculum vita showing I went to a historically black college or university, HBCU, gave a strong, albeit not a definitive indication of my race. If they had any doubts in that regard, googling me would confirm their suspicion. Finally, I really do not know if I want to go into administration right away even if I am hired; but, if given a chance, I'll give it a shot." He digressed and thanked his mother for a delicious dinner. He picked up another piece of baked fish and scooped more fried rice and steamed vegetables on to his plate. "This is really good," he praised.

"Well another letter of invitation came today," Vanessa disclosed. Before leaving the dinner table, Darrell read the letter. He seemed pleased and said he would prepare for his next interview.

As before, Darrell emailed Prof. Kwame the job description before calling. Characteristically, the retired professor was supportive but cautiously optimistic. "I am encouraged by the fact that they are looking for an assistant or associate professor. In many instances, institutions will hire an assistant professor whom they will pay less than an associate professor. On the other hand, I am concerned because this school frequently advertises for professors; I suspect there is a high turn-over rate. I wonder why professors move away."

In spite of his concerns, the professor emeritus encouraged Darrell to do his best as always. "Of course," he added in his usual fatherly tone before hanging up, "don't only look at whether this place will be great for you but also whether it will be great for your family. You need the best environment for your family. I am sure you know that."

Darrell nodded as his mentor spoke. The following day, he flew out west for the interview. He was greeted at the airport by a friendly professor who drove him to his hotel. The next morning, he had breakfast with two professors and an associate dean before going to the campus. The campus was nice but not as elegant as portrayed on the internet. He met his future department chair, if hired, and a number of professors. He knew the interview started as soon as he got off the plane so he was prepared. He gave a lecture in one economics class and a public presentation on economics. Despite his problems through his doctoral program, he had studied at the feet of some of the best brains in economics—at least three of them Nobel Prize nominees and one a laureate—so he was very comfortable in his presentations. As always, he dressed elegantly.

After his presentations, small group and individual sessions, Darrell met with the dean of his college. The charming lady in her mid-sixties expressed admiration and encouraged Dr. Thomas to ask questions. Darrell was getting to be an expert in this regard. First, he stated how impressed he was with the school, faculty, staff, students and administration. His questions eventually led to salary range for the position and possibilities for his wife getting a teaching position in the History or English Department which were in the same college. He briefly mentioned Vanessa's qualifications and teaching experience.

The dean, also dressed elegantly, repositioned herself in her chair before speaking. "Well, that's a very good possibility. It is clear she has a stellar academic credential and considerable teaching experience. I cannot promise for sure but if you are hired, I certainly will fight for her to get a position here." Even if she was being diplomatic, she sounded convincing to Darrell. Although he was determined to be optimistic at all times, he also could not shun reality naively.

Pleased with the interviewing process, Darrell flew back to the south. The nearest major airport to Ghetahzia was fifty miles away. Vanessa and the girls were on hand to pick up Daddy.

"How did it go?" Vanessa asked when they were all settled in the car. As he drove, Darrell explained the interviewing process and said he was pleased with the dean's willingness to fight for Vanessa if he were hired.

Two days after his trip out west, Darrell received two letters. One indicated he did not get the administrative position from his first interview and the second invited him to an interview in a southern university. "Well, this follows the game plan," he averred. "We will keep interviewing till we get a job somewhere."

His mother who was listening could not help but comment. "Honey I told you; God's time is the best. When His time comes, Honey believe me, a job will fall right into your lap."

"I'm waiting anxiously for that day Mama," Darrell confessed. "I only pray it will be a place for all of us."

The first thing that sparked skepticism and apprehension in Darrell's mind about the next interview was the fact that, though the university was four hours away, his letter of invitation did not offer to fly him; it only stated that the university would pay mileage. On the other hand, when he looked at the university on line, he was somewhat pleased to see some degree of diversity among the faculty. The faculty make-up included seventy percent Caucasians, twelve percent Asians or Asian-Americans, seven percent Africans or African-Americans, three percent Hispanics/Latinos/Latinas, and less than two percent Arabs or Arab-Americans. About five percent of the faculty was designated as "other." There were no members of the faculty who were Native Americans, Alaskan Natives, or Pacific Islanders. Similarly, no member of the faculty was designated as having a disability and the ratio of males to females was about four to one. Although Darrell felt this diversity was unacceptably minimal, he was glad to see some diversity nonetheless.

After a pleasant four-hour drive—made so mainly by his music and the beautiful southern scenery—Darrell pulled into the parking lot of his hotel. He quickly registered, when to his room to rest a little and freshen up. About an hour later, his phone rang; two senior professors had come to have dinner with him at the hotel. He knew the interview had begun and, from the type and depth of questions thrown at him at dinner, he was absolutely right. The next morning, two other persons had breakfast with him before driving him to the campus.

With minor changes here and there, the interviewing procedure seemed to be the same and that was fine with Darrell—give a lecture in economics, group presentation, small group interview sessions and one-on-one meetings. At every stop, he had one goal: to market himself as clearly and convincingly as he could. His knowledge about the university, the administration (including names of administrators) would certainly help this effort.

The official interview sessions ended with a final meeting with the dean and associate deans of the college. Once more, Darrell inquired about longevity in the position. When asked to clarify, he said, "I mean, what's the turn-over rate of professors in this university?" The room was quiet for a moment before the dean spoke up.

"I must be frank with you Dr. Thomas. Assistant and associate professors here are expected to publish quickly and extensively. They are expected to write grants and bring in money from different sources. People who do not think they can meet up with these demands usually move on. If you are hired, we certainly hope you will stay with us."

Darrell nodded politely and asked other questions. He wove his way toward salary range and the possibility of his wife being hired in the History or English Department as a lecturer. The deans also nodded politely and gave diplomatic responses.

The end of the official sessions did not conclude the interview. Darrell met Dr. J. Dwayne Coleman, an African-American professor with whom he wanted to speak briefly before leaving town. He asked the middle-age gentleman who introduced himself as J.D., if they could meet somewhere for coffee before he left town; the gentleman consented.

"Tell me the truth Brother; what is it like to work in this institution as an African-American or someone from any other under-represented group?"

J.D. looked directly at Darrell. "I will tell you this in all honesty. I read your curriculum vita and was incredibly impressed; my goodness, how many PhDs does one find around in Economics? How many assistant professor candidates already have two articles in major journals and served as co-PI on two federal grants prior to completing a doctorate? Believe me, you are among a select few in general and particularly among African-Americans." Keeping a serious face, Darrell politely thanked J.D. for the compliment.

Continuing, the African-American professor said, "I also know you have a family of six children. Therefore, if you are offered a job here and you need one badly to support your family, take it." On the heel of this encouragement, Professor Coleman admonished Darrell to be ready for all kinds of discriminatory treatments. Then, he added, "If, on the other hand, you find a job elsewhere, take it. Believe me Brother, that's the truth."

"Why have you stayed here," Darrell inquired.

"I was just about to tell you. I am here because of family and personal circumstances. I was born in a rural area only fifty-five miles from here and my parents, now aging, need me around here. I too have a large family of five children and moving them is not easy. Moreover, when I came here, I ignored all the rubbish—I mean, the horrible and racially hostile campus atmosphere-and got myself tenured; now, with a secure job, I seem to be locked in. Honestly, that's how I feel; I feel locked into a hellish academic prison and, articulated or not, that's the feeling here of many people from under-represented groups otherwise called people of color." The professor stressed that, regardless of their race, ethnicity, etc., women at the university were not much better off although consistently, because of their intersecting identities, women of color got the worst end of the stick. "He took a sip of his coffee before adding, "Believe me Brother, this socially constructed notion called racism is blatant here but again, in my opinion, it is all over this country although much more pronounced in some places than others."

Darrell nodded politely and the professor continued. He cited major problems relative to entering and remaining at the university. He said there were numerous barriers to recruiting people of color in the university. "You see Brother, the traditional requirements for recruitment work strongly against us and this has nothing to do with our qualifications." He made it clear that no one was seeking preferential treatment, the bending of rules, or the lowering of the hiring bar but until the one-sided requirements were modified, people of color would continue to be excluded from predominantly white universities and prestigious schools of engineering, law, and medicine. "To cite just one example, our accent, no matter what, works unfairly but strongly against us."

The African-American professor further stressed that even if African-Americans and other people from under-represented groups overcame recruitment barriers, they often were unhappy people who were excluded from the administration and key decision making processes. For example, except for one or two token positions—-and they were nothing less—there were no person from under-represented groups in a notable senior position in the university. Likewise, people from under-represented groups were largely unhappy because they were isolated, unappreciated, most criticized, barely promoted, if ever, and always the first fired. Touching briefly on the toilsome task of gaining tenure in such a university, he accentuated that, as Whiteness was seen as property, scholarly works by people of color were dismissed as weak, inconsequential, out of place, and the like.

"I mean this is hell Brother where the discrimination and unfair treatments are blatant. I will be remiss if I do not tell you the truth before you get here. Again Brother, I will emphasize, if you have to come here, do but be prepared." Professor Coleman said he wished Darrell had time to meet with other African-Americans so he would not take one person's opinion as the be-all and end-all. To underscore this point, he gave Darrell a list of other African-American and Hispanic professors in the university. "Call any of these people; I have no doubt, they will tell you what I have said and more."

Darrell shook his head in total amazement. "I have heard what you said Brother and believe me, I doubt it not. However, just to crystalize the point further, please give me just one example of blatant racial or gender discrimination in the pro-fessoriate here."

Professor Coleman laughed. "I can quickly give you ten, if you please." When Darrell rejected that number by shaking his head, the professor offered one example. He said an African-American and a Caucasian were going up for tenure. The Caucasian professor did not have an appreciable number of refereed journal articles on his curriculum vita or CV. He appealed to his African-American colleague for support which, according to J. D., was interesting as often, the shoe was on the other foot in that it was professors of color who lacked support. In any case, the African-American professor invited his colleague to join him in writing two articles which were almost complete. The Caucasian professor did and they published the articles jointly. When they went up for tenure, although the African-American professor had a much stronger CV overall, he was denied tenure on grounds that his articles were not in 'reputable' journals and his teaching evaluations were not strong. On the other hand, his White colleague was promoted and tenured. "The African-American had to leave the university while his white colleague is now department chair. That's a typical thing around here."

J. D., could not help but provide a second example from personal experience. He said as he had been at the university for years, he served on a variety of search committees although he always knew that was in the university's interest. In any case, he served as chair of a number of search committees and, when the white candidates were hired, they rose up in ranks while he remained in his same position. "One of such persons not only became my department chair but rose to the levels of associate, and eventually, acting dean. This has consistently been the case although I have applied several times for higher positions," the professor concluded

"Amazing! Absolutely amazing," Darrell marveled. He thanked the professor before heading back to Ghetahzia. He thought over the coffee discussion all the way home. "I remember what Dad said: 'wherever you go in this country, you will see the ugly head of racism and discrimination'," he recalled. "Dad was absolutely right for I saw it during my graduate studies. However, I will not shrink from it; I will face it head-on. As my grandfather said, if I succeed, I will not do so as a black Darrell but as Darrell Dwayne Thomas."

By the time Darrell pulled into his parents' driveway, it was nearly 10 p.m., and a gentle southern rain was falling. The kids and the old folks had gone to bed but Vanessa was up waiting for her husband. She ran to the door. "Hi Honey! How was the trip?"

"It was o.k."

"Just o.k.?" Vanessa questioned as if to say, "I understand this trip was not great." She hastened to get something for Darrell to eat but her husband said he ate a bite on the way. He nonetheless accepted a cup of tea. As he enjoyed his tea, Darrell explained the interview process and the conversation he had with the African-American professor.

"No surprises there Honey; we are not strangers to such news. If you get the job, take it; we will not shrink from racism and discrimination. The only way to combat it and effectively eliminate it-or at least reduce it-is to face it head-on. Some lost their lives for this purpose and losing a job for the same is miniscule."

"I could not put it more poignantly and forcefully Honey," Darrell said with a sense of relief and happiness that his wife saw things as he did. He added, "The gentleman was very honest. As I said, he did not advise me away from the job. He said if I needed the job, I must not turn it down; he only prepared me for the worst and I am armed and ready to face whatever comes. So, let's first see if the job is offered."

I remember reading it: 'Cowards die many times before their death; the valiant never tastes of death but once,'" Vanessa recalled.

"I'll bet if Dad were up he would tell you 'That's from Shakespeare' and probably identify the play.

"Julius Caesar," Vanessa disclosed. "Does that not sound like braggy Caesar?"

"It does," Darrell agreed. "I think it was the same time he talked about death being a necessary end."

"That's right!" Vanessa exclaimed as if to express surprise that Darrell remembered.

"Well, I'm not a literature student but I read some of that stuff," he protested mildly.

"You read?" Vanessa said laughing but fighting to keep the laughter down so as not to wake the children and the old folks. "I don't believe you just said you read some of that stuff. I read Julius Caesar and other books to you when we were courting and after we got married."

With a guilty face, Darrell admitted with a smile. "That's right and quite frankly, often I just was not interested."

I knew what you were interested in but getting through various books was important to me so I introduced to you various classical novels, great plays and earth-moving poems."

"Sometimes I just wanted to grab the book and throw it away but frankly, knowing the gist of those books eventually helped me greatly."

The couple talked for a while before retiring. The next day, Darrell and Dad were off to a historical site. Dad would explain all he knew about the various sites they visited. Upon their return, another letter of invitation was waiting. It came from a university in the mid-west.

"My goodness, you are looking for jobs everywhere; I hear that area has lots of snow," Mama said.

"Mama, that's the American tradition; 'go where the job is'," Darrell emphasized. "I dearly need a job and pray for a good working environment."

Darrell read about the university and realized it was far less diverse than the school where he last interviewed. Nonetheless, he flew out for the interview.

Darrell was now very familiar with the interview process—breakfasts, lunches, dinners, classroom lectures, public presentations, small group sessions, and one-on-one interviews. His answers were sharper, his lectures clearer, and public presentations more persuasive. He almost seemed prepared for each question fired at him. Everyone in the university who heard him was impressed. Finally, he sat to talk with the dean of his college.

"Well Dr. Thomas, we are very impress with you and I can tell you right now, we will do anything to get you here. I know this is somewhat unusual but we knows a sound person and a great teacher when we see one."

Darrell smiled modestly and thank the dean, paying no attention to his grammar. "I too admire this place very much; people have been incredibly nice."

"Have you interview somewhere else?" the dean probed.

"Yes Sir!" Darrell was careful not to prevaricate by stating that he had job offers already. Yet, knowing the reason for the question, he had to give the impression that he was on demand and could be hired elsewhere if this school failed to do so.

"No, no," the dean said. "This university want to keep you so we will make sure no other university pass us in offers."

"True, I'm interested in what you have to offer as a salary but I have other concerns." Darrell said he was concerned about a good environment for his children and the possibility of his wife getting a position as a lecturer in history. He gave a synopsis of Vanessa's background in history and English literature.

"We can take care of your wife. Honestly, we need someone in African and African-American history and that is in my college. It seem she will be a very good match. She may even teach a course or two in the English department. Therefore, tell her to apply and consider herself hire."

Darrell could not believe his ears. Why such quickness in recruiting him and his wife? He did not understand but tried hard to conceal his excitement, again, paying no attention to the dean's horrible grammar. After getting information about the city — schools for the children, living areas, recreation, etc. — Darrell left for the airport with the assurance that his appointment letter would be in the mail.

The smile on Darrell's face said everything when Vanessa met him at the airport. "You have never looked like this after your interviews; there must be great news."

"You bet Honey, there is." He promised to tell her everything when they were seated in the car and once they were, he did.

When Vanessa heard the news, she could not contain her excitement. "Hurray! Both of us got jobs? Honey, this is worth celebrating."

Darrell maneuvered the car onto the interstate highway and accelerated. Occasionally glancing at Vanessa and enjoying the broad smile on her face, he cautioned his wife to hold still to everything until they both received appointment letters. "In addition," he went on, "we need to know about the university. Quite frankly, I did not see much evidence of diversity there. Nonetheless, I was impressed with the place." He said he also thought the mission statement of the university was interesting. He pulled a piece of paper from his pocket and handed it to Vanessa. At the top of the first page was the mission statement: 'The mission of this university is to promote research, academic excellence, and service to community and humanity in conformity with uncompromising ethical and legal standards in the context of academic freedom, human diversity that accentuates skin-color blindness, justice and equality'.

"Honey, we will take the jobs, diversity or no diversity. We are going armed to face racism and discrimination if they show their ugly faces. We will not be deterred or intimidated. Besides, as your dad says, racism and discrimination will be everywhere."

"That's the spirit Baby," Darrell supported.

Back at home, Mama danced when she heard the news and Dad, who seldom showed his emotions, smiled broadly. "What is the university?" Mama sought to know.

"Southwest Achval University in the mid-west," Darrell replied. "It has about twenty-five thousand students and I will be teaching economics and Vanessa will teach African and African-American history."

"Praise God and bless His holy name," Mama said as she started a gospel song. "I lived to see my baby become a university professor! Only God can make that possible and He did. Praise be His holy name!"

As Darrell and Vanessa rejoiced for new positions, Darrell received letters of rejection. The school out west rejected him outright. The school in the south expressed interest in him but regretted that, after his interview, they realized they were not prepared to hire new tenure track faculty members. Instead, they offered Darrell and adjunct position, stating that he would teach one or two courses until a tenure track position became available.

It was easy for Darrell to accept rejection letters not only because of the certainty of employment but particularly because three or four days after he returned to Ghetahzia, the certainty was cemented by the arrival of a contract with Southwest Achval University. He went over it with Prof. Kwame and both thought it was very good. He signed it, made a photocopy, and sent it back. By then, Vanessa had sent in a letter of interest and not long after, her contract came in the mail. She too signed, photocopied, and sent it back.

At last, Dr. Darrell Dwayne Thomas was hired as an assistant professor and his wife, a lecturer. This monumental achievement reinforced his conviction that, "With total reliance on God, tenacity and perseverance always bear fruits." With this invigorating conviction, his gaze was now directed to the future which he hoped and prayed would produce big, sweet, and juicy fruits although this hope was not tantamount to naivety. He had been in academia long enough to see its smelly side. Therefore, while he did not allow doubts and pessimism to ruin the celebration of a mountainous milestone, he nonetheless realistically knew that the professoriate was not expected to be smell free; the only thing uncertain was the timing and extent of the stench.

Chapter II:

WOW! STARTING HERE?

The reminder is a torturous trite and yet true that the only thing constant is change itself. Yes, life is replete with numerous changes with various effects. When, for example, change or a pending change breeds uncertainty, the logical consequences are likely to include doubts, trepidation, and fear. This reality was painfully true for Vanessa and Darrell as Mama Clara and Dad went out of their way to give them a befitting farewell party. The trepidation was fueled by their experiences in the mid-west.

"You must be Vanessa," the dean said as he stood to shake Vanessa's hand.

"If you mean Vanessa Thomas, I am she," Vanessa replied in jest. She and Darrell flew to Achval to sign papers but they could have done so by mail; they went to get acquainted with the area and more importantly, locate a place for their family. While at the university, Darrell called the dean who expressed desire to meet Vanessa.

The dean's office was elegant with sophisticated computers and other hardware matched by expensive furniture. The recherché rug flawlessly matched the furniture, wall painting and the small fish tank in the front right corner. After the salutary pleasantries, the dean offered Vanessa and Darrell seats before asking a few questions. He expressed delight that Vanessa was joining the History Department which was in his college along with the Department of Economics.

Vanessa, attired in an elegant dress that perfectly matched her shoes and purse, took on a diplomatic tune when she quickly noticed that the dean, dressed in a light blue suit, was polite but not particularly friendly, welcoming but not convincingly genuine. As Darrell listened and watched the exchange between his wife and the dean, he could tell easily that Vanessa, who always looked elegant in even the most casual outfit, was not intimidated but certainly perturbed, even disgusted with the dean. He was right for after the dean wished them a safe trip back, they left his office and walked briskly toward their rented car. Until they reached the car, she did not say a word. As soon as she slammed the door shut, she blurted out her anger. "Rats! I could not stand that dean; he made me sick in the stomach. I mean the man is a nerd, a cold and heartless person. He was nauseatingly condescending and outrightly racist with his childish and insulting so-called compliments. Oh the gods save me!"

Darrell knew his wife was disgusted but he did not realize the extent. He had never heard her speak so strongly about someone, no matter how angry she was with that person. "Wow Honey," he spoke softly as he straightened his tie with one hand and the other on the steering wheel. "You really are angry. Please dear, calm down for this is only the beginning. If you let such behavior get to you, you will develop high blood pressure and probably worse before you know it."

"You're right Dear," she consented as she straightened herself in her seat. "I will not allow such a nerd to make my blood boil within me; that plaguing prologue prepares me properly and summons me to battle. We will take up employment here and I am ready for any challenges that come. On account of such a cold, callous creature, the fight against racism will not be abated until the battle is won decisively. Who does he think he is? For starters, he better work on his grammar."

Although in the heat of a serious discussion, Darrell smiled lightly and thought to himself. *My goodness; in her anger, that literature stuff really comes out—anything as old as Chaucer and Shakespeare or as modern as Hughes, Angelou, Achebe, and many more. I still remember when she used to literally shove the stuff down my throat when we were courting and even after we were married.*

For a while, the couple was quiet in their beautiful rented car. Darrell turn down the radio which was not loud anyway. Later, because of their experience at the university, Darrell suggested, and Vanessa agreed that they toured the town, get a nice dinner and search for housing the next day. The university did a lousy job of introducing them to the community but the couple did its homework thoroughly. They looked on line and found many numbers—apartment complexes near the university, single family houses, and realtors in the area. Of course, they were concerned about good schools for their children who ranged in age from six months to six years.

A delicious dinner, couple of glasses of red wine in the evening, a good night's sleep, a hearty breakfast, and reassurance from Ghetahzia that the children were well combined to make for a wonderful start of day. Unfortunately, this wonderful start was short-lived. The downward spiral started when Darrell made the first call to their first choice of apartment complexes.

"Hello, thanks for calling Elegant Dwelling Apartments," a charming voice answered. Darrell asked if the apartment complex had three or four bedrooms available. "Hold on Sir," the lady replied in a suspicious tune. After two or three minutes, another voice, clearly that of an older lady came on the phone.

"May I help you?" Darrell repeated his question. The response was quick and firm. "Sorry Sir, we are all occupied at this time. Thanks for calling." Darrell heard the lady slam down the receiver.

"That was awfully rude," he retorted. "I do not understand."

"Let me try the next complex," Vanessa offered. When she got an answer, she was as clear as she could be. "My name is

Mrs. Vanessa Thomas and my husband, Dr. Thomas and I are looking for a three or four bedroom apartment. Do you have any available? She thought by stating that her husband was a doctor (regardless of what kind) might make a difference. Also, the fact that she was married and looking for a three or four bedroom apartment would mean she was looking for an apartment for a family. Neither appeared to matter.

"Can you hold a minute please?" a lady said politely. After a minute or two, a man came on the phone.

"Hello, how may I help you?" Vanessa, like Darrell, repeated her question. "I'm sorry Mam, the man said. We are overbooked at this time. Thanks for calling." As was done to Darrell the man hung up impetuously.

Darrell and Vanessa were silent for a minute or two. "I don't believe this!" Vanessa blurted out her disgust. "I'm sure they have empty apartments but even if they do not, that's no reason to be sickeningly rude. What?"

"Hold on Honey," Darrell advised. "Come with me." He headed for the door and Vanessa, not asking any questions, followed. Although dressed in a nice jacket outfit, he walked briskly toward the elevator and Vanessa, also in a nice light dress, kept up the pace. Soon, they were at the front desk.

"Excuse me Mam," Darrell called the attention of a Caucasian receptionist at the front desk. "Will you please do me a favor?" After she agreed without asking what, he handed her a piece of paper with two telephone numbers. "Please call those apartment complexes and inquire if they have three or four bedroom apartments available." Fortunately, the lady was not busy and so complied.

"Thanks for calling Elegant Dwelling Apartments, how may I help you?" In response to this courteous telephone greeting, the hotel receptionist inquired about the apartment and was told immediately that there were several two bedroom and four three bedroom apartments available. The receptionist inquired as to the rent of the apartments and wrote down the information. She thanked the person at the other end and hung up. She called the next number and for sure, that complex also had vacant two and three bedroom apartments. Like before, she wrote down the figures. When she got off the phone, she handed the paper to Darrell. He thanked her and walked back to the elevator with Vanessa following.

The couple sat speechlessly in their room where, in one window, the curtains danced gently to the direction of a gentle breeze while a blank television set stared at them. Their suspicion was confirmed. Their black southern accent, although relatively mild owing to many years in higher education, were distinctly noticeable in the mid-west. In spite of improvements in race relations, and despite the passage of the Civil Rights Act (as amended) and subsequent relevant pieces of legislation and judicial mandates, these apartment complexes were determined to keep out blacks and probably other people of color, especially since, with the dawn of another school year, they would soon be overbooked in earnest. Of course, they had to keep out "unwanted prospects" without blatantly breaking the law and if they did, they probably had some of the biggest law firms in town representing them. Conceivably, they shared the same hidden curriculum agenda with many facilities, especially places of employment; that is, "Keep them out and deter their growth but do not get caught doing so."

In the heat of the crisis, the couple was doing everything possible to cool off steam. As Darrell shook his head for the nth time, he asked quietly, "Do we really want to come here Honey? We have fought racism tenaciously in the south so I am sure we can handle it but how about the children here in the mid-west where one would have thought the situation was better?"

Vanessa's response was instantaneous. "Yes Baby, we are coming. We have signed contracts and we will honor that agreement. We will face this monster head on. The children will learn the realities of living in this country as black people, proud, determined, and contributive African-Americans or what some call 'people of color' as though the others are colorless. Neither they nor we will not, and indeed must never, shrink from the reality and evils of racism and all who perpetuate it." She stopped to catch her breath. Needless to say, she was sorely exasperated.

"Mmmmm!" Darrell moaned. He paused a moment before stating painfully, "Just think Honey; we were rejected simply on account of our accent. Accent?" he questioned in total disbelief. "They did not care who we were, how we looked, what we did, nothing like that. Isn't that amazing?" He too could not mask his frustration even if he tried.

Vanessa once more forced her husband to face reality. "Yes, it's amazing but so too are the situations where people are refused interviews and even jobs simply because of their names. As the Bard says, 'what's in a name?' Others are rejected on account of disability while still some are refused because of looks. There is no logic in racism or discrimination; it's simply idiotic, an irrefutable personification of narrow-mindedness. Worse, it is a serious mental health problem."

Mental health?" Darrell asked curiously.

"Think about it Honey. Beyond character—and even character is sometimes debatable—but beyond character, when discrimination, exclusion, denial, maltreatment, marginalization, resentment, inequality, or any combination of these and similar evils is based solely on race, skin color, ethnicity, etc., the underlining malady cannot be anything less." She said that as a consequence of this realization, she vehemently resented the behavior but deeply pitied those affected. "Honey, we must face this despicable monster head-on and nothing else," she concluded emphatically.

Darrell knew this was not the time to present a logical refutation of his wife's points as he often did although she seldom acquiesced without a counter argument. Rather, feeling somewhat embarrassed for sounding weak, caving into pressure, and perhaps self-defeatist, he consented quickly. "I guess you are right Honey so where do we look next?" Vanessa suggested that the first thing to look for now was a good school. As they had checked those too, they drove around to check the neighborhoods. They found a mixed race private elementary school which, in actuality, was predominantly White. They talked with the principal and a few teachers who were on hand. Obviously this was a very short time for them to know a lot about the school but from what they saw, they were convinced this was an excellent school for their children. They promised to enroll their children in this school which went from preschool through sixth grade. They also found an excellent nursery for Clara Louise (whom they called CL) and Nabea.

After choosing a school and nursery, Darrell and his wife went to see a realtor. They explained that they really wanted an apartment as they did not know how long they would be in the area but expected to be around for at least two years.

"I have had a number of clients in your shoes," the realtor assured. "You need a house but do not want to buy one and be stuck with a mortgage thereby making it difficult for you to leave when you want to."

"I think you somewhat understand although not totally. We actually wanted to start with apartments," Vanessa clarified. The realtor shook her head in disagreement without saying why. "So what do we do?"

"Again, I think I have a solution," the realtor repeated. "I have several houses for rent with option to buy. You may live in the house up to five years and if you decide to buy, the rent you put into the house will go toward your fifteen, twenty or thirty-year mortgage, as you please. After five years and you still are not sure, you may continue renting."

"Great!" Vanessa and Darrell said in unison. They asked if such a house was near the school they chose for their children. In a few minutes, the three were standing in an elegant house just a few blocks from the school. For the first time throughout the day, a smile crossed Vanessa's face.

"This is perfect for our family!" she exclaimed. As the realtor was working for the owners, Vanessa's show of excitement was a mistake and clear evidence that she was a novice in renting, let alone buying a house. Vanessa and her husband also did not notice the neighbors staring from their windows as soon as the realtor pulled in the driveway of the unoccupied house.

"Well then, we are set on this one, are we?" the realtor asked. Before Vanessa could agree, Darrell asked to see one or two more houses in the area.

"Honey I just do not think we will find a better house. This is great. There's enough room for the children, an elegant study for both of us, a finished basement, great backyard, and even rooms for visitors. Nothing beats this."

"Oh yes," the realtor disagreed. "I have another house which is bigger but much more expensive."

"Precisely my point!" Vanessa emphasized. She then quickly inquired as to the rent of the house in which they stood. When she was told, and the realtor made it clear that the rent did not include utilities, necessary yard work, and minor repairs, Vanessa looked to her husband as if to say, "Can we afford this?" It was Darrell's turn to smile although he fought hard not to seem sardonic.

"Do you want to see the next house then?"

"I guess," Vanessa replied doubtfully. The realtor led them to the next house which was truly elegant but certainly beyond their pocketbooks as entry level employees, especially so for Darrell. "Let's go back to the first house Honey; I think that's our house," Vanessa requested.

At the real estate office, Darrell and Vanessa carefully read over the lease before signing papers. From their small saving, they were able to come up with the rent for the first four months. They got the keys and drove back to the house. Vanessa quickly determined who would be in what room and where grandparents and other visitors would stay. "Imagine Darrell, it's our own house. For sure, God is great!" She hugged and kissed her husband.

"I agree with you Honey but let's not forget that this is for rent."

I know Honey but if those nerds, for some divine reason become humans and treat us right, we might buy it and make a life here. Oh Baby, let's think positive, I mean positively," she corrected herself.

Although signing their employment contracts assured them definitively that they finally had jobs, obtaining a home was certainly the highlight of the trip to Achval. Yet, the couple did not forget the battle they were most likely to face. Even with this likelihood, back in Ghetahzia, they did not hide their excitement about their new home. They made the children anxious to move. "I have already assigned rooms," their mother informed. "I did not want any fighting over rooms."

Indeed, Mama Clara and Dad went out of their way to give Darrell, Vanessa, and their children a wonderful farewell party. Of course, Darrell's siblings were part of the planning process and some of his high school mates in the area were invited. Unknown to the couple was the fact that Vanessa's parents and siblings were invited and so were their best college friends, Lamont and David along with their families. Also invited were the mayor of Ghetahzia, Mama Clara's pastor, and some leading figures in town. Since the family house was too small, Mama rented a hall.

The party was planned carefully. Darrell, Vanessa and their children were not to see out of town guests until everyone gathered in the hall. The food was truly delicious. Kolu, the young lady from Liberia who was married to Lamont made her trademark Jollof rice which everyone enjoyed. Of course, Mama, Elayne, and their helpers prepared the best southern food one could find anywhere in Dixieland.

At the end of the meal, Mama took the microphone to thank everyone for coming. In tears, she expressed thanks to God for seeing her baby and his family move to a new place where he was to take up his new assignment as an assistant professor and his wife a lecturer. The mayor, Mama's pastor for many years, some of Darrell's friends, Vanessa's father and several other people made brief remarks. Professor Kwame, who could not make it, sent a congratulatory statement with best wishes for the couple. Vanessa thanked everyone on behalf of her husband and children. She was anxious to party hard through the night.

Like the variety of food served, the DJ played various songs to suit everyone—Darrell's children's age group, people of Darrell and Vanessa's age, and also for mama and her age group. Everyone truly had a wonderful time.

Darrell's achievement truly was worth celebrating. As the mayor pointed out in his brief remarks, as far as they knew, Darrell was the first Ghetahzian, Black or White, to earn a doctorate and subsequently become a professor. He truly was a role model and evidence that when God opens doors, no one can close them.

After the party, Mama Clara asked Darrell to wait with her in the living room. When everyone went to bed, she asked him to join her as she knelt in front of the couch to pray. "Baby, I was born in this house and will probably join my Lord from here. I want to bless you as your grandfather Darrell would have done in our rich African fashion." She prayed and prayed and, laying her hands on Darrell, blessed him with tears in both of their eyes. "Go Son and always trust in your God; He NEVER fails." Pausing between lines and accentuating each point, she continued, "Take good care of your family, be charitable and generous, respect yourself, treat others right but never draw back from life's challenges. God bless you son and, from the bottom of my heart, and in the name of my Lord and Savior, I wish you, your wife and children all the best."

"Thanks Mama; thank you very much and God bless you too," Darrell said in a husky tearful voice. "Mama, you have been a great mother and continue to be; there's none like you. I love you dearly and will remember the things you taught me. Your strong faith, your ability to handle hardship and challenges, the way you work with others, your generosity even when you do not have much, and many more are great lessons for us. God bless you Mama," he ended his remarks as he hugged his mother.

"Good night Son and get some sleep. I'm sure you will do well for God will go with you."

Within a week, Vanessa and her family packed everything they wanted to take to Achval. The night before they left, Darrell's friends and brothers came over. They sat outside mama's house drinking light beer, joking, and laughing till late at night. Darrell was up early the next morning. He jogged to Grandpa Darrell's grave. He wished Grandpa could once more say, "Is that you Darrell?" In a way, he could almost hear him saying so although the old man had been dead for years.

"Well Grandpa, I am leaving today. I remember you telling me that if I succeeded, I had to do so as Darrell Dwayne Thomas, not a black Darrell. Well Grandpa, if there truly is a life beyond the grave, please Grandpa, help me succeed for it seems like I am up against the same racism you faced for years although now, it is in a different form." He talked on and on as if his grandfather was listening. He wept a little at times and laughed other times when he recalled funny moments with his grandfather. Still other times, he sat quietly for long moments as if Grandpa would respond to his comments. Incredulously, he could feel Grandpa's presence.

Excitedly, the children too were up early. Grandma made huge breakfast and, with everyone seated, Grandpa Dwayne prayed a long and touching prayer. Finally, the Thomases were off to a new home and a new life, hoping in god for the best.

Chapter III:

GUIDANCE FOR SETTLING IN

A s she moved around the kitchen languorously, Clara seemed to have lost vigor and desire for anything. She sat down as if the world had come to an end.

"Baby please eat something," Dwayne implored as he coughed incessantly for he almost choked on his delicious fried chicken.

"I'm alright Dwayne. You need to drink some water," Clara said with an emphasis on the "you."

"You can't be. You have not said much today and have not eaten a bite. Believe me Baby, the children will be alright. Please eat something."

"Anybody home?" Elayne knocked and, without waiting for an answer, opened the door and rushed into the kitchen. "Oh great! I'm truly starved. Since the children left, I have had no desire to cook anything."

"Your mother cooked but has not eaten a bite," Dwayne informed his six-foot beautiful daughter who, dressed in a casual outfit, had already taken her usual seat at the family table.

"That's true Elayne; I just miss the children too much. Not having Clara Louise and Nabea around is hard to take. I also got attached to Vanessa so much that I did not want to see her go."

"You're right mama; she is something else. I too miss the boys but that's not stopping me from eating. I'm so hungry I could eat a horse." Elayne quickly fixed a plate and "dug in." "Eat something Mama; my brother and his family will be alright."

"I know they will be; the good Lord is watching over them but I still miss them dearly," Mama said sadly. She picked up a piece of chicken and put a small helping of fruits and vegetables on her plate. Just then, the phone rang. Elayne ran to it.

"Hi Mama," Vanessa said.

"Do I sound like your mother-in-law?" Elayne asked laughing.

Also laughing, Vanessa apologized. "I'm sorry Elayne. I just expected Mama to pick up the phone."

"Where are you guys now?"

"We are about forty miles from Achval. We are all tired but have had a wonderful time seeing parts of the country. Nabea slept a lot and when up, she did not seem to care for beautiful sceneries. At times she just whined and whined; but I just wanted to call to say we are alright. Is mama there?"

Elayne handed the phone to Mama who was already standing and waiting anxiously. She spoke with Vanessa and Darrell. Darrell also spoke briefly with Dwayne while all the children wanted to talk with Grandma and Aunty Elayne.

After the telephone conversation, Mama Clara admitted she was much relieved and ate a little more. "I know the God I worship is a good God. He will take them safely," she echoed her unbending faith.

"Achval, 15 miles," the sign board read much to the delight of the Thomas family. It was a long drive from the south to the mid-west but stress and boredom were mitigated by the beautiful scenery and the fun in the car. In a few minutes, another sign read, "Welcome to Achval, The Butter City." Achval got its nickname from the many butter producing factories in town.

As Dad wove his way around the streets trying to get to their house, the children looked left and right around the city that most likely would be their home for months, perhaps years. "Here we are children," Dad said as he pulled into their driveway. The children could not wait to get into the house. In a few minutes, they were in, running around and getting acquainted as quickly as possible. After unpacking as much as they could, they closed the garage, ordered pizza for dinner and, after eating and chatting about the house and the town in general, went to their rooms with sleeping bags.

The four boys were up early and so were the neighbors who looked on curiously. Darrell III, whom the family simply called "D3," surveyed the backyard from one end to the other while Kwame, Dwayne, and Joseph looked on. Mom improvised in the kitchen as she tried to prepare breakfast. In a few minutes, Dad joined her with Nabea in his arms. "She just jumped out and looked all over the place. I guess she is not sure what this strange place is all about," he said laughing.

"She was probably looking for her grandma," Vanessa thought out loud. "Is CL still sleeping?" she asked referring to Clara Louise.

"Sound asleep but, as you know, as soon as breakfast is ready she will be here in a twinkling of an eye. Where are the boys?"

Vanessa put the food on the old shaky table in the dining room before she answered her husband. "So excited about the house, they are checking everything out. I think they are in the backyard." She called CL AND the boys for breakfast.

As soon as the family sat to eat, using picnic chairs, paper plates and cups, the doorbell rang. "Who in the world could that be?" Dad wondered as he went to the door.

"Good morning good neighbor," a charming lady up in age greeted. She handed Darrell flowers and a map of the city. "Welcome to Achval and to our neighborhood." She said she was Mrs. Susan Westville and that she and her husband Jim lived two houses from Darrell and his family. "Jim and I would love to have you and the children over for coffee and cake and home-made ice cream. While you settle in, please let us know if we can be of any help. I know it takes a while to get everything in place. We can help with dishes, directions to shopping areas, whatever you need. We are just glad to have you in our neighborhood. This is actually a very nice neighborhood. Jim and I have been here for years."

Darrell was really touched. He introduced himself and Vanessa who had joined him with Nabea at the door. He thanked Mrs. Westville who preferred to be called Susie.

"Great way to start the day and our stay here in Achval," Vanessa grinned with utmost delight as she took her seat at the breakfast table. "I could not ask for a better way to be welcomed. Bless her heart. I truly would like to know her."

Darrell agreed, adding, "She seemed very genuine."

"But she is White," D3 chimed in as if his parents did not know. Without waiting for his parents to respond, he continued, "The only Blacks I have seen in this area live three or four houses from us. Why didn't they come to welcome us?"

Mom hesitated but opted for her husband to answer this one. "Well Son," Darrell started as he buttered his toast. "I am glad you noticed. We commend Susie for welcoming us regardless of our race, and that's how it should be. All people belong to one family of human beings and so it is very sad that some people focus more on our differences of color, race, nationality, and things like that instead of our very valued humanity. The black family still may come to welcome us but we should not expect it just because they are Black." He explained further that in every race, among any group of people, and indeed in every family, some are open while others are not, some are good while others are not so good and still, others very bad; it boils down to individuals. "So children, never jump to conclusion about someone solely because of his or her race. Likewise, do not accept anyone's preconceived notion of you because of your race. You are as good as anyone in the world. You are not better than anyone and no one is better than you," he concluded as he picked up his cup of coffee.

The boys seemed to be listening but CL certainly was not as she splashed her milk from her cereal bowl all over the table to the disapproval of her mother. Nabea, sucking her pacifier, was very relaxed in Mom's lap.

Darrell was not sure how clearly his children got his message for he delivered it as strongly as he would to adults. Maybe they got it, maybe not. Whatever the reception, He knew this would not be the last time he would emphasize this message. This repetition and emphasis was necessary because it is mind-boggling that the strongest, clearest, albeit simplest messages often do not get through. This was precisely the case with Darrell's message regarding the oneness and equality of human beings. In simplistic terms, he explained that, no matter how poor or rich, strong or weak, young or old, able or disabled, famous or unknown, talented or untalented, powerful or powerless, and regardless of a person's looks, religion, race, ethnicity, nationality, or socio-economic status, he or she was a human being created in the image of the Creator and MUST be treated as such. "What else is there to tell?" Darrell asked. "Not much more," he came back with an answer. "Hence, humanity loses itself and its future when it misses this poignant unmistakable message. Hopes are truly lost when differences among human beings are stressed on the basis of religion which teaches the origin, pith, and importance of the oneness and equality of human beings." Without getting away from the main topic, Darrell explained further that he was aware of the existence of many religions but the world's major religions taught the same or similar lesson regarding the oneness and equality of all peoples.

While Darrell thought over his message, Vanessa moved a few feet from the table to change Nabea to the annoyance of the children. "Thank God I already finished my breakfast," Kwame said.

"Me too," agreed D3.

"But I'm still drinking coffee and may have another toast," Dad informed to the yuck and uuuu from the children. "Mom and I did it for each of you and certainly can do it for Nabea," he emphasized with a smile.

Two days after arriving in Achval, a moving truck rolled before the home of the Thomas'. It was a tough job for Darrell and the movers unloading but soon, the house was transformed into a real home with tables, chairs, couches, beds, dishes, television sets, computers, video games, and many others including bags of "imperishable groceries"—a definite misnomer or, at the very least, an oxymoron. Family and friends gave them as much as they could take and it was cheaper moving them than buying anew. For people starting new jobs, this was a smart idea indeed.

After setting up the house, the Thomases needed to get acquainted with Achval. This was made easy in part because of the map Susie gave them and partly because the streets were laid out well; they ran from east to west, and north to south with very few corner streets. They therefore learned the city quickly and shopped for school materials for the children. Finally, the children were ready for another school year.

The start of the school year brought more apprehension for Mom and Dad than for the children. Although Mom and Dad had visited the school and nursery, they still wondered how the kids would fit in. As it turned out, this was no problem for Nabea and CL who seemed very comfortable, perhaps too active as newcomers in their new nursery and preschool although the overwhelming majority of the children were white. This reaffirmed the old saying that, "Regardless of race, ethnicity, nationality, disability, and any other difference, children are children; only adults set limitations and make distinctions among children."

Vanessa and Darrell did not know what to expect either at the university. Before they started, they had a long conversation about what they thought lay ahead. They agreed to go in with open minds, not being suspicious of anyone and with malice toward none. They were newcomers who had a lot to learn to fit in and so they had to work really hard, expecting nothing on a silver platter. This had been their lives from the south to graduate school but they deemed it necessary to remind themselves once more.

For sure, the reminders were didactic. For example, it is said that, undoubtedly, life's an endless struggle—a long bumpy ride with ups and downs, twists and turns but one must hold on. To give up or give in is to let go and fall off. Success through this struggle comes not by falling off but by soaring over the dark clouds, focusing on the goal and ignoring the bumps and bruises. Doubtless, this requires tenacity, endurance, and yes, opportunities but it is indubitable that ignoring thus allows us to sense the sweet smells that stifle the struggle and shape our gaze to life's joys and opportunities as well as to the possessions, people, talents and abilities we often take for granted. Above all, success comes when we acknowledge the Giver of life itself and ask Him to direct our paths. This Master Planner NEVER fails, even if we think we have.

Again, the reminders were refreshing because, growing up in southern Christian homes, Darrell and Vanessa certainly heard a lot about faith, a Supreme Being, and everyone being a child of God. In the mid-west, their faith would be sorely tested and it remained to be seen if they would hang on or fall off.

On the first day, the college faculty met following the long summer break. The Thomases sat together as new faculty and staff members were introduced. The chair of the Department of Economics introduced Darrell, commented briefly on his background and academic interest, and expressed real delight for having him in the department. A few minutes later, the chair of the History Department introduced Vanessa and said, "No relations to Dr. Thomas," to the laughter of the faculty. Also presented was Vanessa's background and academic interest. At the end of the meeting, several people shook hands with the Thomases and welcomed them to Southwest Achval University, SAU. A few people asked them to have lunch or coffee whenever possible. Vanessa and Darrell were also pleased to meet the "new recruits."

AT the end of their first day of school, the children were full of excitement when Mom picked them up from their respective places—D3 just turned seven and in second grade, Kwame six and in first grade, Dwayne (five) and Joseph or Joe (four) in preschool while Clara Louise or CL (three) and Nabea (six months) were in a nursery. Dwayne and Joseph screamed at one another as each tried to get out a story first while D3 and Kwame attempted to serve as mediators. Nabea was sleeping through it all and Mom quickly stepped in and quieted everyone, promising to listen to each person's story. "Joe started first; let him tell his story," she said.

Joe's story was initially difficult to follow but it boiled down to one teacher who said she liked his hair and another student who wanted to touch it but he refused. Dwayne's story was about his drawing which he thought was better than another presented by the boy next to him. D3 and Kwame gave brief accounts of their day with excitements. At home, the stories were told once more to Dad who listened patiently.

Later in the evening, since the children did not bring homeworks home on the first day, Mom and Dad read to them and kissed them goodnight. Then, it was their turn to discuss their first day at the university. Through the conversation, they suddenly realized both had corner offices; they wondered if this was a coincidence. Furthermore, they noticed quickly that their departments had very few "people of color," the general term for racial and ethnic "minorities." Of course, some consider the term "minority" as pejorative while others maintain it refers more to disproportionate power distribution than numbers. Considering the latter perspective, numbers were revelatory as Darrell was the only tenure track professor or lecturer of color in his department while Vanessa's department, much larger, had five persons of color and that included Vanessa.

"I wonder if it is too late to call Prof. Kwame," Darrell murmured.

Vanessa glanced at her watch. "I do not think it is. Besides," she added with a giggle, "he's retired; he's not going to work tomorrow, at least not in the same sense as we know work."

"You're right Honey and we pray one day to get there too. At the rate we are going, I wonder—just wonder," Darrell laughed as he picked up the phone.

The phone rang at least five times before a voice came on. "Hellooo!"

"Oh thank god you still are not asleep," Darrell stated without repeating the usual "Hello."

"You know me Darrell, I do not go to sleep early and that's more so now that I'm retired. How did your first full day go?"

Thinking about Vanessa's comment, Darrell laughed lightly and said his day went well. He then explained what he and Vanessa observed on the first day. "We just wanted to run this by you to see what you think."

"Academia is a tricky arena and the professoriate even trickier," the retired professor started. "Seems you are going up against several uphill battles: the nauseating realities of the white privilege, the demanding expectations of the professoriate, the tedium of academia, the smelly politics of the university environment, and untrustworthiness, unpredictability, and often, back-stabbing tendencies of so-called colleagues." He hesitated before adding, "then of course never under-estimate the intolerance, closeness, and callousness of cliques; when it comes to discrimination and the exclusion or marginalization of nom-members, they are the worst and unashamedly so."

"Gee, sounds like it is worse than hell although I have not visited nor do I intend to visit hot, horrible hades; is there anything encouraging?"

"Oh yea," the old professor averred. "There can be true colleagues and once in a while, you will find humane and conscientious administrators but in general, such creatures are rare. Your best bet is always to do your utmost best and be as vigilant as you can be."

"What do you mean?" Darrell probed.

"I have pointed some of these out to you before but let me reiterate and perhaps add one or two points as indeed, you caught me on a good evening." The professor admonished Darrell and Vanessa to do or not do several things in higher education especially so since they were members of under-represented groups in a predominantly, almost exclusively, white university.

"First," he said, be over-prepared." This meant, he elucidated, the two had to know their subject matter well. He had no doubt about this for he knew the academic abilities of Darrell and Vanessa. "While disgustingly even freshmen students will challenge your abilities, many of your so-called colleagues will doubt you and worse, overlook you." He lamented the fact that many colleagues would assume Darrell and Vanessa got their positions only because of Affirmative Action, not their true academic abilities. Of course, this would be a misunderstanding of Affirmative Action which was (and continued to be) legal as its constitutionality was affirmed in *Board of Regents of the University of California v. Bakke, Grutz v. Bollinger, Grutter v. Bollinger, and Fisher v. Texas II. "Incidentally," the professor emeritus appeared to digress a little, "believe it or not, the primary beneficiaries of Affirmative Action have been White women."*[3]

Prof. Kwame further explicated that owing to racism and narrow-mindedness, the works of Darrell and Vanessa would be scrutinized more than others. "Is Vanessa listening?" the professor asked.

"I'm on the other line Sir! As during our discussion days in college, I am writing as quickly as I can."

"Very well," acknowledged Prof. Kwame. "To be prepared," he continued, "also means being thoroughly familiar with the sequence of courses, and the requirements of both certificate/licensure and degree programs; this is what renders you great advisers." He further admonished the couple to be familiar with

---

[3] Garrison-Wade et al, 2012

the constitutions of both the university and college as well as the college's policies, procedures, guidelines, and strategies. He emphasized that this was the only way they would know, on one hand, if their rights were infringed and on the other, how to advise, and generally perform in conformity with the university's policies, rules and regulations. Likewise, they were to know the administrative hierarchy of the university adding, "For never in my life have I seen power consciousness as at the university level. Everyone is doggedly protective of his or her position and extremely sensitive about pleasing the immediate boss at whose pleasure he/she holds his/her position."

"As of the first day, I already have seen evidence of this Prof.," Darrell reported. "At our first meeting, the associate deans could not stop singing the dean's praises; it was nauseating."

"There you go!" the retired professor stressed. Continuing, he warned against being suspicious of all Whites. "As it is with individuals in any group of people, some can be open, accepting and non-judgmental." Prof. Kwame was cognizant of the fact that Darrell and Vanessa were not looking for preferential treatments, only plain level playing fields. "In that regard," he said, "do not conclude unreservedly either that you will get justice from administrators who are Black or from other under-represented groups; they can be the worst in their zealous determination to please their bosses. Some also want to prove that they are not as discriminatory as Whites and in proving so, members of their own groups are the first targets."

"If, in showing that they are fair and just means meting out harsh treatments on all sides, that would be tolerable but why focus on one side?" Darrell questioned in disgust.

"That's the problem," Prof. Kwame affirmed. "It must be either their own inferiority complex or a desire to target people they regard as most vulnerable in proving their point. However, meted out and to whomever it's meted, injustice is injustice and therefore abhorrent."

"I could not agree more Professor," stated Vanessa as she turned the page of her notebook.

"What most of these administrators from under-represented groups do not know Vanessa, is the fact that the Whites use them to do their dirty jobs, and be the instruments for the old trick of 'divide and rule'." The professor emeritus said he was absolutely sure there were competent, capable, and qualified—maybe too qualified—administrators from under-represented groups but such persons were appointed rarely as they were threats to the white establishment. Conversely, many incompetent members of under-represented groups were mere token appointees. He added, "When that's the case and the appointee himself or herself—usually they are males for females from under-represented groups are at a worse disadvantage—the appointee will be disgustingly sycophantic. He will go to great lengths to please his boss. He will kill his grandmother for the same if he has to."

"That's serious," Darrell said laughing.

"I'm not kidding," Prof. Kwame stated with utmost seriousness. "These people are horrible.

"I do not mean to defend them Prof., but isn't it true that these administrators often have their hands tied?" Vanessa asked. "They are charged with specific duties which they must perform or lose their jobs thereby becoming examples of the baseless generalization that Blacks, Hispanics and others from under-represented groups are incompetent? I mean, I suspect such administrators are also at a severe disadvantage in predominantly white institutions. Aren't they?"

"Yes, and that was exactly where I was going next," Prof. Kwame assented. "As the literature shows,[4] the problem of administrators of color in higher education begins with the fact that the ruling establishment sees Whiteness as property; therefore, they secure and legitimize their positions of power, and consequently maintain and perpetuate 'White privilege' and

---

[4] E.g. Wolfe & Dilworth, 2015.

domination. From that vantage position, they appoint people of color to inferior positions to portray a sense of diversity. Quite frankly," the retired professor stressed, "that is nothing less than a mockery of diversity. Worse, often, they expect people of color to do their dirty jobs and unfortunately, people of color sometimes acquiesce in light of their vulnerability." The professor added that, on the other hand, it needed to be stated earnestly that some people of color expected preferential treatments from administrators of similar race, ethnicity, nationality, and the like, forgetting that bending the rules for anyone most likely would jeopardize the administrator's position.

Darrell understood the professor. "I think you mean Prof., that a sound administrator ought to execute his or her duties fairly and justly across the board without fears and favors, and this applies to administrators from under-represented groups."

"Absolutely!" the professor agreed. "The observation is that administrators who do so are persons who are qualified and truly believe in themselves. Unfortunately, such persons are rare and when found, unless they have bosses of high moral characters, do not tend to last too long especially in the face of White domination. However, as I said, you caught me on a good night; therefore, I would like to reiterate a few points and direct your attention to a never-to-forget reminder."

Vanessa and her husband loved and admired Prof. Kwame so much that they took his words very seriously. They checked their pens and papers to make sure they did not miss a word. Reemphasizing an earlier piece of advice, the professor emeritus told them to be mindful of the platitude but poignant truth of the professoriate; that is, 'publish or perish'. "You must work hard to publish in nationally acclaimed professional journals. Attend and present at various professional conferences in your fields, not just conferences organized by Blacks for that may seem self-serving no matter how professional the conference although they do not say the same about professional conferences planned by Whites and where Whites predominate. Be sure to write grants and bring in money. We went over the basics of grant writing; improve on those rudiments as extensively as you can; leave no stones unturned."

In Addition, Prof. Kwame wanted to encourage the young couple and buttress their resolve. To that end, he reminded them of the successes of their forefathers despite slavery, gross degradation, discrimination, and unimaginable humiliation. "In spite of these difficult circumstances," the learned professor pointed out, "our people did not despair; rather, they relentlessly persevered and many succeeded in a variety of ways. We are the heirs of these earlier spirits of tenacity and perseverance."

"This reminds me of our discussions which covered African-American, Hispanic and other inventors from under-represented groups," Vanessa recalled. "They succeeded despite the odds."

"You took the word right out of my mouth," Prof. Kwame said. He stressed that such were the vanguards to emulate. Further, he stated that, a cursory review of the literature would show that such vanguards were in academia as well. For example, he said if they did not remember from their undergraduate group discussions, they were to be reminded that, despite gruesome and humiliating segregation laws and practices, in 1823, Alexander Twilight became the first black person in the United States to graduate from college. He graduated from Middlebury College in Vermont. He became the first African-American to be elected to a public office; he served in the Vermont State Legislature. Likewise, although women from under-represented groups were (and still are) usually doubly victimized, in 1862, Mary Jane Patterson graduated from Oberlin College thereby becoming the first African-American lady to earn a bachelors degree in the United States. In a similar triumph from a disadvantaged position, in 1889, Susan La Flesche Picotte became the first female Native American to earn a medical degree. She graduated valedictorian and top of her class from the Women's Medical College of Pennsylvania. Interestingly," the prof., continued, "Susan became interested in medicine early in life when she saw a Native American lady die because a white doctor refused to treat her."

Professor Kwame cited other first African-American graduates. These included Richard Theodore Greener who, in 1870 became the first African American to graduate from Harvard College and Edward Alexander Bouchet who, in 1876, was the first African-American to earn a doctorate degree from an American university. He earned his Ph.D. in physics from Yale. He also was the first African American to graduate from Yale. On the other hand, in 1895, W.E.B. Du Bois became the first African-American to earn a Ph.D. from Harvard. Focusing once more on women, Prof. Kwame shared that in 1921, Sadie Tanner Mossell became the first African-American woman to earn a Ph.D. in the United States. She earned her degree in economics from the University of Pennsylvania.

"There also were vanguards in the professoriate and higher education," the retired professor reminded. He cited Charles L. Reason who became the first African-American professor in 1849; he was at New York Central College. Similarly, Sarah Jane Woodson Early, in 1858, became the first African-American female college professor; she was at Wilberforce College. Also at Wilberforce College, Bishop Daniel Payne, in 1856, became the first African-American college president.

The professor emeritus encouraged Darrell and Vanessa not only to look at their undergraduate notes but also sift through the literature and surf the internet to read more about first African-Americans, Hispanics, Asians, Native Americans, and others from under-represented groups in academia. Look at achievements in law, medicine, mathematics, economics, chemistry, physics, education, music, art, and other fields and disciplines. "Once more, let me remind you that we went over many of these during our discussions in college but when you think you are up against a wall, when you think the world is against you, before you ask, 'why me,' or 'how can people be blatantly racist and discriminatory,' think what those people went through to achieve in the face of de jure racism." He said he did not need to remind them but they were in a predominantly white

university; therefore, reflecting on such vanguards was doubtlessly bound to encourage them and strengthen their resolves.
Before hanging up, Prof. Kwame appealed to Darrell and
Vanessa to read the works of former Harvard Law School professor, Derrick Bell. "A pioneer of critical race theory, CRT,
that's a man after my own heart. The professor and others
advanced CRT in what they saw as delays in advances in civil
rights. This critical theory was geared at not only understanding
but challenging, even disrupting, structural racial inequality,"
the professor emeritus lectured. "Look for his book, 'Race,
Racism and American Law'," he strongly encouraged. He said
if Darrell and Vanessa checked the literature or internet carefully, they would find that Professor Bell resigned from several prestigious positions in his zeal to advance racial equality.
When working for the Civil Rights Division of the U. S. Justice
Department, he was asked to give up his membership in the
National Association for the Advancement of Colored People,
NAACP; he resigned rather than give up this membership. He
resigned as dean from the Oregon School of Law when the
school refused to hire an Asian-American woman as a faculty.
Prof. Bell also gave up a Harvard Law School teaching position
to protest against the school's hiring practices; the school did
not have a single African-American female tenure track professor. Vanessa found out from the literature later that, eventually, the school hired Lani Guinier as the first African-American
female to join the tenured faculty.

Continuing his fatherly advice, Prof. Kwame said, "Working
in a predominantly white university, one of professor Bell's
core beliefs ought to be your guide; this was what the professor
termed 'the interest convergence dilemma', one of the key tenants of critical race theory."

"How did the learned law professor explain this dilemma?"
Darrell asked.

Professor Kwame replied instantly. "He believed that
Whites were reluctant to support any efforts, programs, or the
like that would ameliorate the positions of Blacks unless doing

so was in the interests of Whites themselves. Of course, as can be expected, this idea has been criticized but similarly, it has been endorsed by scholars. This is why his book is extremely popular," the retired professor said, sounding tired.

We cannot thank you enough for your usual fatherly advice; this means a lot to us," Darrell commended earnestly. "But before you go Prof., I would like to know one thing. How did you know so much about predominantly white institutions when you taught in one of the HBCUs?" Darrell chuckled referring to historically black colleges and universities.

Prof. Kwame laughed. He reminded his listeners that, as the literature showed,[5] HBCUs, which made up only three percent of the nation's institutions of higher education, were founded on the same assimilationist values as predominantly white institutions. "As such," the professor continued, HBCUs may shelter Black faculty from racial isolation but not from institutional racism or sexism. Furthermore, you may not know that only fifty-eight percent of the HBCU faculty is African-American, predominantly male, and receives only eighty percent of salary received at all institutions." Professor Kwame added that there was a large number of White administrators in HBCUs. For instance, Howard University did not have a Black president until 1926, nearly 60 years after it was founded. Likewise, "Lincoln University, the nation's first degree-granting historically Black university, did not see its first Black president, Dr. Howard Mann Bond, until 1945, close to a century after its founding in 1854"[6].

"In addition," the retired professor went on, "apart from sifting through the literature for I do not understand much about this internet thing, knowledge about other institutions comes from years of attending professional conferences." Explaining further, he said during such conferences, after the

---

[5] Daufin, 2001.

[6] Morris, C. (2015). White faculty deal with the challenges of teaching at HBCUs. Retrieved from https://diverseeducation.com/article/71289

day's activities, he and his African-American and Hispanic colleagues from various universities spent hours drinking beer and discussing their respective experiences. He often thought naively that because such professors were at rich universities, they had little problem; he was shocked to hear their experiences. Similarly, they thought because he was from an HBCU, he had no problem with discrimination; they were shocked to hear his experiences. With a slight laughter, he said, "Yes, there are similar issues of black professors at black universities and the same holds for white professors at black universities." Out of the blues, he added, "From my long term experience in parts of the world—Africa, Asia, Latin America, The Caribbean, and Europe—I found the same problem at universities in those places; I guess it's just something about colleges and universities."

In ending his remarks, the professor emeritus said, "Regarding my experiences at conferences in the country, through discussions with my colleagues from predominantly white universities, we noticed advantages and disadvantages on both sides but there were definite differences. In my humble opinion, I think problems of marginalization and discrimination are much more pronounced at predominantly white universities but again, that's only my opinion. I must add humbly that the literature overwhelmingly supports my position especially with regard to people of color, be they students, staff, instructors, professors, or administrators, and the situation is particularly worse for women of color."

"Goodnight Professor," said Vanessa. "We continue to be blessed to have you as a father and mentor. Thank you and God bless you richly."

"With all my heart, I say 'Amen'!" Darrell supported.

"Thank you both. I trust both of you and know you will do well in spite of any hardships. As we pointed out tonight and at other times, remember the professoriate is not a bed of roses. Whether at an HBCU or a predominantly white institution, say

PWI, you will face stiff challenges albeit from different perspectives. Good night!"

When they got off the phone, Vanessa and Darrell looked at one another in total amazement. "He's undoubtedly invaluable; I mean, the man is incredibly insightful, and 'intelligent' is not adequate a word; he's a rare gem. We thank God for him."

"We could not ask for a better mentor. He's been there for us and has followed us through graduate programs and now, into our professional lives. Yes, I agree; thank god for him," Darrell reechoed the compliments befitting a devoted mentor.

Doubtless, Darrell and Vanessa were blessed to have a mentor because mentoring is one gem many tenured and tenure track professors of color lack especially in predominantly white institutions. Indeed, mentoring is an invaluable service fueled by a rare gift. The root word, mentor, comes originally from Greek mythology to the teacher of Homer's son. It refers to a wise counselor, an experienced person who guides newcomers, a sagacious individual who tutors learners or a trusted and successful person who sets shining examples for others to emulate. The literature shows that the relationship between mentor and mentee can be so strong that it is possible to mentor at both conscious and unconscious levels. One can mentor unconsciously in that mentor and mentee may not know one another but mentor's life, achievements, approaches, conviction, etc., touch and influence mentee. Conversely, conscious mentoring requires conscientious and devoted effort as the mentor guides, instructs, and/or directs the mentee. Mentors who provide such invaluable services are rare especially when their sense of reward transcends mere satisfaction to embrace the conviction that, by mentoring, humanity is one step better. It therefore helps not only to seek a mentor no matter our possessions, power and position but to be one. Helping others to walk when they are crawling improves humanity and makes the world go smoothly around. This was the sacrificial devotion of Prof. Lumumba Kwame, a southern African-American who not only shed his slave-based name for an African one but gave his children African names. His devotion to his mentees was indescribable; hence, they loved and admired him unreservedly. As a consequence, they followed his advice. Darrell and Vanessa therefore went through the literature and the internet to discover and document everything the beloved professor said. Thankfully, it was all there.

Chapter IV:

STARTING IN EARNEST

The first week at the university was for faculty and staff only. The following week was the first week for students and the actual start of classes. With only one car, Darrell and Vanessa worked out a simple routine to drop the children off in the morning and ride to the university together.

"You look very professorial Sir," Vanessa complimented her husband on the first day of classes.

"Thanks Honey," he appreciated the compliment, probably unaware that in due course, he would shed his professorial outfits for casual ones. "You know you always look gorgeous," he too complimented his beautiful wife.

"That's only to you," she kidded.

"I do not think so but I prefer it that way," Darrell laughed. He took her in his arms, hugged and kissed her. "I thank god for you Honey; you are everything to me."

"I thank God for you too," she returned the compliment. "Before starting at the university, let's pray. We must thank God for bringing us here and ask His Grace to see us through thick and thin."

"Good idea," Darrell assented. They knelt and prayed together.

"We needed that as we truly enter academia," Darrell softly murmured as they stood up.

"We are going into the academe," Vanessa stated emphatically as if correcting her husband.

"Academe?"

"Yes academe," she re-emphasized. "It was first mentioned in Love's Labor's Lost. Do you remember when I read that to you?" Darrell nodded in agreement although he did not remember the play specifically.

I have never professed to be a lexophile," he reminded his wife.

"I am and love it dearly," she exclaimed. "After reading those classical novels, provocative poems and peachy penetrating plays, it's difficult not to love cryptic words, idiomatic expressions, figures of speech, Latin phrases, and the like. I an exceedingly exuberant for minoring in literature, a subject that feeds young breeds the seeds of life and the bread of intellectualism." Darrell nodded politely. He always admired his wife's mastery of the English language. She smiled at him and headed for the door.

There was an unusual silence in the car as the couple drove to the university as if each was thinking seriously about the job and challenges ahead. At the university, Darrell closed the door of his office and reflected and projected for a while before his first class. He prayed a little and thought of his childhood days in Ghetahzia, the wonderful time he had in college especially with the guidance of Prof. Kwame, and the challenges of graduate school and his doctoral program. He thought of his life-long college friends, his beloved grandfather, his siblings and parents, his wife and children, and the prodigious task of remaining afloat in academia, however and whatever that meant.

He caught himself. "Is it academia, the academy or the academe? How do those differ, if at all, from the university? Where does the professoriate fit in?" the questions flowed without answers although he thought he knew what each word meant in spite of nuances.

The young professor reached for a dictionary and looked up a few words. He dropped the book and continued thinking. "Is the so-called academe really a world of scholars? Who then are the intellectuals and academics?" He reached for the dictionary again, flipped through quickly and closed it up.

As he thought, Darrell was convinced that whether the university was an academe or academia, it was a unique world, incomparable, unsurpassed, and unpredictable. "The path to this world contains a series of incremental academic achievements shroud in intellectualism, and any level of achievement could be an end in itself." He was convinced that, at any level, as with most achievements, the achiever was likely to be blinded to the perils of perverting pomposity and the delusion of greatness. This was why Prof. Kwame argued ardently that academia was a pool of hot air manned and supervised by airheads.

"I wonder if the professor was too extreme with that thought," Darrell said softly. He was sure that, given the many wonderful things emanating from higher education, it was not likely that most people there were nincompoops but, on second thought, he felt the learned and experienced professor must have had reasons for his opprobrious criticism of higher education, the professor's professional lifetime place of employment. Again, he caught himself playing with words. "He said 'academia'. Is that synonymous to higher education?" Before he would give it another thought, there was a knock on his door.

"Good morning Professor," a young lady with beautiful blond hair greeted. "My name is Karen and I really need your course. This is my last semester and the course is closed. Please, please Professor, do sign me in otherwise I will not graduate in time which will be a real shame because my entire family, including grandparents on both sides and many friends have already been invited to my graduation."

"We are here for the same reason," three other students pleaded.

"Come in and I will sign your registration forms," Darrell consented to the delight of the students probably not knowing that throughout his professorial life, he would hear similar and other implausible excuses a million times.

When the students left, Darrell looked at his watch. He still had a few minutes before his first class. The more he thought about it, a number of "firsts" ran through his mind: his first real job, the first semester, the first day, his first class, on and on. He also knew the old adage that a journey of a thousand miles started with the first step. Similarly, he reminded himself that there was never a second chance for making a first impression; he had to be at his very best, even if teaching a freshman course. This was a smart idea because it is said that, "Punctiliousness is priceless, scrupulousness simulates sainthood, sedulity sanctifies, and dogged devotion devours difficult duties."

Doubtless, it pays to be conscientious regarding one's duties, obligations, and responsibilities, be they legal or ethical, professional or social, national or community, personal or family. Carelessness in these regards breeds multiple consequences, including disreputability, social ostracism, loss of a job or position, and overall failure. As Darrell recalled these points, he knew he could not afford even one of these horrors.

"Good morning class," Darrell greeted his first group of students. "My name is Dr. Darrell D. Thomas and this is Economics 201, just to be sure we are all in the right room." He handed out a carefully prepared syllabus and went over the requirements of the course, including reading assignments and attendance policies. He directed students to his web page where students could find a copy of the syllabus and other materials related to the course.

Next, Darrell clarified that the purpose of the first class was to give an overview of the course. Subsequently, he took a few questions before asking everyone to introduce himself or herself briefly. Following the introductions, he cleared his throat and started his lecture. He thrilled the sophomore and few junior and senior students over microeconomics topics he of course, considered very elementary: broad definition of economics, decision making by governments, producers, and individuals in the face of limited resources, making economic decisions based on economic principles, and the like. No doubt, he introduced the course, firmly established its foundation, and mapped out its trajectory.

After Darrell's first class, he hung around to talk with students and sign in a few late registrants. The students who left his class had varied views. They were all white except one African-American gentleman and one Hispanic lady.

"This man is very good," one young man stated emphatically. "He sure seems to know his stuff."

"You got to be kidding," a young lady rejected. "I mean, I cannot even understand the man. Why do they hire people like that? And if they have to hire them to make the university look good, why don't they send them to teach African-American history or that kind of rubbish? That's the only thing they know or more correctly, they think they know."

"Admit it; you are simply biased," the first student countered. Dr. Thomas' accent is far better than Dr. Williams' but Dr. Williams happens to be a white southerner so you do not mind it; that's very wrong and you know it. Your bias is especially clear because you never asked why Dr. Williams does not teach history of the confederacy. Shame on you!"

"Don't you ever accuse me of being biased," the young lady came back forcefully.

"You are not just biased but a bigot," the young man would not be intimidated. "Once more, shame on you!"

"I am not!" rejected the young lady emphatically. "I'm simply entitled to my opinion and so are you; so there!" Just then, Darrell was walking out of the classroom and the two shut up.

"How was the class?" Darrell asked.

"Great!" said the young man who admired him. "I think I will learn a lot from this course."

"I hope we all learn from it. See you Wednesday," Darrell stated with a smile as he walked down the hall toward his office. The two students went separate ways.

At his office, Darrell looked over the materials for his next class. His two undergraduate courses were scheduled for Mondays, Wednesdays and Fridays while his three graduate courses, each meeting once a week, were scheduled on Tuesdays and Thursdays.

Darrell zipped through his email messages. One was from his department chair with the subject line, "First Department Meeting." The meeting was scheduled for Friday at 11 a.m. The email asked for confirmation. Darrell hit the reply key and wrote, "I intend to attend." When he reread his short message, he realized he had included a signature that started, Darrell D. Thomas, Ph.D., Assistant Professor, Department of Economics .... He smiled lightly as if patting himself on the back. Quickly however, he swept aside the head-swelling self-adulation stating, "True, titles tend to go to the head and generate a spurious sense of superiority instead of positively transforming personalities. It's truly sad and immodest to feed on such self-glorification."

He wondered if people who employed such self-glorification ad nauseam were plagued by insecurity and/or inferiority complex and therefore had to compensate for same. He recalled Vanessa reading about an insecure one who heinously misused his title so much that he fell into disrepute and so his title hung loose about him "like a dwarfish thief in a giant robe."

"No," Darrell said, still referring to his new title. "Here, it's not so much a title but performance and I know it. I will follow the learned Prof. Kwame's advice to the letter. My performance and productivity will be my defense. Yes, I must produce in a manner that silences every detractor." Just then, the phone rang.

"Hi Honey," Vanessa greeted. She said she just discovered that the assistant dean signed four students into her course without her permission; she only learned the information from the students.

"That does not seem right to me," her husband said. "I do not trust these university lines Honey; so let's talk about it at lunch time."

Since the Thomases were starting on a very tight budget and with six children, they drove home for lunch instead of eating out. This was not only a smart way of saving money but it gave them a chance to talk about their experiences before the day ended. "Baby, I checked the policy manual after I received your call and for sure, it clearly indicates that only the instructor of record can sign students into a course after the course is full," Darrell explained at lunch time.

"I checked the manual too and was sure that's what it said. I am sure Peggy, the so-called assistant dean, will not dare do same to other professors and lecturers."

"Well Honey, let's not conclude with certainty. Maybe she does this to everyone," Darrell pleaded. He suggested that since they were just starting, it would not help to begin with confrontation.

"So what am I to do? Roll over and play dead even though my right is clearly infringed? No, I will not." She insisted she would not tolerate violation of her rights by Peggy—who was Caucasian—or by anyone else.

"I do not mean that Honey," Darrell clarified. He suggested Vanessa wrote the assistant dean like this:

Dear Peggy,
In my first class today, four students (names of the students) showed me evidence that you signed them into my course History 101. The policy manual (pp23-24) is clear that only instructors of record sign students into courses when such courses are full. However, I will accept these students as you have already signed them in. Next time, please be sure to consult me as you do not know if I have signed other students into the course. Thanks Peggy.
Sincerely,
Vanessa
Lecturer

"That sounds great Honey," Vanessa agreed.

"She will not like the fact that you not only ask her to consult you but you also cite the Policy Manual. Whatever she thinks, since this is in writing, it serves as your record and evidence next time it happens. Remember what Prof. Kwame said: 'be very careful what you put into writing, even in an email but document everything'."

Darrell too had an issue to discuss with his chair. He hesitated whether to call or email but quickly reminded himself that an email would be a documentation. He sent one off to his chair Alex or Alexander Brooks, Department Chair and William Peters Professor of Economics. Alex preferred to meet so Darrel went over.

"Alex," Darrell began, "I do not mean to change my current workload but looking over the workloads of my colleagues and sifting through the college policy, it is very clear that I am carrying a huge overload. I mean, five courses with huge enrollments just seem to be too much for a starting professor; I guess it would be even for a continuing professor."

Alex hesitated. "Well, let's see. I think it's because you do not have any advisees as of yet."

"Again, the policy manual is clear on advising as a part of, not a substitute for, course assignments unless under specific conditions as outlined in the manual. Additionally, I understand first semester professors usually get light loads. Two colleagues have told me so. One came last year and another two years ago; each started with two courses and you were department chair. Furthermore, no professor in the department is teaching more than three courses. I therefore do not understand why I am assigned five courses."

"Must have been an oversight Darrell. We will be sure to correct that next semester."

"Like I said, I do not mean to change my current schedule but since it was an oversight and I am carrying such a huge load, do I get any financial compensation? It is stated so in the manual."

Alex seemed very uncomfortable, somewhat exasperated. "Such a fund will come out of department budget and I do not think we can afford it now Darrell. Like I've said, we will correct it next semester, O.K?"

"First Alex, my pay does not come out of department budget; you and I know that. Secondly, if you intend to correct the situation next semester, will I get something in writing to that effect?"

"Well, I'm not sure. Saying what?" Alex was getting red in the face.

"Alex," Darrell tried to defuse the situation, "I do not mean to annoy you but put yourself in my shoes. As you know, this is my first semester; fitting in requires a lot of work and time, reading through textbooks, preparing lectures, etc., while simultaneously, I am starting research for publication and conferences. If there was an oversight in my course assignment, I accept. I also applaud the fact that there will be an adjustment next semester to make up for the oversight. If so, why not send me an email or letter stating that because of an oversight in my course assignment this semester, I will get a lighter load next semester? This will give me chance to research and write, and you know I need to do so if I am to continue working here."

"I will give it a thought," Alex growled lightly. Darrell thanked his chair and left convinced he would never get the commitment in writing.

"Of my seven years of being chair, no one has insulted me like that," Alex snarled after Darrell left him alone in his office. "He needs to be put in his place or find somewhere else. I told Dean Harris about that fool; they are lazy and incompetent jerks who are only good as criminals and trouble makers. He better watch out." He stood up and took a few steps as if blowing off steam. "I wish Dean Harris had listened to me but again, he's such a blockhead and yet so egotistical that he listens to no one except his friend and boss who is no less egotistical. Without consulting any of us, he quickly hired that idiot and his funny-looking wife and now, we are stuck or so it seems; but no, something will and must be done before this nonsense goes any farther."

Vanessa's email did not go down well with Peggy either. Although the note was strong enough to prevent her from repeating the act, she did not back down but rather flexed her muscles in a bid to intimidate Vanessa. "You must understand Vanessa that as assistant dean, I can override decisions. I hope you learn to understand the manual which you cite as a Bible. For sure, that manual does not require me to consult you on anything and I hope this is the last I hear about this."

Vanessa fumed when she read Peggy's email. She knew exactly how to respond but hesitated because her husband advised against confrontation within the first week of teaching. "She may see herself as an ivory-tower and all-powerful assistant dean but her hegemonic power-drunkenness does not extend to my class," she stated angrily in her office. "If she thinks she can intimidate me, she must think again; that is, beyond her preposterous pomposity and maniacal megalomania, if she is capable of thinking rationally." Doubtless, her husband was right; when she was angry, no telling what words and phrases flowed.

Back at home, Darrell once more calmed his wife as best as he could. Fortunately, they completed their first week with no disturbing incidents. At the end of the week, they attended meetings in their respective departments. In Darrell's department, Alex welcomed returning and new faculty members and staff, and went over pertinent issues for the semester. He outlined activities for the rest of the academic year and entertained nominations or volunteers for the various department, college, and university committees.

"As you know," he reminded faculty members, "at the beginning of each academic year, you will be evaluated for the previous year on the basis of your teaching, professional activities, and service; service includes your membership on committees in the department, college and university as well as your activities in the community and with professional organizations."

As an untenured assistant professor, Darrell was barred from serving on a few committees. Of the ones on which he could serve, he did not know which was demanding, boring to serve on, or exciting. He simply agreed to serve on a few, including Student Affairs and Campus Beautification. "I think you will be a great addition to the University Diversity Committee," Alex requested. "In addition, I want you to serve as member of the College Diversity Committee and adviser to students of color in the department. I have no doubt you will be an enormous asset to our students of color from both national and international backgrounds."

"Diversity Committees?" Darrell questioned as if he did not know what the words meant.

"Yes, our University and College Diversity Committees," Alex repeated. "Those committees address all issues regarding diversity. For example, at their respective levels, they monitor the recruitment, treatment, and retention of minority students, staff and faculty. As evidenced by our mission statement and website, this administration from top to bottom strongly, seriously, and consistently emphasizes the importance of diversity. All of us therefore uphold that principle rigidly."

Darrell smiled and accepted the appointments not knowing precisely what his acceptance entailed. "If this is diversity, I do not know what tokenism is," he thought to himself. "And if such committees exist, and if they performs as charged, why don't we have diversity in this place?" He thought he had some answers but refrained from pursuing what he deemed as a lost cause.

Vanessa's department chair, Dr. Brian Anderson, Phillip Russell Professor of History, also welcomed returning and new faculty and staff. Toward the end of the meeting, Vanessa said she had a question.

"Go ahead," Brian encouraged.

"As you know, this is my first semester and I am glad to be here. However, I am assigned five courses, all with very high enrollments. Is this typical?"

The room was quiet for a minute. Then, Brian spoke up. "Not really Vanessa. That must have been a scheduling error." "If so and we are already at the end of the first week, is there any possibility of financial compensation for this error? I mean, this takes up a huge chunk of my time and definitely requires enormous work. Besides, the policy manual is clear on the issue of compensation under such circumstances."

Again, the room was quiet. "I'm not sure," Brian responded. "Check with me later Vanessa. Maybe we will just make up next semester."

"That's fine," Vanessa accepted. "But if we will make up next semester, do I get something in writing to that effect?"

"Again, check with me later and we will discuss such issues," Brian insisted, looking somewhat uncomfortable discussing the issue.

"Forgive me," said Vanessa. "I do not mean to dwell on this ad nauseam but please tell me one thing."

"What is that Vanessa?" the department chair asked.

"Is the policy manual truly authoritative or is it printed simply for purposes of decoration?" A few people laughed and Brian turned red in the face. He definitely did not expect this from a new lecturer who had been at the university for only two weeks.

"Let me repeat once more Vanessa," said Brian. "Please see me later and we will talk about this in my office." Vanessa doubtfully nodded as a few people continued to laugh under their breaths. "I also would like to discuss with you some matters regarding our students of color but, as I have said, please meet me in my office."

Vanessa's phone rang shortly after she returned to her office. She was not sure if it was her husband or a student calling. "Hello Vanessa," the voice said. "I am Lupita, the Hispanic lady who was sitting behind you in the meeting. Ann and I would like to have lunch with you early next week if your schedule permits. If you do not know her already, Ann Kinsman is an

African-American who works as one of the secretaries in the department."

"I will love that; set it up and I will find time."

"Actually, I would like it to be at my house, away from campus. Ann and I take turn meeting at one another's house." Vanessa accepted the invitation with the suspicion that soon, they would be meeting at her house too. She did not mind that as her children would be in school during lunch time.

Darrell also wanted to get a lunch or coffee appointment with one or two of the persons who expressed desire in that regard on the first day but each one gave one excuse or another. The lone exception was Dr. Andrew Barclay, a tenured full professor, known simply to his colleagues as Andy. In fact, he asked Darrell if they could have coffee or lunch the following week. They agreed to meet for lunch on Monday.

At the end of the first week, Darrell and Vanessa compared notes and shared ideas. They placed another call to Prof. Kwame.

"So, how did the first week go for my young professor and lecturer?"

"A mixed bag—some dainty, some doubtful, some doleful," Darrell answered laughing.

"Give me a synopsis," the professor emeritus requested.

First, Darrell briefly discussed his first week of classes. "You were right Prof. An undergraduate student challenged me on an elementary topic like demand and supply. I thought of you as I smiled and responded poignantly." Continuing, he disclosed the workloads for him and Vanessa and discussed his meeting with his department chair. He referred briefly to his committee assignments. He pointed out Vanessa's email exchange with the assistant dean and the workload issues she raised in her department meeting.

"You have had a busy first week," Prof. Kwame observed. "Within the first week, you have called attention to yourselves and now are regarded as people who have stepped out of their boxes to challenge the status quo. Believe me, you are now branded as trouble makers. You really have to be careful although you have only sought your deserved fair treatments." Continuing, he said he had contacted Dr. J. Edwardo Dominguez, a Hispanic colleague who retired from SAU about two years ago. "After working there for more than thirty years, Ed knows a lot about the place. I had not mentioned him for I could not locate him; I just found him this week. He now lives actively but happily in retirement and is willing to give you as much inside information as he can. He still has a few friends there; he himself emphasizes the word 'few' because, according to him, it was difficult to get true friends he could trust. In retirement, he keeps in touch with his few trusted friends on a weekly, even daily basis."

"That will be very helpful Prof., Vanessa said.

"But for now, I encourage you strongly to be on your guard. Leave no stones unturned. I have told you so before. You are fighting against an administration which, when it comes to under-represented groups, is especially stiff, hostile, and fastidious. As such, your only chance of winning is to out-perform them and observe the policies keenly. Believe me, there will be snares, put downs, picky evaluations, non-promotion, and more. Therefore, give them no excuses, reasons, or opportunities to effectuate their preset plans. In other words, do not overlook even the minutest things or routine activities like keeping office hours and attending meetings regularly. Remember what our African elders say; 'when snake is your dancing partner, watch your feet'."

The retired professor warned that the two young people on the line had no choice but be vigilant and work hard. He said this was because the general presumption was they were inept, incapable, and unable to perform the tasks of a professor or lecturer. With that presumption, administrators and even colleagues would look for the minutest evidence to confirm that presumption and exaggerate it exponentially. He admitted this was a generalization but very likely in a number of instances, if not in most instances especially with regard to predominantly white institutions of higher education.

Addressing the workload issue, Prof. Kwame said for a school of that size, it was unusual for anyone to be assigned five courses. Besides, from what they told him, such a workload was prohibited by the collective bargaining agreement and the college policy handbook. He therefore did not think it was a mere oversight that both were assigned five courses with no financial compensation. "I doubt if Darrell you will get that email nor will Vanessa's chair address the issue. I am also sure no 'make-up' adjustments will be made in your schedules next semester; the best you can hope for is getting less than five courses."

"I believe that Prof.," Vanessa averred. "As you say, we will be on our guards. For instance, we have received conflicting messages regarding tenure and promotion." She explicated that on one hand, they were advised to excel in teaching if they wanted to be tenured and promoted. Similarly, Darrell was told successful grant writing was not regarded as scholarship but most professors who were tenured and promoted wrote grants, some funded and others not. "Despite these conflicting messages," Vanessa explained, "we are working on articles for publication; Darrell is considering grant writing. We would like to publish every semester. I would like to publish two to three articles a year while Darrell wants to publish three to four."

"That sounds like a lot. To accomplish such a feat, you may not be talking to one another, let alone your children but if you can accomplish even half as much, you will be paving your ways to tenure. Do not forget conference presentations and grant writing."

It is true that success in duty and longevity in position come not by perfunctory performance but through devotion and sedulity. Cognizant of this truism, and mindful that their works were scrutinized more than others, Darrell and Vanessa were determined to meet and beat the challenge. They also knew that to succeed, they could not work in isolation; they needed honest friends for a genuine friendship is more than a priceless pearl. Identifying such a gem was a monumental task albeit prayerfully possible.

Chapter V:

GETTING ACQUAINTED

I ndeed, it is difficult to overemphasize the complexity of human relationships, especially their communications and interactions. It is inexplicable, for instance, why and how a person genuinely falls in love or vehemently resents another on first sight. True, there is a middle ground whereby an open-minded person may maintain that, "I will accept you as you are until you show me who you are." However, what if any of the extremes exists? It is neither a planned victory for the observer nor fault of the observed; rather it is simply the feeling of the observer. As this feeling feeds on nothing substantive, sometimes not even verifiable about the observed, it grows on everything about him or her. Apparently mindful of this truism, Darrell and Vanessa truly needed genuine friends so as to know who to befriend and who to avoid. They therefore were delighted for opportunities to know one or two persons early in their work at SAU.

"Thanks for coming to lunch with me; I really appreciate it," Dr. Andrew Barclay, popularly known as Andy, said as he and Darrell took seats at a restaurant near the university.

"I thank you," Darrell said with an emphasis on the 'you'. "I honestly was looking forward to this.

Darrell did not understand why, except for Andy, all the people who wanted to have lunch with him 'withdrew into their little corners' and left Darrell isolated. Although he did not know that this isolation would linger for a long time, perhaps never end during his entire stay at SAU, he was grateful that Andy showed up. In fact, Andy was so anxious to have lunch that Darrell wondered why but he was determined to keep an open mind, not be suspicious or speculate ad nauseam. After they were served, he began to understand, as he listened intently to Andy, paying little attention to the bustling around the restaurant.

"I was born in this country but because my father was in the military, we lived in various countries around the world," Andy started. "When I grew up, I too joined the military and served in a number of countries. When I left the military, I did odd jobs as I completed college and eventually went to graduate school. Believe me, working here has been an enormous experience."

"What do you mean?"

"Well," Andy cleared his throat as he picked up his sandwich. He took a bite, chewed for a minute or so before continuing. Dressed in a nice long sleeve shirt that match his gray pants and black shoes, the handsome five foot nine professor elucidated that when he lived outside the country, he learned a lot about other people, cultures, and governments. First hand, he learned the importance of accepting others because often, as a white American, he was the person struggling to fit in and eventually be accepted. He said he found out, sometimes the hard way, the importance of making use of what one has. Mindful that Darrell was listening to every word he said, Andy clarified, "I mean, I learned to appreciate every little thing I have and everything society offers for out there, I saw people who were very poor by our standards but far happier than we can ever imagine. Here, we have everything, or so it seems, but we are among the unhappiest people in the world. Honestly, I learned a lot.

As Darrell's attention remained undivided, Andy turned to his experience at SAU. He divulged that, in all sincerity, people at SAU WERE generally friendly. Most regrettably, however, he observed that deep down, the university generally was engulfed by a false sense of openness and a hypocritical atmosphere of tolerance and acceptance. Worse, the nauseating syndrome of sycophancy forced some to abandon their principles and subsequently sucked them into unceasing unscrupulousness while others went further; they could, in his words, "lick the behind of anyone to gain or maintain a position. It's all dreadfully disgusting!"

"I'll say," Darrell interrupted and both men laughed heartily. As the laughter faded, Andy reached for a glass of water and drank about half of it. He then pulled over a salad bowl and began to eat slowly while half of his sandwich waited.

Darrell entirely agreed with Andy's views about SAU. He disclosed he had found out quickly that people were not very tolerant of difference at SAU, whether that referred to difference on the basis of gender, race, ethnicity, nationality, or even denomination.

"I do not know you Darrell but there's something about you I like. You seem to be a decent man and obviously an extremely bright gentleman. So, I will be very honest with you."

"On my honors, I will do all I can to uphold the confidence you repose in me."

Andy took another bite of his sandwich and a drink of water as a young waitress had come around to refill their water glasses. "For a moment, you sounded like a politician there," HE said. Both men laughed lightly and Andy continued. "You see Darrell," he struggled to explain as if addressing a very difficult topic. "I have been here for more than twenty years and have seen people from under-represented groups come and go; these are the people, you know, some call 'minorities' but I know that's a pejorative term." He paused a little as he chewed. He explained further that within the last five years, the university in general but particularly his college lost very good professors, lecturers, and secretaries simply because, as he saw it, such persons were African-Americans or Hispanics. The regrettable loss of people who left in frustration included Asians, Arabs, Africans, two ladies from the Caribbean, a Brazilian, and a Native American lady.

"Frustration?" Darrell probed for elaboration.

"Yes, frustration," Andy repeated the word. He said people of color left the university because consistently, they endured injustice in a hostile campus climate. "They charge, and I do not doubt them that they are frequently criticized and never appreciated. Rather, they are marginalized, often bypassed for promotion, minimally supported, if at all, conspicuously isolated, and treated cruelly in various ways. Why would anyone stay under such conditions especially when the same treatments are not meted to Whites?"

Andy cleared his throat as he turned his attention to another area. He regretted the fact that the university recruited relatively few students from under-represented backgrounds and among those who were admitted, only a handful remained; of those staying, the graduation rate was dismal. He straightened himself in his chair as he continued, "I mean we do a horrible job of recruitment and treatment of people from under-represented groups; no wonder then the retention rate is atrocious. For sure, we give validity to the terms, 'under-represented groups'. No doubt about it; we create the 'under-represented' status and I think this is unconscionable."

Darrell nodded agreeably but did not utter a word. Andy added that although he could point a finger at one or two persons within the administration, he did not blame any single individual since everyone, himself included, had faults and limitations. He rather blamed the system. He acknowledged the obvious; that is, the system was made up of individuals. However, as opposed to generalizing, he clarified. "I am referring to stakeholders who do not provide a conducive campus atmosphere or a positive workplace climate to boost recruitment on one hand and on the other, retention of faculty, students, and staff from under-represented groups."

"Presently, my wife and I are renting our house as we do not know how long we will live here," Darrell disclosed as he worked on his sandwich.

"That's the thing," Andy tried to speak as he finished the last piece of his sandwich. He averred that generally, people from under-represented groups who went to SAU either as students or employees did not know, after a short time, whether to stay at the university or leave. Comparing this horrible situation to that of Whites, he revealed, "I have seen white men come here with mediocre credentials and yet are encouraged to stay; they get enormous support from the administration when the so-called people of color and women are not treated in similar manner. The worst treatment is meted out to women of color who, in my view, are doubly victimized—first on the basis of gender and second, because of their race."

"I absolutely agree," intimated Darrell. He said as Andy knew, he was hired along with a Caucasian gentleman who held an ABD (all but dissertation) credential while Darrell was a Ph.D.. He said although he could not categorize ABD as a mediocre credential, the truth was, an ABD was not a Ph.D., and yet, the gentleman had a better office space and far better overall treatment than Darrell. For example, the gentleman was actually assigned mentors to enable him complete his doctorate and fit in as an assistant professor. Furthermore, his office was furnished with new equipment while Darrell inherited old ones. Worse still, Darrell found out later that the gentleman was allowed to teach only two courses in his first semester while Darrell, also in his first semester, was assigned five courses, all with high enrollments, including graduate courses, not forgetting his "official" and "unofficial" assignments with students of color in the department and throughout the college. "Such treatment on the onset does not give me any encouragement or hope in the system," Darrell bemoaned.

Shaking his head in disgust, Andy said, "I heard that and it's absolutely detestable. Continuing his reference to women, he lamented further that emphasis on hiring women generally meant hiring white women thereby exacerbating the imbalance although, in this case, culpability rested not with white women but administrators and recruitment personnel. The same were to be blamed for the incessant discrimination against men from under-represented groups. He decried the situation strongly. "This is wrong; the so-called administrators know it and so do I and therefore I have always opposed it as vehemently as I can and will continue to do so."

Andy stopped speaking to listen to an announcement in the restaurant about a car light that was left on in the parking lot. When he and Darrell breathed a sigh of relief that it was not either person's car, HE went on. He admitted he had never supported nor did he intend to support someone solely because he or she was a so-called person of color. He quickly clarified however that he was convinced such persons needed varied considerations, but he would not go to the extent of advocating preferential treatments for them and, in fact, he did not think they themselves sought such treatments especially if they were qualified. Andy stated further that, in line with the standards of the university, and although he was cognizant of the fact that certain groups in the country had traditionally been at a disadvantage in schools and general society, he nonetheless would not support anyone whose work was mediocre either. "On the other hand," He explained, "if a person is qualified and industrious, I honestly believe he or she should receive the same level of support and evaluation, and be given the same chances for promotion, irrespective of gender, race, nationality, and the like; that's the essence of 'justice and equality for all' but, considering the number of lawyers in this country, that's another story." Both men laughed.

"I could not agree more," said Darrell as he finished his sandwich. Dressed in a nice jacket and tie, he said it was only common sense that everyone be expected to be judged on merit, not race, color, gender, or any other external criterion but in the case of SAU, race was the criterion and merit the camouflage.

"MM," Andy nodded. "Isn't that Dr. Martin Luther King's notion of being judged by the content of one's character and not the color of his or her skin?"

"Absolutely! Dr. King was right on the money!" Darrell agreed.

"He was amazing, one of a kind," Andy praised. He promised to support Darrell as much as he could. For starters, he encouraged Darrell to work hard—teach effectively, publish and write grants, present at conferences, and serve on committees. He said if Darrell covered these areas well and abided by the university and college policies, he would be fine and no one could oppose him for his record would not only speak for him but would decisively win his battle. In addition, Darrell was advised to be on top of the advising process. In other words, he was to know the courses approved for the completion of university, department and program requirements. He had to know the alternatives for such courses if some were not available for his advisees. In instances where he was confused, in doubt, or flatly did not know what to do, he was encouraged strongly to ask someone lest he misadvised a student.

Darrell listened intently to every word Andy spoke. More than what was spoken, he appreciated the sincerity of the speaker. As these thoughts crossed Darrell's mind, Andy looked around the semi-crowded but very clean and decorated restaurant before adding softly, "Believe me, judging from previous experience, many will oppose you here singly or in committees solely because of your race and, as I have said, that's terribly wrong especially in such modern times and in light of unambiguous prohibiting statutes which are ignored blatantly, incessantly, and with impunity."

"It seems I am presumed grossly inept, incapable, and inefficient until I prove otherwise but they will pounce on every opportunity to confirm and validate their presumption."

"That is an accurate observation," Andy commended. Reemphasizing his point, he said it was terribly wrong for Darrell or anyone else to be forced into proving himself or herself; each professor was expected to perform his or her professorial duties. It was therefore unfortunate and highly regrettable that Darrell had to 'over-perform' and thereby prove himself. "But," Andy intimated, "that's the name of the game around here."

Darrell thanked Andy as they both rose to leave. They shook hands and promised to meet regularly for lunch, coffee or even dinners at one another's home. Before he got into his car, Darrell once more thanked Andy in the parking lot. "Believe me, I appreciate this more than you will ever realize. Thanks a million and I will see you soon.

As Darrell drove and thought of his conversation with Andy, many things went through his mind. At times turning his thoughts into soft whispers, and as he later revealed to Vanessa, his thinking was along the following lines.

It is incontrovertible that interpersonal relationships are compound complex and delicate. Regarding such relationships, the good book is right on many fronts but four pertinent ones can be pointed out. First, it says no one should be reluctant to accept others for some accepted angels unaware. Second, it says that the measure one puts in is the measure he or she gets out. Next, it commands that we love our neighbors as ourselves. Fourthly, it stresses that one ought to treat others as he or she wants to be treated. To ignore these cardinal points and judge or treat others not in line with what they do or say but on the basis of their race, gender, nationality, disability, and the like is unconscionable, abhorrent, detestable, and totally unacceptable. Yet, many refuse to shed their biases, prejudices, and bigotry forgetting that, irrespective of their earthly powers, possessions, and positions, one day they will stand before the final bar of justice. May the Supreme Judge have mercy on us all!! We especially pray for mercy as some think they can fool the Supreme Judge by getting one or two token friends from under-represented backgrounds as a means of masking their deep-seated prejudice and bigotry. Oh no, the eye above sees us all, our hands, hearts and heads.

A day after Darrell's lunch appointment, Lupita Gomez, commonly known as LG, drove Vanessa and Ann to her house for lunch. "Welcome to our little humble home," she said. "My friend and sister, Ann Kinsman and I have been meeting for years. Three other ladies used to meet with us but could not take it here anymore and left in total frustration. One of them was from the Caribbean, the other from the Middle-East and the third from Africa." LG explained that one of the ladies, did not say which, initially refused to join them as she saw nothing even minutely wrong with the attitudes and policies of the dominant group. Instead, she accused LG and others of sensationalizing the race card. When the powers that be showed her their true colors, she joined their luncheon get-togethers but later left in disgust.

As Ann laughed to confirm LG's narrative, Vanessa expressed thanks and gratitude. "Honestly, I thank you sincerely for inviting me to join you. Heaven knows I need to know this place. Hence, I am very grateful that you two are willing to take me figuratively under your wings and show me around."

"My dear, this place is a living hell for minorities, especially so for women," Ann jumped into the heart of the matter as LG served a simple lunch of soup, sandwiches, and fruit salad. "To be honest, it is hell for any woman but more so for women of color; that is why my sister Lupita here and I have been meeting to provide support for one another. Without Lupita, I would have left long time ago."

"I can say the same for Ann. She has been very helpful," LG stated with a slight but beautiful Spanish accent. She described herself as a Chicana, the feminine of Chicano. "As you know Vanessa," a Chicana or Chicano is difficult to describe." She said although the word generally referred to American citizens of Mexican descent, it had other connotations. For instance, in some circles, it referred to politically active Mexican-Americans. In other instances, it was simply an attestation that people so described were neither Mexicans nor Americans but were proud to have roots in Mexico. However, perceived or interpreted, the truth remained that Chicanos and Chicanas were plagued by multiple problems in higher education. Like others from under-represented groups, this was particularly true relative to matters of acceptance, incorporation, respect and promotion, and appreciation of work and contribution. Although Vanessa had taken courses in Latin American history, she listened intently to Lupita's explanation. Returning to the reason for inviting Vanessa, Lupita said, "To be honest, I grew up not knowing much about African-Americans but graduate studies and especially knowing Ann have made a huge difference in my life. We therefore want to include you in our company although we do not know you but will do so on your honors."

"You can rest assured I will not betray your trust and confidence. In all sincerity, I highly appreciate your confidence and will do everything I can to uphold it," Vanessa promised.

"We trust you and therefore will do all we can to help," LG promised in return. As the ladies ate, Vanessa learned more about Mexican culture and Lupita's struggles as the only Chicana instructor in her department. LG expressed frustration with the fact that all issues of Hispanic students were turned to her as if she was the be-all and end-all on Hispanic issues. Further, she resented the fact that advising and other issues took up much of her time and yet, she was not recognized for these services. Worse still, she was treated contemptuously; to the administration, she was just a Chicana, not a professional colleague. "It's all very disgusting."

Vanessa also learned about the department and college as well as about specific individuals. She told the others about her experience with Assistant Dean, Dr. Peggy Chance, a Caucasian administrator who was known around the college only as Peggy.

"I can tell you about that woman right now," LG jumped in. "She is vicious, vindictive albeit ignominious, inept, and indescribably disorganized. She hangs on power not only because she is Caucasian but especially because she falls in the good graces of the dean and president whose praises she sings incessantly."

"Oh lord, don't get me started about that woman. All I can say is, be very careful with her," Ann warned. "She is a back-stabber, a real witch. I agree, she is incredibly inefficient and inept. She is terribly disorganized and lies all the time to cover up. It is not really known what she does and so she embarks on trivial tasks to seem busy and meaningfully contributive. Whatever she does, she is generally dreaded, even hated in the college by almost everyone. I mean, I have not met one person who speaks favorably about that woman. Heaven knows from whence she comes. She has caused many good people to leave this college. This is why I cannot stand her although I am not a hater."

LG laughed. "Why don't you show her your poem Ann?"

"Oh yea. I'm just a secretary, not a poet but I wrote something small about her. It probably does not make much sense but I wrote it anyway." She pulled a piece of paper out of her purse and read:

> She is a shitty, shaky, fakey, freaky freak
> A stinky, nasty, nasty, snake
> Dreadful, hateful, vengeful
> A creepy sneaky cheat
> With fleeting sneaky feet
> To sweep away the meek and sleepy saints
> In the deep of a grace-seeking night;
> So if you can hear a warning bell,
> Please do avoid Je-ze-bel!
> She smears anything and anyone good in sight!

Vanessa fell over laughing. "That is pretty and really profound," she commended for this was no occasion for incisive literary analysis. Thinking about the label 'Jezebel' which was used to derogate black women who resisted racism and patriarchy, she smiled lightly before adding, "That says a lot about her, my goodness! How did she get her doctorate?"

Lupita started laughing again. She tried on two occasions to stop laughing and get out a word but could not control the laughter. Finally, she got a word or two out in the midst of a continuing soft laughter. "Oh, that's another story and how she gained tenure, a dissertation in itself. I tell you, Ann and I can't stand that woman. Actually, most people in the college cannot stand her."

When Lupita's laughing died down completely, she went on with her insider information. "I have been here for twelve years and am now tenured as a senior lecturer but, as I have pointed out repeatedly, it has not been easy." She said she taught mainly American history but had strong roots in Latin American and African history, and had published in all three areas. "But," she hesitated, "as I have said, I am treated with contempt and disrespect. I am among the lowest paid lecturers in the university despite all I do. I had no mentors and have never been appreciated for my work. Worse, I always get an overload in terms of advising, teaching, and committee service. I mean, the campus climate has never been conducive and getting promotion and tenure was worse than seeking a grain of sand in the Sahara Desert. I therefore almost left. I seriously considered it because there are just too many nasty people in the department and, believe it or not, these include an African-American professor who, in my opinion, has been colonized."

"Save me Lord," Ann chimed in. "Don't get me started on him either; my next secretary poem will be about him; Oh Lord have mercy!"

"You see," LG clarified, "we have three minority professors in the department." She corrected herself and said they were from under-represented groups. "They are one

African-American, one African, and a non-American Asian. You probably noticed that in our first meeting." She explained that the African-American, Dr. Amos Commings, was a full professor with tenure and incredibly nasty especially toward fellow African-Americans and others from under-represented backgrounds. The Asian, an associate professor with tenure, interacted minimally with people in the department except for one or two Whites. The African was an assistant professor without tenure and so was exerting all his efforts toward gaining tenure. "He just does not pay attention to anything going on in the college. He has a lot to fight—discrimination, degradation, and all kinds of rude comments, including some from students."

Ann articulated that although she could not stand Peggy, she had to admit nonetheless that Peggy's nastiness was directed toward all, starting first with people from under-represented groups, then women and finally anyone else. On the other hand, she could not understand why Professor Commings only under-mined Blacks primarily and then other people of color. "That man has been the cause of a good number of Africans and African-Americans leaving this university, among the few hired here; these include not only people from our college but also from other colleges as he serves on all kinds of committees." She became visibly angry adding, "How in the world does this fool get away with such nastiness? They use him to do all kinds of dirty work and yet never promote him but he does not see it. To him, anything White is good and anything Black is sus-pect—a black man who grew up in the hood?"

LG started laughing again. "Ann please tell Vanessa the exchange you had with Professor Commings one day."

"Oh yea, that's another thing," Ann began. "He gives you the impression that he is for Blacks when in fact, he is the biggest back-stabber of Blacks." She said one day Professor Commings told her he was her big brother and she replied, "I am a Kinsman, not a Commings, the family that only opposes Blacks." Vanessa could not stop laughing.

Also laughing, LG said that was why she categorized Prof. Commings as "colonized." Delving into history, she elaborated that, wherever colonialists went, they condemned the people's languages, cultures, governments, and ways of life. To exemplify, colonialists made Africans believe everything African was horrible while everything European was wonderful. Many of the colonized and indoctrinated people believed this and consequently condemned their own cultures, including invaluable components of culture such as language, food, clothes, music, art, family relations, names, and mores. "In the same way," LG explained, "I am not sure how but Professor Commings strongly antagonizes his own people and yet gives the false face that he is concerned about them; hypocrite, liar, nasty snake!"

"Believe me, you will do very well to avoid him as much as possible; he's no good," Ann warned. Conversely, she mentioned a number of African-American and Hispanic/Latino and Latina lecturers, professors, and administrators who were very supportive of others, including students from under-represented groups. "Unfortunately," Ann regretted, "many of them are not in positions to make a huge difference given the political atmosphere of this university." She said the same was true of a number of Caucasians who endeavored to support students, staff and faculty from under-represented groups.

"How about Dean Harris?" Vanessa asked.

The two ladies looked at one another and laughed. "Only two words correctly describe him, 'moronic bigot,'" LG said. "I mean, the man does not know what he's doing but is kept on because, like his haggish assistant dean, he falls within the good graces of the president. He's really a sad case."

Anne said she had taken minutes in college-wide faculty meetings and found the man pitiful; she actually felt sorry for him. She said the dean did not know what he was doing yet, one could cut his bigotry with a knife. With visible frustration, she declared, "He's extremely narrow-minded. I agree, he's a sad case and his grammar, just terrible; even a secretary like me notice it clearly."

"I understand he does not have a doctorate," Vanessa aired what to her was a rumor.

"No he does not," LG confirmed. She further averred that the dean had been working on his doctorate for years but remained ABD, All But Dissertation. To show how putrid was the system, she revealed that, while the manner in which the dean got his masters degree was another long story, the truth remained that the accepted period for a doctoral program was seven years with possible short term extensions. In spite of this clear policy guideline, the dean had been doing his doctorate for more than twelve years and, to the best of her knowledge, without a single request for extension. "Moreover," she expressed with confidence, "if evaluated properly, there is no way he can complete a doctorate but, given the prevailing situation, he will." She twisted her head in disgust. "I tell you, this is a case of dirty politics playing in the hands of a pathetic idiot."

"My goodness, everyone is a bigot, an idiot, a moron, or the like. Are there people around here who do not fall in these categories?" Vanessa questioned curiously.

"Sorry Vanessa," LG apologized without saying why. "We do not mean to give the impression that everyone here is horrible. In all honesty, even though most people are narrow-minded when it comes to issues of diversity, this university has great administrators and internationally renowned scholars." She said two associate deans in the college, for instance, were fabulous administrators but were overshadowed by Peggy, an assistant dean, because of her political connections. Similarly, there were outstanding chairs in a number of departments within the college and presumably throughout the university.

Ann agreed. "As a secretary, I hear various comments, compliments, and condemnations by faculty, staff and students. I also know there are many highly qualified and dedicated people in our college and I imagine throughout the university." She said she knew of a number of professors and lecturers whom students described as caring, considerate, conscientious, competent, and compassionate. She also knew of professors and lecturers whose courses filled up quickly semester after semester because of such instructors' teaching abilities and keen interests in students. "In like manner, beyond Peggy and our 'wonderful dean,' I know administrators who have earned the praises of both students and faculty members. No, not everyone is rotten," she concluded.

This was exactly what Vanessa expected to hear and she was glad it came through loudly and clearly. She was sure that, given the university's reputation, there had to be outstanding professors and administrators on the campus but wondered how many, or more particularly, which ones could be described as narrow-minded, racist, and/or a bigot. She knew they existed and sooner or later, she would find a few. Already, she had learned a lot during the short term she and Darrell had been at SAU.

LG went to the kitchen to do the few dishes and the two ladies joined her. "Oh no, I can handle these few dishes," she protested.

"We know but doing these few dishes together is a neat way of bonding," Vanessa countered and the three ladies laughed. As they did the dishes, Vanessa thanked the ladies for the inside information and once more promised to uphold the confidence reposed in her. She offered her home as the next place for lunch. "Maybe instead of having lunch, one day we might plan a dinner with our husbands and cook some ethnic dishes," she suggested.

"Will both of you cook soul food," LG asked with a giggle.

"Girl, I can burn the pot. Although I was born here, my family is from Mississippi and they sure taught me how to cook good southern food."

Vanessa was not sure whether to tell the others about the dish she wanted to prepare but she did anyway. "A friend from Liberia, West Africa taught me to cook Jollof rice; it's delicious and I am sure you will love it."

"Sounds interesting; actually, I can't wait," LG stated and Ann agreed.

"We will plan it," Vanessa said with conviction. "I do not mean to cancel the lunch meetings but, once in a while, such a dinner including our families will be great." Changing the topic slightly, she once more expressed appreciation to the ladies for their frank and insightful information.

"Believe me, we will support you as much as we can until you are tenured and promoted. If you have a problem to discuss, or if you need a shoulder to cry on, we are here," offered Ann with utmost sincerity.

"That's the truth Vanessa," Lupita endorsed. "In this nasty university environment, no one can do it alone."

Again, Vanessa thanked the ladies before they left for the university.

As Vanessa drove home to pick up Darrell whom she had dropped off to fetch a simple lunch, she thought out loud. "In a 'normal world', life is tough, tedious, and toilsome. In a 'hostile world', life is doubly arduous. In 'either world', no one can make it alone regardless of place, position, possession, and power. Total isolation from others is possible only in one place, the grave; otherwise, the importance of interdependence cannot be overemphasized and this is particularly impelling in a hostile community." She was sure she and Darrell were therefore lucky to have sources of support, even if that meant only one or two persons. In fact, to her, this number was sufficient because, to make a difference, one did not need a noisy multitude but a committed few. She hoped this was true in their case.

Chapter VI:

A SERIOUS ALLEGATION

"I'm calling this meeting to morder," Dean Harris said although some members of the College Administrative Council, CAC were still getting coffee. "I intend to adjure this meeting in time 'cause I have another appointment. Did everyone get the agenda?" the dean asked. Ignoring a seeming catachresis, everyone nodded.

"We have a number of items on the agenda but Item 7 regards a charge of plagiarism against a professor," Professor Aaron Daniels of biology pointed out. "I think this is a serious charge and so ought to be discussed first."

"Are there any objection to Professor Daniels proposal?" the dean questioned. Seeing no objections, and with everyone ignoring his horrible grammar, he jumped to the heart of the matter. "Well, this is a issue of plagiarism that has been brought forward by a department chair against a professor. Both the chair and professor will remains synonymous for now. We will bring in the professor when this committee decide on discipline for him and I am sure we will do so because this is serious. No one should be allowed to get away with this kind of volition."

"I want to believe you mean anonymous and if so, I question the reason for anonymity. I also think you mean violation but could you give us a little more detail?" Professor Andrew Barclay requested.

The dean seemed somewhat uncomfortable. He sipped on his coffee apparently to calm his nerves. He sat upright and straightened his tie which did not match his shirt and jacket. Clearing his throat, he said a chair reported that a professor plagiarized in both the syllabus and in a handout. "As you know, this is a serious charge even against our students, let alone a professor," the dean stated, looking around the room for impressions and reactions and leaving no doubt that he was angry and meant business. From his looks, it was certain that a tough disciplinary action was in order and would be exacted swiftly and decisively.

Andy said he still did not understand. He probed further to see if the professor charged had been informed and if so, what plea he or she entered.

"To my knowledge, the professor have not been inform. The chair brought this matter to this council for our action," the dean once more displayed his inability to handle the English language effectively. A number of professors in the room shook their heads and wondered how this man became dean. This "wonder" clearly symbolized the fact that they had either forgotten or perhaps were not aware of the mysterious and enigmatic inner workings of higher education. Whatever the case, the truth was, the dean was the dean and that was that.

"I think I understand now," declared Professor Phil Smith of Geography who, like his colleagues, paid no attention to the dean's poor grammar. "A professor has been charged with plagiarizing materials in his or her syllabus and handout but has not been informed. Yet, this council is expected to take action against the accused professor, in the absence of any evidence and without knowing the professor by name. Is that right Dean?" The dean nodded in agreement.

"That's what I call jungle justice or justice upside down," Andy bellowed. "In fact, it is no justice; it is injustice; I mean the very worst example of injustice. Where is this professor's right to due process? You mean we are charged here with the task of indicting someone on the basis of rumor? Do you expect us to exact disciplinary action when we ourselves are not privy to any evidence?

The dean rejected Andy's line of questioning. "No Dr. Barclay; there is strong charge here," he said.

Andy was not amused. "Let me ask you Dean." The dean nodded as if prepared for the question. "Let say you go to the bank next door and say you have strong charge that the bank owes you money; therefore, the teller should pay up. Do you think you will get a penny?" Almost everyone in the room laughed.

"No," the dean answered, remaining serious.

"But you have a strong charge; so why would you not get the money?" Andy probe further to the laughter of a few people.

"That's not the same thing here Dr. Barclay," the dean once more rejected.

"Of course it is," Andy replied. "According to your line of logic, if you have a strong charge, you are right and the other party is wrong." With a faint smile, he added, "While your sense of 'strong charge' remains undefined, please Dean Harris, do not insult our intelligence or make us to do something totally illegal and even ignominious."

"I do not mean that Dr. Barclay but what do you suggest?"

Andy laughed mildly. "Excuse me," he apologized. "This is not a laughing matter for we are talking plagiarism here, a very serious charge indeed." He therefore suggested that the professor in question be informed of the charge against him or her and be given a chance to defend himself or herself after evidence was presented. "This professor indicted and seemingly convicted anonymously has a right to notice and a hearing; that is the essence of due process." Dr. Barclay continued to shake his head in total disbelief as to how a matter of such seriousness was being handled.

"Due process?" Clearly, the dean did not understand what that meant. He looked around the room as if searching for the answer in people's faces. "Everyone agree?" he asked. "Is Dr. Barclay right or shall we call in our legal chief?"

"There's no other way," Prof. Daniels stressed. "I am just shocked and utterly disappointed that this issue was put on the agenda under these circumstances." Before abandoning the issue in total disgust, he warned the dean to handle the issue properly. "I hope there is thorough investigation to ensure that there is evidence beyond reasonable doubt that this professor is guilty. I suspect there is no such persuasive evidence and this will be another waste of our precious time." In total disgust, he added, "Honestly Dean, how many more times will we endure this type of situation? Repeatedly, we are plagued by ineptitude, missteps, illogical analyses, and the like when we have better use of our time." It seemed he no longer cared. The dean had to know the truth and he did not mind being the messenger or at least, one of the messengers.

The dean shrugged. Though uncomfortable, he did not know how to rebut Prof. Daniels' statement. In a low tune, he averred in his characteristic grammatical flub, "O.K., I will send this issue back to the chair but I am sure the chair is right; otherwise, he would not have send it to me." Five or six persons in the room shook their heads again without saying a word. Without addressing other items on the agenda, they filed out of the dean's office apparently without knowing what the next step would be.

After another lively class, Darrell was headed to his office with a few students following. "Darrell," shouted Alex as Darrell and the students passed his office. When Darrell looked his way, Alex said, "I have something important to discuss with you."

"Very well Alex," Darrell replied. "I can come now or later after I talk with these students."

Alex took a few steps to the door of his office while Darrell and the students stood in the hallway. "This cannot wait. I am holding here copies of your syllabus and handout. We have here convincing proof that you plagiarized in both documents and therefore you are to appear before the College Administrative Council. It is a shame, indeed an outright disgrace that we warn our students against plagiarism but you as a professor commit the same crime. You will not get away with this one, no matter how you try and I am sure you will try your hardest."

Dressed in an elegant jacket and tie, Darrell was visibly shaken with anger. "You accuse me of being a criminal? A criminal? You better have some proof or you will see the dirtiest side of me." He asked if Alex also saw on the syllabus a statement to the effect that all college and university prohibitions against plagiarism and cheating were in effect.

"I did but that does not mean anything especially when you are the culprit. Again Darrell, believe me, you will not get away with this one."

Darrell lost it. "I see you have convicted me before any trial. I certainly hope you not only know what's plagiarism but also have persuasive evidence. As I am sure you do not, I definitely will be going beyond the CAC to another forum where you will have to defend yourself against defamation. Thank god these students heard your preposterous charge. You better, I mean you better have some proof. Moreover, I will not come to the CAC unless I have union representation and possibly my attorney. Alex, you accuse me of being a criminal? Unbelievable. You certainly are messing with the wrong guy. I maybe new and somewhat quiet but don't be fooled; I respect all but fear none, including you Alex. I repeat, you better have some proof otherwise that venom that undergirds and fuels your rage, malice, and hatred will be your breakfast, lunch and dinner. I mean it and I am determined to grind your nose literally in the dust not only to prove that I am not a criminal but for you to learn the hard way never to mess with me. Alex, if you are out of your mind, I'm not; let that sink into your skull."

Alex was red in the face as Darrell walked away in total disgust. Later that day, representatives from the SAU Seer, a student run newspaper showed up at Alex's office to interview him on the matter. He not only refused to give any interviews but dismissed the students rudely.

Darrell could not control his anger as he explained to Vanessa what he called "a ludicrous charge" against him. He could hardly talk. "B-b-b-baby, I do n-n-not care about a job, tenure, or any other nonsense; my reputation is on the line. A criminal? I, plagiarize materials for an elementary course like Microeconomics? And worse, in a syllabus? Unbelievable! Disgusting!" he vowed to fight Alex to the end until he was totally vindicated. He continued, "Utterly preposterous! Totally ridiculous! I mean, I mean! I cherish no personality trait more than my character and reputation. Alex is definitely in for something he had never imagined."

As Darrell's breathing increased and he perspired profusely, Vanessa put her hand on his shoulder and spoke softly. "Please calm down Honey; we will handle this; please, please Honey." She asked to drive and when given the keys, instead of driving to the kids' school, she drove home. She went into the house with him and got him a cold glass of water. "Please Honey, drink this and lie down for a moment; I will get the children."

Darrell looked at his wife with utmost admiration. "You are the best Honey; I do not know what I'd do without you." He did as she said.

When Vanessa returned with the children, Darrell interacted with them for a short while before going to his doctor's office. He was told his blood pressure had risen precipitously. "I'm hoping this is temporary," the doctor said. "I want to see you next week for an extensive check-up. If the pressure remains elevated, I'll have no choice but put you on medication and usually, that's for life with limited exception. So, if you can avoid it, the better for all of us."

Darrell was disturbed by the thought of being on medication for life. He vowed to avoid it as much as possible. However, he did not know if he could succeed, given his hostile and unhospitable working environment. Thus, he talked with a union representative but unfortunately, the representative only gave 'general diplomatic' advice.

"I'm calling this meeting to order," Dean Harris once more announced at a special meeting of the College Administrative Council, CAC. "This is a serious charge of plagiarism against Dr. Thomas and if proving, will most likely means serious consequences."

Once more ignoring the dean's horrible grammar, Darrell spoke up. "I see you too Dean Harris are bent on convicting me without a right to trial. Well, I insist on my right to due process. I also insist on my right to face my accuser or accusers. Who brought this charge against me and on what grounds? I mean, what evidence has been presented and by whom to show I am a criminal? Let me just warn you; you better have evidence to prove your charge beyond a reasonable doubt. I mean, this is not a civil charge in which you only need to preponderate; rather, this is a criminal charge. Therefore, you must present evidence to prove the charge beyond a reasonable doubt; if you know what I mean."

"Professor Thomas is right," asserted Prof. Barclay. "Who brought this charge against him and on what grounds?"

The dean scratched his head. "A sophomore student pointed out this plagiarism to the chair who brought it to my attention. The last time we meet, this council wanted the professor to be informed. He has being, so here he is. He need to defend himself. I mean, let him show us if he did or did not plagiarize."

"Wait a minute," interjected the union representative who also paid no attention to the dean's horrible grammar. "A charge, I mean a mere allegation has been levied against Dr. Thomas and he now needs to defend himself in the absence of any evidence to prove the charge?"

"That's right," agreed Dean Harris with an air of authority. "The council wanted him here to defends himself and so we need to hear him. I say, let him show us if he is guilty or not; that's why we are here. This is a very strong charge so he must defends himself. Otherwise, he will get the worst end of the log because we do not accept such a calamrous act around here; I mean it."

Heads around the room shook again. Some looked on the floor as if terribly embarrassed. "No dean," objected the union representative. "That's not how it works. He is not guilty until proven innocent. Rather, he is presumed innocent until proven guilty. We therefore must have Dr. Thomas' accuser here to show us how this professor allegedly committed plagiarism. I agree with you Dean; this is indeed a serious charge! It therefore must be handled delicately and responsibly."

"Well, you may be representing your so-call union, idoctic as it is, but you do not tell us how to run this college. I am in charge here," the dean stated with steaming superciliousness. He paused to catch his breath as he was clearly exasperated. Then he added, "Beside, I am not porstponing this hearing."

The union representative was amused. "Are you saying the faculty union is idiotic? Dean Harris, if I were you, I would not go there," he chuckled lightly. "With all due respect, and for obvious reasons, I am not going there either."

"Listen Dean," demanded Dr. Smith, who also showed no interest in the dean's description of the faculty union. "No one is asking you to postpone the hearing, if you want to call it that. If the chair is accusing Professor Thomas of plagiarism, send for him to come with his evidence. He is a member of this council. Why was he not here in the first place? For goodness sake Dean, we have work to do. Moreover, a charge of this magnitude must not be handled slovenly or incautiously, regardless of who is in charge."

Andy and two others smiled lightly as they were sure the dean did not understand Prof. Smith. "Jimmy!" the dean called one of the secretaries in his office. "Get me Dr. Alex Brooks and tell him to bring the evidence he showed me about Dr. Thomas."

Darrell was in total disbelief. "Evidence?" he wondered. "Why wasn't that here in the first place?"

The brief waiting period calmed the dean. "There's more hot coffee and some doughnut," he informed the meeting attendants. "Please help yourself. We want to be sure they are all gone before we leave here, even if that mean putting on a few pound,"he joked apparently in a bid to shift people's attention from the serious matter at hand. No one moved or paid attention to his horrible grammar; everyone was aware of it. Soon, Dr. Brooks walked into the room.

"Yes Dean. Did you send for me?"

"Yes Dr. Brooks. Tell this council about Dr. Thomas plagiarism and show them the evidence. I told them we have evidence for sure; after that, we will see what to do with Dr. Thomas. He should know this is not a cheap school where people can plagiarize and get away with it."

Darrell protested. "Dean, you have found me guilty in the absence of any evidence; that's preposterous, absolutely ridiculous. Do you really know what's plagiarism? How dare you Dean?"

"Dean Harris, let me address his points," offered Dr. Alex Brooks. The five feet two inches tall department chair, somewhat over-weight for his height, wearing a green sweater, white shirt, and black pants, looked angry before he started speaking. He said one of the students brought the syllabus and handout to his office along with the textbook for the course. He said Dr. Thomas had the words "government regulations" in both documents and those were the exact words for the title of Chapter Six of the text. In other places, there were words like, "consumer decision," "economic principles," "opportunity cost," and "labor market." He was convinced that, as these words appeared exactly in the text, they were adequate to convict Dr. Thomas of plagiarism.

"There you have it Council," the dean beamed with a triumphant smile. "I knew Dr. Brooks would prove this charge that's why I asked him to rescue himself from this council. I knew he would come in as a witness so there it is." He swore Darrell

91

was guilty and therefore would receive the maximum penalty although he did not say what that would be.

"I am speechless," averred the union representative. "Totally speechless."

"I do not believe my ears," Andy snapped. "What?"

Darrell continued shaking his head. He told the council how Alex stopped him in the hallway, in the presence of his students, called him a criminal and a disgrace who had committed plagiarism. "I have never been so humiliated in my life and groundlessly so. Is this what you call 'plagiarism'? Is this my crime Alex?"

Straightening himself as if to release tension, Darrell recalled that on several occasions, he presented evidence of students leaving hate notes under his door, some signing their real names and yet, Alex did nothing. "Now," he continued, "do you really think this is evidence that I, Darrell Dwayne Thomas plagiarized? The Heavens help us all — Lord give me serenity!"

"What other evidence do you want?" Alex asked.

Darrell continued shaking his head in disbelief and disgust. He disclosed that since he was charged with plagiarism, he had dug up information about proven charges of plagiarism, sexual harassment, embezzlement, and theft of property but all the people found in those cases still were at the university. "But for me," he went on, "on account of pairs of words, you accuse me of plagiarism, of being a criminal? I am sure you intend a serious disciplinary action but Alex, you and your dean are in for a real surprise. You are barking up the wrong tree; you are messing with the wrong fellow. As I told you, I will grind your nose and the nose of your dean in the dust and in the mud to show I am not a criminal; I mean it."

Andy stood up. "This makes me furious." He said for a baseless charge of this nature to be brought against such an outstanding scholar was bad in itself but to do so in the presence of his students was defenseless. To refer to such a decent man as a criminal was more than insulting. "Let me inform you Dean. If this brilliant scholar goes to court, and I think he should, he will win hands down. In essence, this university in general and you in particular will be disgraced in both national and world-wide fora, and you will have yourself, no one but yourself to blame! That's the essence of your administrative ability or the lack thereof; Heaven help us all." He too no longer care telling the dean in his face.

"I intend to do just that," Darrell spoke up angrily as Andy sat back. "I have been slandered, my reputation thrown to the dogs, my character assassinated, and my rights infringed. The courts will settle this one. I told Alex and meant it."

"You say this is not good evidence?" the dean seemed surprised. "So what should we do?"

"I will say it one more time and if it does not sink in, I will not say another word about it," Andy somewhat threatened to be silent in protest. "This is no plagiarism. Picking out pairs of familiar words or topics is not tantamount to plagiarism; Alex knows it and so should you Dean. Both of you have brutally wronged Professor Thomas." Professor Daniels supported strongly.

"O.K., we will ask Dr. Thomas to leave so the council can decide," the dean murmured.

"Decide what?" prof. Daniels wanted to know. "Besides, if we ask Dr. Thomas to leave, Dr. Alex Brooks ought to leave too for today, he is not here as a member of this council but, according to you, a witness. Oh my goodness, we have better use of our times."

When Darrell and Alex left, Andy did not mince his words. "Dean, I must reiterate the point that you and Dr. Alex Brooks terribly wronged Professor Thomas; there is no beating around the bush. I mean, to humiliate this man in the presence of his students and then drag him before this council first with no evidence and then a ludicrous evidence is defenseless. I am totally disappointed and terribly disgusted. In your maddening haste to convict this man, you advanced embarrassing examples of plagiarism. This is wrong and we must face the facts. As he stated, he has brought convincing evidence of insults and harassments against him and you did nothing. There have been proven charges in this college but no serious disciplinary steps were taken. Now, for something preposterous, you are determined to act on a bogus evidence. That's disgusting, totally disingenuous, and blatantly unfair."

"I absolutely agree," supported Prof. Daniels. He said there was no reason for such an action. He further stated that the dean and his Chair of Economics owed Dr. Thomas, a decent and hardworking man, sincere apologies. In fact, they needed to figure out how they could prevent Dr. Thomas from going to court for if he did, it would be a huge embarrassment for them and the university. "Why would Dr. Alex Brooks call Dr. Thomas a criminal and a disgrace? Alex ought to know better. He refuses to face the truth because, let's face it, he either cannot stand Dr. Thomas or he's intimidated by this outstanding scholar. In his maddening haste to convict Dr. Thomas, he has wronged a good and decent man, and therefore needs to apologize profusely," Prof. Daniels ended his statement.

Some members of the council tepidly supported the dean. "But we need to look again at the definition of 'plagiarism' to see if it applies in this case," Dr. Charles Davidson of History stressed. This view was supported by professors from English, Chemistry, Political Science, and Foreign Languages. Three persons of the twelve-member council did not say a word implying that they were either neutral or too timid to speak.

Professor Daniels was furious. "This is what bothers me to the core. We know the truth and yet ignore it like an ostrich buries his head in the sand. Why ignore or even sugar-code the truth? Any dumbbell knows that these pairs of words which are familiar topics in economics, do not amount to plagiarism and you all know it; we must say so to the dean's face and stop being timid or sycophantic." This brought roaring resentments from two professors who supported the dean indirectly but Prof. Daniels stood his ground. "However you define plagiarism, pairs of words do not rise to the level of plagiarism and you know it," he fought back.

Andy was unequivocal. "Look, I must be going but Dean, if you know what's right for this college and university, you and your chair need to apologize to Professor Thomas and do all you can to prevent him from going to court. I have better use of my time and if you doubt what I am telling you, check with The Department of Legal Services." He stormed out the door. The other council members slowly filed out of the room.

As soon as he returned to his office, the dean picked up the phone. "Alex," he said, "can you come to my office?" In minutes, Alex was across the table from his boss. "Alex, it looks like this is a serious case. We might go to court and according to Andy, we might lose."

"Do you think we need to talk to our law firm to ascertain our options?"

"No Alex, I do not even want it to go that far. I do not want the president to hear about this."

Alex did all he could to calm the nerves of his boss. In the first place, Alex did not think Darrell would go to court. He said Darrell was just starting at the university and had no money. He was convinced Darrell would not dare to contact a lawyer. Yet, to please him, Alex said he and the dean would send him letters of apology and make it look like it was the council's decision. "Since he is just starting, we do not want this matter to go further and fortunately, in all likelihood, it will not." Alex stressed this point because he was sure Darrell was unfamiliar with the legal system and knew no lawyers in town. As such, he was no threat and therefore could be handled very easily.

"I fears he will want some money," the dean disclosed his concern. "You know how they are."

"But he will not get a penny, any privilege, or any concession," Alex replied with certainty. "If he pushes his luck, we can threaten him with expulsion from the university. He has a large family and will not want to be unemployed. There is no way his wife's income can sustain his large family. Of course, his wife can be dismissed too. Besides, he is only an assistant professor although he is on a tenure track." Clearly, Alex had forgotten that according to Darrell's contract, he had seven years to gain tenure or leave the university.

"Hold it," the dean demanded. He dialed the phone. "Paul," he called, "can you come to my office for a moment? We really need you. I promise, this will not takes long." In minutes, the head of the university's legal services was in the dean's office.

"What is this about gentlemen," Paul asked, wanting to know the details like a good lawyer. When he heard the story, he asked a few questions to ascertain the facts clearly. He heard of the charge, how it was disclosed to Darrell, and what the council felt.

"But you must promise me Paul," the dean requested. "I do not want the president to hear about this."

Paul thought for a moment. "But if this professor sues us, the president and most likely the Board of Trustees will hear about it. Similarly, the local papers as well as radio and television stations will pick it up and who knows how far it will spread nationwide, even worldwide through the media and internet?" Paul added further that if Darrell sued the university, based on what the dean and Alex disclosed, the university had a slim to no chance of winning the case. He said he would definitely do his best but, as Alex and the dean knew, he and his legal aids were not legal gods. "In fact," Paul explained further, "in some instances, it is very difficult, perhaps impossible to circumvent the law. Indeed, it is unethical, if not criminal, to do so." He said he and his team of legal scholars at the university as well as the folks in the law firm representing the university were experienced attorneys but in such clear-cut cases, they could only seek a settlement. "As you know," he went on, "the university is regarded as having a deep pocket; therefore, settlements are usually huge and of course, we do not want that."

The dean and his chair of Economics were visibly shaken. "Then what do we do?" the dean questioned.

"Let me be frank," Paul asserted. He said if the professor in question were present, Paul would tell him he (the professor) had little to no chance of winning in court and if he knew what was best for him, he'd would do well to drop the case. Paul emphasized that he would threaten the professor, even if the professor appeared with a lawyer. "But now that he is not here and we are talking among ourselves, I will tell you the truth. If I were in your shoes, I would apologize to the professor and negotiate with him in a way that the case does not go to court; believe me, that will save all of us tremendous headache." He reiterated his plea to prevent Darrell from going to court, even if that meant settling with him in one form or another. To that end, he did not rule out monetary settlement. "However," he averred, "if the case goes to court anyway, as I have said, we will do our best but our chances are slim to none with the 'none' being more likely. Now gentlemen, if you will excuse me, I must run. Please keep me posted on this case and for now, my lips are sealed."

When Paul left, Alex and Dean Harris sat for a moment without saying a word. "Now what?" the dean sought to know.

"I think it will be wise to ask Andy to talk to him; Andy seems to like him, although I do not know why," Alex responded softly. He thought for a moment and murmured, "Maybe we could ask Dallas Davis to talk to Darrell too."

"Who is Dallas?" the dean was not sure.

"Oh you remember him, the funny looking black guy. He is the Assistant Director of our Office of Minority Services. Frankly, he does not seem to be very bright, you know how they are! But, as a member of the administration, he must be on our side." On second thought, he feared because Dallas was not very bright, he might ruin the case; yet, he wanted to take a risk on him. "Maybe when Darrell sees another black person, he will change his mind. You know how they are—calling one another brothers and sisters, something I find very idiotic."

The dean did not understand Alex's drift but added, "I needs you to help me talk with these guys Alex," he emphasized with his usual grammatical flub. He reiterated that he did not want the President to know and so he did not want the case to go to court. "We must do all we can to prevent him. I do not know how but we must try Alex," the dean stated in a frustrated tune.

The department chair was not about to refuse his boss' request nor did he pay any attention to his poor grammar. "Oh sure, I will stay here and help talk with them."

The dean asked Jimmy, his secretary, to brew a new pot of coffee and prepare munchies for four. He said they did not want to be disturbed, no matter who showed up at the dean's office. Jimmy nodded in agreement and, after a few calls, Andy and Dallas were in the dean's office.

Both were offered coffee and munchies but they refused. Instead, Andy wanted to know the purpose of the meeting. "What is this about Dean?" he asked. "I cannot spend the entire day in meetings especially when such meetings regard preposterous charges."

"Please listen to us Dr. Barclay," the dean pleaded. I really mean your help. I mean, I really want both of you to talk with Dr. Thomas. Please help me and the college."

"Talk to Dr. Thomas about what?" Andy thought he knew but wanted to be sure.

Alex went to the dean's aid. "Let's be blunt. The council says we wronged Dr. Thomas." As such, he explained further, the college and university did not want him going to court for that would reflect unfavorably on the university and thereby damage the reputation of the university and the dean. "So, we dearly need your support. We are willing to go an extra mile to protect the good name of the university and the untarnished name of the dean." He added further that the dean had superbly served the university with dignity and devotion; he therefore deserved no less. The dean smiled broadly and nodded in agreement.

"Interesting," Andy seemed somewhat amused although he did not crack even a faint smile. "You say 'the council says' but you do not know you wronged Professor Thomas? You called the man a criminal and do not think you wronged him? You disgraced him in the presence of his students and do not think you wronged him? You accused him falsely and do not think you wrong him? Please think again. Moreover, you are concerned about favorable perception of the university and the reputation of the dean but not Dr. Thomas' reputation, employment and professional life? Isn't that disingenuous, I mean, shamelessly hypocritical, callous, and selfish?"

"Andy, we needs you to help us, not gestize us," the dean pleaded ungrammatically and with Malapropism.

Dallas explained that he was willing to help but did not know Darrell. "He seems like a nice guy but I really do not know him."

"Well you needs to know these black people who come here," the dean demanded. "That's why we have you in minority affairs." Dallas wanted to ask if the dean knew all the white people on campus but he refrained from asking. He just looked at the dean and shook his head in disbelief.

"I do not know Dr. Thomas either although I have gotten together with him once," Andy disclosed. He said he was willing to help but the blatant mistreatment of people from under-represented groups had to stop if the university was to be a truly inclusive institution. "Let's face it; Dr. Thomas was accused falsely and humiliated in the presence of his students because he is African-American."

The dean and Alex rejected the allegation. "No Andy, we were just going by the guidelines against plagiarism," Alex defended.

Andy was direct. He asked as to the number of white professors Alex and the dean checked seriously regarding plagiarism. He said they all knew that there had been at least four clear cases of plagiarism against white professors and nothing was done about them. He reiterated Darrell's point that various charges were proven against Caucasian professors and staff members but nothing of any significance was done in terms of punishment or reprimand. Several other cases were not even investigated. "Frankly, I have lost track of numbers," Andy went on. "Why act now on bogus evidence? How could you act upon an allegation brought by an undergraduate student without investigating? Your raging racism and mind-boggling bigotry blinded you to the blazing truth and robbed you of reason and logic. How could you? Why did you?"

"I told you Andy. This is no time for gestizing; we needs to stop Dr. Thomas from going to court," the dean once more pleaded.

"I know a number of things," Andy endeavored to reveal information from Darrell. He said Darrell cherished his reputation and character more than employment, tenure, promotion, and all that went with higher education. "As such," Andy revealed, "he has contacted a lawyer who already has gained sworn statements from the students who were present when Alex humiliated him. Three of the students are so angry that they are willing to testify on Darrell's behalf in court. I tell you, you have a problem on your hands."

The dean and Alex were stunned. "Has he gone that far?" Alex asked in astonishment. "We really need to stop him and we are counting on both of you to help." He said he and the dean would write Darrell letters of apology and he (Alex) was even willing to send Darrell email about his workload for the following semester. He offered to do anything to prevent Darrell from going to court.

"Would that include monetary settlement?" Andy questioned.

"If that what it take, yes," replied the dean with no one paying attention to his grammar.

Sensing their desperation, Andy promised to help but not until he was assured this would not happen again. "You know I have been here long enough. Although we tell the world we steadfastly welcome and promote diversity, at best, we minimally keep our words and in the worst case scenario, we practice the opposite of what we preach. For example, I have seen people of color leave this place because of prejudice and outright bigotry; frankly, this must stop." He stressed that there was no justification for the repeated marginalization and general maltreatment of people from under-represented groups. He said such people were 'under-represented' only because the majority/dominant group of society made them so. In addition, Andy said if the university were truly inclusive, if the institution cherished and promoted justice, equity, and equality, if administrators and the entire university community understood and appreciated the fact that diversity enriched the institution, community, and nation, the university would reword its admission and recruitment criteria and abandon its one-sided traditional practices. "Believe me," Andy stressed, "the day we genuinely and consistently abide by these principles, the university and the nation will be far better off beyond the mess we currently have." He made it clear that he was not advocating preferential treatment of people from under-represented groups or the hiring of unqualified individuals. Rather, he strongly supported fairness and equal treatment of all people regardless of race, gender, ethnicity, or any other such characteristics.

The dean and Alex nodded as if they agreed. They once more appealed to Andy and Dallas to help in every way they could. To that end, Andy and Dallas left only promising to do their best in appealing to Professor Thomas, not guaranteeing anything.

"I am dying to know why the two of you asked to meet with me," Darrell addressed Andy and Dallas as they took seats in his office. "What is this about gentlemen?" Before they could respond, he apologized for having only one coffee cup in his office. "This is not like the dean's office," he laughed. Andy and Dallas joined the laughter.

When the laughter died down, Andy said, "Let me shut the door," as he rose from his seat. "Believe me, this will not take long or, as Dean Harris always says, 'This will not takes long'." Everyone laughed loudly.

When Andy returned to his seat, he cut to the chase. "Let's be terse; the department chair and college dean have wronged you grossly and you have a valid cause of legal action against this university." In spite of that right, Andy strongly advised against any legal action. "You are starting newly here and you do not want to call such glaring attention to yourself. They have assured me definitively that it will not happen again. In addition, you will receive letters of apology from both the chair and dean, and, all of a sudden, the chair is willing to send you an email regarding your workload issue."

"I have been here a while and am familiar with this kind of treatment," Dallas disclosed. "Since you have vividly demonstrated intrepidity, they will think twice before they do it again. Drop this issue for now and watch what they do. I assure you however, they will not stop completely; you need to be on your guard because from now on, they will do anything to prove you incompetent or worse, guilty of wrongdoing. Therefore, as I advise you to drop this case, I equally suggest you keep all records from this case for the future. One never knows when, how, where, through whom, and to what extent the ugly head of racism either rises mysteriously or is risen anonymously."

"Anonymously?" Andy asked.

"Anonymously," Dallas repeated. "No one, or almost no one ever claims to be racist. Rather, they all defend their racist actions as only following the rules or principles. The worst claim to be color blind but open to principles of fairness, meritocracy, and equality." Andy's nod was not convincing as to whether he fully understood Dallas' drift'.

After a lengthy discussion, Darrell preferred to discuss the issue with his wife before giving any response. As promised, Darrell had a long discussion with Vanessa on the issue. They placed calls to Profs. Kwame and Dominguez who gave their usual pertinent pieces of advice based on years of experience. Ultimately, it was agreed that Darrell refrained from pressing charges. However, the college was to reimburse expenses he had incurred, including whatever he paid his attorney. Furthermore, Darrell was to receive letters of apology as promised but with the understanding that he would share same with his class to assure students he was not a criminal because for sure, he did not plagiarize.

"Those are reasonable demands," Andy registered his conviction after hearing from Darrell in another meeting. "I will pass this information on and if they want me to continue to intercede, they better accept these; my goodness, you are nice for someone else would have demanded much more."

The dean and Alex listened intently as Andy explained the result of the meetings he and Dallas had with Darrell. "I have no doubt these are reasonable, I mean extremely reasonable requests from a man who has been wronged grossly."

"I agree," said Dean Harris, feeling as if a huge burden had been lifted from his shoulders. "We will do so. Thanks you Andy for your help," he concluded with his usual grammatical flub.

Andy later telephone Darrell to say the dean had accepted his demands. As Darrell drove to pick up the children that afternoon, he thought over the matter out loud. "Indeed, it is difficult to argue with, let alone beat sound advice from the elders. They say that success in life comes from, and is sustained by many qualities not the least of which are the resplendent Fruits of the Spirit. These fruits are antithetical to evils such as envy, jealousy, lies, discrimination, bigotry, racism, and tribalism, among many others." He regretted that in both the workplace and general society, irrespective of one's qualification, industriousness, and purity of heart in dealing with others, one would most likely fall into a hostile environment without fault on his or her part. If so, he or she had to be guided by the old adage that, "A lamb among wolves needs little advice regarding vigilance for his life depends on it." The person had to learn further that success in life sprang not from fear and self-defeatism. Continuing his soliloquy in a low voice, he said, "this is because vigilance enables one to see the enemy whereas competence, self-assurance, self-confidence, clear conscience, industriousness, high moral and ethical standards, respect for self and others, honesty, and humility serve as invincible armors for overcoming the enemy. In other words, whether referring to an individual or group, knowing the enemy helps to plan carefully and execute the processes for both vigilance and defense. Conversely, when one is his or her own enemy, the battle is lost before the war begins. So, people who work in hostile environments ought to beware." He was sure there would not be a shortage of snares, unjust treatments, and blatant violation of law albeit often with impunity.

Chapter VII:

SUMMER ONE

D arrell's grandfather's teachings were invaluable at various times of his life. After his exculpation from a preposterous allegation, he could almost hear Grandpa's voice echoing two adages regarding lessons learned from a first occurrence. Grandpa once said, "One whom a snake narrowly misses jumps at the site of a lizard's tail." Another time, Grandpa taught, "An ape falls only once on a rock when he grabs a walking stick." Doubtless, these adages were didactic as he thought of the first ridiculous calumnious charge levied against him. He now knew, more than ever, that he had to perform exceedingly well and in the process, watch every step. As he thought over these issues in his office, his cell phone vibrated. He quickly reached for it and, absolutely sure it was his wife calling, he answered without looking at the caller identification, "Hi Honey."

"Does Vanessa know about your other Honey? This is certainly not she!"

"Oh Andy," Darrell laughed out loud. "I just thought it was Vanessa. I'm sorry," he apologized as he and Andy continued laughing.

"I called to see if you have had lunch and if not, could we meet for lunch?"

"At the same restaurant we met the last time?"

"That's fine although we could go somewhere else," Andy said. "On second thought, that's closer to the campus and I guess that's why it is seldom empty."

"Simple concept of demand and supply Andy," the Economics professor reminded in jest.

"I forgot I was talking to an economist," Andy capitulated.

"Just kidding," Darrell somewhat brushed aside the compliment laughing softly. He quickly checked his email, called Vanessa, and headed out the door.

"Thanks for coming on such short notice," Andy declared. "After that farcical drama …"

"And it was nothing less," Darrell interrupted but quickly apologized and asked Andy to continue.

"I was just saying, after that incredible display of idiocy, I felt somewhat hypocritical interceding to prevent you from going to court when you had all rights to do so." Andy declared that without an iota of doubt, the calumny and humiliation against Darrell were unwarranted and absolutely defenseless. However, he expounded, there was some method to his madness and so wanted to explain.

Before Darrell could respond, a young man showed up to take their orders. Darrell placed his order and turned to his friend. "I do not think you need to explain anything Andy; I knew whatever you did, you were perfectly sincere."

"Yes, I need to explain," Andy insisted. "You see, I figured you had just come and going to court would have shone light on you thereby making you a target for all kinds of things."

"You stated so clearly," Darrell reminded his friend and loyal supporter.

"Yes but I need to clarify further. You see, I know the people in this theatre. They can easily make your life very miserable and force you out of here if you are not careful. I did not want you to start in such a manner and so I agreed to intercede and I am truly appreciative that you heeded my advice." He emphasized strongly that he did not intercede to gain any favor with the administration because, with a few exceptions, he had little to no respect for key figures in the administration.

Convinced beyond doubt that his friend was sincere, Darrell nodded lightly. "I see," he said softly.

Andy continued. "I mean, they may still make your life miserable and that's another reason why I wanted to talk with you." He was sure Darrell had stood against the administration effectively and they most certainly could not fathom that; therefore, Darrell had to be very careful. In that regard, Andy advised his friend to follow the policies strictly and produce as much as he could. He said he was very sure the administration would be checking far more than Darrell realized. "Dallas hinted this and I totally agree with him. You must be extraordinarily vigilant."

"You aren't kidding," Darrell agreed. He disclosed that he had already noticed same clearly. He said it would have been thought that his chair would be supportive of him but quite the contrary, the chair checked diligently for Darrell's faults and flaws. When the minutest evidence was found, the chair would pounce on and exaggerate such so-called evidence. In contrast, Darrell explicated, his department chair offered no compliments for major achievements and contributions. Worse still, the chair sided with anything and anyone against Darrell, including an undergraduate student who challenged Darrell's credentials and work. Darrell was clearly disgusted vis-à-vis the realization that, to Alex, his chair, he could do nothing right. He found it especially incredible that, whenever there was an allegation against him, his chair believed the accuser, regardless of the futility of the allegation and irrespective of the status of the accuser, presumably including a mendicant off the street. Conversely, the chair bent over backwards to cater to professors in his clique or those whom he regarded as threats to his position. Of course, to maintain the position, the chair worshipped the dean, often in shameless sycophantic ways.

"I am not surprised at all and if previous trends are to continue, he will only grow worse. However, you can 'repel' them, so to speak, if you produce far beyond expectation. Again, I find this unfair because, while we are expected to transcend mediocrity, no one else is expected to produce and perform far beyond expectation," Andy expressed resentment as he worked on his bowl of soup while his salad waited.

"I know it is unfair but, in the midst of covert and overt racist tendencies and practices around here, I am armed and ready to perform in a way that will shut them up and leave little or no room for criticism. Of course, I know they will put on their nicky-picky glasses to find something but at least, they will have to look very hard. After all, I have never been perfect nor am I able to achieve that status even if I try."

"I agree," Andy assented. "By the way, did you get an email about your next semester workload?"

Taking diligent care of his chicken wrap, Darrell replied in the affirmative and added that he was informed he would be teaching three courses per semester. Then he added, "Amazingly Andy, Vanessa has been told the same. Our emails came within minutes of one another but in actuality, this is no solace; that's the normal load for every professor in the department."

"Mmm, interesting," Andy wondered. "I think there is some connection."

"I doubt it not," said Darrell. "Whatever the connection, this is another reminder that she and I must be careful and believe me, we are not intimidated and certainly not frightened but will be very cautious. As my former professor and mentor says, 'when snake is your dancing partner, watch your feet'."

Laughing out loud, Andy agreed. "That's a good one. I have not heard that before but you could not put it better." He and Darrell continued laughing softly as they rose to return to the university.

AT the end of the first semester, Darrell and Vanessa were dissatisfied with their productivity; each submitted only one article for publication. They nonetheless reminded themselves of the heavy load during their first semester combined with family activities. They were determined to do better the second semester.

The semester break provided opportunities for family activities. It also enabled Darrell to socialize a little with Andy and Dallas while Vanessa got together once with Lupita and Ann. One afternoon, the children invited friends over for games and snacks. Darrell and Vanessa talked almost daily with their families down south as well as with Prof. Kwame who was aging although he remained as sharp as ever.

During the break, and after lengthy discussions, Darrell and Vanessa decided to convert their rent payment to a mortgage. While this decision was based partly on their work at the university, it was influenced largely by the fact that their children really loved their private school experiences. Seeing the excitement in the children, it was evident that moving them would be more difficult than leaving the university; they therefore decided to stay put regardless of the university atmosphere.

To make their decision official, Darrell and Vanessa called the children to a family meeting. As the children wondered as to the purpose of the meeting, their father asked, "Where would you children want to attend school next year?"

"Oh no," bemoaned D3. "Are we moving again? Please tell me that's not the case."

"Honey, why don't you simply answer your father's question," Vanessa appealed to her son. "Just tell him where you would like to attend school next year."

"Well, that's simple," replied D3. "I would like to attend my current school next year and the year after that."

When D3's father asked if that meant living in Achval for a long time, the lad answered affirmatively. "Well then," said his father, "that's exactly what you will get."

"I do not understand Dad," said Kwame. "What do you mean?"

The children's dad gave one of his trademark broad smiles. "Well children, your mother and I have decided to live here. We are glad you like your schools and because of that, we will not look for jobs anywhere."

The children screamed in unison. They jumped up, danced around, and embraced their parents with thanks and kisses. "Butter City here we are!" shouted D3. The other children repeated the chorus.

Seeing the children very jubilant was truly refreshing for Darrell and Vanessa. They now knew for sure they made the right decision. After all, they had expressed determination to face the illogical social construct called racism in whatever form it raised its ugly head. Besides, it was racism in one form at SAU or in another form at a different predominantly white institution. Although they did not want to generalize, they were convinced that if there were differences, such were miniscule. They therefore prepared themselves for whatever occurred at SAU and, based on their short term experience, they had no doubt that something was coming. The only thing they did not know was when it would come, how often it would come, and how big it would be.

At the beginning of the second semester, Darrell and Vanessa took solace in the fact that they had very high student ratings in the first semester. Of course, there were a few "left fielders" who made disparaging remarks but in general, students were highly complimentary. This was particularly important since most of the courses they taught were required. Equally important was the fact that the criteria for evaluation were biased and some students quickly established negative preconceived notions of professors they deemed as different. Yet, Darrell and Vanessa did well in the ratings.

Before the second semester started, Darrell's courses filled up quickly. His reputation had spread as a professor who explained economics subjects and terms clearly. He was jovial in class but did not tolerate nonsense. Students knew he had stood up even to his department chair. Therefore, like Darrell's high schoolmates, the students called him DDT, a name that stuck even among his colleagues.

The second semester rudely introduced the Thomases to the horrible mid-west weather; it was terribly cold and snowy but they quickly learned to adjust. The young assistant professor and his lecturer wife were also moving up. They bought a new van for the family which made the children very excited. As they moved into the middle class, Darrell and his wife knew what it took to keep them there. Thus, since each one was teaching three courses, they devoted enormous time to writing articles for publication. Vanessa was often the voice of reminder: "You know what they say, 'publish or perish' and I am not perishing in the face of pressure." Darrell concurred although, as a tenure track assistant professor, the pressure to publish rested much more heavily on him.

In spite of their heavy work, Vanessa and Darrell invited Ann, Lupita, Andy, and Dallas and their spouses for dinner one evening. It was a fun-filled evening as they joked interminably about persons and events at the university. No person was targeted more than Dean Harris as everyone recalled three or more occasions of his incredible grammatical blunder, not to mention his masterful and constant display of idiocy. Occasionally, they mentioned serious issues but most of the evening was fun and laughter. Before the guests left, they thanked the Thomases repeatedly and expressed desire to meet on such an occasion at least once a semester, even if they had to rotate the meetings from one family to another.

In the new semester, a lighter teaching load enabled Darrell and Vanessa to work assiduously on articles for publication. By the end of the semester, Vanessa had one article in press and one under review. Darrell had an article in press, one under review and one newly submitted. He also submitted two grant proposals and was working on a book chapter which he hoped to complete during the summer. He served on ten committees at the university, not including six search committees, five committees in the community, and four with major professional organizations. These "officially recognized" activities were separate from the many meetings and mini-conferences he attended regarding students and staff members from under-represented groups. It seemed everything about African-American students was forwarded to him. As such, he and Vanessa spent countless hours advising students of color and attending to academic and personal issues. On two occasions, Darrell was sitting in a hospital at 2 a.m., with a student of color who was a victim of one crime or another. Such "unofficial duties" were performed in addition to the work Darrell and Vanessa did with their graduate mentees: four African-Americans, three Hispanics, two students of Middle-Eastern origin, two foreign students, and one student with a disability. Altogether, they were five ladies and seven gentlemen.

Darrell's dossier covered other activities. During the year, he presented six papers at major professional conferences in addition to several presentations to community, social, and nonprofit organizations. At the end of his first summer session, he called Prof. Kwame to delineate his achievements in the first year.

"My goodness, it must cost a pretty penny to travel to those conferences but, if you keep that up, you should be eligible for tenure in three to four years. Let's hope your grant proposals are funded; that's the kind of performance I expected from you and Vanessa and, unsurprisingly, both of you have not disappointed me." While the retired prof. encouraged Darrell and Vanessa to keep up the good work, he also admonished them to be selective as to which committees they served on. "They will want you to serve on every committee regarding diversity." Additionally, Prof Kwame stressed what the couple already knew. He said they would be asked to serve on search committees not because their services were needed; rather, their presence would be sought to give the impression that the committees were diverse. "In other words," the retired prof., clarified, "it's not you per se but your skin color is used to their advantage when, in most instances, it is to your disadvantage. I mean, they just can't lose while conversely, you might not win if you do not double your efforts. So be on your guard always."

As always, Darrell and Vanessa appreciated the fatherly advice from Prof. Kwame. They knew he was deeply sincere and equally caring. Thus, if their work impressed their critical but caring mentor, they were delighted. Criticism from anyone else would be taken with a grain of salt. Therefore, they were in a good mood when they left for the south for their first summer break since they moved to the mid-west.

As expected, it was another long drive south, a new van notwithstanding. After hours, Darrell pulled into his mother's driveway. Mama Clara and Elayne rushed out with hugs and kisses. "Lord thank you for the children; see how they are big! Good Lord, Nabea is running!"

"Grandma, Auntie Elayne, I want to show you some of the stuff I made in school," shouted Joseph.

"I want to go first," Kwame challenged.

"Grandma and I will see everything," Auntie Elayne comforted. "Let's go in the house. Grandma got a special dinner for y'all."

"Baby, I see you got you a new car. It looks good," Mama Clara complimented. "Son, I know, this must cost some good money." Darrell simply thanked his mother but refused to comment on the cost of his family's new vehicle.

Darrell, Vanessa, D3, and Elayne brought a few things in to the living room where Dwayne was waiting patiently. As he waited, he thanked god for his children and grandchildren. It seemed they all turned out very well and he owed all first to God and then to his lovely wife.

"Hello Son," Dwayne greeted as Darrell walked into the door. "My arthritis got me tied down these days like a couch potato. How've you been?"

"That's alright Dad," Darrell replied as he embraced his dad warmly. "It's really good to see you Dad; I mean you look good."

Without a doubt, Mama Clara had prepared a sumptuous meal for the family. As before, the boys were going to Auntie Elayne and the girls would stay with Grandma. "Yea!" the children screamed when Auntie Elayne announced the arrangement for the summer.

After dinner, although tired from the long drive, Darrell and Vanessa spent some time with the old folks who wanted to know all about the university. Darrell explained a few things, pointing out the hardship he and Vanessa had to endure because of their race. "There's no dodging the fact; most of the nonsense we face is because we are Black," he summed it up.

"I told you Son; wherever you go in this country, you will find the ugly head of racism, sometimes very clear and other times not so clear," Dwayne stated in a frustrated tune. "With all their laws and stuff, it remains a malignant cancer on the body of this country, eating the body and soul of the nation but some people do not know it and those who do, ignore it just like that."

Continuing, Dwayne said the bite of racism was especially venomous in places where the disease itself was under the skin while on the surface, there were false impressions of acceptance of all, inclusiveness, equity, equality, and non-discrimination. "That's when the disease of racism is the worst," he emphasized. "I'd rather know you do not accept me than pretend you do when in actuality, you do not." The former factory worker could not hide his frustration even if he tried.

As Dwayne vented his frustration, his wife Clara chimed in. "Well Baby, we just keep praying the good Lord to keep watching over you and your family. As the good book says, the good Lord made us all and he is no respecter of human beings."

Early the next morning, Darrell jogged to his grandpa's grave where he talked again as if Grandpa could hear him. Sometimes he kept quiet as if listening for his grandpa's voice.

After resting solidly for two days, Darrell and Vanessa sprang into summer action. They volunteered at the senior center where Darrell had worked before. Additionally, Darrell improved his skills in his brother's auto repair shop. Furthermore, the couple spent time with Darrell's other siblings, Deborah and Tyrone. Darrell also visited old friends and enjoyed driving Dad around to familiar places while jointly and separately, the young professor and his wife were invited to speak to youth groups and community organizations. Although aging and therefore experiencing reduced mobility, Mama Clara thoroughly enjoyed preparing meals and running errands for the grandchildren. "Oh Lord, these children's parents kept me busy and now they are doing the same," she would say mirthfully.

After two weeks in Ghetahzia, Darrell drove his family to Vanessa's home to spend time with Grandpa Joseph and Grandma Louise. This was another occasion to talk with the old folks and provide whatever community service they could. They drove back to Ghetahzia, left the children with Auntie Elayne and Mama Clara, and ran off to join David and Lamont, and their families. Vanessa and Darrell dearly looked forward to this reunion.

"Where are the children?" Lamont asked as Darrell and Vanessa ran out of their van to embrace David, Sabrina, Lamont and Kolu, their best college buddies.

"We left them with their auntie and grandparents," Vanessa answered, still rejoicing for seeing her closest college friends. "We wanted to spend this time with you guys."

"What, that's not right," protested Lamont. "We want to see our nieces and nephews too."

"That's right," Kolu supported. "After all, we have seen enough of you guys." David agreed and everyone laughed.

It was a wonderful reunion indeed. The three couples talked endlessly about their college days. They talked lengthily about their work experiences. When Darrell and Vanessa pointed out the challenges they faced, the others encouraged them to be resolute in determination in facing racism head-on.

"That is precisely our resolve," Vanessa informed. "As a result, we have converted our rent payment to a mortgage. True, our children's love for their school played a huge part in our decision but part of it was due to the fact that we remain obdurate in our resolve to face whatever challenges come. I tell you, however, they are terrible. It is just difficult to understand how people can be blatantly unconscionable, unscrupulous, and absolutely unfair."

Lamont could not resist. "My goodness, Vanessa now truly sounds like a professor. What happened to that good old southern talk?"

"I have always sounded like this," Vanessa protested.

"I do not recall that either," David declared. Everyone laughed at Vanessa's expense. When the laughter died down, David added, "However, I think Lamont is picking on you as he did in college."

"I agree," Darrell said.

"The same way you always agreed with her in college and that agreement got you married," Lamont came back to the laughter of the group again.

The three couples really enjoyed being together again. They placed calls daily to Prof. Kwame who invited them the next summer to his home. After three days at Lamont's, they took off for a short vacation trip in the south. They had a great time together but soon, Vanessa and Darrell had to return to school.

Back in Ghetahzia, Darrell and Vanessa packed their van for another long trip to Achval. They promised to send tickets once in a while for family members to visit, beginning with grandparents and then aunties and uncles.

Although they took turn driving and although the children were lively, when not sleeping, the trip from the south to Achval was always long and tiresome. It therefore was a huge relief when Darrell finally pulled into their driveway. Before they got out of the car, Vanessa called both grandparents and Auntie Elayne to say they arrived safely.

Preparing the children for school and for the university was now a familiar routine. While Vanessa did most of the shopping, Darrell did minor repair work around the house in addition to painting here and there. However, they took a few days off to rest prior to the resumption of school and this was well deserved.

Chapter VIII:

THE RATINGS

I n any economy but especially in a depression, repression
or any dwindling economy, it is a blessing to be employed.
This truism notwithstanding, it is equally important to love
and enjoy one's employment and work harmoniously with
co-workers. Such a work atmosphere not only satisfies and
consequently maximizes productivity but it is said that har-
mony with co-workers enhances longevity both on the job and
generally in life.

If the preceding is true, and it certainly seems so, it was
regrettable that Vanessa and Darrell faced a number of stum-
bling blocks and setbacks regarding their relationships with
others at the university. Yet, they appreciated and enjoyed certain aspects of their employment. For instance, on one hand,
they did not enjoy fantastic relationships with their bosses nor
did they have congenial relationships with co-workers except
in very few cases. On the other hand, even in the face of racial
tension, isolation, and marginalization by colleagues and
administrators, and in light of occasional rude comments by
students, they truly loved their students and enjoyed working
with them. Moreover, in the midst of a racist campus climate,
they were grateful for high student ratings. Likewise, they were
grateful for the limited number of friends with whom they could

associate and talk earnestly; such persons minimized the negative consequences of isolation and marginalization. To keep going therefore, Darrell and Vanessa focused heavily on the positives and concomitantly struggled to minimize, possibly eliminate the negatives. They were reminded constantly of this dual challenge as they returned to the university for another academic year.

In preparation for the new year, Vanessa and Darrell worked on syllabi and ordered books for their courses. They prepared course outlines for two semesters. This advance preparation would enable them to focus heavily on writing for publication. Additionally, they worked out schedules and mapped out activities for the family. They wanted to ensure they paid attention to family and work without sacrificing or undercutting either.

When Vanessa and Darrell returned to the university after the summer break, the campus was buzzing with students and faculty returning to school. Darrell's office looked as he left it but some things looked suspicious. As he checked, he was convinced someone had gone through his emails and desk drawers. He could not believe this and so checked further. For sure, he had convincing evidence. For example, email messages which came in when he was out of town were marked as read. As he had not checked his messages the entire time he was down south, he called his department chair. "Alex, could you please come for a moment to my office?"

"Oh sure," Alex responded in a cheerful voice. "What is it Darrel?" he asked when he reached Darrel's office.

"Someone definitely has been here in my absence Alex. Look here, these emails were read when I was out of town." He opened his desk drawer. "Look here, someone was snooping through my drawers."

When Darrell looked at Alex, the latter's facial features had changed drastically. He was quiet for a while and then softly said, "I don't know Darrell; I mean I do not know if someone actually did that and if they did, what would be the motive? Don't you have a secure password?"

"Don't you believe this limpid evidence? I mean, look at the dates on these emails; the dates received are clear and they are marked as 'read'. Of course I have a password but you and I know that secretaries have keys to my office. The administration not only has keys to my office but can bypass my password by logging in as administrators."

"Like I say, I just do not know Darrell; I really don't."

"O.K., Alex, I will call in computer experts and after their findings, I will send you, the dean, and provost letters of protestation; that's all I wanted to show you." Alex did not utter another word but simply walked away. Feeling violated, Darrell knew it was time to heed and earlier advice and get an off campus email address. There certainly was no comfort in the realization that he did not feel secure in his place of work.

At the first department meeting, Alex welcomed everyone to a new academic year. He reminded faculty members to send in their dossiers covering their activities for the previous year. Like everyone, Darrell and Vanessa sent dossiers to their respective department committees. In addition to his presentations at professional conferences, Darrell was pleased to note that one of his grant proposals was funded. Two articles were published and one was in press. He concluded his book chapter and the book was also in press.

Toward the end of the fourth week of classes, Darrell was in his office when his phone rang. "Darrell," Alex said, "could you come to my office for a moment?"

"Sure Alex; I'll be there." He ran over and Alex offered him a seat.

"I have received your ratings from the Department Evaluation Committee, the DEC, and wanted to share them with you. You have five days to protest or accept these ratings before they go to the dean and onward to the provost."

"What are the ratings like Alex?"

Alex pulled out a small sheet of paper. "You were rated in teaching based on preparation of courses or workshops, service on masters and/or doctoral committees, advising, and especially student ratings. In teaching, out of a possible ten points, you got two. You were rated in professional activities based on presentations at professional conferences, grants, unpaid consulting, and publications, among others. For professional activities, you got a three. Finally, you were rated in service based on your membership on university and community/social organization committees, your membership and activities in professional organizations, and on account of your contributions to society. In the area of service, you received three points."

Darrell was speechless. "Are these the department committee's ratings?

"That's right," Alex agreed. "Initially I rated you two points in each category but I am willing to adjust my ratings to be consistent with the committee's." Alex smirked. No doubt, he had achieved a goal and that was the end of it. As he saw it, the young assistant professor had no way out but succumb to his whims and caprices. *This is power and authority young man,* he thought to himself, *and this is just the beginning.*

Darrell smiled lightly as if to say sarcastically, "What a great favor you have done for me?" He still was speechless. A thousand things ran through his mind: was academia this murderously difficult or was this just SAW's way of rating? Was it worth staying in this kind of depressing atmosphere or was this just the department's way of rating him? If he stayed, was there any possibility of overcoming this demoralizing evaluation scheme or in fact, was he too dumb to live up to the rigorous expectations of the academy?? Alternatively, was this the department's way of kicking him out against his will? What could it be? His thoughts rolled on and on without landing anywhere.

"What's your reaction Darrell?"

"I do not know Alex; I just do not know what to say. Let me ask one question; where do I stand in comparison to my colleagues in the department?"

Alex smiled. It seemed he was having a great time seeing Darrell in such agony and disillusionment. Looking directly at

Darrell, he replied, "Well, that's another thing I wanted to say. Even among lecturers and adjuncts, you have the lowest ratings. To be honest with you, we have not had this kind of low rating in this department for a long time, if ever. I personally cannot recall and quite frankly, I am not sure how long we can or should tolerate such poor performance. Moreover, I was disturbed by some of the comments students made."

No doubt, Alex continued to be more than happy to add insult to injury. After all, the young assistant professor had to learn sooner than later the force of his power and authority. *Soon,* he thought, *Darrell would be brought to his knees and be forced into being controlled by the movement of Alex's finger or leave the university. He therefore continued to* beam with joy and satisfaction within, and o*ne could hear his inner voice saying, Welcome to academia and higher education administration at its best and never forget my unchallenged controlling power.*

Not caring to look at Alex's smiling face, and unaware of his thoughts, Darrell asked curiously, "Like what?"

"Many of the students said they had difficulty understanding you because of your southern accent; that is a real concern to me."

Darrell laughed softly as he finally looked directly at Alex who was smiling broadly. "Let me ask you Alex; do you have difficulty understanding me?"

Alex took on a serious face. "Well Darrell, I am not one of your students so it does not matter; the students are the concern here."

"Very well Alex," said Darrell as he saw no need to continue the conversation. Will you please send me the ratings and your concerns in writing? I need that within the five day period to enable me to respond."

Alex wasted no time. He handed Darrell a letter showing his ratings and expressing his concerns especially with regard to his accent.

"Hhhmm-hhhmmm-mmm" Darrell murmured to himself as he walked to his office. "My accent?" he questioned incredulously. As he thought over the matter, he began to empathize with SAU professors and lecturers who were foreign born. He knew most of them had beautiful accents and spoke better English than most citizens. Yet, he thought, if racism and bigotry could drive people to detest his accent even though he was born and raised in the country, how much more non-Americans whose first language was not English? He could not shake off the shock and incredulity.

The looks on Vanessa's face said everything when she got out of the car at the end of the day. It seemed she had been crying. Darrell ran out. He did not have to ask any questions. He held his wife by the hand and led her in. As soon as Vanessa stepped into the house, he took her in his arms where she burst out in tears. "We will not stay here Honey, children or no children; this is too much. I will not allow these people to worsen my blood pressure problem and drive me to an early grave; it's not worth it. That's right Honey. Already, by their dirty deeds, they have inflicted enormous physical and psychological harm on us. This so-called 'racial battle fatigue' cannot and must not go any farther. Our lives and psychological wellbeing are far more precious."

"I know Baby," Darrell comforted as he embraced his lovely wife. "You know why they are doing this; they want to drive us out of here."

Vanessa disagreed. "More than that, they want to drive us underground and that's a resounding NO!" Darrell nodded but nonetheless reminded his wife regarding her statement about staying put regardless of whatever happened. Vanessa agreed but reiterated that, in light of the harm they endured, staying in the hellish hole was not an option.

Darrell nodded again. He and his wife talked over the matter before calling Andy who ran over. When he saw the ratings, he could not believe his eyes.

"This is grossly unfair; absolutely unconscionable. Is this the rating for someone who had this number of presentations, published two articles, has one in press, completed one book chapter, and had one major federal grant funded?" He kept shaking his head. "And look at Vanessa's accomplishments versus her ratings. We will fight this; we must," he vowed.

It seemed Vanessa did not sleep over her ratings. The next morning, she was rushed to the hospital where the doctor said her blood pressure was out of proportion. She was kept for a few hours until her pressure stabilized but, because of her situation, her doctor doubled her medication.

When Vanessa felt better, in line with relevant state and federal laws, Darrell evoked his rights under the Freedom of Information Act and requested copies of the dossiers of professors and lecturers in his department. He was blunt with his chair: "Pursuant to this act, I am willing to pay for the collection and transmission of the materials requested but since they were submitted electronically, it should not cost anything to forward them to me. In line with the act herein evoked, collecting the information should not cost anything unless an outside expert is needed to gather the information sought." Darrell informed his department chair further that the law was clear on the issue of tampering with, or distorting the materials sought in a bid to prevent or obscure discovery. "I am sure," he wrote, "you do not want my attorneys to charge you with such a crime. Finally, please note that, considering my deadline to respond, time is of the essence."

Alone in his office, Alex was furious, uttering obscenities and racial slurs. "I told that idiot Dean Harris about this fool but in his maddening pomposity, he refused to listen to me. If this dirty ... (using the N word) thinks he will spend another year here, he must think again; certainly it will not be under my watch, even if my job, indeed if my life depends on it." Alex raised his hand in the air. "I swear to that; he will not work at this university after this semester; I will make sure of that. Who does he think he is? We know how such people get their degrees; on every occasion and at every gateway, they cry racism, racism, racism, and people let them through. Oh no, it will not work with me. Hell no!"

Despite his blinding fury, Alex had wit about him to call Paul, the head of legal services. He explained Darrell's request. "You must comply immediately," Paul stated firmly. "He has evoked a specific right under the law that cannot be denied. More than that," Paul went on, "tampering with the information requested is forbidden strictly. Alex, please do not get us in another legal mess and ultimate disgrace. Paul hung up before Alex could say another word. Begrudgingly, Alex sent the dossiers and their respective ratings to Darrell.

Darrell had collected statistical data about each professor and lecturer in the department. With the dossiers and ratings on hand, he was in position to comment on his ratings in the three areas of assessment. The courses he taught the first year were considered newly developed although they were on the books; he therefore deserved credit for them. In addition, despite disparaging comments by a number of students, he nonetheless had the best student ratings in the department and that, in itself, spoke volumes given the racist atmosphere of the institution. His publication records were outstanding compared to others in the department. His service likewise dwarfed the others in the department. However, before going to Alex' office, he invited Brenda, the department secretary to come along. He pointed out the clear-cut comparison to Alex.

"Well Darrell, first of all, I am not sure why you asked Brenda to come to my office; she has serious department tasks to perform. You have no right harassing her for your selfish personal purposes."

"I understand that anything pertaining to Dr. Darrell Thomas is insignificant but I wanted someone here as a third party," Darrell said sardonically. "Besides, she is my secretary as she is to any other professor in the department. It beats me as to how or why you forgot that."

O.k., but you had no right snooping around and looking at other people's ratings. This is a classic case of invasion of privacy," Alex charged.

Despite Brenda's presence, Darrell took a deep breath and counted to ten before he uttered a word. He also stepped backward for he heard that once, Alex said he was physically threatened by an instructor from an under-represented group who questioned him strongly. In addition, he did not raise his voice. "I do not know if you and I share the same definition of 'invasion of privacy'; this is public information and even students have access to this stuff on the internet." He stopped again and added softly, "Looking at the ratings Alex, including yours. Nothing there comes close to mine. Incidentally, I taught ten courses last year, including two summer courses. The undergraduate courses averaged forty students per course while the graduate courses averaged twenty-five students. Out of the scores of students enrolled in the ten courses, there is only one comment on these ratings about my accent. Sure, there are few derogatory comments but only one student, I mean one student, complained about my accent, not 'many students' as your letter indicated."

Alex was furious again. "So what do you want me to do?"

"Simple Alex; rate me fairly; that's all I'm asking—fairness and nothing more or less."

"So you are accusing the committee and me of being unfair? That's an insult."

Darrell took another deep breath and said a quick prayer for equanimity and self-control. He was glad for Brenda's presence for, without her, he would likely be misquoted. "O.K. Alex," he said. "This is my response. I will leave it with you for your written reaction."

"I can give you a four in each area and nothing more; I mean nothing more," Alex said angrily. "After all, your publications were not in reputable journals and your service was mainly self-service as you only worked in the black community. The committee raised the same concerns. What do you expect for such a lousy work? Quite frankly, I am sick and tired of your endless complaints which have no bases."

Darrell was stunned but certainly not surprised. Yet he said, "I'm surprised at you Alex. You mean you chair the Economics Department and do not know the major journals in Economics? I'm truly embarrassed. You categorize my service as 'lousy' and 'self-service'? You know you are dead wrong about me working only in black communities as evidenced by my publication regarding regional economic development. But even if I did, how many professors at this university who serve on ten committees? How many times have you categorized my white colleagues as 'self-serving' because they work in white communities?"

"I find it difficult to understand how you deny a glaring truth Darrell. Your publications are mainly in mediocre journals which add little to no scholarship to the profession. For instance, in your maddening haste to counter the highly respected economics literature, you wrote utter rubbish about the limited education or miseducation and consequent unemployment of people of color in general and African-Americans in particular. You then proceeded sluggishly to offer what you term 'suggested solutions'. Honestly, do you truly consider that as scholarship compared to the highly academic articles emanating from this department? You've got to be kidding."

Darrell took a deep breath. "Very interesting Alex," he said. "It is clear you and the committee are only interested in master narratives that confirm to the 'dominant paradigm or Eurocentric perspective, I mean that of the dominant White majority. It therefore comes as no surprise when you are intolerant of counter-narratives. That truism has left me wondering if you and the committee truly understand the depth of scholarship as you are boxed in a narrow-minded pigeon hole with one Eurocentric lens."

Alex gave a mocking laugh. "We do not understand scholarship? I say, you are out of your mind Darrell. How in the world do you think we got here? In any case, my ratings will not change; if they do, they will be lower and actually, they should be."

Darrell was not laughing. Looking directly at Alex, he said, "Let me be brusque with you Alex. If your desire is to push me out of this university, it will not work. If I leave, I will do so on my terms, not anyone else's and especially not yours." He took another deep breath and stepped backward. "Once more Alex, let me be clear with you. I want to respect you as a colleague but rest assured I am not afraid of you, no, not for a moment; so get that completely out of your mind. That's my response and I await your written reevaluation." There was no mistaking of the fact; Darrell was audacious, firm, and intrepid. He thanked Brenda for her time and walked away leaving Alex to fume endlessly.

When Alex sent Darrell's reevaluation, Darrell received a three in each of the rating areas. The dean was copied on the reevaluation with the comment that Darrell had displayed gross insubordination to his chair and supervisor. Darrell did not wait for the dean to call but made an appointment.

On the appointed date, Darrell, Vanessa, Andy and Paul showed up in the dean's office. A faculty union representative was expected but none showed up. Darrell was not surprised because, while he did not want to generalize about unions, he knew that, in the mean, they did not represent professors of color rigorously.

Unlike Darrell, the dean was shocked. "What! I thought this was a meeting between DDT and I."

"It was originally arranged to be a meeting between you and me but the magnitude of the problem prompted me to invite my wife and these gentlemen," Darrell clarified.

"I seen the ratings," the dean stressed. "My only concern is your publication."

Oh angels be my guide, Darrell thought to himself. *What does he know about publications?*

"What about the publications?" Andy questioned. The dean said he thought they should have been better.

Paul jumped in. "That's why we are here Dean. If you look at this man's ratings in the three areas, he ranks highest but is rated lowest in the department. Moreover, he is told, in writing, that his accent is a problem and that his service in black communities is lousy and a self-service." Paul said nothing was said about Darrell's service in white communities. Furthermore, he called the dean's attention to Darrell's masterpiece article regarding regional economic development. He reminded the dean that when the article was published, it was cited by several regional newspapers and television stations invited Darrell to expound on the article further. "In any case," said Paul, "I have nothing to do with department or college ratings but I am here because I am not sure if you realize that these ratings and your letter have serious legal implications."

"What! Court again?" the dean exclaimed. "I do not think we want that again."

"We do not but if these ratings do not change, that's where we are headed," Andy warned. He aspired to be straight with the dean. He said once, he and others talked Darrell, an outstanding professor, out of going to court when his right was infringed. Now, Darrell was told in writing essentially that, because he was black, he did not deserve a higher rating regardless of his performance.

The dean twisted in his seat as if in severe pain. Whether this was his way of denying did not matter to Andy. "Look at what the man achieved—three articles in major journals, a major federal grant, a book chapter, six refereed presentations, etc.. Who in his department comes close? This is blatant unfairness, a clear case of discrimination in writing. I personally will support this man and his wife to go to court."

The dean termed the matter to be serious and rightly so. He called for department chair Alex Brooks to join the meeting.

Alex arrived when Paul was speaking. "Let me be clear again Dean," the lawyer tried to be as simple as possible although he could not avoid his legal jargon. "You know I represent the university but in such a case, with this kind of evidence on hand, we will not survive a motion for summary judgment." He clarified that, essentially, a motion for summary judgment was a process in which one party asked the court to make a judgment without the case going to trial. For this motion to be upheld, the court had to determine that, based on law, no issues of material facts existed to warrant a trial and/or based on law, it would be impossible for one party to prevail if the case went to trial. In this regard, it was normal for the court to consider the materials most favorable to the party which opposed the motion.

The lawyer clarified that in light of the mountainous evidence against the dean and his department, no doubt, the court would determine that the university would not prevail in a trial. "To put it simply," Paul said, "DDT's lawyer will ask the court to rule against us without the matter going to trial. Most likely, the judge will uphold the motion and rule against us."

"That mean we will lose," observed the dean with a smile as he was proud of himself for understanding any theory at all but especially a very difficult legal theory.

"You got it," assented Paul. He said he did not understand why the department committee and chair made DDT's race, accent, and community major issues in his ratings especially when there was only a single comment by one student about Darrell's accent. He called on the dean to be fair because DDT was a good-old American who had a very nice southern accent. He added further that if the dean wanted to be true to himself, he would agree that all in the meeting had heard worse accents from parts of the country. Moreover, Paul reminded the dean that there were southern whites in the college but no one made similar comments about their accents. "Dean, you and your chair have to think again," Paul challenged.

"But Paul, have you looked at all the evidence?" Alex asked in a groggy voice. "The committee and I discussed Darrell's dossier at length. I think he got a very fair rating."

Andy was furious. "Alex, you know and I know that Darrell deserves far better ratings than he got. Why are you masking the truth and asking for trouble?"

Alex reacted with equal fury. "You are not my dean to rate me. Nothing could be fairer than this rating and I wish you would buzz of these discussions. I am not sure from where you picked up your so-called sense of justice."

Andy was determined not to roll over and play dead in the face of such a personal attack. "Alex, the nerve of you to tell me essentially to shut up; you should shut up and get out of town for in all matters regarding Dr. Thomas, you have been blatantly racist, unfair, and unashamedly so. Yes, we need to teach you a sense of justice for you got none. Now, you tell me to buzz off but when Dr. Thomas was about to take your rear end to court, you evoked my help on your knees. Quite frankly, you ought to be ashamed but unfortunately, you have no sense of shame, justice, or decency. The only thing you are good at is playing the hypocritical game; shame on you Alex."

Not surprisingly, Alex was red in the face. "You are completely wrong Andy and you know it. I have treated Dr. Thomas more fairly than anyone in this department. You have no way of knowing so because you come from another department, a department you have almost destroyed with your lousy sense of justice; no doubt, you would like to do the same here. Oh No, it will not work here Mr. Justice."

Andy laughed. "You are out of your mind Alex but let's not divert the issue to you and me. Attack me any time you wish and believe me, I will defend myself forcefully. Let's turn our attention to your horrible treatment of Dr. Thomas. Honestly, you ought to be ashamed in that regard." He threatened that if Alex did not change course in his treatment of Darrell, he would support Darrell in filing a grievance against his chair.

"Go ahead at any time you wish," Alex replied defiantly. He reiterated his point that Andy would not be allowed to destroy his department.

The dean and others sat quietly and probably in amazement regarding the exchanges between Andy and Alex but the latter once more insisted he treated Darrell more fairly than anyone. As such, Darrell did not deserve better ratings.

"Really Alex?" Paul questioned. "Obviously, I am not a professor in your department but even a dumbbell can tell the differences among the ratings. Here they are," handing a pile of papers to Alex. "Point out one person in the department including yourself whose rating is better than Professor Thomas'. Yet, he has the lowest ratings and you endorsed it with a clear conscience?" Paul made it clear once more that his focus was centered on the legal implications of the ratings.

"Look Alex," Darrell declared. "As I told you in your office, I only seek fair treatment and nothing more; you do not even have to like me but for Heaven sake, treat me fairly."

Andy reiterated his point that once, when Darrell's rights were infringed, he interceded but in this case, he would not. "Of all people Alex, you should have known better but unfortunately, you did not and still do not; what a shame?" Alex frowned without saying a word.

The dean thought for a moment. He agreed to give five points to Darrell in each area. Darrell shook his head. The dean offered eight points but even that was unacceptable. Finally, Darrell was rated ten points in teaching and professional activities and nine points in service.

"I will accept a rating less than ten only if you can show me that no one in the department got a ten in service. My record clearly shows I served on more university committees, was engaged in more community activities, and served on more committees in professional organization than anyone in the department, and those activities do not include my numerous and time-consuming unofficial services."

"Two people in the department got ten in service," the dean disclosed.

Without stating that he was aware of the various ratings in the department, Darrell said, "Then to any prudent person, the logic is clear. If my service record is the best, I cannot get less than anyone in the department; that's clear and simple."

"O.K., I don't want court so I give ten in all."

"No dean," Darrell sought to set the record straight.

"But what you want again DDT?" the dean questioned with a long face.

"I will take the ten but it is not for fear of court; it is because, in all modesty, I deserve a ten. Dean, you are not doing me a favor but simply giving me what I earned all along. Unfortunately, you, your department chair and so-called committee do not understand that these ratings speak volume in a hostile racist environment, and whether you believe it or not, ours is nothing less."

Darrell underscored further that he would accept the ratings on two conditions. First, his wife's ratings also were to be changed as she too was rated unfairly. Secondly, he saw a trend in the college, a trend he detested and wanted to end. "My wife and I must not consistently be targets of discrimination," Darrell stressed. "We are not seeking preferential treatments; we only ask to be treated fairly. Why is that so difficult?"

The room was quiet and then Andy spoke up. Alex and the dean, both of you please tell us present here. Why is that difficult?"

Before the dean could answer, Darrell aspired to get things off his chest. "Let me level with you Alex and Dean Harris." Speaking with emphasis, he said if the dean and the college or university administration thought his skin color was, and must be, a vicissitude and an onus to make him reticent, inactive, servile, and blindly acquiescent, the dean and the administration had to think again. "No! It rather invigorates me, boosts my determination to level the playing field, and consequently ensure equality for all." He pointed out that he was not at the university because of privilege or favoritism. Rather, like his colleagues, he was at the university because of what he did. Put directly, the good Lord enabled him to complete graduate school and a dissertation process. The only difference was that most, if not all, of his colleagues did not endure the discriminations to which he was subjected. Summing up, he said, "As I told Alex, if I leave here, it will be on my terms, no one else's. So Dean, you and this administration must, pursuant to law, treat my wife and me fairly. Of course, rest assured that we understand the trickeries, camouflages, subterfuges, and shameless hypocrisy employed here to sidestep, even jettison both the letter and spirit of the law. Believe me, we are not fools; we notice them all. That's right; there is no way you can camouflage your chicanery."

Again, the room was quiet for a while. Andy repeated his question. "Once more Dean, why is it difficult to treat Darrell and his wife fairly?"

"That is not difficult," the dean assured hesitantly. "We will change Vanessa's ratings the same way. I think she too had done well."

"Dean," Paul called, "this man and his wife probably will apply for tenure and promotion one day. Prior to, and at that time, can we expect fair treatment or do we expect to get grievances from them each month and maybe go to court two or three times a year on their account?"

"No, we will do our best Paul. I only hope the president don't hear about this from us here."

"For once, Darrell smiled and looked at Andy as he recalled jokes at his house concerning the dean's grammar. "If we play the game right, there will be no need for court; if not, we will be back here again and probably headed for court from here," Paul warned. "Please Dean, let's do our best."

When the dean agreed, Darrell shook hands with everyone in the room and thanked Andy and Paul for coming. "Vanessa and I also will do our best to keep this university going. As I have said, we only ask for fair treatment."

"Any comments Vanessa?" Paul asked.

"My darling husband has spoken eloquently for both of us and indeed for all who endure unfair treatments. I only find it incomprehensible that people resort to blatant unfairness in the face of conspicuous veracity. How long will people succumb to preconceived negative notions about others especially on the basis of race, gender, nationality, creed, color or any other difference? How long will an institution of this size and caliber practice blatant discrimination, and/or resort to stereotypes and faulty generalizations in the face of the full force of law? Above all, how can we expect justice when we ourselves mete out injustice? I just do not know but my husband and I will stand for our rights and for justice as long as we can; no one will intimidate us or force us into appalling taciturnity and sycophantic acquiescence, with or without tenure."

The room was quiet again as Paul, Andy, and Darrell nodded in agreement. It was not clear if the dean grasped Vanessa's poignant points but he smiled broadly and wished the couple well. In spite of this wish, nothing became of Darrell's protest against the substantiated intrusion into his office. Commenting on this in a telephone conversation, Prof. Dominguez was lucid. Referring to the behavior of administrators, in this case, in higher education, and regardless of their race, religion, etc., he said, "It follows the pattern. With very few exceptions, they speak from both sides of their mouths; they say one thing to you and another to someone else. In practice, they say one thing on paper or in public and do another in private, and this is especially true with regard to matters concerning people of color in predominantly white institutions. I doubt if they will ever change. I earnestly doubt it because they see leadership as a matter of property right, their uncontested property."

Chapter IX:

DIFFERENT PERSPECTIVES

I n the middle of his second year, Darrell knew, without doubt, he and his wife faced a prodigious, albeit unwarranted, crisis at Southwest Achval University, SAU. While in actuality, this was not new, he nonetheless comforted himself with the thought that they were not the only persons from under-represented groups at SAU facing unnecessary crises. However, this solace was ephemeral as it did not change his circumstances.

As Darrell struggled strenuously to comprehend the gargantuan challenges he and his wife faced, the young professor not only critically analyzed the situation but often reflected on teachings from his childhood. Raised in a southern Christian home, his grandfather, who endured the staunch bitterness of racism and segregation more than four score years earlier, taught him to rise above hatred and accept everyone as a human being, regardless of race, color or creed. His father, who also saw the ugly head of discrimination, warned him to be prepared for the same and all its corollaries wherever he went. His mother taught him to accept everyone as a child of God.

Darrell's sound formal education was also a huge help. Looking at his situation analytically and philosophically one Saturday afternoon as he sat at the dining table, he concluded, "Life is a conundrum and people are enigmatic." He was sure he was not afraid of challenges in life, even Herculean ones, for he already had seen quite a number of challenges. At all times, and without being timid, blindly acquiescent, and definitely without sacrificing principles, he went out of his way to avoid extending direct or indirect invitations to challenges through words, actions or inactions. However, when challenges came his way, he welcomed them because of his conviction that life was not only replete with successes but also sporadically stained by strains, stresses, scorns, scantiness, and setbacks. He contended that, pushing aside egos and personal pride, failures would have positive effects if seen as reminders—reminders of our mortality, our human limitations and inabilities. On the other hand, he could not understand gross injustice of humans against others. Why did human beings abuse, reject, maltreat, suppress and oppress other humans? In a case of maltreatment, he wondered if the problem was with the maltreated or the maltreater. He was sure it was the latter.

"What are you thinking about as you are heavily involved in thought?" Vanessa asked as she came down the stairs attired in a simple but beautiful house dress. She looked gorgeous in the outfit but again, she looked stunningly beautiful in almost anything she wore. She was just a natural beauty although incredibly modest about her looks. "Is it about how deeply you love me?" she joked.

"I think about that every second for you are 'as dear to me as the ruddy drops that visit my sad heart'," Darrell responded with a broad smile.

"Oh my goodness, he remembers the line; that's from The Bard. It's a line in Caesar, from Brutus to Portia. I read that to you and hoped you would say it to me one day hoping of course, you would not be under the same pressure as Brutus."

"When you read those lines, that was the end of the reading that evening," Darrell reminded with a chuckle that turned out to be contagious.

"Oh yea, I remember," Vanessa admitted, still laughing. She asked if Darrell wanted a glass of wine on such a nice afternoon.

"That will be great Honey especially if I have it with you."

"With whom else?" Vanessa laughed again as she got wine for both of them. She placed the beautiful wine glass in front of her husband and served the wine like a skilled bartender. She leaned over, kissed her husband lightly before taking her seat. The young professor, smiling from ear to ear, could not take his eyes off his beautiful wife.

"I love you Honey and I thank God for you every day."

It is said true love never fades; it only grows stronger. Its strength withstands and wards off bruises and bombardments. Even in the face of setbacks, scarcity, or sickness, its flavor only grows sweeter and sweeter, and its joy and rejuvenating powers remain immeasurable and endless. This certainly was the case with Darrell and Vanessa for after many years, Vanessa's husband's compliments still touched her immensely. She blushed and beamed with smiles. She returned the compliment. "I love you too Baby and thank god every day that I did not perpetually keep up my walls of resistance." The two laughed and Vanessa continued, "But honestly tell me Baby; what were you thinking about? You were ruminating so deeply that you did not hear me coming down the stairs. Is something wrong?"

"Oh no Baby," Darrell quickly calmed his wife's concerns. He said he was thinking about the maltreatment they and others from under-represented groups endured at the university. "The truth of the matter is …" he hesitated, "I mean, although we do not have very close relationships with many people, most people are at least tepidly friendly, be it genuine or not. Our problem emanates from, and is exacerbated by, a few and unfortunately, a few influential people in the system—vice presidents, directors, deans, assistant deans, department chairs, and chairs of major committees, people Professor James Schiavone referred to in his memoirs as 'Gods From Afar'. This is why I wonder whether the problem is with us or with them."

Vanessa sipped her wine and straightened herself in her chair, her usual seat during dinner. "In short Baby, you mean our problem is with the system for those are the people who make up the system. Without an iota of doubt, it is the system and most certainly not us," she accentuated. Setting her glass of wine on the table, she was articulate and emphatic. "In a world of bigotry, there is no humanity except one's kind. In a world of hatred, there is no logic or vision. In a world of ignominy, there is no discernment. Thus, those who swim perpetually in a pool of hatred and bigotry refuse to see us as colleagues. To them, it is unfathomable that academically, we can perform at their level and even outperform them. Rather, from us, they expect low performance, clear manifestation of inadequacy, or a doleful display of disorderliness."

The young lecturer sipped on her wine glass before continuing. She said the 'haters' expected them—people of color—to wallow incessantly in a lowly position from where they constantly sought help, displayed ignorance, lay at their mercy, and responded unquestionably to their beckon calls. People of color genuflecting permanently in that low position would confirm the haters' expectation and buttress their already inexorable sense of bigotry. If, on the other hand, people from under-represented groups displayed competence, and exuded self-confidence, etc., they would be branded as pompous, arrogant, and out of their place, their place of servility, obedience, chronic incompetence, and taciturnity. In fact, under such circumstances, and if they ever dared stand on their own feet and therefrom insisted on their constitutionally protected rights, they would be quickly branded as trouble makers. "Honey, although we abide my institutional rules and regulations, and even though we make every effort not to call attention to ourselves or offend anyone, you and I already have been called thus and we know several people on this campus who have been labeled in similar manner when they are only trying to perform their jobs as best as they can."

The beautiful and determined lecturer took another sip of her wine and collected her thoughts. She emphasized strongly that, in this twenty-first century, in light of relevant laws and judicial mandates, and in honor of all who suffered, even died to foster justice and promote equality, she, her husband and others from under-represented groups could not, and must not, accept, let alone be shaped by, such convoluted and irrational behavior couched in, and fueled by racism and bigotry. Hence, it was vitally important, indeed actively compelling, for people from under-represented groups to gain the best qualification they could afford; by so doing, they did not have to be at the beckon call of anyone or worse, perish in a genuflecting position. "Oh my good Lord; I sincerely wish every individual, especially people from under-represented groups could listen to me and prepare themselves as best as possible, regardless of hardship and setbacks."

Looking directly at her husband, Vanessa threw out a series of imperatives. "Baby, that's why, if we do not do anything, we must work very closely with the twelve mentees we have chosen. When they graduate, we must select twelve or more students and this must continue until we retire. We must ensure they succeed as Prof. Kwame did for us."

Her husband could not agree more. "Believe it or not Honey, you are not only mesmeric, I mean, tantalizingly gorgeous but also incredibly brilliant; I knew it the first day I met you." The doorbell rang. "Who could that be?" Vanessa did not respond but ran to the door

"Dallas!" she exclaimed. "Welcome! Great to see you!"

"I was in the neighborhood and just decided to drop by the good old southern way—no calling or anything like that."

"That's alright," Vanessa accepted the impromptu visit. "That's the kind of visitation we know—none of that formal stuff. Please come in and, as always, feel at home."

Dallas thanked Vanessa, gave Darrell a hearty handshake and joined the couple at their dining table. He gladly accepted an offer of a glass of wine.

"You came at a propitious time," Darrell informed Dallas. Suspecting the pronouncement would keep Dallas wondering, Darrell elucidated quickly. "My darling wife and I are talking about our problems at the university. We wonder why such raging racism engulfs the entire institution."

Dallas took a sip of his wine. "My brother," he started, "I have been here seventeen plus years and have seen no change; if there's a change, the situation has only gotten worse. I mean, it's blatant albeit untenable. I'm serious," he stressed. "This is one of the most racist institutions of higher education I know and I have visited many and actually worked in three others. Of course, none was free of racism and domination by the White majority, especially the White male majority."

"I imagine they have had to respond to several lawsuits," Darrell conjectured although with an air of certitude.

"Oh yea," Dallas agreed, "but almost none of them goes anywhere." After another sip, he continued, "As you know Darrell, most of us are familiar with Title VI of the Civil Rights Act of 1964."

Before Dallas could continue, Vanessa pulled out a book, flipped through quickly and said, "Here it is in plain language: 'No person in the United States shall, on the ground of race, color, or national origin, be excluded from participation in, be denied the benefits of, or be subjected to discrimination under any program or activity receiving Federal financial assistance'."

"That's the law my sister and it applies to virtually all public schools and a considerable number of private institutions," Dallas concurred. He regretted that the law meant nothing to SAU. He elaborated that this was because the university not only had lawyers on campus but was represented by one of the strongest, some said most crooked, law firms in town and in the state. As a result, Dallas had seen many ugly incidents which passed with impunity. He enumerated that these included: incidents of racial slurs and hate notes left for minority students and workers, including professors; hateful placards left in conspicuous places on campus, some using the N word and calling on people to go elsewhere; white power signs around campus; demoralizing and castigating graffiti left in men's and ladies' bathrooms; blatant discrimination against minorities in hiring and promotion, and on and on. Generally, the university ignored these abuses, including threats to the safety of administrators, faculty, and students from under-represented groups. In a few instances, the university put out statements condemning the incident but did nothing to deter repetition, improve race relations, or stop the maltreatment and marginalization of people from under-represented groups.

"I mean," Dallas went on, "minorities have been treated horribly here with impunity. Yet, if you check our website and, if you look at our mission statement and check through our strategic plan, you will find impressive statements as to how the university is committed to diversity." Perhaps because of his position as Assistant Director of Minority Affairs, Dallas continued to use the word "minority" instead of "under-represented groups" or "people of color" as he angrily generalized, dubbing the racial majority as bogus and shamelessly duplicitous. He said it was especially disgusting because, in actuality, the university's doors were shut to minority students, staff, administrators, and professors. The token few from under-represented groups who made it to the university were treated very badly to the extent that only a small fraction stayed. He contended that the disgust could not be overemphasized. Worse still, mind-boggling was how cleverly racism was camouflaged alongside the side-stepping of relevant laws and judicial mandates. As a result, there were relatively few 'people of color' at the university and those who dared stray into the professoriate encountered low ratings, indicating that their works were not valued. This insult added injury in terms of stiff walls in promotion, tenure, and appointments to senior administrative positions.

"That's a real shame," Darrell condemned. Agreeing with Dallas, he said prior to coming to Achval, he was impressed with the university's mission statement. His only objection to the statement was the reference to colorblindness as that was a denial of racial reality. In any case, upon arriving at the university, he did not see convincing evidence of the diversity that was professed. He further disclosed that he sat on the Diversity Committees of his college and the university but both were a real joke. Worse still, he was amazed as to how cleverly the university authorities used subterfuges in the face of glaring violation of law. Then, he addressed Dallas directly: "But Dallas, you have been here for years; what is your personal experience, if I may ask?"

"Wow! Where do I begin?" Dallas laughed. He divulged that it took more than twelve years for him to get a slight promotion and even then, his junior staff members and even students were held in higher esteem than he was. He was isolated and scrutinized more than any of his colleagues in the administration. The minute they found his minutest fault, it was brought to his attention and magnified exponentially to confirm and validate their preconceived notion of his supposed ineptitude. Conversely, when his white colleagues committed the worst crimes—yes, crimes—such were either swept under the rug or the perpetrators were given minor reprimands.

As Darrell and his wife listened intently, Dallas was determined to spill the beans as much as he could. He said when he came up with a good idea, it was either shot down in preference for a worse one or stolen by his boss and presented as his own. "I mean, I just cannot do anything right or so it seems to them. Worse still, I seem to have no rights; they invade my privacy, reprimand me in the presence of students and visitors, and often treat and/or address me like a dummy. Stated differently, I'm insulted, isolated, unappreciated, over-worked, and under-paid. This maltreatment and isolation create in me what one writer calls 'a feeling of otherness,'[7] a painful and humiliating state. As such, I am most insecure in my position as I can be transferred, demoted, or worse, fired at any time."

"Then why do you stay?" Vanessa probed. "Or, if you have to stay, what do you do about the situation? How long will you allow them to push you around? When will you put your foot

---

[7]   Segura, 2003.

down and firmly assert your right?" She continued her line of questioning before Dallas could respond.

Dallas welcomed the challenge. "My dear sister," he said, "I believe your practical experience in higher education, although already rich in many ways, is nonetheless limited. I'm also sure you have looked at the literature but I encourage you to look deeper with regard to the nature and impact of the campus climate especially for people of color." He pointed out that one writer[8] addressing the topic, covered "educational exclusion" since World War II, "from academic apartheid to affirmative action and, more recently, from race-based criteria of selection to what is called diversity." He elaborated that the writer not only outlined various advantages of diversity in higher education but also pointed out how the courts had confirmed same. "Despite this, other writers have[9] called attention to the notion of Whiteness as property, a property right, evidently, that extends to leadership in higher education."

Dallas added that because of the notion of 'Whiteness as property', the white establishment set barriers to the advancement of people of color in higher education and presumably, in other spheres of employment. "As the literature shows,[10] such barriers," Dallas went on, "include poor working conditions, woefully inadequate financial compensation, and the elimination of Affirmative Action and similar programs as cost-saving measures. This is why I would like to call your attention to the notion of Whiteness as property which is detested by all people of conscience, including Blacks, Whites, and Hispanics. Hence, some scholars[11] have advocated the identification and dismantling of same.

---

[8] Brown, 2002.

[9] Wolfe & Dilworth, 2015

[10] Ibid

[11] E.g. Brunsma et al, 2013

Darrell and Vanessa looked curiously at Dallas, apparently making sense of his words and simultaneously sympathizing with him. Without stopping to interpret their curious looks one way or another, Dallas continued. "So, my sister, you need to understand first that I have a family to feed and bills to pay in the face of such barriers. In the best interest of my family, I must at least ignore, and at best overleap, those illegal and illogical barriers." He said from his experience, he did not harbor a modicum of doubt that racism, bigotry, and discrimination were endemic and enduring in the institution. Most definitely, they were neither new nor limited to a specific segment of the system; rather, they permeated and putrefied the entire institutional system. Yet, at his age and with his experience, he regrettably felt he could do nothing about it; consequently, like everyone else, he looked out for himself and his family. "I'm being honest. I feel detached from the institution and therefore perform my job for my salary. I think that is what industrial psychologists call surface acting and I do so without shame or regret."

"Quite frankly, I see from where you are coming Dallas but your insistence is interesting indeed," Vanessa declared. "So, you will do nothing to defend your right, reputation, and dignity in the face of this notion of Whiteness as property?"

Dallas laughed. "My sister, why rock the boat unnecessarily? Do you know how many people are in the job market? Yes, I am thankful to God for a good education; I have a masters degree and a twenty-five year experience but I am an at will employee. Besides, the competition in my field is indescribably stringent. I therefore will do nothing to hurt my job." He hesitated as he took a sip of his wine and reached for munchies Vanessa brought. He continued, "Maybe both of you will not understand. You see, both of you have sound academic credentials; therefore, you can find a job anywhere but that's not the same with some of us. Unless you have been where we have been, you will not understand." To cite one example, he said within the last month, his department cut one lady of color although there were whites with horrible records and far limited experiences and academic qualifications than the lady. The departure of the lady left him as the only person of color in his department although that was nothing new, and although the department widely publicized its reputation for enhancing diversity at the university. "But," he murmured, "that's the nature of the beast before us and, unfortunately, that beast targets me all the time.

When asked to explain how he was targeted, Dallas said like many people of color in predominantly white institutions, he incessantly experienced microaggressions and various forms of racism. As if those were not enough, he endured blatant discriminatory and humiliating attitudes. For example, when people visited his department, he was called upon to give the impression that the department was diverse. "In other words," he added, "they showcase me to promote themselves and subsequently dismiss me to put me in what they term 'my place'. Often I feel like a zoo animal on display." Dallas further added that, as the only person of color in his department, he resented the onus of "representing blackness" in his department.

Darrell grew serious. "Dallas," he called, "of course we understand the illegality, illogical nature, and negative impacts of racism. For instance, there is no basis for the microaggressions and discriminatory treatments you and I endure along with others of color in predominantly White institutions. However, you talk as if Vanessa and I dropped from some ivory tower. Like you, we were born in poor families in the south. We are no strangers to racism but the way it is manifested here is beyond comprehension. Heaven knows that, like you, we have been maltreated and continue to be unappreciated in this university."

Dallas sat backward. When he sat upright, he reached again for the munchies. He once more reiterated that his sincere aim was to be honest with Darrell and his wife. He agreed totally that the university was rotten to the core. If it were a corporation, it would have folded long ago. From the top to the bottom, most administrators did not really care for the institution; they were only trying to serve their terms and after that, either retire or go elsewhere. Then he threw in a series of questions. "Have you seen the president's contract? Do you know he makes more than the President of the nation and he only needs to serve for a limited number of years? Are you aware that everything in the presidential mansion is paid for by the university? I mean everything—food, drinks, laundry detergents, bathing soap, toilet tissues, and all. In addition, do you have any idea about the salaries of the provost and his vice provosts, vice presidents, deans and associate deans, directors and other administrators? Do you know that often, they create positions to accommodate their buddies while demoting or dismissing minorities as I just pointed out? Have you any idea how much bonuses they get beyond their salaries every year while they increase tuition on one hand and on the other, give nugatory salary increases to professors and staff members? Are you aware of the number and variety of expensive junkets they take? Have you noticed that only a handful of under-represented graduate students receive graduate assistanceships while the children of administrators are given preferences for such positions? I can go on and on. I mean, this whole thing is disgusting but once more, I say, that's the beast we must deal with on a daily basis. As I cannot change the world, I similarly will do nothing to hurt my job," Dallas underscored once more as he accepted a recharge of his glass.

"My brother," Vanessa stated in a low tune, "permit me please to offer one observation and let me know what you think."

"Go ahead," Dallas permitted promptly.

"I guess it goes without saying that all of us detest to the core, the essence of racism, white domination, and the notion of Whiteness as property but, it seems they have succeeded with you. I mean, I think you have been pushed into a position of powerlessness where you feel helpless and therefore forced to capitulate and settle for a ..." she thought a moment before completing her sentence, "well I will not say a callous life but at least a carefree one. Do you agree?"

"I most certainly feel powerless. However, power or no power, I must put the wellbeing of my family first and I hold that position rigidly."

Darrell chose his words carefully. He reiterated his point that he was fully aware of racial microaggression, isolation, marginalization, non-promotion, and other negatives people of color faced in higher education. At the same time, he made it clear that he cared about his family as much as Dallas cared for his; therefore, he would do nothing to jeopardize his family's wellbeing and his children's future. Additionally, as an economist, he was very familiar with the prevailing economic crises and the extent to which they affected communities of under-represented groups. "However," he cleared his throat to make his point clearly and poignantly, "to ignore the putrescence of blatant racism, to accept degradation driven by discrimination, to sacrifice one's self-respect, to accept diminution of one's dignity, and to overlook obloquy in the name of job security is beyond belief. Let's face it Brother; it's an appalling display of diffidence, indeed nothing less than cowardice."

Dallas tried to force a smile but his serious face was unmistakable. "Oh my brother, call me what you may but, let me reiterate; it's easy for you to say that for you can leave today and find another job tomorrow. Many of us have to swallow bitter pills to put bread on the table and keep roofs over our heads."

"But that's not true; it took a while for us to get jobs here," Darrell corrected.

"I agree but eventually, you got a job; if you leave, it may take a while but because of your academic credentials, you will find another position elsewhere. How many of us can do that?"

"It's not that easy Dallas," Darrell reemphasized. He clarified that after all, it was not fun looking for a job and dragging the family all over the country. Stated differently, there was no doubt that his family too needed job security. However, as they yearned for that security, no one needed to remind them of racism and its multiple ugly vices. They therefore were not prepared to flee in the face of one incident or another but ultimately, they refused to abdicate their rights, accept degradation, and sacrifice dignity in the name of job security.

Vanessa could not wait to get her point in. "As you know Dallas, we are the heirs to generations of African-Americans who, despite unbearably difficult conditions, resisted domination, fought back, and many succeeded." She generalized that she, Dallas, and all African-Americans could not afford to abdicate that honorable legacy. Additionally, she reminded Dallas that the nation's beginning was characterized by egregious race relations as the indigenous people of the land, some call Native Americans and others call American Indians, were regarded as savages worthy of elimination. This colonialized racism from the nation's early beginning was extended to other racial minorities.

Focusing on African-Americans, Vanessa praised the heroism of Africans who, while transported unscrupulously by nefarious slave traders, resisted humiliation and this caused their demise. The strongest of the strong who survived the tortuous journey resisted slavery as evidenced by the numerous slave rebellions. The so-called end of slavery was only a political move.

"In what sense?" Dallas inquired. Clearly, he was not acquainted with this depth of African-American history.

"Well," Vanessa responded, clearing her throat, "On March 3, 1807, Jefferson signed an act abolishing the importation of slaves but this act was not to take effect until January 1, 1808." She elaborated that the act did not end slavery. In fact, the plight of blacks was exacerbated by the Black Codes, a series of laws passed in the ex-Confederate states after slavery ended. Similarly, from 1876 to about 1965, despite the passage of the 13th, 14th, and 15th amendments of the constitution which gave blacks legal protection as whites, Jim Crow laws legitimized racism. She clarified that Jim Crow laws overthrew Reconstruction and reimposed white supremacy and thereby resurfaced laws that were reminiscent of the Black Codes. "Interestingly," Vanessa added, "these laws were engineered and supported by white ministers of the Gospel who were convinced that God supported segregation because whites were God's chosen people while conversely, blacks were cursed. This was precisely the basis of apartheid laws in South Africa were whites landed in the mid-1600s, whites who called the blacks 'children of an inferior god'."

"Isn't that something?" Dallas murmured in amazement. He still was curious. "I have heard of Jim Crow laws. Where did they come from and why the name 'Jim Crow'? Who was Jim Crow?"

Vanessa smiled. "The name 'Jim Crow' does not refer to an individual although various persons claimed to have been Jim Crow." She explicated that the name actually came from a minstrel song written by Thomas Dartmouth Rice also known as Daddy Rice, a white comedian who performed in blackface. Vanessa said she used to know the song but did not care about it for obvious reasons. The only line she remembered was a part of the chorus which said, "Eb'ry time I weel about I jump Jim Crow."

Vanessa explained further that there were various versions as to how the song started but eventually, it was used to mock blacks and therefore became the basis for de jure discrimination against blacks especially in the south and borderline states. State and local laws enacted on this basis were fortified by a Supreme Court ruling in *Plessy v. Ferguson* in 1896 which coined the infamous phrase, "separate but equal," a phrase rejected by the same court in the famous 1954 case of *Brown v. Board of Education,* of *Topeka, Kansas.*

"Wow!" Dallas said. "That's amazing."

Vanessa agreed. She emphasized the importance of African-Americans and other people of color knowing their history as they struggled against the evils of racism and all its vices. To exemplify, she said it was important for African-Americans to know that, despite The Black Codes and Jim Crow laws, many Blacks succeeded incredibly as evidenced by a considerable number of first black inventors, college graduates, legislators,

149

and the like. She turned to Dallas and said, "So you see my brother, even during slavery and under the harshest of circumstances, many of our forefathers fought for dignity. Furthermore, for your freedom and mine, and for the very employment you refer to, many died before you and me. No one is asking you to sacrifice your job and family but is your personal dignity negotiable and compromisable?"

Dallas stood his ground. He appreciated and admired the historical account but accentuated that he respected himself and similarly taught his children to respect themselves. He said he would respect himself even more and probably be respected more if he was able to support his family and raise his children in a proper and respectful manner. Then he sipped on his wine glass before adding, "After all, on second thought, in reality, we are far better off than our forefathers during the Jim Crow years. I therefore submit that the racism you over-emphasize is not as widespread as you profess. I have never heard Professor Amos Commings complain about racism and he has been here many years."

Darrell chimed in. "First Dallas, you have confirmed that racism permeates, and is endemic to, the university. Are you retracting or contradicting that statement, and if so, why? Besides, to say that racism is not as widespread as we profess is as admission that it exists and no form or degree of racism is acceptable. Second, we know of Commings and his underhanded dealings. I'm sure you will be the first to admit that as he has undermined you on at least three occasions."

"You are very well informed; I am not his only victim. Though blacker than you and me, he does not hesitate to hurt people especially people from under-represented groups," Dallas interrupted. He apologized quickly and asked Darrell to continue.

Darrell added thirdly that he wanted to make it abundantly clear that his was not an anti-White campaign. As he saw it, racism was abhorrent and therefore unacceptable and intolerable, whether directed at Blacks or Whites. He and Vanessa therefore were not indicting all Whites. He said, "As you know, I associate freely with Andy and quite frankly, I owe that man more than I can say. Furthermore, He is not a lone token exception because when ludicrous charges of plagiarism were levied against me, while some of my colleagues were convinced of my guilt even in the absence of evidence, Andy, Prof. Daniels and Prof. Smith not only supported me but insisted on fairness and justice. In other words, there's no doubting the fact that this is not a denunciation of all Whites for that is as repugnant as a blanket discrimination of all Blacks. Rather, we maintain that the system is putrid and this putrescence, fueled by racism and bigotry is intolerable, regardless of the skin color of the perpetrators and victims."

Darrell stopped as if collecting his thoughts. He directly addressed Dallas. "Let's face it Dallas, how many people from under-represented groups do you talk with on the campus to understand their problems? Do you know about the many who are degraded daily? Have you ever talked with people who are denied promotions and salary increases? Do you know the number whose bosses are far more incompetent than they are?" He hesitated again before adding, "Let's be personal; even you, Dallas; how long have you been here and when was the last time you were promoted? Isn't it true that most of the bosses you have had held only bachelor degrees and often with far less experience than you?"

"You are right again," Dallas conceded. He admitted that while he had worked with at least one very capable and efficient boss, in general, he had coped with some of the most incompetent, indeed moronic and megalomaniac bosses. He also knew of people from under-represented groups who had doctorates but could not even get tenure track positions. Conversely, he knew of Whites with bachelors degrees at the university who firmly occupied incredible senior positions; one white high school graduate earned more than people from under-represented groups who had doctorate degrees although, as most people knew, the gentleman did not possess any outstanding talent worthy of extraordinary remuneration. He said Darrell and Vanessa did not have to look too far for they had a dean who did not have a doctorate and even his masters degree was questionable.

"And that's fine with you?" Vanessa questioned curiously.

Dallas doggedly defended his position again. "Oh no but to keep my job, I rather not look at them but secure my position as best as I can." He said his views and stance were a matter of survival. He stressed he was being as honest as possible. Further, he noted that it was difficult for Darrell and Vanessa to understand his position, let alone empathize with him. Similarly, as newcomers, he was sure the couple did not understand him. They did not understand how difficult it was to deal with African-Americans and others from under-represented groups, people he called, "our people." He said it was doubly difficult even if one tried to help them.

Vanessa did not want to address Dallas' point that she and her husband did not understand him. Rather, she was anxious to throw in a few questions. Before asking, she commended Dallas honestly for looking out for his family. Additionally, she applauded him for not hurting others, as far as she knew, in his zeal to look out for his family. Furthermore, she clarified that increasing diversity on any university campus ought to be the duty of everyone, not just blacks or people of color. After her clarification, she zeroed in on her questions. "But, how many people, Blacks or Whites, have you helped? As you say, and I agree, they preach diversity but perpetuate adversity; certainly, they practice anything but diversity. We therefore bemoan their sense of advancing diversity which is including people who talk, think, and write like them; this is why they have one yardstick for assessing scholarship. It is therefore no surprise when they cry incessantly that they cannot find qualified people of color." She stopped to catch her breath as she was overwhelmed by this insane sense of diversity.

When Vanessa settled down, she continued asking Dallas. "As an administrator, what have you done to increase the number of people from under-represented groups in administration, the professoriate, or even within the student body? Do you know the failure and attrition rate of students from under-represented groups in this university? Are you aware of the multitudinous complaints of African-American, Hispanic, Asian, Native American, and international students on this campus? If you are not aware, why not? If you are aware, what have you done about them especially since you alluded to striving desperately to help?"

"You question me as if I am on a witness stand in a court of law," Dallas protested mildly. "Look, I do not know how many times I will tell you. I honestly do care about these young men and women who are failing or dropping out. Some have come to me for help but most regrettably, I am not in a position to do anything substantive for them."

Vanessa jumped in quickly. "But Dallas, the quest for assistance is not always on 'big matters'. Often, students of color get stuck over relatively minor issues for which they need help."

Dallas said he knew that to be the case but nonetheless stressed that at SAU, more than any other universities he knew, people from under-represented groups were hired often as token appointees, a means of masking true racist policies and invading relevant law. Beyond that tenebrous thickness, people from under-represented groups were exempt from power-sharing and in decision making; the key positions were occupied by Whites, sometimes, qualification notwithstanding. "In spite of this nauseating truism," Dallas continued venting his frustration, "Heaven knows I have tried only to be deterred or forced to justify my actions. For example, if I help one minority student, I have to help three or four white students to demonstrate fairness; white administrators do not have that burden. You see; it's disgustingly unfair and remains doggedly so. Pushed against the rope and feeling frustrated, exhausted, powerless, and angry, what then do you expect me to do other than protect my job for the sake of my family?" He hesitated before adding softly, "You know, I honestly admire you for your stance but, given this rotten system, I will tell you right now that if you continue to advocate strongly and openly for yourselves and others, I sincerely do not see you lasting too long at this university. If you stay, I cannot imagine you will ever get into administration; if you do, undoubtedly, you will either have to go along with the system or be forced out as quickly as you entered."

"Hmm," Darrell murmured as if trying to understand Dallas' perspective. He did not want to comment on the implied basis for his possible longevity at the university or his chances for entering the administration. Rather, he thought a minute of the fact that he and Dallas were on different sides of the university table; he was on a tenure track while Dallas was in adminis- tration, Dallas' level notwithstanding. He therefore wanted to direct the discussion a little differently. "Would you agree then that there is something such as a white privilege?"

"What is that?" Dallas inquired.

Darrell sat up straight as if to be in a good position to express himself as clearly as he could. "That simply means by virtue of their race, Whites get privileges, opportunities, approvals, clearances, etc., that Blacks and members of other under-represented groups do not enjoy."

"Like what?" Dallas was dying to know.

Darrell was equally anxious to explain. "For example, Whites are presumed competent and that competence is mea- sured relative to an Eurocentric realm. Conversely, from that dominant perspective, Blacks and other people from under-rep- resented groups are presumed incompetent, irrespective of qualifications. As a result, incompetent Whites get better posi- tions; Whites do nothing wrong and when they do, it's swept under the rug; Whites cut corners and that's acceptable; Whites get away with murder ..."

"Murder?" Dallas exclaimed.

Darrell knew he had to clarify quickly although he was sure he was not dishing out anything new to Dallas. He explained that, as he saw it, certainly there were exceptions but often,

Whites got away with horrible offenses like plagiarism, nepotism, ineptitude, theft, embezzlement, cheating, lying on their CVs and annual reports, sexual harassment, etc.. From his perspective, it went without saying that, no one, including Blacks, was allowed to commit such horrible crimes. It was therefore regrettable, indeed unjustified that, while in general, Whites got away with commission, Blacks and members of other under-represented groups were publicized, disgraced, and dismissed for false charges relative to these crimes. Referring to Blacks, he added, "I imagine an attempt will land them in prison indefinitely while actual commission will send them to the gallows. Put succinctly, Whites are the beneficiaries of this double-handed game because they have a special privilege called white privilege. In other words, their skin color supposedly ordains them to be superior and therefore entitled to higher and better positions, thereby forcing people of color to secondary, tertiary, or no positions." Darrell bemoaned covert and overt marginalization that resulted from the expectation that people of color in the institution conformed to attitudes and practices rooted in white privilege.

"I contend that this privilege has its roots, at least its similarities, in slavery and post-slavery days," articulated Vanessa. She called attention to a July, 1852 oration by Frederick Douglas when leaders in Rochester, New York asked him to speak on Independence Day. She pointed out that the speech was touted as given later in Congress and it may have been in part or in whole but she had to ascertain that historical fact. She said the reason for pointing out the speech was that a line in the speech was relevant to the discussion. She read from a note: "There are seventy-two crimes in the State of Virginia which, if committed by a black man (no matter how ignorant he be), subject him to the punishment of death; while only two of the same crimes will subject a white man to the like punishment."

Dallas appeared nonplused or perhaps just searching for the right words. "Hmmm," he groaned. "White privilege? I had never thought of it that way but you are absolutely right; they do get away with a lot. I can't even begin to tell you. Some horrible incidents that have been covered up I cannot disclose except when subpoenaed and forced to testify under oath; oh my goodness, it's terrible."

"A little more wine Dallas?" Vanessa asked.

"No Sister," he answered quickly. I must drive home and, as I am not afraid of death, I will not invite it either for it is just as asinine to fear death as it is to invite it."

Vanessa laughed out loud but then stopped abruptly when she realized Dallas' strange statement. "Now, I am aware of The Bard's statement that 'death is a necessary end, will come when it will come' therefore it will be foolish to fear it; but how does one invite death?"

"By doing anything foolish that will hasten its arrival," Dallas answered in the midst of laughter. "Since its coming is inevitable, I will offer no help; I will not pay its way, give directions, hasten its coming, or do anything to help. Obviously I cannot stop its coming but it must go through the troubles and find me by itself." Still laughing lightly, Dallas looked at his watch. "Incidentally, I must be going. I thank you for the wine, your warm company, and the lively discussion. This was a great exchange; let's do this more often."

"We will love that," Darrell concurred as he saw Dallas out. He cleared the table and joined his wife in the kitchen to help prepare dinner as the children were expected home soon.

Chapter X:

HOLDING ON

The discussion at the home of the Thomases lingered for a while in the minds of the three persons involved, Dallas, Darrell and Vanessa. Darrell and his wife returned to it briefly but individually, they analyzed it in their minds from various perspectives. Was, for example, Dallas to be maligned as cowardly, callous, sycophantic, and diffident or was he simply oblivious to injustice meted out to him and others? Could it be that, given his many setbacks and failures directly or indirectly engineered by the system, and the fact that he had endured insults, marginalization, and exclusion, he felt impuissant, frustrated, and therefore forced to throw in the towel and acquiesce, focusing intently on his family and forgetting the system and its putrid vices? Was it that Dallas gave in too much and too soon? Did Dallas' personal greed exceed his need for integrity, pride and dignity, justice, and the welfare of others? Did Dallas fall in that breed of African-Americans who plead they had to bleed to succeed and therefore perceive no need to spoon-feed others who are not equally willing to work hard forgetting that others may not have opportunities or worse, may be messed up by the system? On the other hand, were Darrell and Vanessa, newcomers to the system, myopic, brutally captious, and consequently oblivious to Dallas' frustration and challenges? Did they fully understand the extent to which, as Dallas claimed, the system had isolated, marginalized, humiliated, and blockaded him as a junior administrator of color in a predominantly white institution? Could it be that the anger and frustration of the three parties were misplaced? Did the three focus more on the problem than emphasizing a concerted and sagacious search for solution?

As Darrell's thoughts deeply centered on the conversation at his house, he did not hear footsteps to his office and so Alex knocked. Darrell turned around, saw who it was and so warmly greeted. "Oh hi Alex. How are you and what can I do for you?" It was clear Alex had just come in from the snow for he still had on his winter coat, hat, and boots. He looked very stern.

"Did you get my email about Esther Vickman?" Looking directly at Alex and shaking his head lightly, Darrell replied in the negative. "I suggest you check it and send me an answer today," Alex demanded emphatically and walked away.

The name faintly registered on Darrell's mind. "Esther Vickman," he repeated the name to himself. Quickly he turned to his computer and checked the email messages. He found one from Alex about Vickman. "Oh yea," he remembered, "this is the young sophomore who lectured me on the topic of opportunity cost."

Darrell went over the string of email messages. Ms. Vickman sent Darrell and email stating that he had graded her mid-term exam improperly. She lectured him as to what was opportunity cost and accordingly, how her answer should have been graded. In response, Darrell once more explained opportunity cost. He concluded: "Thanks for the lecture. Whenever you teach the course, I will have a choice as to whether or not to enroll; for now, this is my course and the grade stands."

Darrell's response bothered the student so she angrily forwarded it to Alex who wrote back to her stating, "I will see to it that Dr. Thomas change this grade as your explanation is right on the money." He copied Darrell and demanded an instant change of the student's grade.

To say Darrell was furious would be a huge under-statement. Nonetheless, he regained equanimity and wrote back to Alex also copying the student. He started, "Dr. Brooks," being formal since the student was copied, "this is very interesting. However, I would like to extend the offer to you as well; that is, next time you teach the course, I will have a choice as to whether or not to enroll. For now, this is my course and my grade stands."

Alone in his office, Alex was once more uncontrollably furious; he incessantly uttered profanities and racial slurs. After a while, he went back to the computer and sent the student a message. It is not known what he wrote but never got back to Darrell on the subject. He only continued to threaten that he would ensure the (N word) would leave as soon as possible and that would mean a better university for all. "The profligate never knows what he is talking about so what good is he here?" he growled. "He is just like the rest of them. They do nothing, know, nothing, deserve nothing and yet want to be treated like everyone else—always crying racism, racism, racism! I'm sick and tired of them. Worse, that idiot had the audacity to insult me? I swear he will leave this university. I will make sure of that. Or I will never forgive myself till I die."

Although Alex did not contact Darrell on the Vickman issue, Peggy chance, the assistant dean did. She was laconic. "Darrell, defiance of your immediate boss in the Esther Vickman issue has been brought to my attention. Under no circumstance do we tolerate such act of insubordination at SAU." She copied Alex on the message.

Exasperated, Darrell walked around his office for a few minutes to blow off steam. When he sat down, he pondered over the issue for a while and then replied to all. "Peggy, I find it interesting, indeed inscrutable that a contumelious statement by a sophomore student toward her professor is tolerable while that professor's insistence on his right in accordance with the university's constitution and college policies is deemed an insubordination and therefore intolerable. It is equally unfathomable that, in this case, you as an administrator hastily reached a conclusion without investigation." He was tempted to point out to her the merits and demerits of various leadership approaches: autocratic, participative or democratic, delegative, bureaucratic, transactional, and transformational styles, among others. In educational leadership, he was burning to underscore the invaluable essence of proper communication and interpersonal skills in addition to skills adamantly emphasized by facilitative, democratic, laissez-faire, transformational, visionary, ethical, and other leadership styles. He resisted this temptation on grounds that it would doubtlessly be an exercise in futility. Worse, it would only fuel Peggy's fire of ire and thereby provide another unconscionable excuse for triggering any combination of her dirty and devious deeds. Though he was afraid of neither and none would surprise him, he nonetheless sent off the terse email as drafted.

Darrell's response did not endear him to Peggy. Quite the contrary, if she had an ounce of endearment for Darrell, it vanished as quickly as her delete button could send his response to the recycle bin, never to be retrieved. However, mindful that the plagiarism charge against Darrell proved to be preposterous, and after obtaining inconsistent explanations from Alex about the Vickman case, she appeared cautious in handling issues or cases related to Darrell. Interestingly this deception was diaphanous because, no matter how hard she tried, she could not mask her determination to put Darrell in his place and/or teach him a lesson. Undoubtedly, she was determined to show him, properly or improperly, that, to avoid being in an extremely uncomfortable working environment or even risking expulsion on plausible, implausible, valid or bogus grounds, her authority had to be respected, never challenged, regardless of the invalidity, illegality, or unscrupulousness of her action. This was not a surprise for anything otherwise would not be like the prejudicial, pugnacious, and power-conscious Peggy as people knew her. In fact, were it not for grievances filed and won separately and at different times by two former professors of color, both

Peggy and Alex would not have hesitated changing the student's grade. This was a constant practice directed at professors of color in the college until two of them successfully filed grievances. Only then did the provost enforce an existing constitutional mandate prohibiting administrators from changing grades. "Only instructors of record can change grades," the provost's memo reminded everyone.

Darrell briefly discussed the Vickman issue with Vanessa. Sometimes he rather listened to her gripes than discuss his miseries. This was because her intersectional identity as Black and female put her at a double disadvantage. Most of her colleagues and students showed little respect to women and even less so to women who were African-American, Hispanic, Asian, or from other under-represented backgrounds. No doubt, she was a stronger person; she dealt with instances of humiliation, degradation, marginalization, and exclusion almost on a daily basis. Like Darrell, her work was frowned upon although of sound academic quality. Fortunately, she found support from Lupita and Ann; their friendship grew stronger as, in their socialization milieu, they heavily depended on one another. The group provided an environment for them to express their concerns, vent their anger, and in turn, get support from one another. "Every person of color in a predominantly white institution needs such an environment," Vanessa declared and her friends agreed.

In addition to her socialization milieu alongside her strong family support, Vanessa was inspired by other "people of color" as she skimmed through the literature. This was particularly true of women of color. Among others, she loved the work of Nelly McKay who prolifically wrote about her experiences at a prestigious mid-western university as experiences of a double minority. She made it clear that black women were determined to take their rightful places in academia. Black women, she wrote, would not go back; rather, their aim was to stay in the academy. Likewise, Jan Carter-Black's work, A Black Woman's Journey Into a Predominately White Academic World, was inspiring. The work focused on a forty-year experience regarding "challenges of being African American and female in a majority White university community." Similarly, Sue V. Rosser outlined "institutional barriers identified by women scientists and engineers."

Vanessa also learned a lot from the work of Bryan McKinley Jones Brayboy who interviewed "African American, American Indian, Asian, and Latino faculty members, of junior status, in predominantly White colleges and universities." In similar fashion, the work of Caroline S. Turner was informative. Dr. Turner considered "faculty of color entering the academy." Such faculty "describe factors leading toward their incorporation as well as factors keeping them at the margins." Such faculty, Dr. Turner explicated, remained "underrepresented, and their achievements too often are almost invisible and/or devalued in the academy." Moreover, many described "experiences of racial and ethnic bias in the workplace." Vanessa was grateful for unearthing the experiences of many women of color in predominantly white institutions—-how they were treated or more correctly, mistreated and what coping mechanisms they used to fight back and win in many instances.

Vanessa's experience and familiarity with the literature were helpful when Brian Anderson, her department chair called her in one day. "What have I done again," she kidded as she took seat in Brian's office.

Brian was not smiling. "Vanessa, I am considering recommending you for a refresher course in college teaching," he said.

Vanessa's jaws dropped. "I don't know how to teach? It's that bad? Have you seen my student evaluations? Have you attended any of my classes?" incidentally, she did not point out that among professors and lecturers in her department, she was the only person who held an education specialist degree with emphasis on instructional procedures.

"I have seen it all," said Brian Anderson. "But a number of students in your class are uncomfortable with the way you teach about the cruel transportation of slaves from Africa."

Vanessa was baffled. "I do not understand."

"You present the slave traders as cruel and heartless white people; that's racism to the core if I ever saw one."

Incredulously, Vanessa was quiet for a moment. "Is the information false and misleading or is it based on historical fact? Do you, for once, consider the slave traders as saints? Would you, under any circumstance, support such a ridiculous notion?"

Brian was unequivocal and firm. "Look, I did not call you here for a debate. I'm simply saying if you do not stop your racist presentation of history, you will be sent to a refresher course."

Vanessa equally hit back. "I'm a historian; therefore I endeavor to present history factually. That includes presenting historical facts about the cruelty of human beings against fellow humans, whether that regards the inhumane treatment of slaves by slave traders, cruel efforts by Europeans to annihilate Native Americans or the cruel efforts by Nazis to exterminate Jews and many others, including people with disabilities. Maybe Brian, you need to take a refresher course to know the facts of history. While you are at it, be sure to visit The Charles H. Wright Museum of African American History, the Holocaust Museum, and the National Museum of the American Indian. It's a pity that you chair the History Department but simply ignore these historical facts." Brian was red in the face as Vanessa walked out of his office.

Vanessa relayed her conversation with Brian to Darrell. Once more, she emphasized that acquaintance with the literature was helpful in buttressing her determination to face such a ridiculous charge fearlessly and decisively.

No doubt, Vanessa's keen sense of determination inspired Darrell who had been sifting through the literature as well. As they approached the end of their second year at SAU, they were determined to complete the year strongly. Darrell was administering his grant project and writing new grants. Additionally, he had several articles under review; two of them focused on economic development in developing countries and under-developed areas in the so-called First World. He also was preparing final exams. One afternoon, while he was grading term papers, Alex called. "Darrell, can you come to my office for a minute?" "I'll be right there Alex," he complied instantly.

Upon reaching Alex's office, Darrell found a student sitting across the table from Alex. Darrell greeted warmly and the two responded. Before Darrell could ask for the reason for his summons, Alex blurted out, "This young man, Julius Jones, tells me he is about to fail your course because you lost his paper. Does that sound like justice to you as you always preach? Moreover, does that reflect any sense of responsibility? Darrell, have you any idea as to how such carelessness negatively impacts our institution and plummets our overall student enrollment?" Underscoring his anxiety to hear Darrell's response, he concluded, "I'm all ears."

"Hmmm," Darrell said as he tried hard to maintain his composure. He knew the student. "JJ, did you say I lost your paper?"

"Yes you did DDT," Julius replied.

"How did you reach a conclusion that I lost your paper?"

"I emailed it to you and you lost it. I therefore was very angry in class when you told me you had not received my paper."

"Frankly, I cannot believe you humiliated this young man like that in the presence of his colleagues," Alex snapped. He once more stressed that such a behavior had the propensity of driving students away from the university and that was totally unacceptable.

"One moment Alex," Darrell demanded. "Let me address this young man." He turned to Julius. He reminded him that the syllabus was clear on the requirements of the paper. Julius agreed and pulled out a copy of the syllabus. "Let me see that a minute," Darrell requested. Grabbing the syllabus, he read through.

"Here," Darrell pointed out once more, "it says you are to email the paper to me on the deadline indicated."

"But I did," protested Julius.

Without addressing whether Julius did or not, Darrell continued. "First of all JJ, this is the first time I have heard about the alleged loss of your paper. Second, I was under no obligation to remind you about your paper but did so out of the kindness of my heart. Isn't the syllabus clear about making it your responsibility to meet the deadline and ensure your paper is delivered properly?"

"Yes but I sent you the paper DDT," Julius emphasized, sounding somewhat irritated.

"For now, let's say you did ..."

"If he did, why didn't you grade it but instead lost the young man's paper?" Alex question firmly. "Can you even imagine yourself in that young man's shoes? Do you have any empathy Darrell? Frankly, I'm totally appalled."

"Alex please," Darrell pleaded again. "I will address you later but for now, let me talk to this young man." He turned to J.J. "To what email address did you send the paper?"

"That's on the syllabus, isn't it?" Alex interrupted once more.

"Alex, this is my last time warning you. This young man has accused me of losing his paper. In your maddening haste to indict me, you did not bother to ask me whether I did or not; rather, with childish charges, insinuations, and even opprobria, you concluded definitively that I did. Therefore, let me talk with him or I'll walk away." Darrell turned to Julius again. "Please answer me. To what address did you send the paper?"

"Well everyone knows your email address: <u>DDT@SAU.edu</u>."

Darrell handed back the syllabus. What email address is on the syllabus?"

Julius looked down. Darrell reached and pointed it to him and the young man read slowly, <u>DThomas2@SAU.edu.</u>

"That's why your paper did not get to me. Besides, I gave you a second opportunity to get it to me even when it was late and I did so not in the presence of all your classmates but as you and I walked out the door after class. Was that humiliation?"

"No," Julius said again very slowly.

Darrell was silent for a moment as he looked at Julius. "JJ," he said, "tell me the truth and I will work with you as best as I can. The truth is you did not write a paper; am I right?"

"Yes DDT," the youngster reluctantly admitted with a shaky voice. "I'm very sorry, truly sorry. Please work with me; please!"

"There you have it Alex. I am glad you know humiliation when it relates to others but sad to realize you turn the other way when it relates to me. Yes Alex, I still stand for justice and I truly wish you could see it that way too. You know, justice, respect, and the like are not for one person. This is precisely why our pledge of allegiance accentuates 'Justice and equality for all'."

Alex attempted to say something but Darrell cut him off. He said it was unfortunate that Alex had no sense of justice or the decency to address his colleague respectfully. Darrell said he was raised well in a good old southern African-American culture; otherwise, he would have insulted Alex three or more times than Alex insulted him. Continuing his remarks as Alex and J.J., looked on, Darrell said, "Alex, I have told you that I am not afraid of you; I never will be. The sooner you respect me, the better for you and for your conscience, blood pressure, and overall health which are getting out of whack because of your raging hate and bigotry. Have a nice day Alex but please remember that hatred hurts the hater more than the hated."

Before Darrell walked away, he encouraged Julius to write a paper and send it to the right email address and he still would accept it. The young man's tears rolled while Alex looked red in the face. "Thank you DDT; thank you very much," JJ said.

Walking back to his office, Darrell's cell rang just before he got to his door. "Hi Honey! Did you miss me?" Vanessa said, sounding more cheerful than usual.

"I always miss you," Darrell replied in a groggy voice as he entered his office.

"You don't sound right. Is something wrong?" Darrell said he was alright and would explain when he got home.

"Well then, I will wait to tell you the good news."

"I can certainly use some good news. What is it? Like I say, I'm alright; just one of those annoying things; I'm getting used to them. Actually, they are getting me to be punctilious in everything I do."

Vanessa admonished her husband not to allow racist attitudes at the university to worsen his already skyrocketing blood pressure. She then told him excitedly that Prof. and Mrs. Kwame had agreed to visit them during the summer. "Oh Honey, I'm very thrilled; just can't wait to see them!"

"That is good news indeed," Darrell agreed. He said he was headed home a little early and so would pick up the children.

The children were not excited about their father picking them up for he drove the old car; they loved the new van. "Remember," he would remind them, "this was once the only car we had." Of course, this reminder made little or no difference. The children's love and loyalty had switched to the new van.

At home, Vanessa listened intently as Darrell narrated the Julius Jones episode. "Why is Alex so mean, unprofessional, indeed hateful?" Vanessa asked, struggling strenuously to decipher a horrible situation although she knew it seemed logically inexplicable.

Darrell thought a moment before replying, "I don't know Baby but I intend to talk with him. I mean, this nonsense has to stop." He said he now understood why someone characterized Alex as an evil and demonic person who was always glorifying himself by exaggerating his qualification, flexing his grossly limited administrative authority, and constantly striving to intimidate people, especially faculty and staff of color.

From home, Darrell sent Alex an email asking to meet with him. Fortunately, Alex was at his computer as well. He wanted to know the purpose of the meeting. When Darrell explained, Alex said he could not meet for two weeks. Darrell could not figure out any reason for the long delay but was willing to wait; evidently, he had no choice if he truly wanted to talk with Alex.

On the day of the meeting, Darrell showed up with a colleague. Alex's constitution spoke volumes; doubtless, he did not want to be in this meeting. "What do you want to talk about and why did you come with a third party?" he asked harshly.

"Alex, based on previous interactions with you, I felt it necessary to have someone present for this conversation. I'm sorry for not telling you in advance." He cleared his throat and sat up right before adding, "Alex, you are my colleague and department chair but, as you know, things are just not going right between you and me. I really think we need to talk about it. Don't you?" Alex said he did not think anything needed to be discussed. "Well, I do," countered Darrell. He asked if Alex was willing to listen.

"Go ahead Darrell, but just know I have lots to do."

"Well, as my department chair, I would like to know from you a few things; first, I will be most grateful were you to tell me the things I am doing improperly as an assistant professor. I am referring to anything along the lines of my work and interactions with you and colleagues, my work with students, etc.. Second, what can I do to improve in those areas where I am under-performing? Third, what can I do to improve the relationship between you and me? You and I know it's not going well and this is not healthy for you and me, and by extension, definitely not for the department, college, or university."

Alex scratched his head. Clearly, he was uncomfortable with both the discussion and the presence of a third party. He once more said everything was fine.

Darrell thanked Alex for a positive feedback but added, "I do not mean to deny or contradict your statement nor do I want to appear accusatory but I perceive some serious problems." When asked to explain, he said communication between Alex and him was dreadfully wanting. Regarding him, Alex was incessantly censorious and demeaning. He pointed out how Alex never provided support but frequently excoriated and made invidious remarks. He called attention to how Alex often overlooked, downplayed, and deprecated his academic work and contributions to society; how Alex charged and even insulted him in the presence of students, how Alex ignored collegiality and rather placed students ahead of him, and how Alex specifically told students they knew his course contents better than he did. "I know we give high priority to our students and believe me, I do because I love and cherish my students dearly. In fact, I do not know what I could do without them for they truly keep me going. This truism notwithstanding, the notion that a sophomore student better understands the concept of opportunity cost than I do is unfathomable." He pulled out some papers. "See these Alex." He said students left hate notes, insults, threats, etc., in his mailbox and under his door not once, twice but many times. Darrell reminded Alex further that he, Darrell, had repeatedly taken the notes and other pieces of evidence to Alex and to the administration but nothing was done about it.

"Nothing?" Alex asked.

"Nothing," Darrell repeated. He added that, at the professional level, he had concrete evidence showing how colleagues advised students away from his courses saying he did not know the course contents. Fortunately, that had not worked, at least not as effectively as his detractors wanted. Likewise, prospective masters and doctoral advisees were advised away from him by colleagues who charge that he could not even write well. Also, both male and female secretaries had demeaned him on several occasions. "I have tried ..."

"What's the point?" Alex interrupted.

"What's the point?" Darrell reechoed, somewhat annoyed but struggled to maintain his composure. "It goes without saying that these are not only unbearable and unwarranted insults but serious threats." He painstakingly explained that the point was, unfortunately, except for the hate mails which he shared, it was difficult, if not impossible, to share these lamentable problems with Alex. This was because of the poor communication between him and Alex alongside the realization that no matter the situation, the students and their words superseded Darrell and his views. Likewise, to Alex and others in the administration, the credibility of students and staff far exceeded Darrell's, regardless of the situation. He therefore added strongly, "This is not right Alex. We need to work amicably together. He further underscored that, given his high student rating, he was sure insults and threats from students were from a disgruntled and hateful minority but it was difficult to address the behavior of such students effectively when he and Alex could not work together amicably.

The room was quiet for a moment as if each person was waiting for the other to speak. Darrell broke the silence. "Another thing Alex, no matter what I do right, it is seldom acknowledged. I have seen you heap praises on people for relatively insignificant things; conversely, my praises, if any, are brief and bromidic. I mean, I am not seeking false and undeserved praises but as my colleagues are acknowledged for their achievements, and rightfully so, why are mine ignored?"

Alex cleared his throat. "Well Darrell, if only you could respect your immediate supervisor, you would do better. Instead, you carry an air of arrogance and pomposity."

"That's what I mean," said Darrell. "How am I disrespecting you?" He admitted that he had told Alex he was not afraid of him; that was a matter of fact, not an insult. Furthermore, he admitted addressing Alex roughly in the presence of J.J., but that was a response to his abusive language. With those points established, he challenged Alex to point out one example of his disrespect. Alex could not provide any. "Alex," he spoke softly, "I really want to work amicably with you. You and I are not rivals, certainly not enemies, not as I see it. I therefore have no doubt that working together amicably will be best for you and me, our students, and the university. Will it therefore help if we bring in a third party to work with us?"

"Third party for what? Absolutely not!"

Darrell did not give up. "I once more acknowledge the fact that I talked sternly with you when you addressed me on the issue of plagiarism and when Julius Jones was in your office but you know Alex, both cases could have been handled much better. I was not only accused falsely but also humiliated and demeaned in the presence of my students. I really honestly think we can, and should, avoid such situations."

"Well, there is only one solution Darrell," Alex intimated. Darrell listened anxiously. "If you do not like it here, you can always go elsewhere; it's as simple as that!" After a pause, he added, "Frankly, this university and especially this department will be better off."

Darrell was taken aback, momentarily shocked so he was quiet for a minute or two.

"Did you hear what I said? I could not be more direct and honest with myself."

Darrell remained quiet, looking down on the floor. He was overcome by rage, sadness, and pity at the same time. He lifted his head and looked at Alex directly. "Alex, I heard you clearly and have no doubt you truly mean those words." He cleared his throat and sat upright. "Alex," he continued, "given all that has transpired, I should not be but I'm utterly shocked. Yet, I will continue to do all I can to work amicably with you and I hope in a clear conscience, you will work in like manner with me. I truly pray so because, whether you realize it or not, it is amply evident that your unceasing rage to prove me incompetent and constantly in violation of university rules and regulation has left you blind to logic and reason."

Alex shook with rage. He wanted to say something but restrained himself. Darrell was determined not to light up. He emphasized that it was difficult to understand Alex's uncontrollable aversion because, deep in Alex's heart, he knew Darrell had done him no wrong. Likewise, in no way had Darrell disrespected, demeaned, or ignored his department chair.

Alex clearly did not want to hear more but Darrell continued. "I have never jettisoned the profundity of professionalism nor have I ever compromised collegiality; I have only sought my rights and insisted on just treatment. If this is arrogance, so be it. Therefore, I will reiterate what I said before; that is, as long as I abide by the laws of this land and operate within the policy guidelines of this institution, I will only leave SAU on my terms, not yours or anyone else's. Good day Alex and may the God you and I worship bless you." Alex remained emotionless as Darrell and his colleague walked away.

"Hello Sir! Do you need a ride?" Darrell's children screamed in unison as he waited in the snow for Vanessa following his meeting with Alex. "Where is your junk car?" the children continued teasing when their dad got in the van. Darrell explained that the car was in the garage and would be out soon.

"I think you need to drive it south to Uncle Zac's garage," suggested D3. "The only problem is, I do not think it will make it past the Achval city limits, if it can make it that far," he continued laughing and the other children joined the laughter.

"Children, our second car is not that bad," Vanessa defended her husband.

"Yes it is Mom," Kwame laughed. "Besides, it's not our car; it's Dad's junk. The last time he picked us up in the junk I thought the left door was going to drop in the street; it's a real junk and I think we should give it to charity but I am not sure if they will accept it." The other children agreed. They all laughed again.

Dad took the teasing well. He once more reminded the children, "Don't forget; that's the only car we had at one time."

"You always say that Dad but I think that's the reason why we should junk the junk now," D3 kidded. The children laughed again and their parents joined the contagious laughter.

"One day you will need a ride when your mom is not around; that's when I will not let you in that good and beautiful car," Dad threatened with jocularity.

"It has to run first before you refuse to let us in it," Kwame came back sparking continuous laughter.

Following dinner, homework, and a brief free time, the children were sent to bed. Then, Darrell narrated the conversation he had with Alex. "I do not regret trying to negotiate with him especially when I think of statements from inaugural addresses of two famous presidents, statements that no doubt influenced my action."

"Who?" Vanessa sought to know.

Sounding professorial, Darrell said on Saturday, March 4, 1933, FDR was first inaugurated at the time the depression reached the bottom of the barrel. "The economic crises that triggered and exacerbated the depression ..."

"Excuse me Honey," Vanessa interrupted, "I am not looking for a lecture in economics. What did he say that impacted, or, shall we say, influenced your action?"

"He said the nation had 'nothing to fear but fear itself'. Similarly, I had nothing to fear in addressing Alex directly and poignantly."

It seemed to be Vanessa's turn to lecture. "That's a paraphrase of Sir Francis Bacon's statement, 'There is nothing to fear but fear,'." She said the statement had touched many lives. "Who was the other president and what did he say that guided your action?" she asked.

As if expecting this question, Darrell did not hesitate. "On Friday, January 20, 1961, a very cold winter day, so cold that they almost cancelled the ceremony, John Fitzgerald Kennedy was inaugurated the thirty-fifth president. His inaugural address was laden with memorable lines. He said, 'Civility is not a sign of weakness, and sincerity is always subject to proof. Let us never negotiate out of fear. But let us never fear to negotiate'. Indeed, those famous words influenced me too."

"The line regarding not negotiating out of fear is also attributed to General Tiberius who later became an emperor," Vanessa lectured again. "Similarly, JFK's famous line, 'Ask not what your country can do for you ...' is attributed to two persons, General Omar Bradley and much earlier, Marcus Tullius Cicero, A roman who ...."

"Wait a minute! Who was stopping me from giving a lecture in economics?" Darrell stopped his wife with a chuckle.

Laughing, Vanessa apologized. "Sorry Honey. I just get away with these things. I did not mean to give a history lecture either."

After their conversation, Darrell placed a call to Prof. Kwame to express his delight regarding the retired professor's pending visitation. He informed that he and Vanessa were trying to get the other former students and their families to come to Achval for a great reunion. Darrell also disclosed his last conversation with Alex. "That's terrible," prof. Kwame detested. "What do you intend to do about it?" Darrell desired to speak with Prof. Dominguez and then send a formal letter of protestation although he did not think anything would come out of it. Darrell's letter was worded clearly and strongly. He briefly recapped the conversation with Alex and quoted his words before stating unequivocally that he detested this language as it constituted a threat on one hand and on the other, a clear reluctance on Alex's part to work with him. Darrell indicated that a colleague was present during the conversation with Alex. He copied Peggy, the dean, provost, and the union president. As expected, nothing became of this official protestation. However, Darrell learned later from Prof. Dominguez that the provost did speak with Alex on the issue but Alex called Darrell names and, unsurprisingly, levied unsubstantiated charges against the assistant professor although Darrell was not present to defend himself nor was he ever asked to present his side of the issue.

AT the end of the academic year, Darrell and Vanessa decided to stay in Achval and work on articles and grants but this also meant an avalanche of visitors. They sincerely looked forward to receiving friends and family but this meant enormous work. Nonetheless, they were prepared.

The first people to arrive to visit during the summer were Prof. and Mrs. Kwame. They spent a week before David and Lamont and their families made it to Achval. This was a delightful reunion. Darrell and Vanessa enjoyed showing the guests around the campus and the greater Achval area.

David and Lamont and their families could stay only three days. The Kwames spent an additional week before returning home. A week later, Zach and Elayne drove the old folks from Ghetahzia. Mama swore never to make the trip again by road. A day before they returned, Vanessa's parents, Joseph and Louise made it too. Grandma Clara and the folks from Ghetahzia spent only a week as Zac and Elayne had to return to work. When they left, Tyrone, Deborah and their families showed up. Indeed, it was a busy summer. Yet, Darrell and Vanessa managed to send off articles for publication before school started. Though busy, they and the children could not trade anything for the joy of receiving friends and family in Achval.

Chapter XI:

TWO CONCEPTS

" It's platitudinous but axiomatic nonetheless that, 'every good thing must come to an end'," Darrell said with a huge smile as he sped down the highway.

"What do those big words mean?" D3 shouted from the back of the van. His father continued smiling and the broad smile turned into laughter.

Vanessa, also in the front seat, joined the laughter. When her laughter dissipated, she turned to her husband and asked softly, "Always?" Her question implied either doubt or total denial and if neither, then certainly reluctance to make such a blanket statement. As she thought about it, she scratched her head searching for exceptions to the axiom, if indeed it was an axiom.

"Always!" Darrell confirmed with firm conviction. In actuality, his true emphasis was not on whether the statement was axiomatic or not; while he truly enjoyed the summer, he was simply glad it was over. Without doubt, he and Vanessa thoroughly enjoyed entertaining friends and relatives, but were incredibly busy. In addition to entertaining, they often stayed up late writing articles for publication. As if this was not enough, they had to drive the children to various summer camps and programs. These tiresome activities therefore warranted a special family treat; they spent a week of rest and relaxation in a nearby reserve. Needless to say, it was not a cheap summer. As a result, he felt relieved as he drove the family back to Achval.

Without knowing the cost involved, the children were grateful for a great summer. "Thanks Dad and Mom; we had a great time," they repeated on the way back home. Mom and Dad said they had a great time too.

Resuming school was now a routine process. Darrell and Vanessa submitted their dossiers of activities for the previous year to their respective department committees. As before, in spite of another outstanding year in all areas, both received very low ratings; not surprisingly, they challenged their ratings. This time, Alex asked Darrell to meet with him and the committee.

Probably because of the presence of committee members, Alex was surprisingly professional, even cordial. "Darrell, we just want to know the basis of your challenge. I actually went on line to look at these journals and they certainly are refereed."

Darrell wanted to ask if Alex double-checked everyone else's journals but, as he was sure Alex did not, he refrained and simply explained his publications, presentations, and service. As it turned out, both Alex and committee members did not understand Darrell's international publications. After his clarification, they promised to reevaluate his dossier.

Following his meeting with Alex and the committee, Darrell went home. Incidentally, Lupita and Anne were meeting at Vanessa's house, their first get-together for the year; Darrell arrived a few minutes before the other ladies left.

"How was your rating this year, if you do not mind my asking?" Lupita questioned Darrell.

"I do not mind at all. In fact, it's funny you ask for I was just about to tell you; it was so poor that I challenged it. I mean, I just could not believe Alex and his committee. If they did not understand my publications, they only had to ask."

Lupita, popularly known as LG laughed somewhat sarcastically. "Sorry Darrell, I did not mean to ridicule your statement; I am really laughing at the blatant racism the insensate perpetrators think they are masking." She elaborated that whether the folks at the university understood Darrell's publication or not, he had to become accustomed to challenging it every year for no matter what he did, he most likely would be rated poorly. She disclosed she admonished Vanessa to expect the same. Furthermore, like Vanessa, she directed Darrell to a number of research articles covering the marginalization and under-rating of professors and lecturers from under-represented groups in predominantly white colleges and universities.

Darrell appreciated LG's suggestions before adding, "That's a real shame," referring to the low ratings. "This is scholarly work and so ought to be rated objectively."

Laughing softly again, Lupita agreed adding, "But at SAU, and especially when it relates to people of color or people from under-represented groups, objectivity is not how it should be; it's what they think it should be. In other words, there's really no objectivity; all one gets is strict subjectivity."

When Lupita and Anne left, Vanessa explained how she challenged her committee regarding her ratings. "Well Honey, as Lupita said, we may as well get used to challenging our ratings every year although we very well know such challenges induce little or no changes in our ratings," she emphasized.

A few days later, at Darrell's invitation, he and Andy were seated for lunch once more at what had become their favorite restaurant. A minute or two after they were seated, a young lady approached the table to take their orders. She double-checked the orders and asked if they needed anything else.

"That will be it for me," Andy told the young lady who seemed like a college student doing a part-time job. Darrell said the same. Turning to Darrell, Andy asked, "So, how are things going at the U?"

Darrell took a deep breath and gave out a funny laugh. "Well, as best as can be expected; after all, this is SAU; isn't it?"

"The sound of the sarcasm in that response is deafening. Now, what's the scoop?"

Darrell laughed and Andy joined in. "Well Andy," Darrell came back, "this place is a real hell." He disclosed his conversations with Alex, including the Julius Jones episode, his one-on-one meeting, the hate messages he had received, and the challenge he posed regarding his annual ratings. "These things make me sick. I file official protestations but nothing happens. I have pleaded with Alex for a cordial and professional relationship but all I get is back-handed treatment." In a frustrated tune, he added that in almost every matter regarding him, Alex and a number of people in the department were consistently persnickety, impatient, and often downright insulting. He further regretted that this included members of the Department Evaluation Committee. Worse, the dean and provost were of no help. Pausing momentarily, he said, "There's nowhere to go. It's just plainly unfair. It's equally painful to note that the same or similar treatments are meted out to other people of color across the university."

"Did you get a better reevaluation?"

"Slightly better but nothing much to write home about," Darrell groaned. "I mean, if they do not understand my publications, they only need to ask but I really think that's not the problem."

"If you are writing about international issues, don't be so sure," Andy warned. "My experience is most people here are very parochial in their academic works; while they may be authorities in their areas, or at least think so, when one considers depth and breadth of true scholarship, they just cannot see beyond their noses. I do not say that to castigate or disrespect my colleagues but that's the truth. Believe me, as someone who has lived in various parts of the world, I have had my experiences here." Darrell nodded as Andy had shared some of those experiences with him on various occasions.

The young lady returned with the orders. "That's one thing I like about this place; the service is quick and efficient," Darrell praised and Andy agreed. Returning to their discussion, Darrell's tune changed once more to a serious and irritated one. He regretted that a disgusting realization was the fact that, like him, the system treated people from under-represented groups with disdain, contempt and blatant discrimination. "Here at SAU," he stressed, setting his glass of water on the table, "people regarded as 'different' are marginalized, excluded, insulted, highly scrutinized in ratings, complimented minimally, and taken for granted. They, or shall I say, we are generally given the impression that either, 'if you do not like it here, you can go elsewhere,' as Alex said or 'you must feel privileged to be here, therefore do not dare to try to be like everyone else when you aren't'. By any measurement, this is relegating people to second class citizenship. What! In this day and age? I mean, even gender and age discrimination? Absolutely disgusting! Totally unacceptable!" He paused as if in pain from the frustration. "I just cannot imagine what people with disabilities endure here, that is, if they are ever hired here. No wonder most so-called people of color leave shortly after they get here. If things do not change, and I doubt they will, the attrition rate of such persons will only get worse and that's a real shame."

"Darrell," Andy said as he worked on his half-and-half, this time, soup and sandwich. With a mouthful, he could not complete the sentence so he chewed on while Darrell waited. "Excuse me," Andy apologized as he completed the bite. "I wish I could disagree with you but quite honestly, as I have said in our previous conversations, I have seen many instances on this campus where people from under-represented groups (I mean, people of color) and women were treated contemptuously. Conversely, I know of Whites who were promoted to positions I really did not think they deserved; one only needs to look at the list of recent promotions and unbelievable salary increases within the administration. Of course, there are many Whites here who deserve their positions but I'm just saying, if this university is to live up to its professed public pronouncements regarding diversity, it needs a very good dose of equality treatment, whatever that medication might be."

"Oh my goodness—even if somehow, one could overcome the administration's pertinacity regarding management rights, it still would be difficult, if not impossible, to find a doctor to prescribe, let alone administer that treatment in the face of the phenomena of white privilege and equality contradiction," Darrell stated with emotion as he pounded lightly on the table.

"What do you mean," asked Andy.

It seemed Darrell's turn to finish chewing a bite from his turkey burger which came with fries. He too apologized politely, chewed on, took a drink of water, and cleared his throat, before speaking. He clarified that he did not want to make a sweeping generalization as he was sure, and as Andy had observed correctly, many Whites at the university were highly qualified for the positions they held and some were in fact, under-employed or under-paid. "But," he threw in a familiar conjunction, "because of the phenomenon of 'white privilege,' a considerable number of Whites get away with prohibited acts, ineptitude, and much more. It leads them to praises, promotions, positions, perquisites, and pay increases irrespective of qualification or performance. I mean, if a professor or administrator from an under-represented group attempted some the acts these people get away with, he or she will be condemned, ridiculed, degraded, and ultimately fired."

As he did when he discussed the topic with Dallas, Darrell was anxious to make his point as clearly as possible. To that end, he stressed that 'white privilege' meant not only the fact that, in general, Whites were supported in multiple ways to enable them succeed but also that low standards often were accepted for some Whites but not for Blacks and other members of under-represented groups. On the contrary, as exemplified by Darrell's first year, people from under-represented groups not only received minimal to no support to enable them succeed but incessantly and consistently had to justify their positions by performing above level.

Darrell further observed that, Worse still, as racism was institutionalized, people from under-represented groups were victimized in hiring, retention, and promotion. He was sure such policies and practices were not likely to change unless the traditional criteria for hiring and evaluation were revisited and readjusted to foster inclusiveness. "As the nation increasingly becomes diverse, these predominantly white universities will be diverse as well and therefore must recruit and retain professors and administrators from diverse backgrounds. After all, as the literature and practical experiences amply show, such persons have a lot to offer these universities; doubtless, they can enrich the university and enhance its mission. As such they must not be merely token appointees nor can their absence be justified by offices with racial or ethnic titles." He looked at Andy directly before adding, "That's how I see it here at SAU. I hope other predominantly white universities are better, I mean far better in fostering and promoting inclusiveness."

With still a lot on his mind to unleash, Darrell referred to one of the authors Vanessa suggested. He called Andy's attention to the work of Professor McKinley Jones Brayboy[12] whose article maintains that "language of diversity and efforts to implement diversity are bound to fail in the absence of an institutional commitment to incorporating strategies for diversity into their research, teaching, and service missions." Holding out a copy of the article, Darrell said the professor further argued that, "To advance the agenda of diversity, institutions that truly value diversity must move toward considering wholesale changes in their underlying structures and day-to-day activities, especially if they are truly committed to refocusing the historical legacies of institutional, epistemological, and societal racisms that pervade colleges and universities." Further, the professor detested institutions "that pays lip service to promoting diversity without actually doing much about it." Darrell said without a doubt, this was precisely what was happening at SAU and he too detested it vehemently.

---

[12] Brayboy, M. J., 2003.

"That's very interesting," Andy stated with a plain face as if he harbored some degree of dubiety or, at the very least, a certain lack of understanding of the matter.

"Yes," Darrell said as if he could go on with this topic ad infinitum. He reminded Andy of their conversation when they first ate lunch together in this restaurant. He said because he had experienced what Andy said back then, he understood it much more clearly. In fact, he understood it so clearly that he was able to name and categorize the behaviors of dominant groups—in this case, the "white rulers" at SAU. "This is how and why I have identified 'white privilege'," he declared with emphasis. Admitting he did not coin the term, he added further that he had read extensively on the topic in the literature.

Darrell realized Andy was listening curiously so he endeavored to explain the phenomenon further. He said, "As I have tried to clarify, in part, 'white privilege' means in many, not all instances, a white person, no matter unqualified, is perceived as qualified. Conversely, with the exception of the few token appointments of people of color, appointments often intended to camouflage racism and bigotry, in general, no matter how qualified an African-American or someone from another under-represented group, he or she is perceived as low, inept, and disqualified and therefore is forced to prove himself or herself and in doing so, he or she must conform to the dominant Eurocentric narrative and nothing else, and this is particularly true of women of color owing to their intersectional identity of race and gender."

Darrell thought a minute that maybe he was extreme in stating words like "no matter," but he was unwilling to retract or modify those terms; therefore, he continued. "Hence, when a person from an under-represented group does something properly, usually minor, some Whites effuse puerile praises such as, 'that's pretty good, considering ...' as if to say the person of color was not expected to do anything better." He pointed out that similarly, when a person from an under-represented group occupied a senior position in administration or the professoriate, in that person, most people could not see competence or leadership ability. The first thing they saw were race or ethnicity and therefore the assumptions of incompetence and ineptitude. Regrettably, in many instances, this equally applied to female leaders regardless of race. "In other words," Darrell went on, "amazingly, most people first see a woman, not a competent leader, a despicable attitude indeed."

Andy seemed surprised, even incredulous. "This is true," Darrell assured. Determined to demonstrate various aspects of discriminatory attitudes people from under-represented groups endured in predominantly white universities, he stated that some whites also insinuated often that black professors, who were not qualified anyway, ought to feel privileged just to be at the university. "Alex did not use those exact words but that's precisely what he meant," Darrell stated emphatically. He further expounded that, with that seeming black privileged condition, Black professors had to be willing to accept whatever came their way. Shaking his head lightly, he vowed, "I'd rather be damned than accept anything." He clarified that he was obdurate in that position because his expression was not symbolic of inferiority complex. Quite the contrary, he was so confident and self-assured that he would not accept anything that came his way, even if that meant being without a job.

"Let me stop you Darrell," Andy jumped in. "I am aware of all kinds of forces and discriminatory attitudes toward persons from under-represented groups and I have made it clear that I detest same to the core but, aren't you being racist and won't you term that gross and indiscriminate generalization?"

Darrell disagreed. He denied generalization by reminding Andy that he was aware, and had specifically pointed out, that many Whites were qualified for their positions and others, like many under-represented group members, were under-employed. He said generally, these were Whites who either did not belong to cliques or refused to be sycophantic conformists. Similarly, he denied racism clarifying that he was not advocating White or Black advantage. He emphasized this point despite the realization that the nation comprised a White majority although the numbers were changing gradually but steadily. Stressing the crucial need for equality of racial and ethnic groups, Darrell said he was reminded of a statement by Dr. Martin Luther King Jr., when the learned civil rights leader said Black supremacy was as dangerous as White supremacy. "No, I am not advocating one group above another. Rather, I rigidly advocate equal opportunities in schools and societies, and equal treatment in employment although I am not naïve. I have no illusions for example that, here at SAU, given the prevailing circumstances and under the current administration, reaching such equality is terribly difficult, if not impossible and that's only because of a lack of political will. This is partly why it has been estimated that, given the prevailing rate at which we become associate and full professors in predominantly white institutions, PWI, it will take more than a hundred and forty years for us, African Americans in the professoriate, to mirror our representation in the national population."[13]

Returning to the concept of 'white privilege', Darrell reiterated once more that he did not make up the term. He stressed that his views on the subject were rooted in both experience and the literature. For example, he pointed out that, writing on the topic, Arnold and colleagues[14] indicated that "white privilege" was corollary to the concept of whiteness. They framed it as "an invisible package of 'unearned assets' that White people used to their advantage "without acknowledging it as such. He said the esteemed scholars further penned that, in higher education, white privilege was the "translation of Whiteness as the normative standard into systematic advantages afforded to the dominant racial group."

"Very interesting," said Andy.

"Indeed it is," Darrell assured. "These scholars conceded that, although at times use of privilege by whites might be

---

[13] Jones et al, 2015

[14] Arnold et al, 2016

unintentionally oppressive, as they put it, 'it nevertheless perpetuates inequitable power dynamics and social conditions'."
Continuing, Darrell said the scholars clarified further that, "When institutions expect faculty of color to conform to attitudes, structures, and institutional practices rooted in White privilege, [such] faculty are marginalized both overtly and inconspicuously."

Andy took a deep breath. Darrell's reference to the literature impressed him but also threw him into deep thoughts. Darrell could not read his friend's facial features nor did he give it much thought. "You seem to have no hope in the system," Andy stated in a way as to invite Darrell's reaction.

"No, I do not," Darrell replied quickly and emphatically. He elaborated that one thing which saddened him immeasurably was the realization that, after all efforts, racism and discrimination persisted rigidly. "You mean this horrible creature called racism remains alive although many people have died in the process of squashing it and although we have enacted laws prohibiting it?" He shook his head in disbelief. "In light of prohibiting laws and judicial mandates, I guess the perpetrators are doing a very good job of masking it and that's done superbly at SAU better than anywhere else I know. I tell you, when masked, this creature is more lethal than it was during the dark days of segregation and discrimination; believe me, I was born and grew up in the south. Need I say more?" Although he noticed Andy wanted to say something, he nonetheless added, "And the other thing most people do not know is the fact that civil rights laws prohibit blatant actions, not the minor and subtle ones which have a deep cumulative effect."

Andy sat with a straight face still trying to get in a word. Without giving him a chance, Darrell added, "Let me give you one example of the subtle and not-so-subtle discrimination around here." He said in one of the departments at the university, a young Caucasian professor, noticing that students from under-represented groups were often marginalized and treated contemptuously, called a meeting of the students in his department. He wanted to find out first hand, the students' experiences, impressions, contentions, etc..

"That was incredibly thoughtful of the young professor," Andy commended.

"Very thoughtful indeed," Darrell agreed. "The young professor was highly praised for his thoughtfulness and concerns for the students, and such praise and admiration were absolutely in place. In fact, he should have been knighted for he made a heroic move and genuinely so." Darrell admitted that his suggestion for 'knighting the professor' was an exaggeration but he meant no flattery. Sincerely, he admired the young professor because such a direct contact with students from under-represented groups would enable genuinely interested administrators to know firsthand, the plight, pains, problems and contentions of such students at a university. "But do you know what the administration would have said if I or any other professor or administrator of color did that?" Andy shook his head. "They would have branded the person as a rabble-rouser bent on inciting the students."

"Do you really think so?" Andy seemed doubtful.

"I know so," Darrell stated firmly. He revealed that once, a small group of African-American students went to Dallas' office to acquaint him with the discriminatory treatments meted out against them. Dallas listened carefully and offered to intervene as best as he could. Instead of commending him for listening to the students, the administration berated him for calling the students into his office to elicit their gripes and grievances. The powers that be said Dallas' aim was to make the administration look bad. "Dallas did not call the students; they sought him out to express their resentments," Darrell stated emphatically as he knocked on the table. "In other words," he scowled, "if Dallas had called those students, he would not be knighted but ignited and his ashes thrown down the stream—so much for fulfilling a service dream."

Andy finally found time to throw in his question. "Under these conditions, would you consider leaving us?"

Despite his frustrated mood, Darrell laughed as he straightened himself in his chair. "That would be much to the delight of Alex and certainly several others."

"I suppose," said Andy, "but I am not sure if they realize that will be a huge loss to the university; I mean that."

"Thanks Andy," Darrell complimented with a serious face. Unwilling to be definitive about leaving or not leaving, Darrell wanted to keep all options open. "For now," he accentuated, "I am holding on." He said he would not capitulate. "No, I will not give into pressure and leave within my seven year limit during which I must either be tenured or get out of here. This is not a display of ego but a stance for justice. No one wants to be subjected to such treatment but, as my father prepared me, the way to fight injustice is not to retreat but face it head-on." He paused and laughed a little and then added, "In discussing this, my darling sweet wife, who minored in Literature and is a huge fan of The Bard's, pointed out a relevant statement: 'The better part of valor is discretion, in the which better part I had saved my life.' She thinks, and I agree, for the inimitable Falstaff, this was not a better part of valor but cowardice. No, we will not, like Falstaff, row over and play dead; we will not retreat from these challenges."

While Darrell's resolve did not surprise Andy, he still was curious and so probed a little. "What if, after five, six, or seven years you do not get tenure here and have to leave, will it not be that your time here was simply wasted?"

Darrell disagreed again. "My experience here will be a steppingstone, an armor for the next battle and that's what life's about—we win some, we lose some."

"Mmmm!" Andy groaned with incredulity. "Darrell tell me something," he requested. "In the face of blatant discrimination, marginalization, and non-recognition of your efforts, among others, what keeps you going?"

Darrell laughed although Andy's question was no laughing matter. "Well my friend," he started with a serious face, "a number of things get me going—I mean, they are my reasons and impetus for getting out of bed and going regardless of what goes on at the university."

Andy could not wait to hear what was coming. "I'm all ears," he verbally nudged.

"Well, first is my southern upbringing." Darrell said he was blessed and continued to be blessed with wonderful role models. He cited his late amazing grandfather and wonderful parents who taught him a lot and prepared him for life. Best of all, they led him to God Who strengthened him daily. "Consequently," Darrell revealed, "I read His Word religiously and that really helps." In addition, he stated that he was blessed with other role models such as his undergraduate mentor, professor Emeritus Kwame. Further, he said Andy was a role model who was a wonderful friend and colleague.

"I'm flattered," Andy said with a serious face. "You have had great giants in your life; to be named even remotely among such giants is truly an honor. This is particularly true since what you really need in starting here is a mentor in your area of work. I do not consider myself a mentor but a friend and a colleague; so, I'm very flattered. Thanks! Besides, I have learned a lot from you Darrel; believe me, and I do not mean any flattery, my life and work have been enriched by associating with you, my learned economics professor friend."

"I mean it," Darrell insisted. "True, you have been a close colleague and a friend but beyond those, you have been a mentor to me and God knows there are not enough words to express my thanks and appreciation." He said even when he and Andy disagreed, and that was expected, there was a clear sense of collegiality and mutual respect and no one in his or her right mind could ask for more. Besides, from his review of the literature, a major setback for tenure track lecturers and professors of color in predominantly white institutions was limited or no support from administration coupled with paucity or lack of mentors. Therefore, having a friend who was not just a colleague but a mentor was appreciated highly.

Again, Andy was most thankful. Continuing, Darrell said, "I am also blessed with a family that is second to none. Vanessa and the children are truly a God sent. They do not only support me but cheer me up when things are not going right. No doubt, I cannot do a thing without them and with them and the grace of God, nothing and no one can keep me down, at least not for long."

"That's truly admirable," Andy praised. "Who or what else keeps you going?"

"My dynamic students and the literature," Darrell replied. "I gained strength and happiness from my students. They honestly keep me going. As their facilitator, there is nothing that gladdens my heart more than seeing them grow academically and intellectually. Through them, I have hopes for the future of this country and the world."

"And the literature?" Andy questioned further.

"Yes, the literature," Darrell concurred.

"What kind of literature?"

"Well," Darrell cleared his throat. "Beyond books and journal articles in economics and related areas, I read journal articles in black studies, some of which have been brought to my attention by my darling wife."

"Very interesting," Andy acknowledged. "What journals do you read outside economics?"

Darrell said he read poetry from different cultures as well as journals in sociology, ethnic studies, and social justice. For example, he gained a lot by reading *The Journal of Blacks in Higher Education.* "In one publication," Darrell disclosed, "the journal gave a chronology of key events involving blacks in higher education; that was extremely encouraging."

Andy nodded in admiration. Continuing, Darrell reported that, in like manner, *The Journal of Black Studies* devoted an issue to the struggles of African-Americans and people from other under-represented groups as well as women in higher education. He found this issue very encouraging in that, in some instances, his problems paled in the face of what others encountered. For the same reason, he read biographies, auto-biographies, memoirs, and critical works by and/or about African-Americans, Hispanics, and scholars from other under-represented groups.

"Fascinating again, absolutely admirable," Andy once more praised. "What memoirs and critical works have you read?"

Darrell laughed. "Well, where do I begin?" For starters, he cited the work by Gloria Bonilla-Santiago, *The Miracle on Cooper Street: Lessons from an Inner City*, an autobiography of a Puerto Rican child of migrant farm workers who "defied family, tradition, and expectations" to make it into the professoriate. Despite her academic and professional achievements, she struggled strenuously to gain respect in academia, a world that, in her words, "does not value racial or ethnic diversity."

Darrell also referred to Margo Jefferson's work, *Negroland*, a memoir about an African-American lady who was from a privileged background. Initially, she and her family seemed to be set apart from other African-Americans because of their privileged status but eventually, she too endured insults and setbacks because of her race. In addition, Darrell mentioned *Black Man in a White Coat: A Doctor's Reflections on Race and Medicine* by Damon Tweedy. *"This is a truly scary, indeed depressing one as it shows disparities in the health care system on the basis of race. Reviewed by leading newspapers, this memoir by a black doctor reveals the dark side of health care and shows that race still determines who receives the best medical and health care services."*

"That's incredible, totally disgusting," Andy registered both disbelief and resentment.

Darrell agreed, adding, "But it still happens." He pointed out several fascinating books on the topic of race and racial inequality, including More Beautiful and More Terrible: The Embrace and Transcendence of Racial Inequality in the United States by Imani Perry, Democracy in Black: How Race Still Enslaves the American Soul by Eddie S. Glaude, and Between the World and Me by Ta-Nehisi Coates. Darrell informed that the last was an audacious look at the nation's racial history. It was presented in the form of a letter to the author's adolescent son. The author wrote, "This is your country, this is your world, this is your body, and you must find some way to live within the all of it." Darrell said he could go on and on with listing books, invaluable books and refereed articles about race and racial inequality in the United States because such books helped him understand the world in which he lived.

Andy wondered out loud as to whether Darrell found materials regarding the general problems of promotion and tenure in higher education. Darrell said he did. He made it clear that both Whites and people of color in the professoriate faced many similar problems. He narrated that generally, such persons were under-paid, over-worked, and treated contemptuously by the administration and therefore needed a strong and united bargaining unit. "On the other hand," Darrell elaborated, "people of color face additional biases because of race and/or ethnicity, and the intersectionality of race and gender makes things doubly difficult for women of color."

Explaining further, Darrell said treatments meted out against people of color in predominantly white institutions triggered his interest in reading various memoirs, autobiographies and journal article accounts regarding the struggles of such people in higher education. The experiences of such persons embolden him as many faced discrimination—non-promotion and non-tenure—as they saw it, because of their race, gender, conservative or liberal views, sexual orientation, disability, religion, etc.. "That's just revolting; people ought to be assessed on the basis of performance and not any arbitrary or external criteria."

"I agree," said Andy. "It is equally true that, in general, regardless of race, ethnicity, etc., professors and lecturers are 'the backbones' of universities and colleges, and yet, even after long and tough negotiations with the administration, they only receive negligible increases in salary, if at all, while administrators enjoy lion shares. It's mind-boggling especially when the so-called increases in salary are taken away by heightened health care costs or reduction in one benefit or another."

"It is mind-boggling indeed," Darrell concurred. "While I contend that people of color or people from under-represented groups and especially women in such groups get the worst end of the stick and are subjected to racial, ethnic, and/or sexual biases, the truth is, in the mean, both Caucasians and people from under-represented groups merely feel a sense of unfairness and injustice in higher education. Hence, Professor James Schiavone refers to administrators as *Gods From Afar*, the title of his memoir.

Darrell looked at the problem from another perspective. He reported that, from his reading, he found that in several instances, Whites in predominantly black colleges and universities filed charges of reverse discrimination. In a number of cases, the courts ruled in their favor. He cited Mark Naison's memoir, *White Boy*, in which a Jewish professor relates his experiences in a department of African-American Studies.

"I'm sure, Darrell, you have found positive revelations about the achievements of people from under-represented groups in higher education," Andy probed again.

"I did," Darrell confirmed. He said although Dr. Imani Perry, an African-American female professor at a prestigious university had written extensively on racial inequality and social justice, she stated in an interview that she felt her voice mattered. She admitted that was an unusual experience for women, Black women, in higher education; that is, to feel that when such a woman speaks, people listen to her and therefore she is not fighting to be heard. "Besides," Darrell went on, "you and I know that many people from under-represented groups in higher education have achieved, sometimes monumentally, in research, administration, the skill areas, the professoriate, etc.. We just need more of such persons and that's absolutely possible if there's genuine political will to evaluate them fairly and subsequently recognize and reward their invaluable contributions."

"Absolutely," Andy agreed before adding, "Again, this is truly fascinating. Honestly, I admire the manner and extent to which you have delved into the literature outside economics and related areas. But before we go, I would like to go back to another thing you mentioned earlier. What do you term the 'equality contradiction'?"

"Oh that one," Darrell seemed to have forgotten to address that topic. He sat upright, straightened his tie and smiled broadly. He elucidated that there was a contradiction in the phenomenon of equality when Whites supported equality and treated Blacks as equals only when Blacks sought assistance and appeared to be in need. When, on the other hand, Blacks and other people of color acted as colleagues, and they should, they were frowned upon as if to say, they were getting out of their places. The situation was worse when people of color pursued or assumed leadership roles, and/or demonstrated superiority in one area or another. Some Whites, and he emphasized "some," acted as if such persons needed to be reminded, or worse, treated in a way that they understood unmistakably that they were to lag behind Whites perpetually and thereby remain subservient, a philosophical and sometimes practical return to the damnable days of slavery. As 'some' Whites were overtly or covertly adamant that anything short of this superior-inferior relationship was unacceptable, the so-called advocacy for equality was a glaring contradiction, a blatant and execrable hypocrisy.

Andy seemed to be struggling to understand Darrell's explanation. Darrell suspected this and therefore attempted to clarify as much as he could. He averred that although he had no concrete proof, a good example of his observation related to leadership within the university. He contended that there were some Whites at the university—and he emphasized 'some'—who would never accept a person from an under-represented group as their department chair, director, or the like. Therefore, such persons would put up any fence or fences to prevent someone from an under-represented group from gaining an administrative position. If such an appointment was made nonetheless, such Whites would undermine that person to prove him or her inept and eventually, they would succeed by hook or crook in removing the person from that leadership position.

Continuing, Darrell sought to strike a balanced position. "Sure, as I have said, there are instances in which individuals from under-represented groups have provided superb leadership abilities in higher education. Such persons are to be emulated. On the other hand, there also are instances in which some people from under-represented groups are their own worst enemies and therefore the sole cause of their downfalls but such persons are found in any group."

"I know that when it comes to race relations and the quest for equality, things are horrible here at SAU but, even with your citations of books and journal articles, do you really think that's how it is across the board in this modern day and age?" Andy inquired looking directly at Darrell.

Darrell said he could not speak for every institution of higher education in the country but considering the materials coming out of various departments of African-American, Hispanic, Latin American, Middle-Eastern, Asian studies, etc., the picture did not look good. "Similarly, data from the National Center for Education Statistics regarding people of color in higher education are both revealing and discouraging."

Without waiting for Andy to put in a word, Darrell added, "from my experience here and from my interactions with people from under-represented groups in other predominantly white universities, I think this is true in most places although I'm sure some places are worse than others." He cited instances at SAU in which leadership roles by African-Americans were detested by alumni and alumnae as well as other external donors. "In several instances here at SAU," he clarified, "external donors have withheld contributions to the university to protest the appointment of African-Americans or members of other under-represented groups to leadership positions. I know of similar problems in at least four universities; that's terribly disgusting."

Andy agreed again but Darrell was not done. He said he bemoaned "the barbarous hypocrisy" of the system and vehemently detested the double-talk of stakeholders in higher education, noting exceptions. He hesitated a minute before adding, "You know Andy, not only have I read about Blacks and people from other under-represented groups but I also have read feminist materials because while the perspectives may differ, the struggle is the same—among others, a struggle against oppression and marginalization, a struggle for full and equal participation or put differently, parity of participation in all sectors, an insistence on social justice, and, above all, more than equal representation, a struggle for the human rights of individuals." To exemplify, he pointed out that he had read the writings of feminists from the 1940s to the turn of the century.

"My goodness, you have been reading indeed," Andy aired his admiration. "Who have you read in the area of feminism?"

"Quite a number, as you can imagine and all of them were impressive. However, I started with Simone de Beauvoir, a French philosopher, existentialist, and feminist whom some believe is the mother of the modern feminist movement."

"Never heard of her," Andy admitted.

"I had not either until I delved into feminist literature." Darrell discussed de Beauvoir's treatise, Le Deuxième Sexe (The Second Sex). Underscoring his admiration for the feminist theorist, Darrell said while he applauded de Beavoir for her intellect, wise counsel, and fascinating analysis of gender relations, he was touched when de Beauvoir admonished women not to be confused by a democratic age in which " men proclaim women equal while also acting to ensure that women can never be equal." He said he saw a striking parallel with race relations.

Andy was stunned again. He nodded politely as he could not believe the extent to which Darrell had delved into the literature to enable him understand and perhaps, to some extent, live with the situation he was facing at SAU. However, Andy seemed unsure of what to think. On one hand, he admired Darrell and Vanessa for standing up for justice but on the other hand, he was not sure if they were making the right decision. Why did they want to subject themselves to such hardship when they could go elsewhere especially since they were highly qualified? On second thought, since their qualifications were never in doubt, why did they have to leave solely because of their race? From yet another perspective, while Andy was cognizant of discrimination and inequalities at SAU, he wondered if Darrell was over-stressing or sensationalizing the racism and discrimination cards. Alternatively, was he (Andy) too "white" to understand fully let alone empathize?

Andy's thoughts and questions were in place. In fact, he deserved commendation because, unlike many people in privileged positions who only see such issues from their advantaged positions and/or perspectives, he was struggling strenuously not only to understand Darrell's predicament but also to be as fair and balanced as possible.

As Andy thought over Darrell's situation, it seemed Darrell's turn to voice his curiosity. "I understand there is a search for a new dean. Aren't you applying? I honestly think you ought to give it a serious thought. I know I will support your candidacy tenaciously, for whatever that's worth. Beyond me, I am absolutely sure of many others who will support you."

Andy laughed. "Well thanks for your confidence but definitely not." He said he was not as conformist or acquiescent as the administration would like; therefore, his chances of ascending to such a senior position were slim, if not nonexistent. Besides, on principle, he would not take an administrative position within the administration in its current form.

As the two men stood to leave, Darrell thanked Andy for the get-together and complimented his buddy for standing up for principle. "Very few people these days place principle above position. Most will kill their grandparents for a position, qualified for that position or not."

Andy took the compliment with humility. This was much to Darrell's admiration. He realized that, in a tertiary education world where academic credentials tended to transform people into pompous creatures, it was a rarity that one person possessed the enviable qualities of humility and principle. To him, it was such a quality that made a real human being and hence, a quality to emulate.

Chapter XII:

TOILING TOWARD TENURE

On a quiet evening, after Vanessa sent the children to bed, she returned to the kitchen to make a cup of tea. On second thought, she realized her husband had been in their study since the family ate dinner. She went over and knocked lightly. "Who is it?" a voice asked from within.

"A stranger."

"My mother told me not to talk to strangers," the voice from within came back.

Vanessa opened the door to a nicely arranged study with two sophisticated computers, full bookshelves, and stocks of professional journals as she and Darrell were subscribers to a number of online and print journals. "You better talk with this stranger or else ...," she threatened banteringly. Darrell repeated his instruction not to talk with a stranger, no matter who the stranger was. His wife put her arms around him and kissed him lightly and both smiled broadly. Indeed, this was a special room where they worked assiduously with varied memories. For the most part, they worked separately and often quietly at their individual desks. Other times, they exchanged ideas and other times, they had memorable interactions. Still other times, in the same place, they had some of their strongest disagreements, even heated arguments.

"You been here since dinner. I'm making tea; would you like to have a cup with me? I also have some incredibly delicious biscuits; your mother made them," Vanessa enticed her husband as she continued to hug him lightly.

Darrell did not draw back from such a beautiful queen. "That will be great Honey. Actually, it's time to take a break from this article." Vanessa scored a touchdown. She knew the mention of his mother's biscuits would do the trick and it did. Those biscuits reminded Darrell of his childhood days. He narrated many childhood stories to Vanessa and the children.

After another kiss, this time a long one, Darrell and his wife moved to the dining room. As they enjoyed tasty tea and delicious biscuits, inexplicably, their conversation drifted to their college days—how they met, their sessions with Prof. Kwame, on and on. "That man is one of his kind," Darrell articulated with palpable sincerity and appreciation.

"You know what I'm thinking Baby?" Vanessa asked. With an ehn-ehn, her husband shook his head. "I think we ought to give him his bouquet while he is alive." When asked to explain, she said it would be a great idea for them to join Lamont, David, and any other mentees to honor Professor Kwame on his eightieth birthday.

"How?" Darrell probed.

Vanessa sat up right to explain. "Well, given that we had lengthy discussion sessions with him in college and we all took notes, we can honor him with a festschrift." She said this would include the collection and systematic organization of the notes. The accumulated volume would be presented to the professor during an honoring surprise party on his eightieth birthday.

"Great idea!" Darrell shouted. "Let's do it! Sounds great!" Wasting no time, the two started calling. Lamont and David bought the idea enthusiastically. They offered to spearhead the collection of notes from Professor Kwame's former mentees no matter where they were. Since such notes could be submitted to them electronically, organizing and compiling them would be a manageable task.

Everyone agreed that the proposed program was to be a surprise. As such, Mrs. Kwame was not to know anything about it. The organizers therefore contacted Prof. Kwame's first son, Mandela Tolbert Toure Kwame who was also a professor; he bought the idea instantly.

After days, in fact weeks of telephone calls, emails, and faxes, the stage was set and arrangements in place. Forty-three of Prof. Kwame's mentees could make it. Ten of them were coming in from outside the country—Europe, Africa, Canada, the Caribbean, and Latin America and more than sixty had sent in notes and comments. The visitors were to stay in a hotel in Prof. Kwame's home town until the evening of the program. Dr. Mandela Kwame was to arrange to take his parents out and then, the surprise.

The arrangement worked like magic. At precisely eight o'clock in the evening, the limousine drove to the home of the Kwames where their son had promised them a special birthday treat on his nickel. Dressed in very elegant suits on their son's insistence, the Kwames looked wonderful. They rode to a rented and well decorated hall where scores of people were anxious to surprise a man who had impacted their lives immeasurably.

As soon as the Kwames entered the dimly lit hall, the lights were turned on full blast and everyone screamed, "Happy Birthday Prof., Kwame! We love and appreciate you!" Everyone rushed to get a hug and some kissed him over and over on the cheeks.

Over exuberant to see his mentees, the retired professor had tears rolling down his face; he too could not stop hugging them. His mentees also brought in some of his best professional colleagues, including former presidents, deans and fellow professors. Prof. Dominquez made it and so did Dean Minston, long retired. The former met Darrell and Vanessa for the first time.

After a well-planned delectable dinner, Prof. Kwame's mentees gowned him and his wife in a true African tradition. Then, Vanessa gave the appreciation remarks. She was selected because among the ten mentees who graduated summa cum laude, she was one of four ladies; one was deceased and two could not make it.

Vanessa's remarks were touching. She too was tearful as she thanked the retired professor on behalf of all the men and women he touched, not only his mentees. "Our limited research shows you mentored seventy-seven students, served as adviser to nearly two thousand students, and taught thousands over your thirty-three year teaching experience. Of your mentees, thirteen percent graduated summa cum laude, thirty-one percent, Magna cum laude, and forty-four percent, cum laude. Without you Professor Kwame, most of us would have dropped out of college; because of you, a hundred percent of your mentees and ninety-eight percent of your advisees graduated. All your mentees, without a single exception, are doing well in both our professional and family lives. Moreover, you have not left us; even in retirement, you still check on us." With her tears rolling like a stream, she said, "Thank you Prof. Kwame; we cannot thank you enough, only God can."

Following Vanessa's moving remarks, Lamont unveiled two volumes of notes taken by Professor Kwame's former mentees. AS Prof. Kwame walked to the podium to receive the volumes and respond, the audience gave a standing ovation that lasted almost three minutes.

The retired professor and his wife were in tears. He could hardly speak. He thanked God for giving him an opportunity to work with young people. He also thanked his mentees for such a thoughtful program. He encouraged them to mentor others. As his tears flowed, he could no longer speak. There was another standing ovation. The remarks were followed by a dance that was opened by the honoree and his beautiful bride of fifty-four years. Indeed, it was a well-planned and well deserved program.

Planning the Professor Kwame appreciation program at the end of the semester complicated the schedule enormously but Darrell and Vanessa survived. Likewise, they survived the Christmas break and rested a week before resuming school.

Shortly after classes started, Darrell was very surprised to see Dean Harris at his door one afternoon. "Hello Dean," Darrell greeted. "What brings you to my humble office?" Dean Harris courteously returned the greetings and upon entering the office, was offered a seat.

"Unlike your big and luxurious office Dean, I have only one coffee cup in my tiny office; so please forgive me," Darrell stated in jest.

The dean laughed lightly and accepted the apology. He then disclosed the purpose of this visit. "I came to ask you a favor Darrell," the dean said. Darrell's mind wondered into a thousand different directions. The dean continued. "You know the people call Regional Evaluation Team or RET?" Darrell said he most certainly did. "Very good," said the dean. With his trademark horrible grammar, he informed that the team was coming to the university in two months and particularly to the college. As a result, he wanted Darrell to be on the inner committee.

The dean praised Darrell for his impressive economic background. He especially referred to Darrell's article on regional economic development which went viral upon publication. He then asked Darrell to present a paper on the economic implications of higher education in the region with emphasis on the contributions of SAU. "Do you think you can do that for us?"

Darrell did not hesitate. Grateful that the dean sought him ought to make this request, he accepted at once. The dean said in addition to his request, he had two assignments for Darrell. "Wow!" kidded Darrell, "how many things do you want me to do Dean?"

"Just a few," Dean Harris laughed. He said he was appointing Darrell to both the college and university strategic planning committees. "I think you will have a good view if you serve on both committee." Again, ignoring the dean's grammar, Darrell accepted the assignments.

Planning for the RET visit took up enormous time. Eventually, the visitors arrived and at the first meeting, Darrell and others, including Lupita, quickly realized the dean had bamboozled them into serving on a committee to give the impression that the college was very diverse. "The dean is a snake in the grass," protested Lupita as she and Darrell ate lunch at the meeting site.

"You're not kidding," agreed Darrell. "He deceptively used us to give the visitors a false impression of diversity within the college; this college and the entire university are far from achieving diversity." Furthermore, Darrell was convinced the chicanery was most likely the work of either Alex or Peggy than that of Dean Harris.

Following the RET VISITATION, Darrell and Vanessa excluded themselves largely for the rest of the academic year as they wrote articles and prepared for conference presentations. This burden seemed to be more heavily weighed on Darrell as he would be applying for associate professorship; he knew it and so was up to the task.

The pressure to publish kept Darrell in his office for long hours. One day, Dallas showed up in his office unexpectedly. Somewhat breathless, he asked, "Darrell, have you seen a copy of the SAU Seer today?" When Darrell replied in the negative, he showed him a copy. "See the headlines? My boss is being praised for doing this and that; this was my project; I did it and he presented it as his own and took credit for it. This was what I was talking about at your house one day. My boss seldom, if ever, recognizes my achievements. Rather, in many instances, he steals my ideas, plans, and accomplishments and presents them as his. If it is anything he will not present, he shoots it down regardless of its merits. He acts as if nothing good can come from me. Look at this," — showing the lines to Darrell. "Can you believe this? Look at that line and see this," showing Darrell a copy of his original manuscript from which his boss copied verbatim.

Shaking his head, Darrell was stunned. "My, my, my!" he stated in disbelief. "Now that's plagiarism, if they were ever looking for one but I know that charge will never surface. Oh my goodness." He thanked Dallas for bringing the paper to his attention. Furthermore, he warned Dallas to be on his guard for no matter what he did, his boss would be watching vigilantly for faults to confirm his unshakable belief that Dallas was inept. "I know you have far more experience than I do but I tell you, I have learned a lot within these TWO PLUS years at SAU."

At the end of the third year, Darrell and Vanessa once more entertained their mentees at their house. Subsequently, they started planning for the summer. After a lengthy discussion, they decided to spend the summer in Achval. They needed the time to write articles for publication. Darrell was also completing his first book in economics. In the middle of the summer, Grandma Louise called to say Grandpa Joseph, Vanessa's dad was sick and had been rushed to the hospital. Vanessa wasted no time; she flew down south to be with her dad. Unfortunately, Joseph did not make it. Darrell then decided to drive the children to their grandfather's funeral. "Oh Honey, I am not sure if that will be necessary," Vanessa stated on the phone.

"Oh yes Baby," Darrell insisted. He said although the drive was long and tedious, it was nevertheless very necessary, indeed a solemn obligation, for him and the children to pay their last respect to Joseph, his father-in-law and the children's grandfather. He suggested that, to save the wear-and-tear on their vehicle, he wanted to rent a small van instead. Vanessa was not sure the professor of economics was making the best economical decision but Darrell had no doubts.

It was a sad funeral indeed but it goes without saying that in general, funerals are not exciting occasions. At the service, Vanessa spoke passionately about her father and so did her siblings; their mother was unable to say a word. Her facial expressions spoke volumes.

After the funeral, Vanessa and her siblings sorted out some legal papers regarding their dad. Darrell and Vanessa asked Louise to travel back to Achval with them but she and Vanessa's siblings did not think that was a good idea, at least not for now.

"Mom, you get to fly back and we travel by road?" Kwame asked begrudgingly.

"That's how we came Baby and that's how we will go."

"That's not fair," Kwame stated emphatically. His mom had heard that statement on numerous occasions: "That's not fair! It's not fair!" Sometimes laughing, she would tell them that many things in the world were not fair.

Back in Achval, everyone prepared for another summer. This time, they were not expecting many visitors for Mom and Dad had to do research and write. Of course, this did not prevent the children from attending summer programs and participating in fun activities; Mom and Dad made sure of that.

Even in the midst of work, the family was glad to have Grandma Clara for a couple of weeks. Likewise, Darrell and Vanessa were elated when Lamont and Kolu dropped by for a couple of nights on their way to Canada. Similarly, at the end of the summer, the family was treated to another week of rest and relaxation at a different reserve.

The beginning of the fourth year was a little different; the college had a new dean named Samuel Scott. Inexplicably, Darrell was not a member of the search committee, one of the very few times he was not asked to serve on such a committee. In any case, Dr. Scott, who was a native of the mid-west, was two or three years older than Darrell. Unlike his predecessor, he was very smart with impressive academic credentials. On the other hand, like Dean Harris, he was very conservative. Being conservative was not the problem; from the onset, his academic credentials notwithstanding, it was very clear he was intolerant of difference. "I guess they always hire one of their kind to maintain the status quo; I mean, one who will neither promote diversity nor foster structural change but perpetuate dominance of the racial majority," Darrell told Vanessa. He was sure some would see such a statement as racist but he stood by his words.

Also, at the beginning of the new year, Vanessa was preparing her dossier to apply for tenure and promotion. She got enormous assistance and guidance from Lupita. Anne offered secretarial services where needed.

As Vanessa put her dossier together, Darrell made an appointment to talk with Alex on the same issue. "I am thinking about beginning my dossier for tenure and promotion," he disclosed.

Alex was disgusted that Darrell had lasted this long at the university. Gaining a permanent position there was the most revolting thing he could think of. "I do not think you are anywhere near ready," he snapped. "My goodness, you are just beginning your fourth year."

"I know Alex and that's why I am not going up this year; I want to apply next year."

"I do not think you will be ready even then. He explained that, since becoming department chair, he knew no one who had gained tenured in five years.

"Alex," Darrell called his chair's attention, "you are implying that because no one has done it, no one can do it. Do you really mean that or are you willing to look at the situation with an open mind?"

"I am telling you no one has done it and if anyone will do it, let me be honest with you; it will not be you for you are nowhere near accomplishing such a feat."

The outright insult and callous put-down did not surprise Darrell. Instead of being angry, he reminded Alex of his publications, grants, and conference presentations. He said by the end of his fifth year, he would have a book out. In addition, he would have an appreciable number of published articles with a few in press. He was convinced that, with those publications along with his grants, conference presentations, service, and teaching evaluations, his record would be equivalent to, and in many instances better than, records others had presented in the department to get full professorship although he was only going up for associate professorship. Besides, he gave Alex a list of individuals who gained associate professorship within five years, one of them in four but none had more publications than Darrell who was in his fourth year.

Despite Darrell's persuasive presentation, Alex still was not convinced and so disagreed unequivocally but Darrell was not persuaded to abandon his plans and course of action. Alex had never supported him on anything so he did not expect him to do so especially since Alex had made it clear he did not want Darrell at SAU. He therefore informed Alex only as a matter of courtesy but expected nothing positive out of him.

Unlike Alex, Andy and Prof. Kwame told Darrell separately that a superb performance would win his battle. Similarly, Vanessa heavily relied on her performance in applying for tenure and promotion. By the time her dossier reached her Department Evaluation Committee, to so-called DEC, she had accumulated an outstanding record for a lecturer. She had outstanding ratings in teaching, her record of service was remarkable, her publication record equivalent to that of an assistant professor seeking promotion, and her conference presentations incredible. Yet, as she prepared to give her required presentation to the DEC, she left no stones unturned. She rehearsed her presentation with Darrell and consulted Lupita and Prof. Dominguez. Based on their advice, she researched the records of assistant professors who were promoted in the department within the last ten years.

Generally, lecturers are not expected to do research, present at professional conferences, and publish refereed journal articles. Rather, they are expected to teach, advise students, and serve on committees. SAU's deviation from this practice did not intimidate or even bother Vanessa. She was prepared for tenure and promotion. As a result, her presentation to the DEC was awesome. In attendance to support her were Darrell, Andy, Dallas, Lupita, Anne, and a few friends. To conclude the presentation, she said, "I am aware that these evaluations are on an individual basis. However, in searching the records of the department for the last ten years relative to assistant professors who were promoted, not only lecturers, I find that my record herein presented stands equal to, and often is much stronger than, many of these records. I therefore appeal to the committee to recommend tenure and promotion to the position of senior lecturer based on my record."

In spite of her strong record and eloquent presentation, the committee was split on Vanessa's application; it voted 2-2 with one abstention. The recommendations of the department chair, Brian Anderson were lukewarm, at best. At the college level, the committee voted 4-3 in favor and the new dean's recommendations were lukewarm. At the university level, the committee voted 7-4 in favor but ultimately, the provost denied Vanessa's application. She challenged the denial and after two months and several hearings, she won her case and therefore received tenure and promotion to the position of senior lecturer.

The gruesome experience Vanessa endured to gain tenure and promotion dampened the joy and excitement that would have otherwise accompanied the monumental achievement. Nonetheless, she and Darrell invited a few friends to celebrate. To Vanessa however, celebration was premature, perhaps unnecessary because, without doubting her husband's academic record, her concerns centered largely on his chances for tenure and promotion. She could not put anything beyond the hostile, racist political climate at the university.

Vanessa's concerns were not misplaced. In fact, Darrell regarded her experience as a prologue to his struggle. He therefore held no illusions at the beginning of his fifth year when he was preparing to apply for tenure and promotion against the advice of Alex, his department chair.

In light of Alex's opposition, prior to applying, Darrell showed his records in teaching, service, and research to several professors in his department and asked their opinions about going up for tenure and promotion. Each one felt strongly he was more than prepared and therefore not only encouraged him to apply but also promised to support him; these included Professors Lucretia Dennis, Bernice Marks, and Donald Clement.

With Vanessa's assistance over a period of several months, Darrell methodically put his dossier together. In addition, he sought letters of endorsement from professional colleagues, including Andy and professors from other universities. He was endorsed by Prof. Dominguez and prof. Kwame in strongly worded letters. Furthermore, Darrell made an unprecedented move; he obtained a letter of endorsement from his parents. In his narrative, he stated unequivocally that he was aware that he was operating in academia, and in a professional world with myriad and varied emphases; therefore, he cherished letters of support from various circles of the professional milieu. Yet, he placed the letter from his parents above letters from professional circles. He explicated that, although they were high school graduates, his beloved parents not only knew him best but were his greatest teachers, his true mentors. Next to them, he underscored, no one knew him like his wife and Prof. Kwame. "These people, and my late grandfather, made me into whom and what I am; I am indebted to them for life."

Darrell's presentation to the DEC was a thriller. He systematically covered the three areas of teaching, service, and research, citing his philosophy and achievements in each area within five years at the university. Like his wife, he compared his decked against the records of associate professors who were promoted in the department within the last ten years. He argued persuasively that his record as an assistant professor stood a firm ground against the deck. He therefore appealed to the committee to recommend him for tenure and promotion.

The committee members had a lengthy discussion about Darrell's application. In the end, they voted against his application 3-2, citing five years as a relatively short period at the university to warrant tenure and promotion. Alex's recommendation, unsurprisingly was a resounding "No!" At the college level, the College Evaluation Committee, CEC also deliberated for a long time before voting 5-2 in favor of the application.

After receiving the various recommendations, Dean Scott wrote a very weak letter of support. Subsequently, he informed Darrell of his action and why. "As you know Darrell, I am new. Therefore, beyond the recommendations of the Chair and

DEC, I consulted faculty members in your department and a number of them sent emails opposing your promotion." Under the Freedom of Information Act, Darrell requested copies of the emails and was shocked to discover that Professors Lucretia Dennis, Bernice Marks, and Donald Clement strongly opposed his application in contrast to the promises they made.

"I'll be damned," Darrell shook with disappointment and fury when he read the emails. "Oh my goodness!" Because he was new in the department, and given the fact that he was determined to gain full professorship, he resisted the temptation of individually forwarding the emails to their senders with the subject matter, "Thanks for your support."

The University Evaluation Committee, UEC also deliberated a long time before voting on Darrell's application. The committee voted exactly as it did with Vanessa's; a vote of 7-4 in support. Eventually, the provost denied the application also citing brevity of time at the university.

After discussing his final ratings with Vanessa, Darrell called Andy and later, Profs. Dominguez and Kwame. Separately, each one stated the obvious; that is, although an unwritten rule for assistant professors was a minimum of five years, promotion was based less on the length of time one spent at the university. Rather, the emphasis was on a professor's performance in the three rating areas. Besides, Darrell was in his fifth year. It was agreed therefore that a challenge was in place and Darrell proceeded accordingly.

When Darrell appealed for reconsideration, the provost summoned him to his office, an unprecedented move. AT the provost's office, Darrell was somewhat surprised to see Alex and Dean Scott. "I have received your letter Dr. Thomas and so wanted to meet with you, your dean and department chair." For more than half an hour, this was the only straight forward sentence the provost spoke. The rest of the time, he was excruciatingly verbose and vaunting. "Based on my years of experience here at the university, and believe me, that's many years of rich and unparalleled experience, I know a president and a

Board of Trustees exist in this university but when it comes to these crucial matters of decision making, decisions which affect the length and breadth of this university and especially its academic personnel, I assure you beyond a reasonable doubt, the buck stops with me and for now, I do not think our position, reached with thoughtful care and sound academic analysis, will change, although, as you know, we are humans and truly, no decisions are indelibly carved in stones," the provost pronounced.

As he listened, Darrell fought hard to fish some meaning out of the provost's statement. He also knew Dean Scott was intolerant of diversity but he did not know the extent of the dean's bias and worse, his indescribable lack of honesty. On the other hand, Alex could not surprise Darrell, even if he tried. Thus, his negative statements rolled off Darrell like water on a duck's back. Yet, he felt obliged to address Alex directly and firmly in the presence of his bosses. "Dr. Brooks," he said, being formal, "I have never understood and indeed, will never understand your rigid hatred and your blatant bitter bias toward me. Since my arrival, you have never seen anything good within my person and my work; as such, you have tried fiercely to push me out of this university. In fact, you stated firmly that I ought to leave the university for doing so would be in the best interest of the college and university. I'm therefore not surprised by what you say to the provost in my presence or absence. I only hope and pray that, beyond your hatred and blinding biases, my record will speak loudly for me. In addition, as I have told you before, I will always rise above your mordant hatred to embrace a professional and cordial relationship." Alex stood speechlessly with a long face.

After addressing Alex, Darrell turned to the provost. "I still maintain my appeal that you take another look at my record and reconsider your denial. If, on the other hand, your position is immutable, I am sure you will communicate same in writing." In another lengthy sentence, the provost agreed.

Following the meeting, Andy called Darrell at home to inquire as to how things went. "Unfavorably," he said, declaring that this was not a surprise.

"How did you find the provost?" Andy question again since this was Darrell's first time in such a meeting with the provost.

"My goodness, I do not know what to say Andy. I think the man is a cockalorum who is further plagued by the dual malady of prolixity and braggadocio. Similarly, I did not know Dean Scott was diseased by the triadic syndrome of mythomania, tendentiousness, and sanctimoniousness. These guys really need help."

Andy could not stop laughing. "Very interesting description and diagnosis of your bosses; from where in the world do you get such words and vivid descriptions?" Darrell was laughing too hard to respond.

When he received a letter denying his appeal for reconsideration, Darrell filed a challenge. After months of deliberation, the matter went to an outside arbitrator. In the pleading, a union representative, acting as claimant, outlined how the collective bargaining agreement was violated. In response, Paul, the head of the Legal Department, argued that indeed, there was no violation of the CBA and that Dr. Thomas was not entitled to promotion and tenure.

At the hearing, Darrell was represented by a lady from the union. She made a few introductory remarks but quickly deferred to Darrell to state his reasons why he deserved tenure and promotion. Darrell was prepared. Alluding to *Sweezy v. New Hampshire* without citing the case specifically either because he did not know or such was not necessary, he said he was aware of what the court termed the university's "four essential freedoms;" that is, the university's freedom to determine who may teach, what should be taught, how it ought to be taught, and who may be admitted to study. Fortunately, he pointed out, the university not only heeded this ruling but developed policies and guidelines for its enforcement. In that light, he clearly delineated the university's guidelines and requirements for tenure and promotion. Consistent with these guidelines, he presented his records in teaching, service and research. Using a PowerPoint, he showed how his work met, and often surpassed, the stipulated guidelines. Additionally, he compared his record to the records of people promoted within the department within the previous ten years. Furthermore, he argued that he deserved to be promoted because, at the various levels of his evaluation, there was not a single negative comment about his teaching, service or research; the only thing that was mentioned was the length of time he had spent at the university. "As I have pointed out, there is nothing in the collective bargaining agreement, the university's constitution, and college policies that bases promotion and tenure on duration at the university." He reminded everyone at the hearing that he was indeed in his fifth year. Besides, the only thing regarding duration was a line stating, "If a tenure track professor has not earned tenure in seven years, it lies within the dean's discretion to give said professor year to year contracts but the professor will no longer qualify for tenure at the university." He therefore called on the arbitrator to rule in his favor since the university had not presented anything to show he was lagging in the three areas of assessment.

Responding on behalf of the university were Paul, Alex, and Dean Scott who argued that Darrell could not receive tenure and promotion. However, apart from the heavy focus on the alleged brief duration of Darrell's tenure at the university, they presented nothing substantive to show why Darrell could not be tenured and promoted.

The arbitrator took three days to go over all the pieces of evidence presented to her by both sides. Fortunately, she sided with the view that, commensurate with the collective bargaining agreement, promotion and tenure were based on performance and much less, if at all, on duration at the university. It seemed she could not agree more with Darrell: "As there is nothing in the collective bargaining agreement, and the university constitution and policies to suggest duration—specifically brevity of tenure at the university—as a reason for denying promotion and tenure, the claimant must prevail on both grounds. This is particularly undeniable given that the claimant has excelled in the three areas of assessment. This point is indisputable because the respondent has provided no evidence on the contrary," the arbitrator concluded.

Since the arbitrator's conclusion was final and binding, Darrell received tenure and was promoted to the rank of associate professor. When he received his letter of tenure and promotion from The Board of Trustees, Vanessa wanted to throw a party to celebrate but Darrell persuaded her otherwise. "The battle has just begun because, while there is no doubting of the rugged road ahead, I nonetheless will apply for full professorship. Besides, if we celebrate anything, it is not my promotion but the fact that justice always prevails over injustice, truth over lie, and right over wrong; it's an indisputable evidence of the existence of a just Supreme Being Who exacts justice without fear of anyone."

Vanessa quickly reached for a book on the shelf, flipped through quickly and read a portion of a poem by James Russell Lowell:

Truth forever on the scaffold, Wrong forever on the throne,

Yet that scaffold sways the future, and, behind the dim unknown,

Standeth God within the shadow, keeping watch above his own.

Chapter XIII:

THE RESEARCH

During their childhood and adolescent years, Darrell and his siblings grew sick and tired of the number, variety, and repetition of didactic adages and sermonic pieces of advice. Many proved to be useful later in life but one Darrell frequently repeated was what his father often said: "There is no easy way to success." Although somewhat a trite, this proved incontrovertible during his doctoral studies, in a variety of other instances but especially during his tenure and promotion hearings. He thought his records loudly spoke for him and yet, he was treated as if he had done nothing to warrant tenure and promotion. In spite of what he called "a glaring injustice," he did not despair. Thus, after the gruesome experience, he and Vanessa decided to take the family down south for a week or two with the old folks.

Visiting Ghetahzia was always relaxing and rewarding in many ways especially since Mama Clara and Dwayne were getting up there in age. A quick swing by Vanessa's home and a visit with Lamont and David were refreshing; then, it was another long trip back to Achval.

A new academic year and professional era dawned for Darrell when he started back at SAU for his sixth year as a tenured associate professor. He quickly ignored the title and focused on the goals and challenges ahead. In his academic pursuit, as always, he would perform his job as best as he could, maintain a cordial professional relationship with colleagues, and support students tenaciously. Beyond those, he vowed to do several things. Without a doubt, he would go for full professorship. Toward that end, he believed he knew the prodigious obstacles ahead although he could not harbor such belief with certainty.

Without wallowing in speculation and skepticism, Darrell began the journey toward full professorship with confidence, determination, and faith alongside careful and systematic planning. He knew that, in addition to ensuring maximum performance in teaching and service, he had to continue presenting papers at professional conferences, publishing articles, writing grants, and whatever it took to get there. In fact, he was working on his second book and after another year, he planned to take a sabbatical leaf to conduct extensive research and serve as a visiting professor in a prestigious department of economics.

Darrell's plans were not solely self-centered. In addition to the graduate and undergraduate mentees he and Vanessa chose, he selected three doctoral students with the aim of guiding them to completion and into whatever fields they chose but hoped at least one would gravitate toward the professoriate. Further, he decided to work with at least four assistant professors by supporting them to gain tenure and promotion; two were African-Americans, one Caucasian, and one Hispanic. Additionally, he was determined to befriend professors from under-represented groups in other predominantly white universities. Through and among them, he would conduct a survey to discover the extent to which their experiences were similar or dissimilar. He also planned to increase his contacts with Professors Kwame and Dominguez as well as other retired professors of color to learn from their long and rich experiences. At the same time, an extensive and continuous review of the literature was in place to enhance his understanding of various terms, concepts, ideologies, and perspectives relative to the problems and successes of professors from under-represented groups in higher education, especially those in predominantly white institutions, PWIs. This survey was to include an extensive coverage of appellate and Supreme Court rulings regarding people of color in higher education throughout the nation. Furthermore, he was determined to continue reading books and articles in black studies alongside memoirs, biographies and autobiographies relative to people of color especially those who were in PWIs.

The aim of Darrell's research was not only to unearth the extent and varied impacts of the problem but also catalog a few approaches toward solution. In that regard, special emphasis would be placed on delineating strategies for increasing the number of students, staff, faculty and administrators from under-represented groups in higher education and enabling them to succeed. This was crucial to Darrell owing to the realization that, when problems persist, it is easier to play the blame game than seek lasting solutions. Likewise, it is much easy to pinpoint what's wrong whereas it takes effort, ingenuity, risk, selflessness, etc., to make it right or at least strive strenuously to do so.

Commensurate with Darrell's research plans, he, Vanessa, and his doctoral students worked the phone and surfed the internet for days. They compiled an appreciable list of faculty of color, FOC. Darrell talked lengthily with each one. He followed the conversations with open-ended questionnaires to sample their views and experiences. These responses were mixed. A few professors and lecturers from under-represented groups employed in predominantly white universities and prestigious schools of law, medicine and engineering gave critical, even condemning responses. Conversely, the overwhelming majority gave informative responses which highlighted specific problem areas, including the paucity and struggles of African-Americans and others from under-represented groups in higher education.

As opposed to respondents who either condemned Darrell's research or gave bleak pictures, four respondents from different predominantly white universities give a different picture. They were not entirely satisfied with the level of diversity in their institutions but appreciated the genuine efforts their universities were making toward that end. For example, although the strategies in each institution were slightly different, generally, the universities established reward mechanisms for vice presidents, deans, directors, department chairs, and other administrators who vigorously promoted and sustained diversity of professors, staff, graduate assistants, students, guest speakers, and even courses of instruction. Contrariwise, these universities publicly reprimanded, and in some cases, imposed mild to moderate penalties on administrators who failed to promote diversity assiduously. In addition, the universities published an annual report on diversity in which, based on statistical data, colleges were ranked in terms of their efforts in promoting diversity.

Interestingly, as opposed to other institutions which complain incessantly that they could not find qualified individuals from under-represented groups, the four universities included in the survey hired some of the most qualified scholars, administrators, and staff members from under-represented groups.

Darrell ascertained that, in hiring, the four universities surveyed recruited professionals from under-represented groups without making short cuts, or giving preferential treatments, or any exceptions to such persons other than leveling the hiring field. As the universities did with Caucasian employees, they sometimes pursued experts from under-represented groups at a high cost. Stated differently, the advocacy of the four universities for diversity was not merely to increase numbers but to foster racial equality and equitable power distribution by seeking and promoting the best individuals from under-represented groups and among women of all races. As a result, the four universities were highly ranked nationally for promoting and sustaining diversity at all levels of operation. These rankings were objective in that they were not influenced by contributions to newspapers, magazines, or rating agencies by the universities.

While Darrell and his small core of researchers were encouraged by the reports from four institutions, the bleak picture from the majority of responding institutions reminded Darrell of the country's history of racially and ethnically motivated discrimination and segregation. He painfully recalled conversations with his wife and discussions with Prof. Kwame in which he learned about The Black Codes and Jim Crow laws which legitimized segregation and discrimination of Blacks and other sub-groups.

For a brief moment, Darrell's memories of the nation's odious history gave way to encouraging efforts exerted by subgroups of the population. He appreciated the fact that the Civil Rights Movement, the Civil Rights Act, the Voting Rights act, and the mandates of Affirmative Action combined to open doors for African-Americans and other people of color, including access to higher education. Furthermore, African-Americans and others from under-represented groups had exerted efforts through conferences, workshops, publications, and other relentless endeavors to maximize recruitment, retention, and promotion of people of color in higher education, including prestigious schools of law, medicine, and engineering. He was specifically touched by efforts by faculty members of color who, through concerted actions, were making a difference in their universities.

While Darrell's appreciation was in place, his research revealed the cold truth; that is, despite relevant laws and judicial mandates, irrespective of successes triggered by the Civil Rights Movement and Affirmative Action, and regardless of laudable efforts by determined and conscientious professionals of color, the research indubitably confirmed a paucity of people of color in higher education as lecturers, professors, and administrators. For instance, the survey found that a huge proportion of African-Americans in higher education was concentrated in Historically Black Colleges and Universities, HBCUs as well as other institutions regarded as predominantly black universities. Conversely, the statistics was incredibly dismal in predominantly white universities, PWUs. When the statistics were broken down further—professors, administrators, women of color, etc.,-the result was shamefully appalling. Likewise, the statistics varied among groups: African-Americans, Hispanic (divided further into Chicanos and Chicanas, other Latinos and Latinas), Asians, and on the basis of sexual orientation. At the bottom were Native Americans or American Indians, Pacific Islanders, and people with disabilities. SAU was a glaring example of this dismal statistics because overall, its diversity rate was 2.37%, far less than the mandated twenty percent.

Amazingly, the websites of all the predominantly white universities (PWUs) included in the survey had impressive statements about diversity. They accentuated skin color blindness and touted diversity as a crucial and indispensable part of the university's mission. They therefore expressed rigid determination to promote and maintain diversity. To symbolize their determination, many not only had large committees on diversity but also established offices, centers, and even institutes of ethnic or racial studies: African-American Institute, Institute for Africana Studies, Hispanic Studies Center, Latin American Institute, Asian Institute, Middle-Eastern Studies Center, etc.. On the other hand, when administrators from the same universities were asked to provide reasons for the low level of diversity in their institutions, the responses were very similar across the board. Such PWUs claimed they could not find qualified African-Americans, Hispanics, and professionals from other under-represented groups. They argued that it would be reverse discrimination and, in fact, unconscionable to knowingly hire unqualified blacks and other people of color.

Despite their strong arguments for hiring the most qualified, unsurprisingly, the PWUs included in the study provided no reasons, not even comments for the hiring of Whites with mediocre credentials. In like manner, nothing was said about the barriers these institutions posed to the hiring of people from under-represented groups. Similarly, nothing was said about the fact that the few people from under-represented groups who stayed in these universities in general, were not only forced into professional stagnation but were treated contemptuously, with very few exceptions.

In addition to discovering stiff barriers to the hiring of African-Americans, Hispanics, Asians, and others from under-represented groups in PWUs, Darrell's survey found that when hired in administration, most people from under-represented groups were assigned to junior positions in student services and promoted infrequently, if at all. Such persons who went into the professoriate were unhappy as they were marginalized and isolated—treatments Darrell, Vanessa, and others had endured at SAU. Some were so isolated that they refused to participate even in social activities organized by their departments and colleges.

Several respondents to the survey item regarding social participation commented along the line of, "They do not encourage any professional relationship so why join them for a social activity?" Other responses were to the tune of, "I have a few friends of various races and backgrounds with whom I socialize but in general, you know they do not want you there so why join them for anything?" Other stated that they refused to attend because they were invited to diversify the gathering racially and ethnically, not because they were colleagues or that their presence was important. "No one will use me for his or her purpose," one professor articulated. Overall, respondents indicated that their receptions by students and colleagues which ranged from indifference to rejection, and from degradation and derogation to outright hostility, buttressed their resolve to stay away.

Female respondents corroborated Vanessa's experience at SAU; that is, they were doubly victimized. They were isolated and treated contemptuously on the basis of racial and gender bias. Insults against them, even from students, were more frequent than those levied against their male counterparts. Yet, in general, the insults and harassments were ignored by the administration. This was the case even when male students made rude lewd comments toward them. As one writer put it, such comments were "microaggressive student- teacher bullying," often framed as subtle and backhanded compliment intended to diminish or change the teacher's behaviors.[15] In response, women of color refused to be sexualized—forced into specific gender roles—or racialized—compelled into meeting certain racial expectations.

When hired in PWUs, both male and female professors and lecturers from under-represented groups reported that they were overloaded while their works were under-valued. They were overloaded in that, usually the only person or two of color in their departments, they were asked to serve on numerous committees to ensure such committees were diverse. Additionally, alongside their regular teaching and service loads, they were called upon to handle all issues of diversity—recruitment, advising, and retention of student of color, hiring and retention of professionals of color, etc.. Some professors of color referred to this additional but unofficial assignment as a racial, ethnic, or cultural taxation while others regarded same as a hidden curriculum intended to overburden them.[16] However termed, it seriously impinged on their time and interfered with their teaching, service, and especially their research and publication agendas. They resented this additional onus because, as they saw it, recruitment and retention of students and faculty from under-represented groups ought to be the concern and responsibility of everyone, not only people of color.

While they reported overloads, faculty members from under-represented groups in PWUs reported that in general, their professional activities, including their publications, were undervalued; Darrell was a living witness to this phenomenon. Therefore, he could identify with respondents who revealed that their works were characterized as self-serving, mediocre,

---

[15] Cothran, 2016

[16] Arnold et al, 2016

and unacceptable. Many pointed out that their publications in Afro-centric, Hispanic, Asian, or even international refereed journals were disregarded or rejected outright, regardless of the qualities of such journals as evidenced by many factors, including the top-notch materials of these journals, the credentials of their editors and review board members as well as the high rate with which they rejected submitted manuscripts. These respondents totally resented the tunnel vision idea that white colleagues had one Eurocentric measuring rod for quality of professional work against which all others must either measure up or fail. This affronting orientation not only detracted from, but directly contradicted the advocacy for genuine diversity, if there were ever such advocacy. Along these lines, one respondent protested vehemently: "It is an insult and therefore totally unacceptable that I must constantly explain and/or defend the quality of my scholarly works when my colleagues' are accepted without question." The professor resented the rejection of his counter narratives.

Darrell's gruesome experience during his tenure and promotion bid was similar to other professors in PWUs; many relayed horrid, almost incredulous stories. They repeatedly underscored that a combination of the extra burden covered up in hidden curricula and the devaluing and sometimes total rejection of their works impeded possibilities for retention, promotion, and tenure (RPT). This was frustrating because, as Darrell experienced, often, this was because committee members, plagued by narrow-mindedness, myopia, racism, and bigotry, often did not understand the thrust of such publications nor did they appreciate the quality and diversity it brought to the professoriate.

Most respondents to the survey (92.8%) reported they experienced low ratings because racism was institutionalized. This was exemplified by the fact that criteria for teacher evaluation by students, rating of service, and perception of professional activities were based on traditional standards that rigidly resisted different approaches and perspectives. They pointed out poignantly that, without changing these methods of evaluation, women—including white women—and all who looked and sounded differently would continue to be rated poorly and undeservedly so.

A substantial number of respondents (88.7%) vented their frustration regarding the manner and extent to which their professional works and community services in ethnic or racial communities were rated. Like Darrell, respondents were livid that research and services in these communities were either disregarded totally or rated poorly on grounds that they were self-serving. One respondent addressed the issue eloquently. "I find it both baffling and insulting," he wrote, "that when I conduct research in my ethnic community, regardless of the quality of my methodology, my findings are not regarded as emanating from a top-notch professional activity. Similarly, my services in the same community are dismissed as self-serving. Conversely, when my white colleagues conduct research or provide services in my ethnic community, they are applauded tumultuously." The respondent added that his rating changed only slightly when he conducted research or provided services in white and/or mixed race communities. "Either way," he concluded, "I cannot win."

Another respondent was equally angry about the diminution of his research in international circles. "My research is rejected in part or in whole on grounds that my findings do not apply to this country." In disgust he emphasized, "This rejection is a direct contradiction of the university's emphasis on diversity, globalism, academic freedom, and service to a wider community. If this is not a contradiction," he stressed, "these emphases must be for particular professionals, not the entire population of the professoriate and, needless to say, such narrow focus is a shame and a disgrace."

One respondent resented the fact that in her predominantly white institution, when it came to people of color, promotion and tenure decisions were influenced strongly by notions of congeniality, likability, power structure, hidden agendas, subjectivity, conformity and/or acquiescence to authority. She resented such an improper evaluation process as these notions were not established criteria for promotion and tenure decision making.[17]

Flabbergasted by his research findings, his own experiences notwithstanding, Darrell called as many respondents as he could to discuss his survey further. One point not included in his questionnaire was whether respondents were familiar with the academic works of their administrators relative to areas such as justice and equality. His findings in this regard, although not totally new, shocked him further. He found that a considerable number of administrators who steadfastly impeded the hiring and promotion of professors, staff and administrators from under-represented groups were articulate speakers and prolific writers regarding equality, justice, fairness, and inclusiveness. "These are among the strongest advocates of social justice, at least in their speeches and writings," one person informed. Another said a number of white administrators in her university had written extensively about social justice, democratic equality, the Rawlsian theory of justice as fairness, and Critical Theory, specifically, critical theory as expounded by Max Horkheimer regarding liberating people from circumstances that enslave them. It was further revealed in the telephone conversations that one person had written a dissertation regarding methodologies and justifications for deconstructing racism in higher education; this work earned him a position in a predominantly white university where he did everything but promote equality, be it on the basis of race, gender, or anything else.

As Darrell listened to respondents to his survey narrate their experiences, he took notes quickly but shook with amazement. Cognizant that these hypocritical practices did not apply to all white administrators, he nonetheless occasionally whispered, "My, my, my!" At another time he murmured, "Life

---

[17] Ibid

truly is a conundrum and people are an enigma; may Heaven forgive us all!"

In addition to reviewing and cataloging the views of respondents and following up with telephone calls, Darrell continued to review the literature extensively; this included hours he spent surfing the web. For instance, cognizant that he did not coin the terms "white privilege," he surveyed the literature on the concept, focusing on a variety of definitions and examples. Likewise, he went over terms and concepts such as "white nationalism," "the white culture," "denial of social justice," "social closure," "abstract liberalism," "cultural racism," and "blaming the victim mentality." In like manner, he thoroughly reread critical race theory. In addition, his review led him to concepts such as "the token appointment," and "institutionalized racism." Understanding these concepts gave him a clearer insight regarding the forces against him and others from under-represented groups in PWUs.

Darrell's understanding widened further as he reviewed the literature with emphasis on the experiences of people of color in predominantly white institutions. Along those lines, for instance, one study[18] presented a literature review and synthesis of 252 publications covering a twenty year period. Among many others, it was found that faculty of color remained seriously underrepresented throughout the nation as they made up only 17% of total full-time faculty.

Another study[19] synthesize over 40 years of research and literature to discuss the intersectionality between race and privilege as it related to the need for diverse and equitable leadership in higher education. Among other things, the study underscored inequitable distribution of power along racial lines in higher education especially in predominantly white institutions. Therefore, the study posited a need to acknowledge and extract systematic oppression in such institutions.

---

[18] Turner et al, 2008.

[19] Wolfe and Dilworth, 2015.

Darrell's review led him to another study,[20] among several others, which covered the experiences of women of color in higher education. Because of their intersectional identity as both women and people of color, they are marginalized concomitantly along the lines of gender and race. Adding to this view, a study[21] showed how the intersection of gender and race influenced pretenure faculty members' perceptions of the clarity of tenure expectations. Still, another study[22] covering barriers to recruitment and retention of faculty of color, highlighted the experiences of four faculty of color navigating the tenure process in a predominately white research institution. The study found marginalization, racism and sexism as barriers to recruitment and retention. To that end, a study[23] threw light on the issue of retention as it showed that faculty of color were more scrutinized than recognized. To clarify, the study showed such faculty members were simultaneously invisible in that not only were their accomplishments viewed as unimportant but they also experienced a lack of belonging. At the same time, they were hypervisible in that they experienced heightened scrutiny.

Darrell's literature review led him to additional studies covering various issues regarding people of color in predominantly white institutions; these included online harassment of faculty of color as well as the survival and coping mechanisms of people of color in higher education as they dealt with microaggression and other forms of discrimination, marginalization, non-promotion, etc.. However, the experiences of a Native American professor especially struck Darrel. The professor[24]

---

[20] Mensah, 2019.

[21] Lisnic, et al, 2019.

[22] Diggs, et al, 2009.

[23] Settles et al, 2019.

[24] Mato, 2003.

described his first ten years as "horrible years," as they were "distinctly alien and unfriendly." The professor stated that the message he received was "subtle but clear, you are not welcome here."

Darrell was equally amazed by findings from semistructured interviews with forty-three white Millennials regarding their views on diversity. In analyzing responses of the Millennials, the researchers[25] pointed out how the dominant white majority used diversity ideology to maintain and perpetuate dominance and inequitable distribution of power. For instance, they pointed out that institutional practices and policies promulgated under colorblind ideology "fail to challenge existing racial practice and oppressive norms; but rather seeks to accommodate present inequalities and divisions by casting them in a positive light." It is further contended that colorblind ideology sees "whiteness as property" and therefore "it rationalizes contemporary racial inequality as the result of nonracial dynamics." Besides, this ideology's insistence that "everyone be treated without regard to race" is tantamount to a denial of "the causes and consequences of racism." Stated differently, colorblind ideology accentuates the notion of "racism without racists."

Alongside the preceding, Darrell's literature survey led to four tenants of diversity ideology, namely, diversity as acceptance, commodity, intent, and liability.[26] Essentially, diversity as acceptance implies that the ruling powers accept the notion of diversity but do nothing to address issues of power asymmetry. This ideology therefore contributes to oppression as it supports maintenance of the racial hierarchy.

Diversity as commodity refers to the fact that the dominant white majority endorses diversity only because it helps them learn something. In other words, diversity is tolerated only when it benefits whites but such whites do not have "to focus on the structural disadvantages that people of color are

---

[25] Burke et al, 2017

[26] Ibid

likely to experience" nor do whites concern themselves with issues of power distribution or equity.

Diversity as intent requires the ruling majority to only have an intent to diversify and be inclusive. Therefore, as seen in strategic plans, goal statements, etc., they use the language of diversity to reflect a sense of justice and equality. In other words, they express an intent as to how the institution should be without making further efforts to ensure same. Thus, this ideology maintains the status quo with no equitable results because it emphasizes intent, not structural change.

The ruling majority sees diversity as liability because, as they see it, diversity has many shortcomings. For instance, diversity is regarded as being "incompatible with other values, such as meritocracy." Furthermore, diversity is regarded as a liability because, for example, admitting people of color in predominantly white institutions places on onus on whites to accept and/or interact with them.

Once more, findings from the literature left Darrell shaking his head. Yet, he was determined to delineate approaches to solving, or at the very least, minimizing the problem. To that end, he was fortunate to get sagacious suggestions from respondents to his survey as well as from his literature review.

In advocating a compelling need to include people from under-represented groups in PWUs, Darrell was mindful of the fact that, to a considerable extent, "people of color" were often part of the problem, not always the poor innocent victims. Furthermore, he was careful in outlining solutions in light of the finding that a number of "people of color" had outlined advantages and disadvantages of both marginalization and inclusion. Additionally, he was cognizant of the fact that the need and method of incorporation differed among groups and sometimes within groups. Similarly, he was aware that some of the "so-called solutions" to problems of marginalization, non-retention, non-promotion, etc., of people from under-represented groups in higher education exacerbated rather than minimized the problem thereby maintaining or worsening the status quo. These verities were the basis of his refusal to outline stringent and specific approaches to incorporation. However, he was comfortable with some broad approaches and strategies for including people from under-represented groups in PWUs. After his survey, Darrell wrote an extensive narrative highlighting the findings of his study and delineating strategies for including, retaining, and promoting people from under-represented groups in predominantly white universities. The cogent points in his narrative were presented to a colloquium comprised of professors and lecturers from under-represented groups and administrators from various universities. The gist of his presentation follows.

The aim of this survey was to discover experiences as well as outline the views of people from under-represented groups, PFUGs IN PREDOMINANTLY WHITE UNIVERSITIES, PWUs. It was conceptualized that findings from this survey would be crucial in both our advocacy for incorporation and in advising PFUGs who already work in and those interested in working in PWUs.

An initial challenge in advocating incorporation of PFUGs into PWUs is a consideration of justification. To that end, it is realized that although The Civil Rights Movement, laws, and judicial mandates paved the way for the incorporation of all races into the professoriate, and although minimal successes were realized in that regard, the truth remains that stiff barriers still exclude Blacks and other racial and ethnic groups from PWUs. This is particularly true of women frequently referred to as 'women of color'. Thus, although we are cognizant of arguments emphasizing the merits and demerits of marginalization, it is postulated that such barriers must be removed to enhance access to, and promote equal treatment within, all institutions of higher education but especially in predominantly white universities, PWUs, where these barriers rigidly marginalize people from under-represented groups. This is impelling in light of existing anti-discrimination laws, the increasing changes in the nation's demographic picture, and in line with the inescapable reality of not only a rapid trend toward globalization, but the fact that we now live in a global village.

Indeed, it is difficult to deny that the demography of the nation is changing rapidly. A quick review of the literature or surfing of the web shows that currently, more than one-third of the nation's population comprises people from various under-represented groups. The largest of these groups are Hispanics followed by African-Americans. If demographic projections are right, in about four decades, more than fifty percent of the nation's population will constitute people from under-represented groups thereby rendering them the majority. Hence, it behooves PWUs to attract, rather than avoid students from under-represented groups. Accordingly, PWUs must not only establish programs and centers to accommodate this influx of students but must also recruit lecturers, professors, and administrators from under-represented groups. Beyond the fact that these professionals will reflect the new demographic blend, they will serve as role models although in reality, "serving as role models" ought not to be a requirement. More importantly, these professionals will bring to the academic and intellectual arena, new, different, and dynamic perspectives from their racial, ethnic, cultural, and national backgrounds. Doubtless, as the literature amply shows, this diversity will enrich academia and maximize its productivity.

Naturally, recruitment is the means by which people from under-represented groups (PFUGs) can be incorporated into PWUs as students and professionals-professionals who serve as staff members, lecturers, professors, and administrators. Consequently, the hiring of such persons must be genuine, aggressive, and continuous, not on the basis of tokenism, self-gratification, or simply for purposes of meeting the letter of the law. Failure to do so will put PWUs at the risk of violating anti-discrimination laws. Regrettably, this is precisely what a considerable number of PWUs have done and continue to do; this trend must change. Moreover, exclusionary policies and practices of PWUs make such universities to miss talented teachers, researchers, community workers, and administrators with different abilities and from varied racial and ethnic backgrounds. To cite one example from history, imagine if Woodrow Wilson, FDR, Edison, and Einstein had been discriminated against and excluded because of their learning or physical problems; what a loss it would have been.

In addition, if PWUs are to incorporate people from diverse racial and ethnic backgrounds, their traditional criteria for hiring have to be revisited, revised, and rendered amenable to promoting diversity. This is because many of the recruitment requirements are not only deliberately excogitated to exclude people from under-represented groups but they are not good predictors of success in higher education.

Furthermore, it is absolutely bogus to maintain that PWUs cannot find qualified people of color. This is nothing less than a cop-out. These are the same institutions which rigorously seek talented athletes from under-represented groups and use such athletes to institutional advantage while they overlook high caliber academic students from similar under-represented backgrounds. Yes, they use those athletes like dishcloths and dispose of them after a few years because less than two percent of college athletes become professional players.

Doubtless, highly qualified professionals from under-represented groups are available. If predominantly white universities sought such professionals as they seek talented athletes from under-represented backgrounds, they would surely find them. Besides, if PWUs truly want to include such persons, they can easily develop a pipeline for them toward the professoriate and administration in higher education. For example, by providing doctoral studies assistanceship and by mentoring such persons in and through doctoral programs, their ranks will soar in the professoriate. This is precisely what's done for white students but, with very few exceptions, students from under-represented groups are not availed to such opportunities. This indefensible denial is partly because administrators in PWUs do not want anything or anyone to threaten their racial and masculine hegemonic authority. This point is illustrated by the failure of SAU to offer graduate assistanceship to students from under-represented groups.

A quick survey shows that Southwest Achval University (SAU) has a total of 347 positions for graduate assistants, GAs. For students from under-represented groups, the breakdown is as follows: African-Americans, 14 or 4%; Hispanics, 12 or 3.4%; Asians, 10 or 2.8%; other, 5 or 1.4%; total, 41 or 11.8%, implying that 88.2% are Caucasians. No Native Americans or students with documented disabilities hold a graduate assistanceship (GA). Moreover, of the 41 GA positions allocated to students from under-represented groups, only 5 or 1.4% are doctoral assistanceships.

Lamentably, regarding PWUs, the statistics from SAU are the rule, not the exception. It therefore goes without saying that, if not changed, and changed drastically, such numbers will contribute minimally to the incorporation of PFUGs into PWUs.

In advocating incorporation, we are aware of, and truly appreciate the establishment of offices, centers, and institutes for ethnic, racial, gender, national, and/or international studies. Such centers are symbolic of the move toward diversity. As students of color enroll in PWUs, these centers are necessary to enhance accommodation and provide programs that would meet their needs. However, one notices sadly that these centers, like the people they are intended to serve, are marginalized within the universities in which they are established. Worse, these centers often are seen as ends in themselves. This is the case when PWU administrators recruit token candidates, establish such centers, and thereafter throw their hands in the air and scream, "We have done our part and that's it." Put differently, it is unconscionable to use token recruits and ethnic studies centers to camouflage racist policies and obviate diversity by keeping out people from under-represented groups. Hence, if PWUs truly want to diversify, and it is to their benefit to do so, they must avoid token recruitments and the establishment of symbolic centers.

Alongside the advocacy for avoiding tokenism, it is difficult to overemphasize the fact that much needs to be done to retain people from under-represented groups in PWUs. The universities need to create an inviting and welcoming atmosphere in which everyone, including women and people from under-represented groups (PFUGs), feels welcomed, valued, appreciated, and has an opportunity to excel on the basis of merit, and irrespective of race, ethnicity, gender, sexual orientation, disability, and any other criteria.

In line with the foregoing, it is a grievous mistake for PWUs to advocate skin color blindness. Such orientation not only contradicts the establishment of racial and ethnic studies centers but it also detracts from varied racial, ethnic, and national realities. The needs of various racial and ethnic groups must be seen clearly, acknowledged and addressed effectively, not ignored as if they do not exist. Similarly, higher education in general and, in particular, predominantly white institutions MUST genuinely and effectively foster structural changes to address the manner and extent to which people of color are marginalized, treated contemptuously, rated unfairly, and denied equitable distribution of power. Many scholars of color have offered recommendations to that end and indeed, the literature is replete with similar suggestions.

In reechoing the loud vociferous voices for change, I contend that predominantly white institutions must understand that, to retain professors and lecturers from diverse racial and ethnic backgrounds, PWUs need to revisit the traditional criteria and methods for promotion and tenure. For example, some community services rise to the level of scholarship. Besides, working among people of one's race or ethnicity is not necessarily self-service; any service to the nation has broader than local implications. Likewise, scholarship need not be measured on a single rod. In like manner, by now, administrations in PWUs ought to know that student evaluations have never been characterized as the best measures of teaching effectiveness. They are ineffective instruments in that regard and therefore objectionable when influenced further by biases of students toward professors who look and/sound differently. This is not to be misconstrued as a clamor to jettison student evaluations; rather, the advocacy is that such evaluations be only a part, possibly a small part of the overall process of assessing teaching. Other methods to be considered include peer evaluation and the use of trained evaluators of teaching efficacy.

Equally crucial is the finding that incorporation of people from under-represented groups is not satisfied only by the number of such persons in higher education. When they are incorporated, they must participate in power-sharing and key decision making. Relegating such persons to junior positions except for token administrators in high positions does not ensure true diversity.

It is equally important to reiterate and reemphasize the point that, to promote diversity and maximize its positive consequences, the administration must vigorously recruit students, staff, professors, and administrators from under-represented groups and create a positive and inviting campus climate for all races. Such a climate will encourage people of color to come and stay at the university; otherwise, the attrition rate for same will be high and, unfortunately, this is the prevailing situation. For example, professors of color hired are often treated contemptuously and therefore tend to move on; administration can, and ought to do all it can to retain all professors, including those from under-represented groups. Of course, it is in the best interest of the university for all professors, including those from under-represented groups, to perform superbly and abide by university policies and guidelines; those who cannot meet these requirements will not be retained. However, this does not, and must not lead to over-scrutiny of people of color on the basis of likability, congeniality, and conformity. Similarly, they must not be rated on account of their races, ethnic backgrounds, or any criteria unrelated to their performances in the three areas of assessment.

Likewise, administration will do well to insist on quality performances by faculty but also remove barriers to tenure and promotion for all professors especially those from under-represented groups. It also helps to minimize, preferably eliminate the isolation of such professors thereby eradicating their feeling of 'otherness'. Naturally, this means removing discriminatory behaviors and racial biases against people of color in the professoriate. These horrible vices have lingered so long in predominantly white universities that they are engrained in the systems of such institutions. As a result, removing such vices seems impossible but where there is a moral and political will, it can be done.

In addition to the foregoing, it behooves administrators in higher education to work amicably and respectfully with the faculty; this is because the faculty are the engines that propel the college or university while administration guides and directs this propelled movement. In that light, the administration of a university ought to raise faculty morale with the aim of achieving four things among the faculty: loyalty to the university, devotion to program or programs, commitment to students, and service to the university as well as to local, national, international, and professional communities. A deficit in any or all these areas will likely hurt the university or college in more ways than can be enumerated.

In a similar vein, it behooves faculty unions to work amicably with the administration. Instead of doing so, and instead of fighting tenaciously and incessantly for their members where such members' rights are infringed, such unions usually engage in endless criticism of the administration thereby fueling the ire of management to the detriment of the faculty. No doubt, there are many reasons to criticize such administrative systems and, to be fair, unions occasionally fight for their members and even win. However, criticism of the administration ought to be cautiously and strategically meted out. In fact, the administration ought to be lauded where such praise is truly deserved, even if such instances are few and far in between. In other words, the faculty union ought to convey the message and conviction to management that, "We are working together in the interest of the institution, students, employees, and the grater community but, in that endeavor, we insist that you treat our members with respect, fairness, and with appreciation for their efforts." If, on the other hand, the union takes an antagonizing posture, it only invites a dog-eat-dog battle in which the administration insists on increasing salaries and benefits for its members while shamelessly fighting to minimize payments and benefits to the faculty. In response, faculty members selfishly fight to increase their incomes and benefits with no regard to losses to the administration. In the long run, the faculty get the short end of the stick. Put succinctly, there must be some degree of cooperation, collaboration, and mutual respect even where there is mutual suspicion, apprehension, and mistrust.

Before ending this presentation, I must briefly direct a comment or two to people from under-represented groups hired in PWUs. I refer to my father's advice in admonishing them to work sedulously. My father often used the trite but true statement that, "There is no easy way to success." It is therefore important to collaborate among ourselves and others willing to work with us in the professoriate. My wife and other women are shining examples in this regard; that is, they found success in working with other women regardless of race and ethnicity.

Furthermore, if we are to succeed in PWUs, we cannot and must not be our own worst enemies; we must not hurt ourselves with mediocre performance, violating university regulations and policies, and blaming everyone but ourselves when we fail.

Doubtless, I am cognizant of our challenges. I know the sad truth; that is, when one considers the extent to which African-Americans and others from under-represented groups have progressed, the progress, no matter how measured, is minimal. In fact, some statistical evidence seems to suggest deterioration. For example, considering the percentage of African-Americans within the nation's population, while a good percentage now comprises high school and college graduates, the number incarcerated is appalling. Yet, there has been some progress and with progress comes responsibility and we must live up to this challenge.

In meeting the numerous challenges of our time, especially in PWUs, we cannot afford intra-and-inter-group fighting. It therefore will be asinine for blacks to antagonize one another on the basis of shades of skin color, accents (for people from the south and those who are not U.S. born), etc.. This is no different from other forms of racism. Similarly, we need not reject others on account of race, ethnicity, and nationality. For example, some are angry when blacks support other racial and ethnic groups for they argue that such groups hate blacks. Likewise, women from certain ethnic groups maintain that no one oppresses them more than their men. While such arguments might have merits, they are nonetheless divisive. Instead of such in-fighting and succumbing to fissiparous tendencies, considering the manner and extent of our isolation and marginalization as a group, we need a united front if we are to succeed in PWUs. Again, this advocacy does not imply in any way that we must not differ or disagree on various issues. Rather, I only appeal that we be united when it comes to our survival and success in PWU for there is power in unity.

Additionally, in working in PWUs, we must be mindful of cliques and intra-and-inter departmental rivalries. Often, falling in one camp automatically implies being an enemy of the other. Of course, each one of us has a choice and a right to belong but if your aim is to excel in the professoriate, be sure to focus on the activities that will enhance your objectives, not deter them.

Finally, I am aware of efforts aimed at emasculating, even eliminating Affirmative Action and laws that open doors for us despite supportive court cases. As an economist, I am aware of conservative African-American economists who join others in blaming us. Similarly, I am aware of publications that throw out statistical data to underscore the point that indeed, diversity exists in higher education including PWUs. Therefore, we who advocate genuine diversity, social justice, and insist on nothing less than equality are only noise makers, a disgruntled few, a disloyal, rebellious, rancorous, even riotous group, and a noxious set of unreasonable captious citizens. These detractors must not hurt us; rather, we must tighten our belts, work sedulously toward diversity and ensure our proper places in higher education, even in predominantly white institutions, PWIs. In this regard, we cannot afford to despair as many set examples for us to emulate. The long list of such persons goes from Alexander Twilight, the first black person to receive a degree from a U.S. college in 1823, to Mary Jane Patterson who, in 1862, became the first black woman to earn a degree in the U. S., to W.E.B. Du Bois, the first black person who, in 1895, earned a doctorate from Harvard. Many other African-Americans, Hispanics, Asians, Native Americans, and people with disabilities were pioneers whose struggles and successes must invigorate us. Whatever our challenges, and however difficult they may be, we must embrace and transcend this rich legacy.

Chapter XIV:

A PITIFUL PAINFUL PURSUIT

B orn and raised in the south, Darrell was not a stranger
to racism, discrimination, and segregation. He however
thought the racism he experienced was nothing compared to
those experienced by Native Americans, African-Americans,
Hispanics, and others who lived decades before him. For
instance, he was saddened and at the same time amazed to learn
of his grandfather's experiences in the south as a black person
in the Jim Crow era. In like manner, during his under-graduate
years, he was touched by the experiences of two elderly gentlemen, Mr. Vasquez and Mr. Howard; the latter preferred to
be called Big Billy. These senior citizens taught him crucial
lessons. From them, he learned that racism was chronic to the
nation and that justice was an elusive phenomenon. Further,
he learned that life was replete with bumps and bruises but
each bump and bruise ought to make one a better and stronger
person; each ought to buttress one's resolve to continue life's
bumpy ride without ever giving up. "Sometimes," his grandfather once said, "I honestly feel sorry for people who deliberately hurt or abuse me only because I am black. I believe
they have a problem, not me." He said that must be the reason
why the good book called on everyone to pray for those who
hurt them.

As Darrell grew older and encountered his own experiences, his grandfather's words became increasingly didactic. This was particularly true during and after his gruesome experience at SAU and following his extensive survey of other professors and lecturers in predominantly white universities, PWUs.

As his children were getting older—Darrell Dwayne or D3, the oldest just turned twelve and Nabea, the youngest was six—Darrell began to combine these teachings with his own experiences as the bases for instructing his children. Moreover, the powerful, albeit informal instructions he received during his childhood, adolescent and young adult years were invigorating as he was determined to attain the rank of a full professor, racist policies and attitudes notwithstanding.

In the first semester of his seventh year, Darrell followed through with his plans and took a sabbatical leaf in a renowned university; the schools Department of Economics was one of the most prestigious in the country. He learned a lot during his sabbatical as he taught two courses and extensively conducted research. The administrators were so impressed with him that they offered him a tenure track position in the university. Before talking with Vanessa, he knew he could not accept the offer. For one thing, he knew that, as a private institution, the university rarely offered tenure. For another thing, he did not want to move the family. Besides, as he saw it, the university was not less racist than SAU although the two schools were miles apart in terms of academic standards, size, fiscal might, favorable national and international reputation, and professional collaboration among colleagues. He therefore politely thanked the authorities and said he was flattered by the offer but could not take it. In a phone conversation, Vanessa concurred quickly.

In many ways, the sabbatical leaf was stressful for Darrell had never left his family for any length of time beyond two or three days attending professional conferences. Although he, Vanessa and the children talked every night, they missed him dearly. He too missed his family. A couple of visits to see the children and return visits by Vanessa helped but they could not wait for him to return to them. From a professional perspective, the sabbatical was extremely successful. Darrell collected enormous data for conference presentations, publication, and public speeches. Yes, he was now invited often to speak in many social, community, and professional fora.

The data Darrell collected during his sabbatical leaf, the enormous free time he had, and the support he received from experts in his field combined to bolster his publications. He and a couple of nationally and internationally renowned economists wrote two articles which were submitted for publication before he returned to Achval. Shortly after he returned, he completed his second book. While he truly liked the articles he co-authored, he was very impressed with his book. Although he did not consider it his magnum opus, he predicted it would do well in the professional world, at least he hoped so.

Upon returning to Achval, Darrell kept his nose to the grindstone in his avid determination to gain full professorship. His zeal, coupled with his extensive work with students of color, often uncharacteristically kept him away from the family and this was causing a strain on his marriage. At times, he could barely talk with Vanessa and the children. He missed family meals, and this frequently forced Vanessa to make excuses on his behalf to the children. He went to bed late, and got out early. One evening, when the children went to bed, Vanessa demanded a discussion.

"Oh, oh," Darrell exclaimed, "I remember in college, when you said you wanted to talk, it meant something serious. Am I in trouble?"

Vanessa was not smiling. Sternly, she told him how he was forsaking her and the children in his rigid pursuit of full professorship. "Do you mean this is more important than your health, wife, and children? When last did you see your doctor despite the high blood pressures and other health complications you and I have incurred? When was the last time you talked with the old folks down south?" She started sobbing softly.

Darrell struggled to control his anger. Of all people, he could not fathom his wife's failure to understand his pursuit. "But Honey, this is not only for me; it is for you and the children. Beyond that, it achieved, it will be another conquest for African-Americans."

Vanessa was not buying what she described as "that crap." She emphasized he would not be the first, nor the last, African-American to gain full professorship so if he wanted to make history, he had to look elsewhere. Besides, she thought nothing ought to matter more than his health and family. She was very angry as she pointed out his selfishness.

Vanessa's points were not just accusatory but poignantly truthful; Darrell could not avoid the vividness, veracity, and vehemence of her argument. He began to sob mildly. "I'm sorry Honey; you are absolutely right; I have been selfish, self-centered, and inconsiderate." He said he would give up pursuing full professorship as tenure and the rank of associate professor were enough.

Darrell's frank admission calmed Vanessa. He went over and put his hands around her as tears still streamed down her face. He apologized repeatedly and said seeing her cry hurt him more than anything. "You and the children are everything to me. I'm sorry Honey, truly sorry; please forgive me." He began to sob again.

Vanessa stood up and hugged her husband. "You are the greatest thing to us Baby and I just could not imagine you being selfish; it's just not like you." She said he did not have to abandon his ambition of becoming a full professor but only needed to balance his pursuit with proper health care and family responsibilities as he had always done. Then she broke his heart. "Because you were very aloof, we could not tell you news from Ghetahzia and the folks from there said they could not reach you on your phone." She started weeping again. "I'm sorry Baby but your mother is grievously ill; the doctor does not think she will make it."

Darrell dropped his hands and flung into a seat. As if that was not enough, he sat on the floor with both legs stretched forward. He raised his hands in the air. "What! When? Why? Why?" Tears ran down his face. Vanessa revealed that the children already knew; only he did not as he never gave her a chance to tell him in an appropriate way.

As this was not the time to play the blame game, Vanessa quickly focused on consoling her husband. She knelt next to him and put her hands around him as she explained the details. "The doctor thinks despite the magnitude of the problem, she may be with us for another four to six months."

Oh Honey," Darrell sobbed on, "I cannot imagine losing my mother." He promised to fly down in a day or two, as soon as he could get a reservation.

When Darrell's plane touched down, Zack and Elayne were waiting for him. When he saw them, he broke down again. The two put their hands around their brother and comforted him. "You cannot cry around Mom," Elayne insisted. She said Mom was taking it very well as she saw death as going to her Lord.

"We have all cried our eyes out," Zack informed. "Dad has been especially difficult to calm. As you know, Mom means everything to him as she is to all of us."

Darrell's tears continued to flow endlessly. Instead of driving directly to the family home, Zack stopped briefly at Elayne's for his brother to wash his face and freshen up.

Throughout the visit, Darrell was strong although when he and his father were together, they both cried interminably. On the other hand, Mama Clara was encouraging. She was full of words of wisdom.

Darrell visited a few days and flew back to Achval. Immediately after summer school, he and the family drove to Ghetahzia. By then, Mama Clara's condition was deteriorating. Within a fortnight after they arrived, she passed away quietly at home while her children, husband, and children-in-law stood helplessly around her bed.

Friends and family from far and near attended Mama Clara's funeral. The attendees included the mayor and entire city council of Ghetahzia. Many spoke passionately about her love and caring spirit. Her husband Dwayne spoke only a few minutes. He said his life would never be the same without Clara and in fact, he did not see how he could continue life without her. Darrell, the youngest, gave the eulogy in a river of tears. It was truly touching.

Without Mama Clara, it was a melancholy summer. Darrell, Vanessa and the children did not want to stay very long but to comfort Dwayne, they spent another two weeks.

Back in Achval, nothing seemed to matter to Darrell, not even full professorship. He went through his eighth year without publishing a single article; he attended professional conferences minimally. Without a doubt, in terms of performance, professional output, and overall enthusiasm and zest for life, this was his most lousy year since coming to SAU. In his ninth year, he resumed writing but even then, not with the same vigor and enthusiasm. Eventually, in his twelfth year, and after substantially strengthening his resume in areas of publication, grant writing, conference presentations, and overall service, he applied for promotion to full professorship.

There were major changes in the leadership personnel throughout the university by the time Darrell applied. To the relief of most people, Dr. Peggy Chance, the great Jezebel, had retired. Moreover, the university had a new president and provost. Similarly, Darrell had a new department chair, Dr. Arthur Davis, and a new dean, Dr. Joshua Peterson. These new leaders did not indicate, in any way, they were better in race relations than their predecessors. Darrell therefore did not expect much support; he hoped however, his record would win his battle.

Darrell was the first to admit he had one lousy year. Consistently, he said his eighth year at SAU was definitely infested with lice. He therefore described the year as pediculous, but his wife said it was a pernicious year that was to stand "accursed in the calendar."

Despite one lousy year, Darrell's dossier was impressive. He obtained strong letters of support; three strongly worded letters came from the school where he took his sabbatical. Yet, he was rejected by his department committee and chair. The college committee and dean gave tepid support and so did the university committee. The provost rejected his application outright. Rejection of Darrell's application did not surprise him. No matter what his survey revealed and although he made the results of his survey available to the authorities at SAU in addition to a number of intellectual for a, the university continued to use traditional, often arbitrary standards for evaluation. Even then, he perceived a miscarriage of justice for if he were rated honestly, his performances in the areas of teaching, service, and research were more than adequate to pilot him smoothly to full professorship.

Although Darrell's rejection was not a surprise, it discouraged him tremendously especially in light of his conviction that he was treated unjustly. Thus, uncharacteristically, he threw in the tower. Part of this was because the university hired new people and it seemed the more new people, the more stonewalls he faced. Andy and others who supported him had retired making it an even more lonely community. Nevertheless, Vanessa encouraged him not to give up. "It is not like you to capitulate in the face of challenge Honey; why begin now?"

Vanessa was right. Darrell had come too far to give up. He therefore decided to wait two or three years before reapplying. This waiting period was a bitter sweet one. Sweet in that he won several local, state and national awards because of his community work, teaching, and writing. He published in prestigious journals and presented papers in national and international professional for a. On the other hand, he was deeply saddened by the loss of some of the dearest people to him. Within a year of losing his mother, his father passed away. Shortly after that, he lost Prof. Kwame. He and Vanessa took these losses very hard.

Meanwhile, as some of the children were in college, Vanessa's mother moved to live with them.

In his fourteenth year at SAU, Darrell was preparing his dossier for what he considered his final attempt to gain full professorship when a visitor knocked on his door. He looked up and there stood Dr. Commings. "May I come in?"

"Of course," Darrell replied as he stood up to receive the visitor. "It's a pleasure to see you Sir. How are you and what brings the professor to my humble office?"

Professor Commings took a seat. He looked pretty serious and this made Darrell wonder. "May I close the door?" Commings asked. Without answering, Darrell walked to the door and closed it before taking a seat across the table from Prof. Commings who was dressed in what Darrell considered an old-fashion jacket. Darrell fiercely fought back laughter as he thought even Commings' tie looked funny and certainly did not match his jacket. Growing increasingly curious, he shifted his focus from Commings' outfit to the professor himself.

"I understand you are preparing to apply for full professorship," Commings said. Darrell nodded in agreement but wondered how Commings found out. "I am here to tell you that I will support you with all my heart." He paused as his eyes flickered and became teary. Darrell could not understand.

"I am sure you are wondering why I am supporting you."

"You're not kidding; I am dying to know," Darrell confirmed.

Commings' teary eyes turned into a sob and this only compounded Darrell's curiosity, perhaps bewilderment. "I am an old man now," Commings confessed and he was not joking for he certainly looked it. He said he had been at SAU for many years. "During all these years, the powers that be have used me to do their dirty works. Frankly, I have hurt more people than I can count and all these years, I thought I was just being fair." He disclosed he got nothing out of his dirty works and now old and fighting cancer, he wanted to do something right.

Darrell finally understood. He felt terribly sorry for Commings. "I'm truly sorry to hear that. I thank you for pledging support but frankly, as you and I know, I do not think a letter of support will do much. I have been turned down once and have no doubt will be turned down again. I am prepared to go for arbitration and if that fails, I will give up and work toward retirement."

Commings stopped sobbing as he gently wiped his face. He once more expressed deep regrets for being led by the nose against his people. "Sometimes," he disclosed, "I honestly thought my actions would put my people to the challenge and thereby force them to rise to the occasion. Often, however," he went on, "in all honesty, I also knew I was hurting people." Frankly, I have no excuses. Whatever I did led to nothing good for me; it only ruined my reputation and extricated me from people of my race, background, and ethnicity." Once more, he said he was truly sorry. "As I have said, I got nothing out of the system other than loss of sleep and animosity from others. I do not know why I did all I did. I trusted people unreservedly and thought the feeling was mutual only to find out later that I was leaning on a broken stick. Yes, they eventually showed me their true colors as they used me for their purposes; I'm truly sorry." His eyes became teary again especially when he mentioned he had not mentored anyone although scores of students, staff, and junior faculty needed his support and/or guidance.

Paying no attention to the illogical string of excuses, Darrell comforted his visitor once more. After a lengthy conversation in which Commings disclosed some of the dirty tricks of the system, he left. Darrell could not wait to tell Vanessa.

"This confession not only confirms but transcends all we have heard about this man," Vanessa said after listening to Darrell's encounter with Commings. "I do not want to comment on his regrets and crocodile tears. He must have known he was hurting others." She said although her commitment to the family was a consideration, it was mainly because of Commings that she vowed not to pursue doctoral studies at SAU as he had made it clear that he would not support her. If she went beyond his advice, he would only be agitated the more thereby ensuring her failure. This was lamentable indeed especially since she could not avoid him in the Department of History. "Let him live with his conscience and I sincerely wish him well," she concluded.

In the second semester of his fifteenth year at SAU, Darrell once more filed for full professorship. This time, the department committee voted 3-2 in support and the college committee supported with a 4-3 vote. Letters from the department chair and Dean Peterson still were tepid. The university committee voted 8-3 to support his promotion. Yet, the provost rejected his application. At this time, it really did not matter to Darrell. Nonetheless, he challenged the rejection; he thanked god his collective bargaining agreement included this provision. So, with his challenge, hearings on the matter were scheduled.

After weeks of hearings, Darrell and the university's administration agreed to defer the matter to arbitration. With little help from his union, Darrell went through three arbitration hearings. Sandy, the new director of legal services was brutally aggressive in her determination to deny him promotion. As he learned later, she and the administration were angry with Darrell for conducting what they called a survey intended solely to embarrass them.

At the third hearing, Darrell had had it. He informed the arbitration officers that this would be his last appearance. "I have presented strong and convincing evidence to warrant promotion to full professorship. My dossier is as good as, and in many instances better than, others who gained full professorship in this university and particularly in my department. I have the record to prove it and will publicize it if necessary. Besides, pursuant to our collective bargaining agreement and the guidelines for tenure and promotion, the administration has given no valid reason why I should be denied. I therefore urge this forum to render a decision based on facts, I mean, my record and not on the basis of arbitrary, biased, and/or irrelevant grounds."

The three arbitration officers deliberated for a week turning over facts and numbers. Eventually, they voted 2-1 in favor of

Darrell's promotion. This vote was probably because, consistent with their agreement for arbitration, he and management each selected one arbitrator and the two arbitrators chose a third. Since the decision of the arbitrators was binding, Darrell was promoted. However, it really did not matter to him; the thrill, pride, and joy that would have accompanied promotion were lost in the painful pursuit. He had only continued the pursuit to prove a point and this realization was terribly annoying.

Although he now perceived his promotion differently, he used it to make a point. He called his children together and explained what it took to gain this final promotion. As they were no longer little children, he addressed them like adults for he knew his words would reverberate beyond them. He said, "As my grandfather and parents taught me, I am telling you now that, as long as you live in this country, you will face obstacles, etc., based on racism but do not ever let that discourage or deter you. Besides, do not be suspicious of, and certainly never ever hate people of other races, economic standards, nationalities, and the like; rather, accept each individual as he or she is until that person reveals his or her true character. In addition, in facing racism, you and I must stand on the shoulders of giants before us and make them proud. At the same time, we must insist on justice and equality, support everyone marginalized by the system, and subsequently pave the way for future generations of people from under-represented groups to take their rightful places in society, with race, ethnicity, gender, creed, disability, and the like being no impediments." The children nodded as if to say they fully understood.

Chapter XV:

THE MESSAGE IS CLEAR

L ife's truly an enigma with graduated stages. As we progress through developmental landmarks, we value things,
places, activities, outfits, and even people at each stage but as
we progress, when we look back, some become meaningless,
even absurd. In combination however, these experiences shape
and mold us into whom we become. Darrell's situation was no
exception to this phenomenon.

After obtaining the coveted position of full professor, Darrell
sat quietly in his office and looked back. Was it worth the tortuous effort? Sure, there is some value, a sense of achievement
in becoming a full professor but was it really worth it? Whether
it was, or was not, then what? What had he really accomplished
and what next?

As he could not answer his own question as to what was
next, Darrell's heart sank as he thought of Dr. Coleman, an
African-American professor he met years ago when he was
interviewing for jobs. The brother, who preferred to be called
J. D., said after gaining tenure, he felt locked into an academic
prison. Was this Darrell's fate? He had no answer and thought
it would be necessary to discuss his thoughts with his brilliant wife.

Of course Vanessa did not know what her husband was thinking. Similarly, he had no idea what she was planning. In a marriage, when the left hand does not know what the right hand is doing, at best, the relationship is couched in secrecy; at worst, the doom of separation larks in the distance. Fortunately, Vanessa's secrecy was innocuous.

Aware that Darrell did not want any celebration of his monumental achievement, Vanessa nonetheless planned an elaborate celebratory dinner and dance. Her children, Lupita, and Ann helped enormously.

Invited to the program were very special people to Darrell. These included his and Vanessa's siblings and their families as well as Lamont and David and their families. Also invited were Prof. Kwame's son Mandela, and prof. Andy Barclay who was now retired. Likewise, Vanessa invited the president and provost of the university as well as her college dean and the department chairs from Economics and History. Similarly, all the faculty members from Economics and History were invited although they were informed of the secrecy of the celebration. Regrettably, none from the university showed up with the exception of Lupita, Ann, Professor Commings, and one newly hired African-American assistant professor who was not in their college but admired Darrell for mentoring graduate students and junior faculty members.

As they did with Prof. Kwame's surprise party, everything was secretive. On the day of the celebration, Vanessa promised to take her husband out to dinner and that's how he got to the hall. Needless to say, he was incredibly surprised.

The program was planned meticulously. The children individually congratulated their dad, and so did Darrell's siblings on behalf of their parents. Lamont and David made brief comments and so did Mandela Kwame. Retired prof. Andy Barclay spoke passionately about his association with Darrell and the principles for which they both stood, namely, the quest for justice and equality for all especially in higher education.

After the brief remarks, Nabea introduced her mother to the rousing applause of the audience. With tears streaming down her face, Vanessa congratulated her husband and said how much he meant to her and the children. Darrell was full of tears as he heard his wife, children, and closest friends speak movingly about him.

After Vanessa's remarks, D3 took the microphone and announced, "And now, ladies and gentlemen, Full Professor Darrell Dwayne Thomas, my great, dynamic, and wonderful dad!" the audience erupted again in applause.

"For the first time in years, I am speechless. What can I say?" Darrell started. He said he had only a few words of thanks to God and the many people who touched his life. He remembered his late grandfather and parents, his ever-supportive siblings, the late Prof. Kwame, and the retired Prof. Barclay. He remembered his lifetime friends, Lamont and David whom he called true brothers. He then turned to his family and spoke very warmly about his children but especially about Vanessa. "Without this God-sent angel, I am not sure if, and how I would have completed college but with her unflinching support, I stand before you today; words are inadequate to express my love and appreciation to her." Tears streamed down his face and his daughter Nabea when up and hugged him to comfort him. The audience applauded enthusiastically again.

The remarks were followed by a dance and yes, Darrell and Vanessa still could take a step or two. As they did in college, Lamont and David teased them all evening but not without a reciprocal tease. Indeed, it was a memorable night for Darrell and all who attended.

After obtaining a full professorship status, Darrell relaxed during his sixteenth year at SAU from publications and rigorous professional activities. In his seventeenth year, with their first son D3 headed to graduate school, he resumed rigorous academic work; he just could not stay away from writing as this was his passion. In the second semester of that year, he took another sabbatical; this time, he did not go out of town but conducted research from home and traveled a little.

By the time Darrell and Vanessa started their twentieth year at SAU, he was the second most senior person in his department in terms of longevity. The first person, Prof. Lucretia Dennis, was facing health issues and extremely inactive. Darrell therefore tried knocking on the doors of administration.

Before making any moves, Darrell made an appointment to see his dean, Dr. Joshua Peterson. "It's good to see you Darrell," the dean warmly received his visitor. "How are things with our full professor?"

Darrell did not know what to make of this adulation but refrained from reading too much into it. He simply replied, "So far, so good, we thank God." The dean, at least ten years older than Darrell, was well built and seemed he worked out regularly; he looked very good for his age. He smiled broadly and directed the conversation toward the purpose of the appointment.

"Well, I wanted to see you because I am considering getting into administration, if I am supported," Darrell cut to the chase. He drew the dean's attention to the fact that the college was very large with many opportunities for him to get into administration if his dean supported.

"By all means," the dean concurred. He revealed that Darrell's department chair position would soon be vacant and, like everyone else, Darrell ought to apply if he was interested. Besides, Darrell was right as there were other positions likely to open in the college and throughout the university. "I honestly encourage you to apply when these positions become vacant. You have risen to the position of full professorship and going into administration is definitely a good and logical move." The dean also pointed out that the college and university administrations were not diverse and Darrell's addition to the administration would be one step toward addressing that problem.

Of course, Darrell knew his department chair was leaving at the end of the semester. Likewise, he was aware of the limited diversity in both the college and university but did not want to cite that as a reason lest he be seen as playing the race card. Moreover, as his grandfather taught him, he was seeking a position based on his merit, not his race; if his acquisition of a position would diversify the administration racially, that would be a fringe benefit. He therefore politely thanked the dean and promised to apply.

A few weeks after Darrell's conversation with the dean, the dean notified the department that Dr. Davis was leaving sooner than he thought. The dean appointed an untenured assistant professor of economics as acting department chair. This somewhat surprised Darrell but he rationalized the dean's action on grounds that the dean knew Darrell would be applying for the position. Certainly, this was not the best rationalization but at least for now, it appeased Darrell. Vanessa, on the other hand, was not so convinced. She said the fact that the dean knew Darrell might be applying for the position ought to have been a logical basis for being appointed acting chair. "That way," she argued, "you would be moved easily into the position." Darrell nodded politely but still harbored some doubts. Perhaps, subconsciously, he was denying the truth.

As expected, the dean set up a search committee for a new chair. Darrell applied and submitted all the requirements for the position. He was convinced he had a very good chance; yet, he was neither naïve nor complacent. He admonished Vanessa accordingly, "Knowing the system, I will neither be over-confident nor will anything surprise me; I'm ready for anything."

The committee of four men and one woman, all White, thoroughly reviewed the applications it received. Eventually, in line with the dean's instructions, the committee recommended three finalists unranked; Darrell made the list which did not include a female candidate although two made the second round. Certainly this raised his hopes but he was cautiously optimistic, in fact, suspicious. Psychologically, this was a good posture for ultimately, the position was offered to Dr. Michael

Sunders who received tenure and promotion to associate professorship less than six months earlier.

Without telling her husband "I told you so," Vanessa's words were encouraging. "You were right to be cautiously optimistic," she stated calmly. "The powers that be have shown their true colors again." Darrell nodded in agreement but vowed he would not stop knocking on the doors of administration, at least not for now.

At the end of their twentieth year at SAU, Darrell and Vanessa faced a number of tragedies. First, Darrell's brother Zac died in a horrible accident involving a drunk driver. In addition, Vanessa's mother, who had been ill for a protracted period, passed away. At her request, she was buried down south next to her husband.

Darrell continued to write but had slowed down considerably. By the beginning of his twenty-second year, he was determined to continue his quest for an administrative position. By this time, his children were grown and he and Vanessa were proud grandparents. D3 (28) was married with two children who were named, D4 and Vanessa. Kwame (27) was also married with one daughter, Clara. Dwayne (26) was married with no children yet and Joseph (25) was engaged. Clara Louise or CL (24) was also engaged. The baby, Nabea (22) just graduated from college and landed her first job.

Throughout his twenty-second and twenty-third years, Darrell saw a few internal search advertisements for positions within the university. He ignored most of them but showed interest in a few. In some cases, the positions were not closely related to his background and experience. In other instances, he learned from reliable sources that specific candidates were already earmarked for the positions. There were at least two instances when he showed interest in advertised positions. In both cases, after he filed the necessary papers, he was told the positions were closed only to learn later the same positions were re-advertised.

At the beginning of Darrell's twenty-fourth year, still reluctant to throw in the towel, an internal memo caught his attention; this was a search for someone within the university to serve as vice provost for economic development. The memo said the successful candidate would advise the provost and administration regarding the university's contribution to local, regional, national and international economic development. "Wow!" Darrell exploded excitedly in his office, "I can do that." Knowing he was the most senior professor of economics in the university following the retirement of Professor Dennis, he was very sure of this one. After all, he had published articles, books and book chapters on economic development as related to local, regional, national and international entities. No one in his department came close.

"I still counsel cautious optimism," Vanessa advised. She said if the job was clearly cut out for him, it would have been offered to him. Still excited, Darrell countered that, like other positions, the university had to advertise to fulfill legal requirements. "When have they ever cared about legal requirements?" Vanessa reminded her husband. "I once more maintain that if they really wanted you to have that job, they would have offered it to you and then advertise it afterwards and even so, only if they showed tepid interest in meeting legal requirements."

Darrell was not listening. It seemed his excitement made him both blind to the truth and immune to logic. Thus, with unbending certitude, high hopes, and without paying any attention to his wife, he applied for the position and submitted the required letters of recommendation along with his curriculum vita, or CV. After two weeks, the position was offered to Dr. Sundurs, Darrell's chair who had not gained full professorship. The administration argued Darrell did not have any administrative experience.

"It seems I just cannot win," he told his wife in total disgust. "I am denied an opportunity to get into administration and then I'm told I cannot get a position because I do not have an administration experience. How am I to get such an experience? How did those now in administration begin?" He said he had no malice against Sunders for Sunders, like everyone else, was simply doing all he could to rise in the system. Yet, the truth remained that Sunders had no administrative experience when he was offered the position of department chair; now, he was vice provost.

While Darrell bemoaned his rejection and what he called "gross and indefensible injustice," he was in for more surprise. When the position of department chair became vacant, he thought he had a shot at it but this was not to be. The position was offered to a Caucasian colleague, Dr. Henry Benson, an assistant professor with tenure.

Again, Darrell had no hard feelings toward Dr. Benson; he couldn't. He was sure that, like everyone else, the young assistant professor was seizing every opportunity to inch his way up in the administration. Who wouldn't? However, Darrell was taken aback one day when, before a college faculty meeting started, Dr. Benson sat next to him apparently with the aim of rubbing it in. "They have been asking me for years to serve as department chair and finally, I said, 'yes'," Dr. Benson divulged.

"That was very nice of them as they always know how to choose," Darrell replied. The new department chair turned red in the face, offering no response.

Darrell relayed his encounter with Dr. Benson to Vanessa while sipping tea with her later that evening. He made a last minute observation. "I think I finally got the message; for sure, they do not want me in administration." He therefore vowed to stop trying. He said it proved his research right; that is, in predominately white universities, there was little to no power-sharing except for token appointments of people from under-represented groups and to the powers that be, he was not conformist enough to be considered for any appointments. "When token appointments are made," he reminded his wife, "the administration repeatedly publicizes it as if to say, 'see how fair and inclusive we are'!"

Darrell rationalized that for him, the issue was deeper than he could explain. Citing a few baffling situations, he said when it came to him, seniority was out of the window. Beyond the administration's reluctance to appoint him to administrative positions, he had not been offered the chairmanship of any major committee in the department or college; such were offered to assistant and associate professors. Such positions were offered to him only when no one else wanted them and of course, he refused them under those circumstances.

Vanessa was not absolutely sure. She thought her husband's statement was a generalization since not all predominantly white universities were exactly like SAU in all respects; in fact, no two institutions of higher education were exactly alike. On the other hand, Darrell's statement contained some truth, especially given the specific SAU examples he cited. Nevertheless, she said, "Well Baby, let's just wait and see. If the good Lord intends for you to go into administration, a position will fall in your lap."

"You remind me of my mother," Darrell declared. Before he could say another word, the house phone rang and Vanessa reached for it. "Andy!" she exclaimed excitedly. "Where are you?"

"Enjoying retirement in the best way I can," Andy replied laughing. "That means I sleep whenever I wish and for how long I wish; eating all I can, working when I want to, and that's more than most people think, and traveling as much as I can afford; with my beautiful queen of course," Andy once more laughed. He said talking about traveling, he and his wife Rosemary were coming to Achval in two weeks.

"Definitely you must stay with us; oh no, no hotel or anything like that," Vanessa insisted. "We have lots of room here." Andy accepted the invitation before telling his wife. Later, Darrell talked with him and, like Vanessa, insisted that Andy and Rosemary stop with them. He promised Vanessa would cook Jollof rice which Andy loved. Again, Andy was grateful for the invitation.

Andy and his wife arrived late Friday night. Since they had dinner on the road, Vanessa prepared tea and coffee along with tempting desserts. Tired from the long drive, the Barclays retired for the night. Early the next morning, they got a quick breakfast and took off; they did not make it back for lunch. It seemed impossible to see everyone who invited them.

As promised, Saturday evening, Vanessa prepared a delicious Jollof rice meal along with all kinds of goodies. "My goodness, this was a sumptuous feast," Rosemary praised. Vanessa said she and Darrell were so glad to see her and Andy that they wish they were spending a week. Unfortunately, they had to continue their journey early Monday morning.

After dinner, the two couples had a chance to talk a little as they sipped on wine. "Any improvements at the U?" Andy asked.

"Not a chance," Darrell came back instantaneously. He said race relations were actually deteriorating at the university. "If you can believe that," he murmured. He sipped on his wine glass before adding, "There is just no political will to effect any constructive change in race relations." To clarify, he said, for more than twenty-five years, he had served on diversity committees at both college and university levels and some of the committees were very large. From different perspectives, the committees outlined strategies for increasing diversity at the university. Likewise, for years, he served on strategic planning committees from which diversity was touted as a university priority, indeed a paramount necessity. Yet, the statistics regarding diversity at the university remained constant at best while in most instances, they retrogressed, sometimes considerably. "This is because, despite all that is said and written, there is no political will to make a difference. As someone penned in the literature, we only have diversity as intent but no constructive effort to institute structural changes."

"What is your specific situation like?"

Darrell said nothing had changed. To him, two things were clear. First, he had no doubt the university did not want him in administration. Second, he regretted that the usual courtesies of seniority were not extended to him. In instances where he should get priority in the selection or scheduling of courses, preference was given to assistant and associate professors. Furthermore, he still faced isolation and endured many instances of disrespect and outright insults, not only from administrators and colleagues but even from secretaries, graduate assistants, and other students. Of course, he did not let any abuse or rude behavior get away unchecked. He would not allow any violation of his rights or any insults and rude behaviors to get away with impunity, regardless of the sources of such behaviors. What was frustrating and totally incomprehensible was the fact that some of these behaviors occurred in the first place. "The thing is, Andy," he continued venting his frustration, "often, the chair and dean are appraised of these incidents but do absolutely nothing."

"I know," Andy affirmed. "Their constant inaction sends a message to staff, faculty, and students. It's truly disgusting." Darrell could not agree more.

Sunday was another busy day for the Barclays but later that evening, they took Darrell and Vanessa out to a nice restaurant. It was nice to hear about their experiences in retirement. Early the next morning, after a nice breakfast, they got on the road.

In his twenty-seventh year, another tragedy struck. Darrell's sister, Deborah was diagnosed with a fatal illness and was going fast. Darrell made it to Ghetahzia in time to talk a little with his sister but they lost her. She left her husband with four children. No doubt, this was another sad moment for the family.

Back in Achval, Darrell kept working steadily. In his twenty-eighth year, the position of associate dean for administration became vacant again in his college for which the dean preferred an internal search. "I know I had vowed never to try again but have nothing to lose so I will give it one last shot," he told Vanessa. He applied again but the result was the same; the position was offered to someone his junior.

"I have had it," Darrell snapped. "I will not apply for another position till I retire and if I am offered one, which is extremely doubtful, I will not accept because I am sure such will not be a genuine offer. I will not allow them to use me for their purposes." He insisted that what happened to him at the university was by design, not by chance so there was no need knocking his head against the wall.

About three months after Darrell's last failed attempt to get into administration, he received a phone call from the dean's secretary asking him to attend a meeting with the dean. "What is this about?" Darrell inquired. The secretary said she was only asked to set up the appointment. "The good Lord willing, I will be there," he told the secretary in laughter as he hung up.

"Thanks for coming Darrell," the dean greeted. "Would you like some coffee? Jimmy makes wonderful coffee and I do have two cups for coffee-drinking visitors."

"What happens if you have more than two visitors? Does that mean you watch your coffee-drinking visitors display their coffee-drinking artistry?"

"Oh no," the dean laughed. "If I'm serving, I always serve myself first. If Jimmy, my dependable secretary is serving, he is instructed strictly to serve me first. You know what they say, 'among my mother's children, I love myself the best'." The two laughed heartedly.

"I am dying to know why the dean called me into his office. Am I in trouble as usual?"

"No, no, no," the dean rejected. He said he was serving as chair of an internal search committee for Associate Provost of the university, a person who would be third in command, next to the president and provost. He disclosed that after seeing the credentials of the candidates for the position, he wanted Darrell to apply for he was most suitable for the position. "This is indeed your golden opportunity to get into administration and, on my honors, I will support you doggedly."

Darrell set his coffee cup on the table and looked at the dean in total disbelief. "Are you kidding?"

"I kid you not," the dean affirmed sternly. "I strongly encourage you to apply. Of course, I cannot, and certainly do not, guarantee definitively that you will get the position, but, after seeing the credentials of other applicants, I have no doubt you have a very good chance."

Darrell took a sip of his coffee. He was glad after all that coffee was served for it calmed his nerves. "How much do you know about this position? I mean, are you aware of the number and type of people who have held this position at SAU?"

The dean seemed baffled. He just did not know from where Darrell was coming. "No Darrell, I do not but what's your point?"

Darrell was fighting hard to control his emotions so once more, having a cup of coffee was extremely helpful. He took another sip and looked directly at Dean Peterson. "Within the last thirty years, no person of color has occupied that position and that may be true from the time the position was established. Only one Caucasian female has held the position and she did not last more than two years." He said he found it not only contradictory and disgustingly disingenuous but painfully preposterous that the university which felt he did not have administrative experience to be even an acting department chair, let alone Associate Dean for Administration and worse still, Vice Provost for Economic Development, suddenly thought he could be Associate Provost.

Darrell stopped momentarily to catch his breath. He sipped on his coffee again. "What's the matter Darrell?" the dean questioned as he struggled to understand the situation.

"Nothing Dean," Darrell replied "but I want to ask you one question."

"By all means, go ahead Darrell," the dean permitted with trepidation.

"Are you really convinced I am as ignorant as you think I am?"

The dean shook his head. "No, no, no. I never thought of you as being ignorant," he said with an emphasis on 'never'. "You will be the last person in the world I would think of in those terms. Why would I be asking you to apply if I thought of you negatively?"

"Dean Peterson," Darrell said, looking directly at the dean, "you do not want me in that position and you know it. If I apply, I will never get the position and one does not need to be a rocket scientist to figure that out. You want me to apply so your search committee can show it considered a diverse pool of candidates. In other words, you are deviously using me for your advantage; that is wrong Dean and you know it. Moreover, I am not a simpleton who will not notice the deception or, if you will, mind-boggling skullduggery."

The dean was quiet for a while. Then he spoke softly. "No Darrell, you are wrong. I honestly want you to apply for this position and sincerely think you have a good chance of getting it. If you apply, as I have said, I will endorse your candidacy strongly."

"But you did not think I was good enough to be Acting Department Chair. You did not even think I was good enough to be a full professor. You were not willing to support me for an external consulting position. Why would you think now that I am good enough to be Associate Provost? Does that make sense to you Dean?"

As the dean thought over Darrell's words without a response, Darrel said, "Look, I have to be going but need to register my profound regrets that this university and, to some extent, the nation continue to discriminate against, and marginalize so-called people of color despite relevant pieces of legislation and judicial mandates." He said both he and the dean knew this was wrong and if the university and nation were to be truly pluralistic, and it seems nothing could change that, they also had to be truly inclusive. He accentuated that the muddle-headed sloganeering and lip service about inclusiveness had to be translated into practical reality.

"Do you have suggestions as to how we can get there? The dean asked calmly.

"Suggestions have been offered repeatedly but where there is no administrative or political will, there will be no genuine and lasting change; rather, we will continue to have lip service commitment to diversity and inclusiveness," Darrell empha-sized. He registered his joy in the fact that, to many people, promoting diversity was the only way. Unfortunately, a large proportion of the population still did not see life in that manner and therefore were living with the same one-sided lens. Thus, there was a dire need to rationalize and vigorously promote and ensure diversity. To that end, one had to start with the realiza-tion that, without doubt, there were problems in every commu-nity of the nation, including affluent communities.

Focusing specifically on communities of sub-groups of the population, Darrell also admitted that, without doubt, there were multifarious and humongous problems. However, when students from such communities fail in school, the problem was to be addressed from economic, sociological, and pedagog-ical perspectives. Pounding lightly on the table, he added, "We must not jump to conclusion and attribute the failure to race and ethnicity. When students from these communities make it to higher education, they ought to be given the best support to succeed, not be the targets of discrimination and exclusion, atti-tudes which force some out of college and thereby confirm the biased notion of their academic inability. This is very sad Dean."

Darrell paused to catch his breath for he was clearly exas-perated. As he straightened his tie, he emphasized strongly that when people from sub-groups of the population served in higher education, they did not seek preferential treatment but equal opportunity in teaching, service, research and adminis-tration. "Let me tell you something Dean," he endeavored to make things clear, even if it seemed he was lecturing. "We, as a people, have come a long way but we have a long way to go. Given the consistency and level of our marginalization and exclusion, we would have been far worse off than we are but in general, we are a determined people. Sure, we have seen our ups and downs but again, in general, we do not allow set-backs to deter us. Does that sound racist? It probably is but it is also true."

The dean still was very quiet. He sometimes nodded politely as if he agreed with Darrell. Other times, he made a face as if he disagreed vehemently. Whatever was the dean's position, Darrell stood his ground. "No Dean, I will not apply for that position and be made a fool as you already think I am. Thanks for the offer Dean and have a wonderful day." Darrell stood, shook the dean's hands and headed for the door.

Two months after "laying it" on the dean, Darrell was summoned to another meeting with the dean. Darrell arrived on schedule and in attendance were two department chairs and someone simply introduced as a community developer. "What is this about again Dean?" Darrell asked as he took a seat across the room from the dean.

"Well Darrell," the dean began, "I was serious and sincere when I last encouraged you to get into administration. Another golden possibility has arisen and I once more sincerely want to encourage you toward that end."

"And what's that?" Darrell asked tersely.

The dean explained that the college, and especially his department, had embarked on a seven year local and regional development project; he wanted Darrell to direct the project. "This position comes with no change in salary but relief time and, as director, you will be given a small operating budget," the dean clarified.

Darrell smiled. "So you think I'm qualified to direct this project?"

"Of course," the dean nodded. "You are the most qualified and senior professor in the Department of Economics; this is an ideal position for you. In all honesty Darrell, I encourage you, even plead with you, to take this position. It will be a huge service to the department, college, university and the region."

Darrell smiled again. Soon, the smile gave way to a serious face. "Dean," he said, "it is mind-boggling to note that you still think I'm ignorant. Why Dean? Honestly, tell me why? Why do you keep insulting my intelligence and person?"

"There you go again," the dean frowned. "I have never thought of you in those terms and never will. Seriously Darrell, this is an honest offer; take it or leave it."

"This so-called seven-year project directorship is not an honest offer and you know it. You simply want to know when I will retire and this is your disingenuous way of asking. You are worse than a snake in the grass Dean and you ought to stop. I'm not as idiotic as you think."

Furthermore, Darrell resented the fact that the administration was anxious for him to retire as a way of saving money, never thankful for his long term service. "This so-called budgetary management on the basis of retirement is not limited to people from under-represented groups but directed at all senior professors." He emphasized that this lack of appreciation for service and dedication to the university was at the apex of ingratitude and had to stop.

Darrell stood up as he continued to vent his anger. He said he would not tell the dean when he would retire and no one could force him into retirement. "I will leave this university on my own terms, not yours or anyone else's. Besides, I will neither apply for, nor accept any administrative position. You and this administration have made that message clear to me." He dashed for the door.

Darrell kept his promise. Instead of pursuing positions in administration, he continued writing and speaking in addition to his usual professorial duties. Never abandoning his lifetime concern for African-Americans and others from under-represented groups in education in general and higher education in particular, he made notations to himself under the rubric, Reflections and projections, Analysis and Synthesis.

Looking back on life, he had no doubt his experiences in Ghetahzia, college and graduate school were not only invaluable eye-opening educational experiences but they also strengthened him enormously. He could not thank God enough for the wife and family God gave him; without Vanessa and the children, life would have been meaningless; he was not even sure if he could have made it thus far. Of course, he never forgot the many others who influenced his life positively. He was also thankful for an opportunity to mentor scores of under-graduate and graduate students, and appreciable number of doctoral candidates, and junior faculty members.

Focusing on the problems of African-Americans, he wrote that the problem centered on key areas: the family, education, and the greater society. "We have lots of problems by ourselves," Darrell wrote "but history has impacted us tremendously; there is no dodging of this fact." He argued that what happened to the Native Americans or American Indians was not fortuitous but carefully planned and executed systematically; consequently, those who were not eliminated ended up in reservations. Similarly, what happened to African Americans was by design, not by chance. He contended that, without trying to remove every blame from African-Americans, the truth was, by careful crafty design, for African-Americans who were not removed to Liberia, Haiti, Panama, and other places, the history of the country negatively impacted family life and screwed up their priorities thereby creating huge problems in their community. "When thirteen and fourteen year olds become mothers to fatherless children or children who know not their fathers, we have a problem. When fathers are only sperm distributers, we have a problem. When children show no respect to parents, we have a problem."

Considering possible solutions to the multi-faceted problems, Darrell wrote, "If anything is to change therefore, we must start with the family. Parents must give children hope, examples to emulate, pride to hold on for life, and opportunities hinged on wings with which to fly." He lamented that this was unlikely because the system was set up deliberately to reproduce itself. Consequently, this horrible lifestyle remained stagnant one generation after another. To change this trend, major changes were necessary, not just the few breakthroughs that were realized in the African-American community and the communities of other under-represented groups.

Again, without overlooking problems within the black community, he emphasized the indispensable need to face and solve the problem decisively. He continued, "It is true that often, we waste opportunities. However, without making excuses, part of this is due to a poor, disorganized and/or dysfunctional family system. If, for lack of means, parents cannot give their children opportunities, those parents ought to direct their children to the opportunities that exist and encourage them to make the best use of them. This is not possible when the parents themselves do not know what opportunities exist; someone has to tell them. Likewise, this is not possible when the parents are not around or when around, have other priorities."

Darrell frowned on the education system which he said was not helpful. "Inner city schools continue to be the worst. The drop-out rate is astronomical. Teachers usually are not qualified and those who are qualified are extremely frustrated as they deal daily with terrible children and lack teaching equipment and proper facilities. These schools are not subsidized adequately; they function just to meet the letter of the law. As such, most students who graduate from these schools are not high school material and those who graduate from high schools in the same communities (the so-called hood), are not college material. Their drop-out rate therefore is not a result of race and ethnicity but poor preparation."

Similarly, he turned to the greater society which he described as a broad entity comprising many and varied sectors, including the government. While never ignoring or even sugar-coding problems in the black community, he wrote, "In general, this entity continues to ignore the root problems of Blacks and others from under-represented groups. For example, for such persons, the problems of poverty, dysfunctional homes, poor neighborhoods, lack or dearth of role models, etc., are exacerbated when they attend poorly equipped and staffed schools. Often, they do not have guidance counselors to direct them and worse, they lack opportunities for progress." Then, Darrell's frustration surfaced in a series of questions. What excuses were there for the nation with the world's best economy to have a very high illiteracy rate? What explanations could anyone give for the nation to be plagued by a huge problem of homelessness, with thousands of people sleeping on streets? What possible reasons could be provided for the nation to face a mind-boggling problem of hunger to the extent that many people eat dog food or from the garbage? With this truism, why are farmers paid not to over-produce? What explanations, if any, could anyone give for the rate of poverty and for the nation's many other problems?

Darrell used materials from his notation for speeches and much less now, for publication. At the end of his thirty-first year, he applied for retirement and this was granted. He cleared his office gradually.

On his last day at the university, Darrell reminiscence for at least two hours. After these years, had he accomplished anything? Could he have done better elsewhere or was he too hard on himself? After minutes of thinking back and forth, he would stand to leave but sit backwards and think again. He knew only history would prove his gains and losses. Whatever they were, he thanked God for the opportunities he had.

About the Author

Professor Sakui W. G. Malakpa was born in Wozi, Lofa County Liberia. After losing his sight in high school, he studied at the school for the blind in Freetown, Sierra Leone before enrolling at Albert Academy, a secondary school also in Freetown. He later matriculated to Florida State University in Tallahassee, Florida where, in three years, he earned a bachelors degree cum laude and in another year, he earned a masters degree with a 4.0 GPA. He then went to Harvard University and earned a second masters degree and a doctorate in Education before accepting a professorial position at the University of Toledo; he is now a full professor with tenure. Also, while at the University of Toledo, Professor Malakpa returned to school and earned a law degree.

Professor Malakpa has presented academic papers in various parts of the United States, Europe, and Africa. He has published refereed journal articles, an academic work, a biography, and two novels. He currently has several manuscripts being considered for publication. He is married with children. He can be reached at sakui.malakpa@utoledo.edu or smalakpa@ hotmail.com.

REFERENCE NOTES AND BIBLIOGRAPHY

A s seen above, for this work, the literature was utilized for broad background information, ideas, examples, and, in some instances, direct quotes. To that end, special acknowledgment and appreciation are in place for the *Journal of Black Studies* which devoted an entire issue, Vol. 34 (1) to many of the issues this manuscript addresses. Similarly, references were made to Shakespeare and the Bible. Likewise, websites provided vital background information. Thus, for a number of chapters in the text, the following reference notes give the issues and topics this work gleaned from the literature. Often, the manuscript clearly indicates that the materials are from the literature or websites. In other instances, footnotes are used to cite the references used. As such, these notes are included followed by a bibliography (not references) as the sources cited are credited once more for providing background information or addressing similar issues as this work.

Reference Notes

Ch.1: The Interviews: The traditional requirements to hiring and barriers to recruitment; means of excluding PFUGs

273

from PWUs. No PFUGs in administration—lack of power sharing; token appointments.

CH.2: Wow! Starting Here?

Ch.3: Guidance for Settling In: Prof. Kwame's advice about Affirmative Action; his reference to the literature regarding vanguards in academia (e.g. Alexander Twilight, etc.). Also, the reference to Prof. Derrick Bell. Discussion of the origin and meaning of "mentor."

Ch.4: Starting In earnest: Frequent reference to Shakespeare throughout the manuscript: Julius Caesar, Love's Labor's Lost, Macbeth, Henry IV, etc..Economics topics;

Ch.5: Getting acquainted
The double victimization of "women of color."
Hiring women means hiring white women although this is no fault of white women.
Discussion of Chicano and Chicana.

Ch.6: Serious Allegation, Reference to "fruits of the spirit," from the Bible. Galatians 5:22-23, New International Version.

Ch.7: Summer I:

Ch.8: The Ratings:

Ch.9: Different Perspectives
Incidents that pass with impunity: racial slurs and hate notes left for minority students and workers, including professors; hateful placards left in conspicuous places on campus, some using the N word and calling on people to go elsewhere; white power signs around campus; etc..
Colonialized racism directed first at Native Americans. Slavery, the treatment of slaves and the so-called end of slavery as was indicative of Jefferson's signing of the end of slavery on March 3, 1807. Black codes and Jim Crow laws and the case of Plessey v. Ferguson. Whites in South Africa in mid-1600s.
White privilege;
July, 1852 oration by Frederick Douglas

Ch.10: Holding On
Inaugural statements by FDR and JFK and the historical explanations /attributions.
Ch.11: Two Concepts
White privilege again.
Racism institutionalized; traditional criteria for hiring and evaluation;
Token appointments; offices with ethnic or racial titles.
For a female leader, most people first see a woman, not a competent leader, etc..
References to Dr. Martin Luther King Jr..
Fact that civil rights laws prohibit blatant actions, not the minor and subtle ones which have a deep cumulative effect.
Memoirs and critical works from black studies
Ch.12: Toiling Toward Tenure
The allusion to *Sweezy v. New Hampshire*
The reference to James Russell Lowell.
Ch.13: The Research
Efforts by faculty members of color who, through concerted actions, were making a difference in their universities.
Darrell's survey and its findings were a combination of the fictional character of the work, e.g. Statistics from SAU, and a survey of the literature, especially from the internet; e.g. discrimination against women of color; overburdening workload and undervalued professional activity, barriers to recruitment, retention, and promotion, exclusion from power-sharing administrative positions, etc..
In other instances, it is stated clearly that the literature was reviewed; e.g. for white privilege, white nationalism, etc.. Similarly, Darrell's suggestions for solutions are a combination of fiction and information from the literature; e.g. mixed approaches to incorporation (advantages and disadvantages of marginalization), and

the cogent points of his narrative presented to a colloquium; e.g. demographic changes.

BIBLIOGRAPHY

Alex-Assensoh, Y. (2003). Race in the academy: Moving beyond diversity and toward the incorporation of faculty of color in predominantly white colleges and universities. *Journal of Black Studies, 34*(1), 5-11.

Arnold, N. W., Crawford, E. R., & Khalifa, M. (2016). Psychological heuristics and faculty of color: Racial battle fatigue and tenure/promotion. *The Journal of Higher Education, 87*(6), 890-919.

Assensoh, A. B. (2003). Trouble in the promised land: African American studies programs and the challenges of incorporation. *Journal of Black Studies, 34*(1), 52-62.

Biancuzzo, Dennis (2009, June 20). The culture of white privilege. Retrieved Oct. 1, 2009 from http://blog.pennlive.com/harrisburgcrimewatch/2009/06/the_culture_of_white_privilege.html

Bonilla-Santiago, G. (2014). *The miracle on Cooper Street: Lessons from an inner city.* Bloomington, IN: Archway Publishing.

Brayboy, B. M. J. (2003). The implementation of diversity in predominantly white colleges and universities. *Journal of Black Studies, 34*(1), 72-86.

Brown, R. H. (2002). Overcoming educational exclusion: Is diversity an appropriate model for democratic higher education? *American Behavioral Scientist, 45*(7), 1061-1087.

Brunsma, D. L., Brown, E. S., & Placier, P. (2013). Teaching race at historically white colleges and universities: Identifying and dismantling the walls of whiteness. *Critical Sociology*, *39*(5), 717-738.

Burke, M. A., Smith, C. W., & Mayorga-Gallo, s. (2017). The new principle-policy gap: How diversity ideology subverts diversity initiatives. *Sociological Perspectives*, *60*(5), 889-911.

Carter-Black, J. (2008). A black woman's journey into a predominately white academic world. *Affilia*, *23*(2), 112-122.

Coates, T. (2015). *Between the world and me*. New York, NY: Spiegel & Grau.

Cothran, D. L. (2016). Why do you talk, you know, like "that"?: Using scm and evt to explore the microaggressive student-teacher bullying of expectancy-violating black women. *Journal of Black Sexuality and Relationships*, *2*(3), 11-23.

Daufin, E. K. (2001). Minority faculty job experience, expectations, and satisfaction. *Journalism & Mass Communication Educator*, *56(*1), 18-30.

Diggs, G. A., Garrison-Wade, D. F., Estrada, D., & Galindo, R. (2009). Smiling faces and colored spaces: The experiences of faculty of color pursuing tenure in the academy. *The Urban Review*, *41*(4), 312-333. DOI 10.1007/s11256-008-0113-y

DiTomaso, N. (2013). *The American non-dilemma: Racial inequality without racism*. New York, NY: Russell Sage Foundation

Essien, V. (2003). Visible and invisible barriers to the incorporation of faculty of color in predominantly white law schools. *Journal of Black Studies*, *34*(1), 63-71.

Fenelon, J. (2003). Race, research, and tenure: Institutional credibility and the incorporation of African, Latino, and American Indian faculty. *Journal of Black Studies,* *34*(1), 87-100

Garrison-Wade, D. F.,Diggs, G. A., Estrada, D., & Galindo, R. (2012). Lift every voice and sing: Faculty of color face the challenges of the tenure track. *The Urban Review,* *44*(1), 90-112.

Giroux, S. S. (2010). *Between race and reason: Violence, intellectual responsibility and the university to come.* Stanford, CA: Stanford University Press.

Glaude, E. S. (2016). *Democracy in black: How race still enslaves the American soul.* New York, NY: Crown Publishing

Grollman, E. A. (September 2, 2013). On racist and sexist discrimination in academia. Retrieved Jan. 7, 2016 from http://conditionallyaccepted.com/2013/09/02/racism-sexism-academia/

Hall, R. E. (2006). White women as postmodern vehicle of black oppression: The pedagogy of discrimination in western academe. *Journal of Black Studies, 37*(1), 69-82.

Jayakumar, U. M., Howard, T. C., Allen, W. R., & Han, J. C. (2009). *Racial privilege in the professoriate: An exploration of campus climate, retention, and satisfaction. The Journal of Higher Education, 80*(5), 539-563.

Jefferson, M. (2015). *Negroland.* New York, NY: Pantheon Books.

Jones, B., Hwang, E., & Bustamante, R. M. (2015). African American female professors' strategies for successful attainment of tenure and promotion at predominately White institutions: It can happen. *Education, Citizenship and Social Justice, 10*(2), 133-151.

Lisnic, R., Zajicek, a., & Morimoto, s. (2019). Gender and race differences in faculty assessment of tenure clarity: The influence of departmental relationships and practices. *Sociology of Race and Ethnicity, 5*(2), 244-260. DOI: 10.1177/2332649218756137

Mato, C. (2003). Native faculty, higher education, racism, and survival. *Nunpa The American Indian Quarterly, 27*(1), 349-364.

McKay, N. (1983). Black woman professor-white university. doi:10.1016/0277-5395

Moore, Wendy. Reproducing white power and privilege: The manifestation of color-blind racism in elite United States law schools. Retrieved Oct. 1, 2009 from www.allacademic. com/meta/p105017_index.html

Pasque, P. A., & Nicholson, S. E. (2012). *Empowering women in higher education and student affairs: Theory, research, narratives and practice from feminist perspectives.* Sterling, VA: Stylus Publishing.

Perry, I. (2011). *More beautiful and more terrible: The embrace and transcendence of racial inequality in the United States.* New York, NY: New York University Press.

Rosser, S. V. (2004). Using power to advance: Institutional barriers identified by women scientists and engineers. *NWSA Journal, 16*(1), 50-78.

Segura, D. A. (2003). Navigating between two worlds: The labyrinth of Chicana intellectual production in the academy. *Journal of Black Studies, 34*(1), 28-51.

Settles, I. H., Buchanan, N. T., & Dotson, C. (2019). Scrutinized but not recognized: (In)visibility and hypervisibility experiences of faculty of color. *Journal of Vocational Behavior, 113*, 62-74.

Turner, C. S. (2003). Incorporation and marginalization in the academy: From border toward center for faculty of color? *Journal of Black Studies, 34*(1), 112-125.

Turner, C. s. V., González, J. C., & Wood, J. L. (2008). Faculty of color in academe: What 20 years of literature tells us. *Journal of Diversity in Higher Education, 1*(3), 139-168.

Tweedy, D. (2015). *Black man in a white coat: A doctor's reflections on race and medicine.* New York, NY: Picador.

Ware, L. PEOPLE OF color in the academy: Patterns of discrimination in faculty hiring and retention. Retrieved Oct. 1, 2009 from http://www.bc.edu/bc_org/avp/law/lwsch/journals/bctwj/20_1/05_TXT.htm

Weems, R. E. (2003). The incorporation of black faculty at predominantly white institutions: A historical and contemporary perspective. *Journal of Black Studies, 34*(1), 101-111.

Wolfe, B. L., & Dilworth, P. P. (2015). Transitioning normalcy: Organizational culture, African American administrators, and diversity leadership in higher education. *Review of Educational Research, 85*(4), 667-697. DOI: 10.3102/0034654314565667

Websites

www.biography.com/people/simone-de-beauvoir-9269063
Visited Feb. 14, 2016
www.iep.utm.edu/beauvoir/
Visited Feb. 14, 2016
en.wikipedia.org/wiki/List_of_**African-American_first**s
Visited Nov. 24, 2011
www.nytimes.com/.../**us**/
derrick-bell-pioneering-harvard-law-**profess**...
Visited Nov. 24, 2011

articles.latimes.com/2010/jul/27/.../
la-me-david-blackwell-20100727
Visited Nov. 24, 2011
www.math.buffalo.edu/mad/madhist.html
Visited Nov. 24, 2011
A Modern History of Blacks in Mathematics
chemistry.about.com/od/famouschemists/a/black-
chemists.htm
Visited Nov. 5, 2011
Black Chemists–African American History &
ChemistryHomeEducationChemistry
www.nlm.nih.gov/exhibition/aframsurgeons/new-
frontiers.html
Visited Nov. 24, 2011
Opening Doors: Contemporary African American Academic
Surgeons Home > Frontiers in Academic
Surgery
www.thecrimson.com/article/2011/10/7/
law-school-bell-black/
Visited Nov. 24, 2011
Derrick Bell, First Tenured Black Professor at HLS, Dies |
News | The Harvard Crimson
www.fas.harvard.edu/~amciv/faculty/gates.shtml
Visited Nov. 24, 2011
Henry Louis Gates, Jr.–History of American Civilization
Program Information
www.learner.org/discoveringpsychology/.../history_
nonflash.html
Visited Nov. 24, 2011
The History of Psychology
www.aas.emory.edu/history.html
Visited Nov. 24, 2011
Welcome To Emory University's African American Studies
DepartmentSpring 2009
www.infoplease.com ›
Visited Nov. 25, 2011

BIBLIOGRAPHY

Famous Firsts by Hispanic Americans â€" Infoplease.com
en.wikipedia.org/wiki/**Hispanic**_and_Latino_**Americans**
Visited Nov. 25, 2011
Hispanic and Latino Americans–Wikipedia, the free
encyclopedia
www.uncmirror.com/
legacy-of-**first**-**hispanic**-**professor**-lives-on-in-e...
Visited Nov. 25, 2011
Legacy of first Hispanic professor lives on in educa-
tion hall–UNC
www.nlm.nih.gov/changingthefaceofmedicine/.../biog-
raphy_239.ht...
Visited Nov. 25, 2011
Changing the Face of Medicine | Dr. Antonia Novello
mia.albizu.edu/web/about_cau/carlos_albizu_founder_
of_cau.asp
Visited Nov. 25, 2011
About CAU–Carlos Albizu, founder of CAU. Carlos Albizu
University–Miami, Florida.
www.mfdp.med.harvard.edu/woc/timeline/index.htm
Women of Color as Leaders in Public Health and Health
Policy Conference
CHRONOLOGY OF ACHIEVEMENTS OF WOMEN OF
COLOR IN HEALTH AND MEDICINE
journals.lww.com
Visited Nov. 25, 2011
Staying_Connected__Native_American_Women_
Faculty.32[1].pdf
www.allacademic.com/meta/p105017_index.html
Visited Oct. 1, 2009
(Examination of two elite law schools)
www.law.cornell.edu/constitution/**amendment**xiv
Visited Dec. 27, 2011 (Also looked up 12th, 14th, 15th, and 16th
amendments from the same site.)
en.wikipedia.org/wiki/**Dred_Scott_v._Sandford**
Visited Dec. 27, 2011

www.colonialvoyage.com/eng/**africa/south_africa/
dutch**.html
Visited Jan. 14, 2012
en.wikipedia.org/wiki/
History_of_**South_Africa**_(1652–1815)
Visited Jan 14, 2012
abolition.nypl.org/home/
Visited Dec. 23, 2011
(Jefferson signing end of slavery on March 3, 1807)
www.biblegateway.com/
passage/?search=Galatians+5%3A22-23...
Visited Feb. 4, 2012
(For fruits of the Spirit)
(For Jim Crow)
en.wikipedia.org/wiki/**Jim_Crow**_laws
Visited Dec. 15, 2011
www.ferris.edu/**jimcrow**/what.htm
Visited Dec. 15, 2011
www.ferris.edu/**jimcrow**/who.htm
Visited Dec. 15, 2011
(About minority populations)
money.cnn.com/2009/05/14/real_estate/...**minori-
ties**/index.htm
Visited Jan. 1, 2012
www.marketingcharts.com/.../
one-in-three-**us**-residents-a-member-of...
Visited Jan. 1, 2012
en.wikipedia.org/wiki/
Race_and_ethnicity_in_the_United_States
Visited Jan. 1, 2012
articles.cnn.com/.../**us**/census.
minorities_1_hispanic-population-censu...
Visited Jan. 1, 2012
www.now.org
Visited Jan. 2, 2012
(Origin of Affirmative Action)

(For JFK's Inaugural Address)
www.bartleby.com
en.wikipedia.org/wiki/
Inaugural_address_of_John_F._**Kennedy**
(**FDR's Inaugural Addresses**)
en.wikipedia.org/wiki/
First_**inauguration**_of_Franklin_D._**Roosevelt**
www.historyplace.com/**speeches/fdr**-first-inaug.htm
(About James Russell Lowell)
www.brainyquote.com/quotes/authors/j/**james_russell_
lowell**.html
www.bartleby.com
(More About Prof. Bell)
en.wikipedia.org/wiki/**Derrick Bell**
Visited Dec. 26, 2011
www.npr.org/.../
stand-up-speak-out-**derrick-bell**-told-law-students
Visited Dec. 26, 2011
Others
www.pbs.org/shattering/theprogram.html
www.apa.org/pi/oema/surviving/background.html
www.historyplace.com/**speeches/douglass**.htm -
Visited May 26, 2010
Frederick Douglas' Speech–The Hypocrisy of American Slavery.

About Max Horkheimer and Critical Theory
*plato.stanford.edu/entries/**critical-theory**/*
Visited April 28, 2013